WHEN THE BOUGH BREAKS

O'JUNEA BROWN

Developmental Editing provided by Janna Harner

Line and Proof Editing provided by The Fiction Fix

Cover design created by Designs by Charly

To every woman who fell victim to mental, physical, and/or emotional abuse.

To every woman who was convinced they couldn't walk away and start over.

To every woman who believed for a split second they weren't good enough and it was their fault.

The cost of giving up is yourself, and you're far too valuable for that.

Fuck Them.

Fix your crown babe. You made it.

AUTHOR'S NOTE

Writing a book is already hard, but writing a book from the deepest, darkest parts of your soul can and will drain you. There were days and nights I had to step away because it got too real and raw for me.

But before you start reading, I want to speak to those who have either crawled out of their own darkness or are working on it. I want you to know that even though it may seem like you will never find your footing again, the universe will always help you stand upright. It is never, ever the end. Don't ever let anyone tell you you're not who you believe you are. You were put in this world for a reason, and if anyone makes you believe any differently, they do not deserve you.

You are original. You are beautiful. And you are so loved.

CONTENT NOTE

Please note, this story has very dark elements. As always, your mental health matters. If you find yourself wanting or needing to know all content warnings prior to or during reading, I have made them available on my website.

A complete list of on-page, off-page, and historical trigger warnings can be found on my website at https://ojuneabrown.carrd.co/

Suicide Prevention Hotline: 1-900-273-8255 or 988

Domestic Violence Hotline: 1-800-799-SAFE

Sexual Assault Hotline: 1-800-656-HOPE

National Drug Helpline: 1-844-289-0879

PLAYLIST

Jaws – Sleep Token
Circle With Me – Spiritbox
Nowhere To Go – Bad Omens
LABOUR - The Cacophony – Paris Paloma
Alkaline – Sleep Token
The Cost of Giving Up – Poppy
Bury A Friend – Billie Eilish
Worst Behaviour – KWN, Kehlani
Decode – Paramore
Just Pretend – Bad Omens
Dead Throne – Arankai
Feel Me Now – If Not For Me
Sweat – ZAYN
Granite – Sleep Token
Like A Villain – Bad Omens
Don't Hurt Yourself – Beyonce, Jack White
The Summoning – Sleep Token
You Should See Me In A Crown – Billie Eilish
THE REV3NGE – Joey Bada$$
Bodies – Drowning Pool
Heads Will Roll (Remix) – Yeah Yeah Yeahs, A-Trak
End of You – Poppy, Amy Lee, Courtney LaPlante

PROLOGUE

Have you ever had someone unexpectedly come along and sweep you off your feet?

I mean, full on walk right up to you and snatch the carpet out from under where you stood?

It's a whirlwind of emotions, and it feels exactly like the Disney Princess love stories. But sometimes...just...sometimes...

Those fairytales aren't worth living.

And sometimes, those fairytales are the flames of hell in disguise, but we don't find out until we're too deep into the relationship to start over.

And that means...

We get to learn the hard way.

CHAPTER

ONE

(7 Years Ago)

Do I even know the person staring back at me anymore?

I look away in disgust and turn the faucet off, knocking over my mixed drink from the overly nice guy at the bar. I curse under my breath when I hear the glass shatter; I stumble, catching myself on the wall.

Whoopsie.

"Shit, Maevis. How drunk are you?" a random classmate asks as she strides through the bathroom door. She glances down at the mess on the floor and back up at me. A sly, wicked grin sweeps across her face, and I roll my eyes, preparing for whatever mean-girl bullshit I'm about to endure. Two girls join her in the doorway. "Better yet, what did you take and how much? I want some of whatever you have."

The three of them burst into laughter.

I glare; I know she's attempting to insult me, but I couldn't care less right now. The numbness reverberating through me was the intended goal—I wanted to avoid any and all thoughts of my parents. This wasn't my first time chasing this feeling when it comes to them, but their unexpected phone call this afternoon was more than enough grounds for taking the first drugs offered to me. For a second, I hear my mom's voice in my head, reprimanding me about my chosen finance major, and that quickly bleeds into a barrage of questions about settling

3

down, marriage, and babies, with a follow up question from my father about politics.

I cringe at the thought of crotch goblins of my own. I need another drink.

Shaking my head free of those I consumed a large amount of alcohol and a good bit of drugs to forget, I focus on the now five girls who have accumulated in the doorway.

"Fuck off. It was an accident," I say, grabbing some paper towels and crouching to clean up my mess. My reaction time is too slow to catch myself as I feel a hand push into my shoulder, sending me knees first into the shattered glass with a yelp.

I might be numb from whatever pills were handed to me, but I would need to be on some much more serious shit to not feel the pain slicing through my skin.

I wonder if that dealer is still outside.

I squeeze my eyes shut, their laughter echoing off the walls before they leave. A moment later, I hear the door swing open, and I prepare to endure their bullshit again. I can admit when I'm too far gone to defend myself, and right now is one of those moments; I don't even think I care. But I relax with the famil- iarity of the two hands that clutch my shoulders.

I bite my lip, embarrassed to know one of my only friends found me like this. Still, I'm grateful to know I can trust them to get me the fuck out of here and into my bed before my high fades.

"You can't keep doing this, Maevis," they scold while lifting me effortlessly to stand, their eyes inspecting every inch of me. "We have to get you cleaned up."

I roll my eyes and look away, ashamed at being repri- manded by not only my parents, but now friends as well.

"Don't do that," they say, gripping my chin and bringing my focus back to them.

"You don't know what it's like. You don't know how tiring

it is, the pressure of maintaining the perfect image. The perfect fucking life. The perfect fucking daughter, day in and day out. Don't tell me what I can and can't do. If I want to feel...“ I spew , trailing off while they stare at me in silence, allowing me to vent. "If I want to be numb for a night, then let me be that."

Their eyes soften as they grab my jacket I had thrown over the door of a random stall, holding it up for me to put my arms through. Once I have it on, I wobble as their hands grip my shoulders again, turning me to face them.

"I understand way more than you think I do. I know what it feels like to try your best, striving for your own happiness only for others to continuously break you down, but that doesn't mean I'll stand here and watch you self-destruct. Pills, alcohol, and whatever else you can get your hands on for a temporary high isn't going to get your parents off your back, Maevis. You're smart enough to know this. Now, let's get you back to your dorm to sober up and find you some food, yea?" they rush out on a single, stern breath. I blink, their voice and strong scent bringing me out of my substance-induced dark hole. "You're going to have to pay, though," they add.

Nausea hits me like a deep wave, and the common sense they're trying to speak into me rolls in right behind it.

I don't want to think about it right now.

I wet my lips before throwing my head back on a deep, long breath. Dizzy and avoiding eye-contact as the high pulls me under, I grip the door handle. "Does it ever get better?" I whisper.

The silence lingers for a moment before their hand falls on top of mine, pulling the door open.

"If you start living your life for yourself instead of everyone else, yes."

I know they're right. But for right now, that's not an option.

So, I'll stick with my decision to cling to the drugs that make me feel nothing at all instead of wishing I were dead. I may be intoxicated, but I'm present enough to know this is real life, not the fucking movies.

I was born into a life, a family that's anything but rainbows and sunshine.

TWO

Graduate from college. Get married. Pop out a few kids.

That's what everyone who's a part of the patriarchy tell a woman like me.

Thankfully, I have a brain and know how I wish to live my life. I'm positive it's not to please the men in this world.

My focus snaps back to the elongated table in front of me as Rose elbows me in the ribs. I'm lucky enough to have my best friend working with me at Stark Financial, supporting me every step of the way towards my dream position as Chief Financial Officer. She's always had a knack for noticing when I drift off into my imaginary world where I'm a childfree billionaire on my yacht, a sweet mocktail in hand.

"And Miss Moore, how do you feel about the projected numbers for the upcoming fiscal year?" Brady asks with a stern look on his narrow face, as if I'm a child. But I know what he's doing. He's on my side and always has been. As CEO of Stark Financial, he doesn't want to show favoritism. He wants to show the other executives at the table that I'm capable of the position I'm hoping to be promoted to in the upcoming months.

Brady is one of the very few men I trust in this business.

If not the only.

"I think we're right on track to make a much higher profit than last year," I reply confidently. "And if I'm being honest, with the outreach I've done to our top contributors, I believe this upcoming year will be our best out of the last five."

I suppress a smirk and dip my head toward my notepad, as if I'm taking a very important note.

Nailed it.

I write it on the notepad and tap my pen, purposefully catching Rose's attention. She reads it and lightly kicks me under the table with a devilish grin.

"Are there any other questions before we end this meeting?" Brady asks while gathering his things into a neat stack in front of him. Phil, the snobbiest employee here, raises his pen in the air, and I hollow my cheeks when I see Brady fight to not roll his eyes. Instead, he nods his head, cueing Phil to proceed with his question.

"Exactly who is in the running to replace Frank when he retires this year?" he asks with a haughty attitude that is truly sickening.

Brady leans back in his chair and tilts his head to the side.

I study him as he ponders his answer and notice for the first time how attractive he is for an older gentleman. His flawless brown skin glows under the sunlight beaming through the windows of the conference room, and the confidence etched across his face blended with his success speaks volumes.

"I think the person in the running for the position right now is exactly the person who has worked their ass off to prove their worth to this company over the past several years." His answer makes my heart swell, because I know he notices everything I do to move this company forward, both on and off the clock. "Additionally, I believe their credentials, both via degree and merit in the workplace, would secure their position exponentially."

"Right, but who is he?" Phil follows up, and my nostrils flare in irritation. I know he feels entitled to the position. Phil has been here two fewer years than me and doesn't put in half the work I do. But because he has a dick between his legs, he thinks he's entitled.

Brady sits forward, folding his hands on the smooth wood table and settling his hardened gaze on Phil. "When the successor is chosen, I can assure you, he or *she* will be the best candidate for the position. *Additionally*, the person chosen, whether male or female, will have earned it through their experience, work ethic, and *attitude*. Does that help answer your question, Phillip?"

Phil stiffens in his seat and sternly nods.

Brady ends the meeting and stands with his items in hand, exiting the room after his final parting words.

Rose and I start chatting about where we're going for lunch when Phil slams his laptop shut and glares in our direction. My eyes narrow, and I hear Rose tsk with a *'here we go'* under her breath.

"How can I help you today, Phi—"

Phil cuts me off before I can finish. "Listen here, Maevis. Just because you walk around with a pretty face doesn't mean you've earned that position. I'll jump off the roof before I let you become CFO over *me,*" he snaps.

I huff a laugh and continue gathering my things, pressing my lips into a thin line when it dawns on me—he waited for the room to clear out before addressing me. My eyes roam over the sorry excuse for a man across the table before I cock a brow.

"Phil, I've played nice all these years, even with your snobby attitude with nothing to back it up. But I'm going to be honest with you." I lean over the table, watching his eyes narrow in anger. "If you ever interrupt me again, I'll make sure you're unable to speak for the rest of your life when my fist meets your throat."

Phil rears his head back with rounded eyes.

I offer the fakest smile I can muster before Rose laughs and makes her way toward the door as I follow. Pausing in the doorway, I turn around to face the asshole standing slack-jawed at the table.

"And when I get that promotion, make sure you do a flip when you jump," I say, followed by a wink as I close the door behind me.

THREE

When Rose and I finally make it to my office, Anika waits inside, her feet propped up on my desk. I give her a fake evil glare and smile when she raises a coffee cup in the air.

"Coffee with oat milk, zero sugar, because you're weird as fuck, but at least you're gorgeous," she says, dropping her feet to the floor and rounding my desk. She hands me the coffee with a kiss on the cheek. She squeezes Rose's hand with a smile and plops into a chair in front of my desk.

Anika has been my secretary from the start of my career at Stark Financial, and she's been like a little sister ever since.

"Any big plans this weekend?" she asks while scrolling on her phone.

I settle into my leather chair behind my desk and take a sip of the coffee. I fight my eyes from rolling to the back of my head at how perfectly she made it.

"I'm having dinner with Ross at my house tonight," I say, waiting for them to lecture me. When neither says anything, I glance up from my computer to see Rose and Anika staring at me with their noses scrunched in disappointment.

"Can we please not do this, you guys?" I ask with a pleading look.

"Can we please stop acting like he hasn't cancelled on you the last twenty times?" Rose snarks.

I sit back in my chair and release an exasperated sigh. "It has not been twenty times. Maybe a handful, but not twenty.

And come on, you two; you know how much I love him. He has his faults, but everyone does. We're trying," I attempt to reason with the two of them. "He's just been...busy while preparing to take over the family business from his father."

Anika rolls her eyes and turns her head to look at Rose as if I'm not even in the room. Rose never takes her eyes off me; they soften a little and her shoulders relax. "He was amazing when you two first met. Maybe you just need to find that spark again and he needs a break from work. Hopefully, this dinner tonight will lead to a little reverse cowgirl and—"

"*Can we please not?*" I beg mid-sip of my coffee, resulting in some of it falling out of my mouth.

My two friends laugh, and I join in, but when the laughing fits and jokes are over, both of their faces turn serious.

"He does treat you right though...right?" Rose asks with a furrowed brow, Anika providing the same facial expression. I bounce my leg under my desk where they can't see and pinch at the fabric of my pants. As much as I want to explain our situationship to my two best friends, I know it won't be smart to share the darkness that has unfolded over time with my fiancé unless I'm ready to call it quits.

Ross was amazing at the beginning of our relationship, the perfect fairytale prince who jumped out of a book and into my life. But recently, it's as if a dark shadow is slowly blanketing over the Ross I had come to know and love over the years.

"Of course he does. Why would you even ask that?" I reply and quickly take another sip of coffee.

"Because we care about you. And if that motherfucker ever gives you anything less than princess treatment, we will dispose of him in Lake Michigan," Rose replies.

Anika reaches toward Rose, lifting her hand in the air for a high-five. "I second that motion."

I smile, blowing my two friends kisses from my desk.

"Okay, let's get out of her hair. She has a big day tomorrow," Rose says while raising from her seat, Anika following suit.

I've been working my ass off, and tomorrow is the final nail in the coffin for securing my dream position and watching Phil die of disbelief.

My smile widens when I notice them smiling just as wide as I am.

"When you get this position, you better demand I remain your secretary, or I'll never speak to you again," Anika says while making her way to the door.

"I promise," I reply between laughs and bid both women goodbye, Rose closing the door to my office behind them.

When they leave, I rest my forehead on my desk and release a deep breath.

I hate lying to my friends, but I know how girl code works. The moment I tell them about Ross' odd and unfavorable behavior lately, there's no returning to their good graces for him. I know the stress from his job is eating him alive, but I just want the flame we started with to reignite, sooner rather than later.

I glance down at the ring on my engagement finger and force myself to take a breath. Unease settles in my stomach when the excitement I used to feel about walking down the aisle doesn't spark the emotions I felt in the beginning of our engagement.

Unfortunately for me, I begin to compare our relationship to my *relationship* back in college.

Were we officially dating? No.

But he was the sweetest and most caring human I'd ever met. My mind drifts back to the nights I spent cuddled up to him in my dorm room while we watched the Underworld series on repeat. Silently, I cringe and curl into myself as bits and pieces of my drug addiction try weaseling their way back into my memories before I force them back out.

I smile when I think about how often he convinced me to stay in our dorms instead of partying. My heart skips a beat when I admit he was convincing me to stay inside to prevent me from taking whatever drug was the newest fad that month while drinking myself senseless at whatever frat party I could find.

My phone buzzes on my desk, bringing me out of my joy-filled daydream.

Grabbing it, I squint at the unknown number and hit decline. At the same time, a knock hits my door, startling me. Anika pops her head in with a sleek, gold envelope.

"This just landed on my desk with your name on it. Need anything from me before I head to lunch?" she questions with a broad smile.

I let her know I'm good for now, opening the envelope as she leaves. I prepare myself for a handwritten letter from Ross telling me he's cancelling our dinner tonight. With an eye roll, I pull a flat, white card from the envelope, and my breath catches when I don't recognize the handwriting.

See you soon.

I flip the card over multiple times, searching for a name, but there's nothing. There's not even an initial to sign off.

The hairs on the back of my neck stand, like someone is watching me, and I startle myself so bad, I let out a shriek, clapping my hand over my mouth.

Quickly, I swivel in my chair to look out the large window behind me, and I swallow another scream when I see a tall man in all black looking directly at me from the sidewalk. His hood is pulled down far enough so I can't see his face, but there's not a doubt in my mind he's looking at me.

When I stand from my chair, he turns to walk away, blending in with the heavy Chicago foot traffic, until someone else walks up to him—a woman, wrapping her arm around his waist. They both point up toward my building, and he removes his hood, dawning a wide smile as he gestures to another building and she nods along.

Tourists.

Dropping back down in my seat, I press my palms into my eyes and let my head fall back. For the past few weeks, I've felt like someone has been watching me. I convinced myself I was just paranoid and letting my anxiety win, but now, I'm not so sure.

But why me?

I'm a nobody.

The smart thing would be to report the note to the police, but I have enough on my plate right now. Instead, I pull up my emails and jump right back into work.

A possible stalker isn't going to get me the promotion.

I make a mental note to tell Ross about what happened at dinner tonight and see what he thinks. My eyes glance over to the little white card on my desk, and I run my fingers over the handwriting.

"See you soon," I mumble to myself. "At least be a little more original," I add with a laugh and get back to work.

CHAPTER

FOUR

Like clockwork, the keyring falls from my grasp, and I scramble to pick it up so I can finally unlock my door. Since I started feeling watched, I've prepared my keys before I get out of the car, and every night, without fail, I'm left fumbling with them on my porch.

Rushing inside, I slam the door shut and rest the back of my head against the solid surface, taking a deep breath before silencing my alarm system. My heart finally steadies when I realize I made it inside unharmed.

What a terrible fucking way to live.

This paranoia is slowly killing me from the inside out. I wake up, go to work, and go home with the inkling someone is watching me at every moment, and today's fiasco with the unmarked note has only heightened my paranoia.

With shaky hands, I secure the second deadbolt on the front door before I drop my work bag and purse on the loveseat next to the bay window.

My father insisted I get a home with an attached garage, but did I listen? Absolutely not. "Dad, I'll be fine. Stop being para-noid," I lectured him on multiple occasions. *Now look at me.* I can't even take a shit in my own home without thinking I'm going to be murdered and found like Elvis on the porcelain throne.

But my heart fell in love with this single-family home in Chicago, right around the corner from my favorite bookstore.

16

The landlord said the garage wasn't available for use when I signed my lease, which was annoying, but the neighborhood is quiet, so I'll happily park my car on the street and dash into the house like my life depends on it.

My phone ringing causes me to jump before I flip the screen up and see Ross is calling.

"H-hey, babe, where are you? I thought you were meeting me here for dinner tonight?" I ask in a hopeful tone. Something rustles in the background before he finally responds.

"Maevis, baby, you know how things can get at the office. The paperwork got stacked a mile high within the last hour, and if I don't get it done, the big man is going to have my head. We talked about this, remember? I know you want my attention around the clock, but without a job, I can't provide for my favorite girl. Save me some leftovers, yeah?"

I sit there silently, waiting for his secretary to throw some snide remark about our conversation in the background like she usually does.

"I'll pick you up tomorrow around seven for dinner, yeah?" he asks when I don't speak.

Eventually, I sigh. "Sure thing, Ross. Call me when you—" There's more rustling, and then I hear her high-pitched voice in the background. I can tell she's moving closer to the phone while begging him to hang up and *get back to work.* I want to ask him why she's still at the office so late, but he starts speaking before I can.

"I'm so sorry about tonight, baby. I promise I'll make it up to you." He offers his typical apology with an offer to make it up to me. I can hear him telling his secretary to be quiet, and I take a deep breath before speaking.

"What if I bring dinner to your office? I can be there in less than thirty minutes; I can bring my laptop as well to catch up on somethings," I offer in a hopeful tone that quickly dissipates when he declines my offer.

"Sorry, Maevis—as much as I would love that, I really need to focus tonight," he says, and I begin to plead my case about how I won't bother him while I'm there. But he cuts me off with the typical 'I love you' and disconnects the line.

The engagement ring on my left hand glistens under the light fixture above, making me feel some type of way. We've been together since my last year of college, with him finally popping the question last year.

We're exactly three months out from when I'll be walking down the aisle to become his wife, and he can't even keep dinner date promises. This is the fourth time he has canceled on me in three weeks.

Anika and Rose are starting to sound like they know my fiancé better than I do.

Slipping into something more comfortable, I search my freezer for my favorite Lean Cuisine meal that's loaded with sodium yet promises to help you lose weight.

Gotta love diet culture.

My phone on the counter rings, and I dash to grab it, hopeful it's Ross calling me back to change his mind. My heart sinks when I see the name flash across the screen.

Mom.

I take a deep breath before answering, bracing myself for whatever belittling she has prepared for me tonight. "Hi, Mom," I answer in a cheerful voice, hoping to throw her off.

I can hear her take a swig of something before she speaks. "Maevis, how are you, darling?"

I scratch the top of my head before attempting to speak, but she cuts me off. "How are you and Ross doing?" she asks nonchalantly. Every time she calls, it's either regarding Ross or both of us. It's never just about me and my wellbeing.

"We're fine, I guess," I answer while shrugging my shoulders, thinking about the cancelled plans from moments ago.

She's silent for a moment before her usual verbal assault begins. "I was thinking—Ross let his mother know you weren't too keen on having kids. Have you lost your mind, or are you just dumb?"

I remain silent, my eyes squinted and my mouth half open.

Why is he getting our parents involved in our intimate conversations?

"I mean, honestly, Maevis. Are you still planning on working while married? There's nothing wrong with being the woman of the house. Raise the kids, cook, clean. I did it, and I turned out great," she continues. The grip I have on the countertop has my knuckles turning white.

"I don't quite think my sole purpose in life is to pop out babies at the convenience of my husband, Mother. If that's—"

"Oh, well, that's where you're wrong, sweetie," she cuts me off with a mocking laugh. "The women of this family have always lived to serve our husbands. That doesn't stop in our bloodline just because you came along. If Ross wants—"

I make the executive decision to place my phone on the counter and let her speak to a non-existent person on the other end. With a smug smile on my face, I continue making my dinner as I hear her talk in the background, unable to decipher anything she's saying. Unfortunately, she must have realized I wasn't listening and hung up, because my phone rings again with her name flashing. After the second attempt, she gives up, and I let loose a breath, thanking heaven above that's over with.

Ripping the box open, I get that same eerie feeling, like someone is watching me through the small window in my kitchen. Slowly, I turn to look, finding nothing but the usual tree branches swaying in the wind. But the closer I investigate the tree in my backyard, the more my eyes make out the silhouette of a man.

And the more I concentrate, the faster my heart rate skyrockets.

My palms are so sweaty, the fork I grabbed to puncture the film of my frozen dinner slips from my hand, and the sound of it meeting the tile floor is my undoing. Dropping to the ground and scooting my back against the cabinets, I reach on top of the counter to locate my phone and quickly dial 9-1-1. Just as I press the call button, my alarm system chimes.

"*Disarmed*," the robotic woman's voice says from the main box. Reaching behind me, I grab a knife from the drawer and drop back down to the floor.

"*Armed*," the robotic voice chimes once more.

Did my alarm system just disarm and arm itself?

"9-1-1, what's your emergency?" I hear an exasperated voice say on the other end. They must have been speaking while I was listening to my alarm system go haywire.

"Hi, yes, could you please send someone to 409 Maude Avenue? I-I feel like I'm being watched, and someone may even be in my home. P-please send someone," I say with a sob.

Within five minutes, flashing lights pull up in front of my home, and I wait for the police to ring the doorbell as I clutch the knife to my chest. I run to open it, placing the knife on a side table, feeling eyes watching me from every hallway I pass.

As I throw open the door, the officer behind it looks me up and down, his eyes bulging as he introduces himself. Wondering what he's looking at, I glance down, only to realize I never put a shirt on when I changed clothes. Here I am, standing in the doorway of my home in sweatpants and a forest-green lace bra that's completely see-through. I snatch my coat from a nearby hook as I explain what's going on.

A few minutes later, two additional squad cars arrive, and

officers search my home for any intruders while I wait with two officers outside.

"All clear," a female cop calls from the front door.

Dread and embarrassment wash over me when I realize I may have been overreacting. Tears rim my eyes as I hang my head and mutter an apology to the officers.

"Hey, don't be sorry. I'd rather you be safe than regret it later," the pretty brunette chimes from beside me. "Call us anytime you need."

I thank the officers before setting all three locks and arming my alarm system. After everything that just happened, I now have zero appetite. Pouring myself a glass of wine, I climb upstairs, turn on my favorite television show, and bury myself underneath the covers.

After tonight, I think it's a good idea to hire a therapist to help with my paranoia. I can't live like this anymore. My mind is on constant high alert for a stalker who doesn't even exist. But then, I remember the handwritten note delivered to my office earlier.

Or does he?

My attention returns to *The O.C.* on the TV. Seth is finally asking Summer out on a date. My shoulders relax, and I take another sip of wine. Placing the glass on the nightstand while conforming to the pillows surrounding me, I feel my eyes grow heavy with exhaustion.

And just like that, my dreams consume me.

FIVE

The car is eerily silent as Ross drives us home from our movie date. I glance over at him, his eyes focused on the road. He insisted we go see a romantic comedy, even though he knows action movies are my favorite. I can tell he's annoyed I didn't enjoy it as much as he did. Sneaking another glance at him, I can't help but compare us to the couple in the movie.

Do we share the same laughter and interests? *Did we ever?* I don't even know if any of our interests are similar anymore. Hell, I don't even know the last time we laughed so hard, we couldn't breathe.

"So, did you like the movie?" I ask to break the silence. Ross looks over at me, forcing a weak, thin smile, and nods his head. I don't know what's going on tonight, but he seems so... distant. I stare out my window for a moment, thinking about how we used to be.

How *he* used to be.

"Hey, do you want to grab that cookie skillet we love from that one restaurant?" I ask gleefully, knowing he can't resist that dessert. I watch him roll his eyes as he declines, and irritation floods me. "Okay, did I do something? You've been super quiet all night. Not to mention, you wouldn't even so much as look my way during the movie. What's going on?"

I notice Ross tighten his grip on the steering wheel until we reach my house. He puts the car in park, turns the engine off, and releases an exasperated sigh. "Why does there always have to be something wrong, Maevis? Everything turns into an issue with you."

When he finally speaks, I'm caught off guard. "I didn't say I was upset. I was just asking—"

"I heard you. And I'm telling you, nothing is wrong. Since when did you become so clingy?" he cuts me off, annoyance flooding his expression. I blink a few times to make sure I'm not hallucinating and hearing him correctly.

"Ross, how am I clingy? All I did was ask if something is wrong, because you've barely looked at me all night, let alone spoken to me. I just wanted to make sure you're okay. That *we* are okay. You've just been...distant lately, that's all," I explain.

I watch silently as he runs a hand down the side of his face, producing a fake, mocking laugh while studying me. I shake my head in response, gripping the handle to let myself out. "Let me know when you get home," I mutter, attempting to open the door when I feel him grip my arm and yank me back toward him.

Alarm floods me as I let out a small yelp and eye him cautiously.

"You want me to show you affection? You want my attention? Fine. I'll give it to you," he snaps before gripping my face tight and pulling me toward him until our lips meet. The kiss is forceful, and not the kind I would welcome. It's almost as if he's trying to show dominance, as if he's proving to himself he can have me whenever he wants. I press a hand into his shoulder to create space between us, but he knocks it away. His hand reaches beneath my shirt, palming my breast so aggressively, I wince.

Using both of my hands, I push away from him as hard as I can until he releases me. I attempt to catch my breath and jump out of the car, but I make it three feet before he catches up to me, snatching me by the shoulders and backing me up against the car again. The craziness in his eyes sends my fight or flight into overdrive, and I'm stuck, unable to choose between the two. I search his face for answers; I've never seen him like this. When he sees the fear in my eyes, his face softens, and he pulls me into him. His hand runs up and down my back in an attempt to soothe me.

"I-I'm going to go inside for the night. Thanks for the movie," I mumble and attempt to pull away. His grip tightens, and I stiffen. He reaches for the passenger door, opening it and instructing me to get in. Against my better judgement, I get in and sit down. He walks back around to his side and joins me. After sitting in silence for a few minutes, I reach for the radio, and his hand darts out, swatting mine away.

"What the fuck has gotten into you?" I shout with rounded eyes. Jolting backward from startlement, I listen to his maniacal laughter.

"Me? You ask what has got into *me*? Have you looked in the mirror lately?" he asks between laughing fits. I stare, trying to figure out exactly what he's insinuating. When he realizes I don't know what he's talking about, he laughs louder. "You've let yourself go, Maevis."

My breathing halts within seconds as I narrow my gaze, tears threatening to form. "I don't see anything wrong with me…"

The smallness of my own voice makes me shrink into myself.

"Look harder," he snaps back, and I gasp.

"You don't get to speak to me like that, Ross. There is *nothing* wrong with me. Where is this coming from?" I question on a shaky breath. We sit in silence a few more moments, our elevating breaths the only sound until he slaps the dash, and I jump.

"And with this job you just won't let go. Are you fucking

your way to the top or something? You keep talking about this new position you're working for and some presentation. There's no way you're doing all this just on smarts and wits alone. So, what gives?"

I harden my jaw, trying to process everything he's saying, but it's not registering. This can't be the same man I fell in love with. This can't be the same man I agreed to marry with stars in my eyes. Heavy tears slip down my cheeks before I quickly swipe them away.

"I think we need some time apart for the rest of the night. I'm going to go inside now," I whisper, turning away from him. His hand darts out, squeezing the top of my thigh, and I freeze as I await his next move.

"I'm sorry. I didn't mean what I said. I just...I want what's best for you, Maevis. When you become my wife, you'll have an image to uphold, and I don't want anyone thinking any less of you when compared to me," he says in a soft tone, leaning over to place a kiss on my shoulder as I continue staring out the window. "I have faith in you, baby. And that's why I'm still with you. I know you'll get yourself back together. How about I pay for a spa day? Get something done with that hair of yours. And I know a damn good nutritionist. I'll get you in touch with him asap."

His words send ice through my veins, a sudden piercing in my chest, and I fight not to crumple over from the pain.

Rather than spiral into another argument, I nod in agreement and flash a fake, convincing smile. When he finally releases my thigh, I release a long, weighted breath and step out of the car.

"Have a good night, sweetheart," he says from the driver's seat.

"Good night, Ross," I reply and close the car door.

He doesn't even take the time to make sure I get into my

house. Afraid of my potential stalker, I race inside and reset the alarm before falling onto my couch in a flood of tears. No amount of time can help me process how my relationship has arrived at such a deep, dark place. No amount of time can help me crawl out.

Because what Ross wants, he *always* gets.

CHAPTER
SIX

I'm not sure if I've ever been so excited to wake up at six in the morning for work.

Unfortunately, my excitement doesn't override the eerie feeling I fell asleep with last night. I push back my covers and survey my room to ensure I'm alone. Tip-toeing to the top of my stairs, I release a deep breath when I notice my alarm is still armed, the locks on my door still in place. With the meeting of a lifetime only hours away, I push down any anxiety and panic begging to escape their confines.

And it was worth it, because by nine, I'm already relaxing at my desk after nailing my yearly roundup presentation. I started working for Stark Financial right after college, and today marks my final evaluation pre-promotion.

One of the higher-ups, the Chief Marketing Officer, subtly hinted she heard the CFO position is mine—if I could provide strong financials and profitability strategies for the upcoming fiscal year, that is. At the end of my presentation, she gave me a discreet wink before clapping with the rest of the table.

After following up on a few emails, I reward myself with a quick trip to the corner bakery and then head back to finish the rest of my afternoon agenda. Halfway through my second sip of coffee, I realize Ross never even wished me good luck for my presentation. He's known about it for a month, and he couldn't even send a simple text. Frustration gets the best of me as I crack the pen in my other hand, sending jet-black ink splattering across my lavender blouse.

I'm jumping out of my seat to try to do damage control on the mess I've created as Rose pokes her head around the door to let me know I have a special delivery. Noticing my issue, she lets me know she has an extra blouse in her car. Before grabbing it, she pads over to my desk and places a large arrangement of valerian and lavender flowers next to my computer. My eyes wander to the top, where a mini envelope is poked into the blooms.

Well...it's a good thing I didn't call him and go on a rant like I was about to do.

"I guess I've been a little too hard on him. Ross really does know how to treat a lady," she comments with a bright smile before turning to run out the door to fetch the extra blouse from her car. I offer her a forced smile back before thanking her and grabbing the card as she exits my office.

Picking up my phone, I quickly dial Ross' number to thank him for the gift. I'm interested to see if he sent them for all the canceled dinner dates or as good luck for my meeting.

The phone rings for so long, I almost hang up before he finally answers. "Hey babe, I'm in a meeting. Could I give you a call back?" he asks, exasperated as usual, as if I'm the biggest burden.

"Sure, no problem. I was just calling to say thank you for the flowers. I'm shocked you even knew these were my favorite."

The line goes silent for a moment. "You there?" I ask, confused.

"I didn't send any flowers, Maevis," he deadpans on the other end.

My eyes go wide at his statement. Anika makes her way into my office, and I quickly question if anyone else had received an arrangement. She shakes her head no and eyes me up and down with a quizzical look.

"Do you happen to know who dropped them off?" I ask, holding my breath as I await her answer. Again, she shakes her head. "They were on my desk when I got back from the bathroom, and Rose said she would run them into you."

Though I'm hopeful I'm overreacting, my hand holding the small card instantly begins to shake. I quickly open the mini envelope, and the room begins to spin as I read the immaculate handwriting written in bright blue ink.

An exact match to the note from yesterday.

"Babe, are you there? Is there a card with it?" Ross asks in a panic before I quickly hang up and fall back into my leather chair. My breaths become shallow as I read over the note again and again, trying to process what it means.

My phone is a constant buzz in the background—I've already missed three calls from Ross as time stands still. My mind keeps telling me to answer it, but my hands won't release the tiny white card.

Just as I'm about to pass out from panic, Rose comes back through my office door, chattering about a new brunch spot, before she notices my face is one of dread. Dropping the blouse on my desk, she rushes to my side. "What's wrong? Did something happen? Did you take your anxiety medication today?"

My best friend takes better care of me than my own fiancé.

Without a word, I slide the card over to her. After reading it, she looks back at me. "What's the big deal? You don't like Ross to watch you sleep?" she asks with a nervous giggle.

I shake my head no before thrusting the card back at her. "The flowers aren't from Ross, and that's not his handwriting," I say in a low whisper. Rose almost topples over at my statement, and the three of us lean over the card to read it again.

"You looked beautiful while sleeping last night. Sweet dreams, Duchess."

My friends shoot their gazes back up to me in alarm. I drag my hands down my face and wait for one of them to speak, because I can't.

"You have to call the police, Maevis," Anika speaks first. Rose nods quietly before promptly standing above me. "I agree. This could be...this could turn out bad. What if someone really was watching you?" Rose rambles on while pulling her phone from her pocket, presumably to call the authorities for me. I place my hand on top of her phone with widened eyes.

"Don't. I don't...I don't want to cause a scene. Let me speak to Ross about it first, okay?" I beg her. The disappointment etched across both their faces lets me know I'm being a moron, but I already have too much on my plate to fit this issue on there as well.

"Promise me," Rose says in a stern tone. I cock a brow before realizing she's making me promise I'll call the police to make a report.

I nod a few times before offering a small, tired smile.

"I promise," I whisper.

My chest tightens slightly, making me sit up straight. My own body is trying to warn me about the repercussions of lying to my best friend.

Because that's exactly what I just did.

CHAPTER
SEVEN

During my panic attack about *my secret admirer*, Ross had called my secretary to make sure we were still on for dinner tonight. Naturally, he also informed her he wouldn't be able to pick me up—he would meet me at the restaurant. The stress ball on my desk was getting overworked with my rage. A single tear slid down my cheek as I thought about how not only was he making me drive myself to the dinner date *he* planned, but he never mentioned my monumental meeting in the message he left with Anika. Throwing the stress ball across the room and watching it bounce off the wall did little to relieve my stress.

As much as I debated driving my car off Lakeshore Drive and straight into Lake Michigan, I decided it was better to go straight home and sink into my couch instead. I park the car and gather my belongings before my phone rings through the car speakers. I throw my head back against the headrest and let out a sigh before answering. "Hi, Daddy," I say with closed eyes.

"Maevis, what is this I hear about you backing out of your wedding?" he scolds through the car speakers. My eyes snap open at his question.

"Who said I was backing out of the wedding?"

"Your mother also let me know you don't plan on giving Ross any children. Is that right?" he asks, anger lacing his tone.

"Well, that was a conversation between Ross and I, but

that's correct. I've never really wanted kids, and up until a month or so ago, he didn't care," I explain in an aggravated tone. I calm myself down, reminding myself all my father has ever wanted for me was a good life. I assure myself he means well and take a few more breaths as I await his reply.

"Maevis, the whole point of having a wife is for her to bear children. Am I missing something here?"

The rage that consumes my mind has me seeing red as my hands clutch the steering wheel.

"Maevis, are you there? Do not fuck up your chance at living an easy life. Your mother and I provided you with that at home, but our coddling you stops here."

"*Coddling*?" I yell into the open space of my car. "You and Mom forced me to move back home because you were paranoid I would end up with someone who wasn't up to your standards. I never asked for the handouts you gave me. The handouts that abruptly stopped after college, by the way."

My breathing is so elevated, my windows are beginning to fog. "If you and Mom want us to have children so bad, adopt them and give them to us yourselves," I say before ending the call. I let out a scream, attempting to alleviate the frustration of being an only child with overbearing parents.

I gather my things again and ignore another incoming call from my father.

Thankfully, it's still daylight, and I don't have to run to my doorstep in fear of someone following, but I'm still cautious, casting multiple glances over my shoulder. I close the door behind me and turn off the alarm, kicking off my shoes before I head into the kitchen. As I do, a deep voice rattles through the room, shaking me to my core.

"Hello, Duchess. Before you get any ideas, slowly set your phone on the table behind you."

I turn to see a man seated in the loveseat by the bay

window. His black and white mask covers his entire face but leaves his short, dark hair hanging freely around it. He's sprawled out, an arm on each one of the arms of the chair, his long legs spread in front of him.

Tears spring to the back of my eyes; my paranoia has finally come to life, and it's sitting right in front of me. "P-please don't hurt me. Whatever you—"

He cuts me off before the rest of my begging ensues. "I'm going to stop you right there before you tell me I can have whatever I want," he says with a tilt of his head. His chest rises and falls with a deep breath, and it's then I realize exactly how big he is. He's in an all-black sweatsuit, but I can still see how muscular he is beneath all the fabric. "I'm not here for money or material things. So be a good girl and put the phone on the table like I asked."

Shakily, I reach into my blazer pocket and place my cell phone on the end table nearby. As I glance at the door and then back at him, he releases a husky laugh. "I assure you, I'm faster than you, so let's not try it. Lose the blazer and have a seat on the couch."

His words send a chill down my spine as I accept my loss and follow his instructions. As soon as I sit, he leans forward, resting his elbows on his knees. "Before we start this conversation, I need you to understand something. If you scream, I'll have to tape your mouth shut, and that's the last thing I want to do. I'd much rather stare at those pretty lips of yours instead," he says as his gaze falls to my mouth. It lingers for a moment before moving to my breasts, which are spilling over the blouse Rose loaned me. I quickly adjust my shirt, pulling it as high up as it can go, earning a low growl from him.

Focusing back on my intruder, I notice his eyes are the only detail of his face I can see due to his mask. They're such a deep, emerald green, I get lost in them for a moment. My gaze travels to his large hands hanging between his legs, the ivory skin the only other part of him I can see, aside from his neck.

"So, Maevis," he begins, and my heart flutters at the sound of my name on his lips. I gulp audibly from embarrassment. "What do you do for work?"

The nonchalant question has my mouth agape and eyes blinking in confusion.

"I'm not here to hurt you, so let's be adults and have a civilized conversation. What do you do for work, beautiful?"

I swallow before I tell him I'm an accounting manager and analyst, adding the company name when he asks. Part of me believes he already knows the answer, but I keep my mouth shut. His questions are non-invasive until his eyes drift to my left hand. "What's the ring for?" he questions. My eyes glance down at the gaudy diamond on my finger. A single tear rolls down my cheek, and my mouth runs dry as he adds, "Who's the lucky man? Woman?"

I'm not sure why, but his voice sounds annoyed. When I don't answer, he lifts a leg and kicks the coffee table across the room; I jump and fall back onto the couch in fear.

"Take it off," he seethes.

My hands shake at the change in his demeanor along with his command, but I stay frozen. He stands from his seat and stalks over to me, resting a hand on the back of the couch, caging my head in.

"Take the fucking ring off, or I'll do it for you."

Shaky hands remove the ring from my finger and clasp it in a fragile fist. Holding out his hand, he points with an index finger to his palm, waiting for me to hand it over. More tears fall as I place it in his hand and cower even further into the couch cushions.

Pocketing the ring, he grabs my ponytail at the base and yanks my head to the side while turning me until I'm flat on my back on the couch. The room spins, and I shut my eyes as tight as I can, accepting the assault I'm positive is about to take place as I feel him climb on top of me.

His lips press to my ear, and I flinch as he starts to speak. "I've waited so long to feel your body pinned beneath me, Duchess. Let's play a game, shall we?" he asks in a mockingly playful voice. My eyes remain tightly shut, counting the seconds as I listen to the synchronization of our breaths. I lose count, unsure of how long I've remained silent, when I feel his hand grip my jaw. His grasp tightens as my eyes widen with fear, and I quickly shut them again. When I still don't respond, I hear him growl as he lifts my chin.

"Open your fucking eyes and look at me."

My breathing is so sporadic, I'm convinced a panic attack is about to consume me. Opening my eyes, I'm met with his green ones. "The game is *truth or dare*," he says before producing a knife from his pocket. I can't help but scream, and he claps his hand over my mouth. "Remember our deal about screaming, yeah?" he asks, and I quickly nod in understanding. "Now, any time one of us doesn't complete a dare or answer a question, the other gets to have a little *slice* of fun with a body part of their choosing."

I whimper at his words.

"I'll go first, and so help me, if you scream when I remove my hand..." he says before slowly peeling his hand from my mouth. I dart my tongue out to lick my dry lips, and a sound suspiciously close to a groan comes from his throat.

"Are you happy?"

His question is such a hard blow, I feel like he hit me in the temple as hard as he could.

More tears fall as I ponder his question.

"Are you happy with him?" he asks again with additional clarification.

The added explication sends me over the edge, and sobs begin to rack my body. When minutes go by without me answering, he presses the tip of the knife into the hollow of my throat, and I yelp. "I really don't want to mark this pretty brown skin, Maevis, but I'll happily draw blood if I must. Then, I'll clean it up with my tongue just to get a taste of you."

His statement sends a jolt of panic through my system.

"No!" I yell in answer, my breathing so fast, I can see my chest rising and falling while my entire body shakes.

"No what, Maevis?" he asks, waiting for more details.

"No, I'm not happy," I follow up, seemingly giving him the response he was waiting for.

A rumbling, husky chuckle vibrates his body atop mine before he drags the knife to the middle of my chest. He doesn't draw any blood, instead pulling my blouse down to expose my bra. His gaze stays there until I release another sob, and his eyes find mine once more.

"Don't worry, Duchess. My time here is up. We'll have to finish the rest of our game later," he says before fixing my blouse and climbing off the couch. He pockets his knife and runs his thumb across my bottom lip. He turns to leave, but when he reaches the door, he looks back at me one last time.

"You know you're worth more, right?"

I never turn to look at him, fearful of what he might do if I move.

"W-what?" I stutter, keeping my eyes glued to the ceiling as tears fall down my face.

"You're worth more than that asshole could ever give you. You deserve better. You know it, I know it. Don't be as stupid as he makes you out to be," he says while twisting the doorknob.

A sea of tears spills down each cheek as his words repeat in my head.

How does he know about my relationship?

It clicks in my head—my assumption was correct. Every question he asked was only to create small talk because he already knew the answer to every single question.

"Don't bother calling the police. Wouldn't want any bad blood between us. See you soon," he says before he exits.

My body shakes as tears fall hard and quick. My brain is telling me to get up and lock the door, but my body refuses to listen. I'm unable to move, silence taking over as I remain on my back in shock, staring up at the blank, white ceiling.

CHAPTER

EIGHT

An hour.

That's how long I laid in the same spot on the couch, trying to gather myself and attempting to process what just happened.

I wanted to call Rose and scream for her to help me, but I knew she would only insist I call the police, and when I inevitably refused, she would do it herself. I couldn't call Ross because...well, I just flat-out didn't want to. He wouldn't believe me; he would chalk it up to me wanting attention.

After telling myself I'm okay, I jump off the couch, lock the door, and set the alarm. My pulse speeds up when my memory snaps into place. I realize the alarm was on when I came home, yet...he was still sitting here.

I press my forehead against the coolness of the door and then shoot upstairs to get ready for the dinner I'm now hesitant to even attend while simultaneously changing my alarm code on my phone. Regardless of how the night goes, I know I need to address the issues in my relationship.

Plugging in my flatiron, I stare in the mirror for a moment. I abhor straightening my hair instead of letting my natural curls flow freely, but every time we go out, Ross makes a point to comment how much he likes my hair better when it's straight. I release a frustrated groan into the bathroom and snatch the plug out of the outlet. Grabbing my hair product, I begin working it through my hair, giving my strands the love they deserve.

After throwing my thick curls into a bun, applying minimal makeup—because Ross likes a more natural look—and donning a little black dress that shows a bit more thigh than I'm used to, I realize I'll need to walk to my car alone. Thankfully, I remember this is Chicago, and I can get an Uber in less than ten minutes. Opening the app, I gawk at the price of an Uber on a Friday night. I close out of the app and glance over at the couch where I was just pinned underneath a masked man I don't know. Terror creeps its way back in, along with another feeling I can't quite pinpoint.

Swallowing my pride, I re-open the app and request an Uber that is only five minutes away. At least that way, I'll have a witness if anything were to happen to me.

The Uber drops me off on the corner of Dearborn Street at La Grande Boucherie. Excitement had finally bloomed in my chest on the ride over. I've begged Ross to take me here for over a year. I texted him updates the entire way but haven't received a reply, so him meeting me in the lobby would be too much to hope for. I'm approaching the host desk when I hear a voice— one I've loathed from the first day I heard it.

Ross' mother.

Ross waves me over to their table without standing to greet me, continuing a conversation with his mother instead. When my fiancé finally decides to speak to me, I'm met with a condescending tone. "Hello, darling. How was your day? Mother and I were just discussing your current position at work," he says before setting his lips in a thin line. My eyes flash over to his mother as she sips her glass of wine and looks at me disapprovingly, as per usual.

"Hello, Margaret. How are you doing?" I ask with a tight

smile, trying to be courteous. After ten seconds of no reply, I try to answer my fiancé's question. "Today was great. I—"

Ross cuts me off before I can explain my day while reaching for my hand, but I slide it away to put my napkin in my lap. He narrows his gaze at me for a split second when he notices I don't put my hand back out for him to take. I flash a smile, unsure of my own actions in the moment. "I had a brief phone meeting for a large merger that could possibly bring in the biggest deal of my career. He's a piece of work, though. Real quiet and dark type I can't quite get a read on. Anyway, who were the flowers from?" he asks with inquisitive eyes.

I swallow my panic down before taking a sip of water from the glass in front of me. "The new girl I trained sent them to me as a thank you. She transferred to our New York location last week after her training was complete."

The lie rolls off my tongue so effortlessly, my smile afterwards is genuine because I'm so proud of myself. My entire life, I've never been good at lying. I remain so focused on pleasing those around me, I've never really had the mental capacity to lie to save myself from a conflict. Still, I want to move on from the conversation before either of them can interrogate me any further on the subject.

"Anyway, I did my final presentation for Stark Financial, and I feel like the Chief Financial Officer position will be mine sooner rather than later," I say, slightly too enthusiastically. Ross murmurs a congratulations before his mother speaks, cutting our interaction short.

"Oh, sorry, dear. I'm just confused. Didn't you say this last year as well?" she inquires with her nose turned up. I shrink into my chair instead of telling her to mind her own fucking business.

After ordering myself a diet coke with extra ice, I finally brave speaking. "Well...yes, but I—"

She laughs, holding up her hand. "I'm no good at listening to excuses. I just don't want to keep seeing my son fund your lifestyle."

"Excuse me?" I question, a little louder than I should.

"Ross informed me and his father about the heathen you cared for years ago when you two met in college. Heard you blew a good chunk of your time and money on him. Just how does a twenty-eight-year-old woman in your position afford a million-dollar home in Chicago with such an insignificant job?" she inquires with her nose turned so far up in the air, I'm shocked she doesn't flip out of her seat.

"Mother, that's enough," Ross admonishes from across the table. His mother gives a sly smirk before shrugging her shoulders nonchalantly.

I wait for Ross to say more in my defense, but he just stares at me as if he doesn't know how to defend me in front of his mother. My heart plummets further when a look flashes across his face as if he's disappointed in me.

"Throwing one's life savings away for the hopes and dreams of someone who didn't even stay with you is quite embarrassing, is it not?" she croons from beside me.

Vertigo crashes into me; I don't feel balanced in my chair with this amount of anger bubbling over. Neither she, nor anyone else in my family, knows what happened while I was away at school.

And it's none of their business.

I stare at the bare plate in front of me, trying to ground myself, but she just restarts her verbal assault. "More importantly, how is Mallory doing these days?"

Did she just ask him about his fucking secretary while I'm sitting right here?

"Where's your ring?" Ross asks suddenly, his brow

furrowed as the two of them stare at my hand wrapped around the glass of diet coke I'm clutching for moral support.

"I-I must have left it on the counter when I was doing my hair."

He lifts the corner of his upper lip in a grimace at my answer, his eyes roaming over my curls in disgust. Meanwhile, his mother's eyes raise from my hand to my hair. "That's what you doing your hair looks like? Would a straightener kill you?" she asks with a shake of her head. Such an insult from anyone would hurt, but an insult of that caliber coming from another minority woman has me seeing red. My own gaze travels over her perfectly straightened dark hair against her brown skin. While it's quite gorgeous, I feel the sadness in my soul when I remember her telling me how 'unprofessional' her curls are for the real world.

Don't be as stupid as he makes you out to be.

"Ross, you used to date women of such high caliber. Hopefully, the children this one breeds for the family come with—"

Without a word, I violently stand from the table and throw my napkin in front of me. "Enjoy your date with your mother," I hiss at Ross before turning in Margaret's direction. "Always a pleasure, *Margaret*." I plaster the fakest smile I can manage on my face before grabbing my purse and phone and darting out of the double glass doors of the beautiful restaurant I had waited so long to visit.

I'm standing on the curb, doing my best to flag down a taxi because an Uber would take too long, when someone wraps a hand around my arm and yanks me back onto the sidewalk. I stumble as I try to catch my footing.

"What the fuck was that, Maevis?" Ross asks with fire in his eyes.

When he notices me giving the exact look back to him, his hand darts out and wraps around my wrist, violently pulling me back toward him. My eyes flare in alarm at the force he uses, and instead of him releasing me, his grip tightens until I wince in pain. Never changing his expression, he releases me and repeats his question.

"Are you kidding me right now?" I shout, making pedestrians glance in our direction, though none of them stop. *Typical Chicago nature at its finest.* "Your mother can't talk to me like that, Ross! I'm an adult, not an animal to be bred at someone's fucking expense! She used the word *breed.* What is this, the 1700s?"

My words are coming out like rapid fire in a warzone.

"I'm a woman with her own job, her own finances, and where the fuck does she get the idea that you give me money?" I whisper-scream, licking my lips like a crazed woman.

He looks me up and down. "I gave you money for your nails two weeks ago."

My stalker's words play in my head for the second time tonight. *You're worth more than that asshole could ever give you.*

I clench my jaw so hard at his words, I feel a muscle pulse. "My fucking credit card was locked because I had a fraudulent charge, and I paid you back the same fucking day in cash when I got home!"

I stomp back over to the curb as I spot a bright yellow taxicab at the light.

Please God, if you love me, change the light.

The light turns green, and my arm flails so ridiculously, the cab driver looks like he doesn't want to stop until I twist my face into a pleading look. He pulls over to the curb, and I swiftly grip the door handle.

"If you get in that car, don't expect me to come after you," Ross warns from behind me.

You deserve better.

That's three times my stalker has intervened in my relationship within an hour.

Without turning around, I open the door and get in. Before closing it, I stare into the deep brown eyes I had fallen in love with. The brown eyes I used to be able to lose myself in at any time of day. The brown eyes that would comfort me in my times of need. Unfortunately, those brown eyes no longer hold the same love and comfort they did in the beginning of our relationship.

"I expect nothing less from someone who can't get off their mother's tit at the age of thirty-three."

His mouth falls open at my words; his eyes resemble a deer in headlights. The sight of him is making me sick to my stomach, and a deep, dark part of me I've never explored wants to pound my fists into his face until I see puddles of red.

Snapping out of my vision, I vaguely question my sanity before focusing on the man I agreed to marry in a few short months. "Fuck you and your ego. I deserve better than this," I spit before I slam the door shut, apologizing to the driver and giving him my address as he pulls out into the heavy Friday night Chicago traffic.

CHAPTER

NINE

The taxi drops me off at home for double the price an Uber would've cost me, but it was worth every penny. If I had to deal with one more second of that mommy and son duo, I was going to set my dinner fork upright, aim it at my eye, and slam my head on the table.

I reach my front door, fumbling around in my purse for my keys, and dread begins to set in when I don't find them after what feels like an eternity of searching. I squat on my porch and frantically check for the keys as I watch the taxi driver pull away.

"No, no, no, no," I whisper as the darkness closes in. My hair unravels from its bun, and dark curls fall into my eyes. I dump the contents of my purse out in pure hope that I see my keys amongst the extra tissues, lipstick, and mascara.

"Who are you talking to out here, Duchess?" a deep male voice inquires. I stumble forward before two large hands grip my shoulders from behind and steady me. Even though the thought of him is terrifying, the tone of his voice wrapped in silk is one I could never forget even if I tried.

"Please, don't...please don't hurt me. I listened to what you said earlier. I didn't call the cops. I'll forget it ever happened," I plead as I fight back the forming tears.

I hear him tsk from behind me as he squats to whisper in my ear, "That's a shame. I don't want to forget any of it—especially you squirming beneath me with my knife pressed to your throat."

My body goes rigid as his hand comes around, holding out a key ring in front of me—my house *and* car keys.

Duplicates.

My mouth goes dry at the sight.

Slowly, he stands, moving to position himself in front of me, and holds his hand out. The left side of my brain tells me to scream for help while the right side tells me to place my hand in his, allow him to help me stand. Listening to the right, I force myself to look at him, but I'm met with his chest. He has to be at least six-three against my five-foot-five-inch height. My eyes trail upward until they meet his behind the mask he's wearing. We stare at each other for a moment before he quickly unlocks the door, pulls me inside, and disarms my alarm.

MY alarm.

The fact that he already knows the new passcode sends chills down my spine.

"Upstairs. Now."

His command has me frozen, knowing my bed is upstairs.

"Please, Duchess," he adds softly. His softened tone throws me off, and I eye him suspiciously.

My legs begin to shuffle toward the stairs, and I lean down to kick off my shoes, but instead, I'm met with him kneeling to remove them for me. I'm stunned at the sight, and he has to instruct me to keep moving to walk up the stairs. Once I make it up, I stand in the hallway until he tells me where to go.

"Bathroom."

I draw in a shaky breath—the only bathroom up here is connected to my bedroom. I walk until I reach the correct room and nervously hand-fuck the wall until I find the light switch. I feel his hand on my shoulder, leading me to the bed, and my lips tremble with fear.

"Sit here," he says before going into the bathroom. I hear rustling, then the knob of the tub turning and water flowing. I consider making a run for the front door but force myself to remain seated. I've never been a runner, and now wasn't the time to test my athleticism. He hasn't threatened me so far, so I'd rather not piss him off.

Chills travel up my spine when I think about us on the couch earlier, how I was at his mercy, and yet, I'm deciding to trust him in this moment. My brain goes into overdrive when I think about his knife pressed to my throat as his weight kept me pinned. I catch myself overheating and begin to question my own thoughts when I finally snap out of whatever trance I put myself in.

A few minutes go by before he comes back out, and I can still hear the water running.

He instructs me to go in the bathroom, get undressed, and get in the tub. I turn back to look at him when I notice he isn't following me into the bathroom. Standing near my dresser with my phone in his hand, he tilts his head slightly, and I can tell it's a warning to not do anything stupid.

Wandering over to the vanity, I look at the bathtub and notice piles of bubbles from the bubble bath I keep on the ledge, and my body begins to tremble as I peel my dress off, followed by my bra and underwear. My morals tell me to resist his demands, but the events of dinner have me batting them away. If he truly wanted to hurt me, he would have done it earlier.

Afraid he's going to enter the bathroom unannounced, I quickly step into the tub and slide down into the perfectly heated water.

"Are you in?" he calls from the other room.

I sit quietly for a moment, biting my lower lip. "Y-yes. I'm in," I answer on a shaky breath.

He saunters in with his hands in the pockets of the same black sweatsuit he wore earlier. His gaze travels over the bathtub,, where I sink further under the bubbles to ensure he can't see any part of me below my neck.

"If you don't want me to touch you, I won't."

His husky voice hurls me into a whirlwind, his scent of musk and pine sending me into overdrive as I squeeze my legs together underneath the water. The scent seems familiar yet

foreign to me, and my brain short-circuits while trying to figure out what it reminds me of. I'm pulled from my thoughts when he clears his throat, and his scent encapsulates me once more. *Who have I turned into? A masked man I don't know has me naked in a bathtub and is asking for permission to touch me.* He grabs a washcloth and liquid soap from nearby, holding them up while waiting for my approval. I force a hard swallow before I make my decision. It's been months since Ross last touched me intimately, and I'm about to let a stranger give me a bath.

Is this considered cheating? People in hospitals get sponge baths all the time, so this can't be considered cheating after the night I've had.

You're an idiot for that comparison.

I gaze at his hands, and the size of them has my mouth popping open as I imagine them wrapped around my neck, choking me until the edges of my vision go black.

"Duchess?" he asks, snapping me out of my lurid thoughts.

I nod slowly, my gaze never leaving his.

He stalks over, kneeling next to the bath to begin at the nape of my neck and work his way down my back. "Want to tell me why you left in an Uber but came back in a taxi?" he questions as I turn my head to look at him, his mask illuminated in the dimmed light of the bathroom. I can see slight strokes of grey in the black paint that I missed before.

He knew I took the Uber. He was watching me even when I thought he wasn't.

I inhale and release a shaky breath before turning my gaze away from him again.

"I'd rather not be embarrassed twice in one night," I reply under my breath. He pauses before dunking the cloth in the water and raising it to the front of my neck, slowly working it down. Our eyes meet again when he stops right above my breasts, and I nod to give him the go-ahead. When he runs the cloth over my right breast, he clears his throat, and I can feel my nipples harden at his touch.

"Tell me what happened. That's an order, Duchess, not a request."

After a moment of tense silence, I spill my word vomit as if he's Rose or Anika and we're gossiping about work drama. I can feel his hands moving as he washes the rest of my body, and he stops to glance at me while I speak. But when I finish, I notice his hands resting in the water right above my leg. Our gazes connect again before his fingers slowly move toward my inner thigh.

"And did you end things with him? That family?"

His words cut through me—not because of his language, but because I'm embarrassed to tell him I let them speak to me that way. I might have left the restaurant, but I didn't tell his mother exactly what I thought of her. I let Ross sit there while she berated me like I was a worthless piece of trash instead of reprimanding him in front of her.

I swallow as his fingers reach the apex of my thighs.

"You haven't stopped me yet," he states with a tilt of his head. "If you want me to stop, you need to speak."

My breathing goes ragged as I lick my lips, running through every possible scenario in my head. For as still as he is, I'm everything but that in this moment.

"I have self-control, Duchess, but it can only hold out for so long with someone as perfect as you. I need an answer," he says with hardened green eyes behind his mask.

Memories of hearing Ross' secretary in the background of our late-night phone calls while he's at the office briefly play in my head before I realize I don't give a fuck anymore. Everyone on this Earth might think I'm stupid, and it's partially my fault for following along with their games. But I know what my fiancé does behind my back, and I'm done being the one constantly fucked over, the one being used like cattle in a field to save the hungry.

I'm hungry.

I want the salvation.

"*Now,*" his voice cuts through the silence.

My breathing turns rapid as my hand grips his forearm. "Take the mask off," I say breathlessly, and he shakes his head no. "At least tell me your name," I plead, and again, he declines before beginning to pull his hand away. I grip his forearm once more, tighter, and pull his hand to hover over the area I know will definitely be considered cheating.

"You sent the bouquet of Valerians. That was you...right? Can I call you *V?*" I ask, and he nods his head.

"Sounds a little *V for Vendetta*-ish, but it's better than nothing," I joke and hear him cut off a chuckle. I smile while studying his mask once more. "The correlation isn't too far off," he replies, and we both fall silent again.

We stare at each other for what feels like eternity before his hand grabs the back of my neck and the fingers of the other slide down to plunge into my entrance, leaving me stunned as I inhale a sharp breath.

This is definitely considered cheating.

Regardless, I never open my mouth to tell him to stop. His massive fingers drive into me repeatedly, stopping every so often for him to rub my most sensitive spot before pulling them achingly close to the edge of my entrance and rubbing my clit in perfect timing with his thumb.

"Are you ever going to realize what you're capable of? What a woman like you deserves?" he asks, anger lacing his words. When I don't answer, his grip on the back of my neck tightens before he forces me underwater with one violent, quick push. I fight to bring my head above the surface as he thrusts two fingers back inside me, effortlessly driving me to the edge of my release. Then, just as quickly as he started, he stops and pulls me up for air, still gripping the nape of my neck.

I gasp as I fight for air. "Are you fucking crazy?"

"I can be," he retorts. "Leave him, Maevis."

My eyes blow wide at his statement.

"You think I didn't notice the heavy makeup only below your left eye? When did he hit you? I'll fucking kill him. Tell me it was him so I can break his neck," he lashes out.

When I don't answer, he thrusts me back under the water as I claw at his arms.

This time, I'm under for much longer as his thumb makes tiny circles around my clit, adding just the right amount of pressure for me to climb the ladder of my climax. As I flail and my lungs beg for air, my vision begins to blur, my limbs slowly going limp.

Just when I thought he was going to let me drift away into the abyss, he plunges three fingers into me and brings me up for air at the same time. "What do you want, Maevis?" he growls from beside me.

I know what I want, but I'm afraid to speak life into it.

He repeats his question again, startling me from my thoughts. "Have it your way then," he says before preparing to force me underwater again, but my arms fly out, gripping the sides of the tub.

His fingers curl inside me, hitting the perfect spot, sending shudders through my body before he pulls them out. I want to protest him leaving my body, but I focus on the question at hand.

"I-I want them to burn," I confess as we both pause, our heavy breathing filling the silent void. I turn to look at those deep green eyes, now filled with fire and desire. "I want them *all* to burn. I want to take back control of my life."

He nods in understanding before his fingers work their way into my pussy again, a moan escaping before I can stop it from leaving my lips. His other hand releases my neck as he works my nipples, pinching and releasing them. The pairing of pain and pleasure is my undoing as I squirm at his touch, and his fingers curl inside me at the perfect angle again. I involuntarily arch my back, and the orgasm that ripples through every inch of my body is something I've never experienced. My ears ring with my own screams as I finally teeter over the edge and free-fall at his mercy.

Trying to fill my lungs with air while my heart beats out of my chest from the adrenaline of my orgasm has me seeing stars as he effortlessly lifts me from the bathtub, soaking his clothes in the process. He places me on the vanity chair in the bathroom as he wraps a towel around my body to dry me off. My heavily lidded eyes raise to look at the man who just gave me the best orgasm I've ever had in my twenty-eight years of life.

"Why didn't you kill me?" I whisper and instantly want to take it back.

He stops his work before his hard eyes set on me. Raising the towel to gently wipe underneath my left eye, he reveals the bruise I had worked so hard to hide from the world and curses behind his mask.

"Because that was never my intention. This right here," he says, running his thumb over the tender bruise. "This will lead to a much darker place, one without the release I just gave you in the end."

Tears fall from my eyes for the twentieth time in one day.

Taking the towel, my masked stalker wipes them away before he helps me stand and leads me to the bed, my hand in his. Not once does he ogle my body as I stand naked before him. Instead, he pulls the covers back to let me crawl in and tugs them over my body once I'm settled.

Grabbing the television remote from my dresser, he skims the menu until he finds the streaming service he wants and searches for something specific. My mouth snaps shut when he finishes typing in the search bar. I bite my bottom lip to refrain from saying the wrong thing as he hits play and *The O.C.* blares from the speakers.

He kisses the top of my head, sending a wave of shock through me as he turns to leave. Involuntarily, I catch the hem of his sweatshirt before he's out of reach.

"Could you... Would you mind... I..."

I can't get the words to form before he turns around to remove my hand and gently place it back on the bed. "Tell me you want me to stay, and I will."

I stare at him dumbfounded. I can't register his words quickly enough as they play in my head for a solid minute.

He wants to know I need him, that I can't get through the night without him. He needs me to confirm that even though he pried his way into my life, I trust him enough to know he won't murder me in my sleep.

"I want you to stay," I say shakily as I pull the covers under my chin.

He nods his head. "I'll stay. But Maevis?"

My eyes connect with his, showing he has my full attention as my body relaxes with the knowledge he will stay.

"You're going to burn that misogynistic army of assholes to the fucking ground, starting tomorrow. The fire within you is slowly catching flame, Duchess."

I blink slowly, trying to process his claim.

"Every fire gets hungry, and I'm just here to provide the gasoline for you to feed its rage."

His words send a wave of electricity through my body, but a flash of hurt comes with it when he leaves the room, choosing to sleep downstairs instead of staying up here with me.

Why does a man I don't even know make me feel safer than my partner of six years?

And why am I allowing a masked man who has invaded my privacy multiple times to stay here? A man who almost just *drowned* me.

A man who also gave me an orgasm sent from God.

My brain tosses and turns through my questions and morals as I listen to Seth and Summer argue on the television.

He's not wrong when it comes to me not knowing who I am.

Not only do my fiancé and his family treat me like I'm beneath them, but my entire life, my own parents have dictated all my decisions—where I went to college, the sports I played, what I wore. Ultimately, they bribed me with a place of my own in the city, with the stipulation of me coming home and switching colleges to get away from the boy they didn't want me to date. They didn't approve of anyone until I met Ross, if I'm being honest. Being able to move away from them was a little slice of joy in a world that was steadily burning around me.

I slowly drift off to sleep as I accept I'm letting a complete stranger rearrange the life I worked so hard to build.

A life I'm not even sure is right for me.

A life I know, deep in my heart, will send me six feet under before I reach middle age.

A life that now, for some reason, feels safer with a masked man willing to hold me underwater until I see the change I need to make within myself.

CHAPTER

TEN

I would be a liar if I said waking up to a note from him instead of his physical form was what I desired.

Stay focused on what, exactly? I run through last night and pull my pillow over my face, screaming into the void. Throwing it to the side, I reach for my phone on the nightstand and flip it over to see twenty-three missed calls and three voicemails from Ross.

I don't have the mental capacity to even check my text messages, let alone listen to the voicemails, and I definitely don't have the bandwidth to go into work today. After I call in and shoot Rose a text, my phone rings almost instantly.

Rose's name flashes across the screen, forcing a smile from me.

"You called off too, didn't you?" I giggle into the phone.

"Obviously! Who the hell would I even speak to if you're not there?" she replied in a high-pitched voice. "Coffee at our spot in thirty?"

I'm up and dressed in a comfortable Champion sweatsuit with my hair thrown into a bun in less than ten minutes. As I descend the stairs, part of me was hoping to see my masked admirers' long legs sprawled out on the couch. I hold my

56

breath as I peek down the rest of the stairs and try to ignore the fact that my shoulders slump forward when I see an empty couch.

Throwing on my sunglasses, I thank God for whoever invented large frames to hide the bags under my eyes.

By the time I get to Jitters, Rose has already secured our favorite table in the back corner, along with our usual orders. A smile dances across my face when she notices me, and her hand waves frantically—she's matching my exact outfit in a different color. I plop down in the seat across from her. "A large part of me wishes this was alcohol after the night I had," I confess and take a sip of my iced coffee.

"Well, on the bright side, our coffee is free this morning," Rose sing-songs in her usual cheery voice.

"Please tell me you didn't waste your reward points on me," I say, feeling awful about not getting here before her to pay. But Rose shakes her head with her lips twisted to the side and a worry-free expression. "Nope. I went to order, and the barista said the drinks were already paid for."

It feels like the café has been turned to a sauna as the room begins to spin. Rose continues sipping her latte without a care in the world.

"Did...did you ask how it was already paid for?"

Rose has been a carefree soul ever since we met our freshman year of college, but right now, I need her to be a bit more focused.

"They said some guy came in about an hour ago and paid for two drinks and two breakfast sandwiches," she says with a shrug. I flare my eyes, and she finally catches on to my distress. "Oh shit," she mouths while setting her drink down on the table and licking the whipped cream from her lips. "It's him, isn't it? Your stalker!" she concludes loudly, and I have to shush her.

"What the fuck happened last night?" she whispers, leaning toward the middle of the table.

I make her swear to secrecy before I explain.

It takes her fifteen minutes to stop cursing Ross' mom before I can move on. "Can't we just poison her and get it over with?" Rose pouts over her cup. I laugh and reprimand her at the thought of murder before she demand I continue with the rest of the story. By the time I confess the night I had with my masked man, Rose's jaw is damn near touching the top of the table.

"You cheated on Ross?" she whisper-screams across the table before a devilish smile sweeps across her face. "To be fair, we both know him and his secretary have something going on."

My stomach was in knots at the thought of me cheating, but it unravels itself shortly after, because I know deep in my heart that she's right. I just don't know how to catch Ross and his secretary in the act.

And do I really want to?

I know things have been rocky lately, but do I really want to throw away years of a steady relationship? A shudder travels through me at the thought of having to start over in the dating pool.

"So...what did he look like? Did he hurt you? You got him to remove the mask, right?"

I'm perplexed Rose isn't more horrified at the situation I had somehow landed in, but I'm also relieved she isn't reprimanding me for my questionable choices with a masked stalker. I open my mouth to answer her questions when the bell to the front door of the café chimes. I lift my head and connect with Ross' steel narrowed gaze.

"Shit," Rose and I murmur under our breath. At the same

time, I flip my phone over to see thirteen more missed calls and two additional voicemails.

I bite my bottom lip as he saunters over to the table in his expensive peacoat, Rolex gleaming in the café lighting. The way he drips of money and luxury have the other women in the café gawking.

If only they knew the real him.

When he reaches our table, I cower, and Rose narrows her eyes at my reaction.

"Do you have any idea how many times I've called you?" he hisses while snatching my phone from the table and looking at the missed call notifications. The flames in his eyes grow wild, and he grips my elbow, pulling me upwards to stand. "We're leaving."

Rose swats his hand from my elbow, and my eyes blow wide. "Get your hands off her," she whispers, almost in shock at her own action. "She will let you know if she wants to leave. Do you want to leave, Maevis?"

I gawk at my best friend and swing my gaze over to my fiancé, who is giving me a look that says, *"you'll have to deal with me sooner or later. Might as well get it over with."*

Reluctantly, I grab my crossbody and push my chair in. I can see the hurt wash over Rose's face at my decision, and it kills me, but I know that if I don't leave with him now, I will have to deal with the consequences later.

"I'll call you later," I tell her before Ross grips my upper arm, flashing Rose an I-told-you-so smile and pulling me toward the exit.

The car ride is filled with a suffocating silence as my anxiety consumes me.

I never should have left the coffee shop.

I never should have left my best friend.

When he pulls in front of my house, we sit in the car for a

moment before I push the passenger-side door open and head toward the front door. My teeth press into my bottom lip, hoping he doesn't follow, but I hear his footsteps behind me. My hand shakes as I unlock the door, and he follows me inside. I place my crossbody on the hook by the door and turn around, only to be met with Ross' hand shooting up to grip my throat.

In one, swift motion, he slams me against the wall, forcing the breath from my lungs, and I grip his forearm with my hands. The crazed look in his eyes tells me all I need to know.

He didn't bring me here to talk.

He pulls me from the wall by the grip on my throat, turning and forcing me to walk backwards to the couch my stalker had me on the night before. His grip gets tighter, and I begin to stiffen in panic. His opposite hand begins tugging at the waistband of my sweatsuit, pulling them down to my ankles and completely off.

"I'm so sick of you not looking presentable in public. If you're going to be my wife, you need to look the part," he says while planting kisses down the side of my face. "I'll have to take my baby shopping, now won't I?"

The grip on my throat causes my eyes to sting with tears. I make every effort to tell him to stop, but the lack of air inhibits me. He rips my underwear down my thighs in one movement, and I begin to buck him off me as he finally releases my throat. I gasp for air, and the wild look in his eyes widens with confusion. "We have one little fight, and now you're going to act like you don't want me?" he asks while attempting to raise my sweatshirt.

Little fight?

My hands shoot out to grab the hem of my sweatshirt, stopping him in his efforts.

"What the fuck is going on with you Maevis?" he lashes out.

The fact that he's genuinely confused about this entire situation angers and scares me at the same time. He hasn't made an effort to be intimate in months, and now he feels entitled to *take* whatever he wants?

I snap my legs shut and push him further off me.

"It was not just some *little fight*, Ross. You and your mother belittled me like I was someone who didn't even deserve to be at the same table. You didn't even so much as slightly defend me. Instead, you reprimanded *me* for leaving. And you think I'm about to spread my legs for you?"

My chest heaves as anger spills from me, my breaths harsh and rugged as he stares at me in disbelief. He swallows and runs his hand down the side of his face before sucking in his bottom lip and huffing a laugh.

"Are you fucking laughing?" I ask while standing to retrieve my undergarments. I'm met with a backhand across the face that has me flying backwards onto the couch and clutching my cheek.

I'm suffocated with fear when Ross forces himself between my legs, pinning my arms to my side and baring his teeth. "I don't need to *ask* for permission to get between your legs. If you're going to be my wife and bear *my* last name, this belongs to me to have whenever the fuck I please," he seethes while pressing himself against my core.

I buck furiously as he presses his lips to mine. My mind races a million miles per minute, trying to figure out how I'm going to get out of this.

My phone blares from Ross' pocket, and my eyes fly open. He curses under his breath while he reaches over to his jacket and pulls my phone out. *Stark Financial* flashes across the screen, and my heart flutters in relief at the timing.

"Ross, I have to answer that. They know I'm off work. They wouldn't call me if it wasn't a dire emergency," I say. He grips the phone like he wants to smash it on the floor, and my heart skips a few beats in angst.

"Please," I whisper while holding a hand to my cheek, where I can feel it already beginning to bruise.

He shoves the phone at my chest and stares back at me, waiting for me to answer it in front of him. "Put it on speaker," he instructs with a cynical smirk. I swallow down my fear and slide the button on my screen to answer the call, reluctantly tapping the speaker button right after.

"H-hello. Maevis speaking," I stutter into the phone.

I release a breath when I hear my boss on the other end. "Maevis! I know you called off, but is there any way you could head into the office? Roxxon is threatening to pull out of our deal, and you're the only one he has a level head with."

I squint and scrunch my nose at the request. I have no idea who Roxxon is, but I will do anything to get out of this situation right now. "Yes, of course. I can be there in thirty minutes. Would that work?"

My boss agrees and disconnects the call with a grateful thank you.

Tremors race up my arms as I clench my phone to my chest, waiting for a response from Ross. He clenches his jaw so tight, I can see his temple pulse. Pointing his index finger at me, he runs his tongue across his teeth. "This discussion isn't over, Maevis. It was a stupid fucking fight. Get over it if you know what's best for you."

I nod in fake understanding and pray to God he leaves quickly.

He grabs his peacoat from the floor and puts it on while holding my stare. He stalks back over to me, placing a kiss on my forehead, and I have to force myself not to flinch to avoid another conflict. "I'll see you after work," he adds while running a thumb over my cheek where a bruise is already forming. "Make sure to put some makeup on that."

My lip trembles at his instruction, but I hold my emotions at bay until I see him get into his car from my living room window. When he pulls away, I release a scream that could shatter glass—but I'm unable to wallow in my own sorrows for long. The moment the scream leaves my lips, my front door flies open.

A lump is stuck in my throat, my eyes blowing wide when I see V standing in the doorway, his chest heaving and his bright green eyes blazing with fury under his mask.

ELEVEN

I'm at a loss for words as I drink him in. His muscular build takes up most of the doorway as he forcefully grips the door-knob and frame. I suppress the whimpers fighting to be released from my throat thanks to Ross' behavior.

"Don't," he commands from the doorway, and I sit up straight at the sound of his voice. "Don't you dare give him the satisfaction of controlling your emotions."

I blink back my tears and make sure not to raise my hand to my cheek while praying the bruise doesn't show yet. I blow out a puff of air, and he slams the door shut, startling me. He stalks over to the loveseat and drops down, hanging his hands between his legs while keeping his focus on me.

"I-I have to go into work," I stutter, forcing myself to look away from him. My eyes snap back up to his face when I hear him laugh.

"You honestly think that phone call was real?"

I open and close my mouth in confusion. "I know my boss' voice. He called and said—"

"I know exactly what he said because it was me, Duchess."

Whatever small piece of reality I was clinging to is ripped away from me. I know my boss' voice. It sounded exactly like him.

"It's quite easy in this day and age to take a sound bite and use their voice as you please," he says nonchalantly, sitting back in the chair. "I was too far away to get here quick enough to rip his head from his shoulders." It dawns on me he used artificial intelligence to change his voice. Not only did he know Ross was here, but he was also smart enough to know Ross would make me put the call on speakerphone.

But how did he know we were here?

"Do you enjoy being used by someone who views you to be subpar?"

His question might as well have been a knife to my gut. I roll my lips inward and avert my gaze.

"Look at me," he snaps, and I'm too afraid not to do as he says. Hesitantly, I slide my gaze back to his. "Do you like that he treats you like shit? Is it the money? The gifts?" His questions make my nostrils flare—none of those things matter to me, but I don't have the confidence to tell him I don't feel like I can do any better than Ross.

I just don't feel like starting over.

"Or is the sex just that good that you can't walk away?"

I shoot up from my seat. "Get the fuck out."

His lips are set in a hard line, parting when he sticks his tongue out to run along his full bottom lip. Slowly, he stands, but I don't move. Instead, I point directly at the door, still insisting he leave. I'm about to fold when the scent of him sends me through an unnerving wave of nostalgia. The frustration of not being able to pinpoint his scent irks me.

"Tell me you truly want me to leave, and I will. I'll walk right through that door and never step foot back in here again," he says, tilting his head toward the door. My heart races at the thought of never seeing him again, never hearing his rough, velvety voice again.

How can I care about not seeing a man when I've never even seen his face?

"Say it," he shouts, dragging me from my stupor and causing me to jump.

I lick my lips and turn my back, walking to the kitchen for a glass of water. But before I get there, his arm is wrapped around my waist, spinning me around and forcing my back against the archway. I'm boxed in against the wall, both of his hands resting on each side of my head. He towers over me as I stare at his chest, refusing to meet his hard stare. His muscles strain against his black t-shirt, and I resist reaching my palm out to feel him.

"Tell me you want me to go. Tell me you don't want me to touch you. Tell me you didn't fall asleep last night wishing I was in bed next to you. Tell me all of that, and I will vanish from your life like I was never here," he says on a single breath, tipping my chin upwards with two fingers to meet his gaze. The look of worry is a fleeting emotion in his eyes before he falls back to his hardened expression behind the mask.

"I can't do that," I whisper, and I see his chest rise and fall with the breath he was holding while awaiting my answer. I reach up, tucking a single nail under the edge of his mask. But his hand catches my wrist with a subtle shake of his head, and I drop my hand.

"Did he hurt you?" he asks in a low, steely voice. I go rigid and shake my head in response. Confusion runs its course when I'm unsure of why I lied to him. His large hand loosely wraps around my throat, catching me by surprise. But unlike my reaction with Ross, my body leans into his touch, and I'm ashamed of myself.

"You wouldn't lie to me, would you, Duchess?"

He quickly squeezes my throat and loosens it while staring into my eyes. I take the opportunity to once more try to remove his mask, but then he grasps each of my wrists. In the blink of an eye, they're pinned above my head with his weight pressing me into the wall. The surge of heat that soars to my core has me pressing my thighs together in response.

V brings his face down until our eyes meet. His breath smells of mint while the rest of his natural scent of musk and pine puts me in an immovable trance.

"You like this, don't you?"

His question causes my breaths to quicken. When I don't answer, he tightens his grip on my wrists, and I involuntarily press my pelvis into him. Embarrassed again, I squeeze my eyes shut, turning my head away from him.

"Look. At. Me."

His words are harsh and clipped. When I open my eyes and turn my head back to him, his green eyes are filled with desire, and I find myself barely able to breathe.

"He doesn't even fuck you the way you want, does he?" he questions while leaning closer to me until his mask grazes my ear, sending a shiver down my spine. "Manhandling you to bring you pleasure and pain until you beg for mercy."

A soft moan leaves my lips, and I smash them together to suppress any other noises from escaping. "You yearn for the moment you no longer have to be in control, when you know you can hand yourself over to be used and pleasured without truly being hurt," he continues while forcing a knee between my legs. "It gets you off knowing I could take you right here, right now, doesn't it, Duchess? You would put up a fight, but you truly and honestly want me inside you. Don't you?"

He grinds his hips into me, and I can feel his hardness through his pants. I slouch against the wall from the adrenaline rushing through me, but his hold on my wrists keeps me upright. "You dream of fighting me off you all while quietly giving me full consent to use you however I see fit."

I squirm beneath his hold, but I know deep down that I don't want him to let me go.

He releases my wrists to grab my hips and hoists me

against the wall. My lips part with the shock of how easily he lifted me.

"I can give you exactly what you crave, Duchess."

His fingertips dig into my hips, and I hear him fight back a groan of his own. My lashes flutter, my eyes heavily hooded in lust. I'm ready to admit I want him to use me against this wall when the doorbell rings and there's a pounding at the door.

"Maevis, open this fucking door right now, or I'm breaking it down!"

My eyes fly open, and I have to suppress my laughter. Rose is barely five feet tall; picturing her trying to knock my door down is my undoing. V places me back on the ground, tucking a fallen curl behind my ear.

He's going to leave. I don't want him to leave. Do not leave me.

"Stop depriving yourself, Maevis," he says. My real name rolling off his tongue sends heat spreading through my body. Rose twists the knob of the front door that was never re-locked, and he steps away from me. I instantly feel his warmth seeping from my body.

I wrap my arms around myself, my eyes never leaving the silhouette of my stalker as he walks away from me. I swallow as my stomach turns at the same time he does to leave out my back door.

CHAPTER

TWELVE

Rose and I melt into my couch for the remainder of the day, watching re-runs of *The Nanny* while eating as many tacos as possible from the food truck down the street until she leaves later that night. I didn't fill her in on all the details about Ross, purposefully leaving out the physical details, but it's safe to say that she's no longer a fan of my fiancé.

Not that she really has been these past few months.

I deeply wanted to tell her about my stalker being in the house moments before she arrived, but I kept it to myself. That probably didn't help in the long run, because I had three different dreams about him last night, waking up in a sweat, the sheets thrown from the bed, leaving me disoriented as the sun shone brightly throughout my windows. I can't tell if I'm upset or thankful that I woke up at the part in my dream when he had me bound and gagged against my will.

Forcing myself out of bed, I prepare for my day at the office and head out to my car with an iced coffee in hand. I freeze when I note an unmarked car parked out front, the passenger door quickly opening. Shuffling backwards has me stumbling over my own feet, an unknown bald man already two feet away from me with a large manila envelope in hand, thrusting it in my direction. Reluctantly, I grab the envelope from him as he smiles and tells me to have a good day. My mouth pops open in confusion as he races back to the car, and it pulls off in seconds.

I walk to my car with a fast pace, throwing everything inside and locking the doors.

Ripping open the envelope, my eyes blow wide when I read the first words in large red lettering at the top.

NON-DISCLOSURE AGREEMENT.

This asshole sent me an NDA for hitting *me?*

I skim over the first page of the document before my head pounds from the anger and betrayal. I can barely think while I punch the button to call Ross. The call almost goes to voice-mail when he answers. "Good morning, beautiful. How did you sleep?"

I'm slack-jawed at his greeting. He has to know about the NDA. I place the call on speakerphone and set it on the dash before I grip the steering wheel as tight as I can, gritting my teeth before blowing out a breath.

"Ross. A fucking NDA? Are you kidding me right now?"

The line goes silent as I wait for him to respond.

"Ross!" I follow up, only to be met with another ten second moment of silence.

"I'm not sure what you're talking about, Maevis," he finally retorts.

I feel like I'm going to explode when a deep burst of laughter escapes from me. My head spins as I try to decide what to do with my relationship. Instead of asking, I tell Ross we need to talk and let him know to meet me at the bistro around the corner from my job after work. He counters and insists we meet at his place, which I decline. I can hear the tone shift in his voice when I don't yield to his demand.

"Then I guess we won't be seeing each other today," he responds.

My blood is boiling, and I don't want to go another day without figuring out what the hell is going on in my life, in our relationship.

I know what I need to do, but do I have the will to do it?

I place my forehead on the top of my steering wheel, letting the dreadful feeling of defeat wash over me before conceding. "I will meet you in the middle and be at your office at five-thirty this afternoon."

Picturing the smug smile on his face at technically getting his way once again, I end the call before he can reply. I take a long sip of my iced coffee, letting it cool me down from the heat of the moment before I shift my car into drive.

With the sun shining even brighter than it did through my window this morning, I quickly pull my visor down instead of searching for my sunglasses. A piece of paper falls into my lap, and I swallow when I recognize the handwriting.

You deserve better. And I'll be the one who gives it to you.

- V

CHAPTER

THIRTEEN

Today, like every day, but especially today, I am beyond grateful my friends work in the same office as me. Either Rose or Anika had a large iced coffee waiting for me on my desk, a vanilla scone perched on top of the lid. Did I have an iced coffee on the way here? Yes. Am I ashamed I finished it and am about to start another one? Not at all.

I sent a text to each of them to say good morning and thank them for my sweet treats.

Unfortunately, that was the only highlight of my workday. The hours dragged at a snail's pace, and every client I spoke with must have had a stick the size of a witch's broom up their ass. Thankfully, it was lunchtime, and I was about to place my usual pick-up order for the bistro around the corner when the app disappeared and an incoming call came in. Ross' name flashed across the screen, and I debated sending it to voicemail for a few seconds before disinterestedly pressing the green circle.

"Hi, Ross," I said into the phone without an ounce of enthusiasm.

"We need to reschedule our talk for later. I had a last-minute meeting scheduled with a high-profile client."

I could feel the grinding of my teeth settling into my jaw. I know he's lying, and I've had just about enough of his shit. "No," I reply firmly. "I will be at your office at five-thirty."

The silence on the other end irritates me even more. I say

his name into the phone and repeat it again when he doesn't respond.

"Maevis, this is quite possibly the biggest client I will ever have the opportunity of picking up. I refuse to let you fuck this up for me, so take your bratty little attitude and—"

"I said I will be there at the time we agreed on. Figure it the fuck out."

I press my finger into the screen to end the call so quickly, I almost drop my phone. I observe the screen proudly as his name flashes across with two missed calls. On the third call, my lip curls up into a sneer when I read his name.

Ross (Fiancé) with three red heart emojis.

I snatch my phone off the desk and navigate to his contact card. Erasing the emojis and word 'fiancé' from his name, I press save and toss it in the drawer. Digging my fingers into the curls atop my head, I consider pulling until I force myself to scream instead. My office door flies open, and Rose comes waltzing in with a coffee in one hand and a bagel in the other. She stops halfway to my desk when she notices my current state.

She rolls her lips in and narrows her eyes. "I would ask if I should come back, but I already know it has to do with that douchebag fiancé of yours, so let's chat," she says while finding her way to the chair directly in front of my desk and plopping down.

Once again, I vent to Rose about my relationship while holding back rage-fueled tears begging to be released. In the middle of her voicing her opinion about my potential marriage, Anika called to inform me a package was delivered. I roll my eyes, prepared for a bouquet of flowers from Ross, probably insisting we change the arrangements of our discussion after our chat. He loves ordering flowers from the shop across the street when he fucks up because they get here in less than thirty minutes. I'm convinced he has their number on speed dial.

Anika knocks on the door before cracking it a bit and poking her head in. I roll my eyes again, playfully this time, when I see her adorable face. "Anika, you don't need to knock every time. Come in."

She's balancing a small black box in her hand, a small white bag in the other. I narrow my eyes, reading the name on the front of the bag as she walks over to me. I blink, trying to figure out why she would have a bag from the sandwich shop I missed out on ordering from.

"Here you go," she chimes while placing the items on my desk and flashing a smile at Rose, who offers one back. Confused, I ask her who delivered the items, and her eyebrows shoot upwards on her petite face before she props a hand on her hip. "Listen, I don't know who it was, but he was fine as fuck."

Rose chuckles and takes a sip of her drink, waiting for Anika to provide more details. Meanwhile, my heartrate picks up—I wonder if it was V. A pang of jealously races through my chest, and I'm unsure if it's because of her finding him attractive or the possibility of her seeing him without a mask.

Did she get to see him without a mask before I did?

"What color were his eyes?" I blurt out, and both women eye me suspiciously.

Anika looks me up and down before confirming. "Blue."

I blow out a breath and take a large sip of my iced coffee.

"Deep, ocean-blue actually. Super tall, muscular. Had tattoos all over his fingers with rings," she continues before pulling a chair from the wall and sitting down. "You know, he actually reminded me of this guy I met a long time ago that..."

Rose and I groan, and Anika stops talking and glares at us. She has a bad habit of starting stories she either never finishes or forgets the reason for. "Sorry, what happened with the guy?" I ask, waiting for her to continue.

Anika looks to the side and back at Rose and me while scratching the base of her long, thick ponytail. "I don't remember who I was comparing him to."

Rose and I stare at her, our mouths wide open in astonishment. How does she do this with *every* story? I point to my door while fighting to hold back my laugh. "Get the fuck out," I say while my laugh slips through.

The three of us have a laughing fit before Anika dismisses herself when she hears her phone ringing. "I'll come back when I remember the story," she calls from the doorway. Rose and I look at each other, still laughing and shaking our heads.

But the joy is short lived when I hear my phone buzzing in the drawer again, and my shoulders drop. Rose nods toward the two items Anika placed on my desk and raises a brow. "Well? Open them. Don't make me wait."

I reach over and drag the white paper bag over to me. I unfold the top and peek inside. My eyes narrow, tilting my head in bewilderment. "It's...it's my exact order from the sandwich shop," I say, confusion sketched across my face.

"And that's weird why? You order delivery all the time," Rose counters.

"It's weird because I never placed the order."

Her eyes bulge before she smacks her lips and nods toward the small black box with a purple silk ribbon wrapped around it. I slide the bag to the corner of my desk and grab the box with both hands, pulling it in front of me. Rose leans forward as I tug on one end of the ribbon and the bow falls apart. Removing it, I lift the lid of the box and slam it back shut when I see the contents.

"What is it?" Rose asks with a bit too much enthusiasm. "Show me!"

I try to pull the box out of her range, but she's too quick. She snatches the box, putting it on the corner of the desk in front of her, and throws the lid off. Her mouth drops open as she pulls out a one-piece black lace lingerie set.

"Well, this is new for Ross, I think...right? This isn't his thing," she says with a scrunched nose. "What an odd way to apologize. An apology I hope you don't accept."

My phone buzzes in the drawer again, and I snatch it open out of anger. But my anger dissipates when I see the name flashing across the screen.

"V."

A lone, single letter, one I did not save in my phone. I run my tongue across my bottom lip and take in a deep breath before accepting the call.

"You sent the food and the lingerie, didn't you?"

His husky laugh sends a wave of heat between my legs, and I sit further back in my chair as Rose eyes me suspiciously. I swivel my chair around to look out the wall of windows behind me out into the busy streets of Chicago. "V... This..." I swallow while trying to figure out what I want to say.

"I am an engaged woman. This has to stop," I finally force out, unsure if I believe my own words. I hear a soft chuckle and the rustling of him adjusting the phone. "I love the way you lie, Duchess."

My lips part at his statement, and the line goes dead.

When I swivel back around to face Rose, she's chewing on her cheek with rounded eyes. "It was him, wasn't't? The masked man. He sent you these! Holy shit, Maevis, are you fucking him?"

My heart is beating a million miles an hour.

Am I fucking him? No.

Would I? Yes.

I bite my bottom lip before focusing on my best friend. "I

am not fucking him, Rose. I don't know why he sent these things to me. I don't even know how he knows my damn order from the sandwich shop."

This time, I follow through with pulling my hair as hard as I can before dropping my head back in my chair. Rose rounds the desk and sits on top of it on the side of me. "Mind if I say something about your current relationship?"

I pop my eyes open and study Rose. "Since when do you ask permission to speak your mind?"

She laughs before looking down at the ground then back at me. "I think you've become so complacent in your relationship, you don't even realize what you truly deserve. Ross had everyone fooled and still does. Not me, but everyone else. I think it's time you move on and find someone who will treat you like the princess you are," she says before reaching back and picking up the lingerie with her index finger, letting it hang. "Or maybe you just need someone with a mask to fuck the Sonic rings out of your pussy while donning this ensemble."

My mouth drops open, and I reach to snatch the lingerie from her hand. Instead, she holds it out of reach and presses her palm to my forehead. The tears threatening to run free are held at bay as we laugh uncontrollably again.

I don't know where the course of my life is going or how I got here, but I know one thing is for sure...

Ross is going to meet me at five-fucking-thirty.

CHAPTER

FOURTEEN

The rest of the day flew by since I was dreading my meeting with Ross. Rose offered several times to accompany me as backup. Secretly, I would have loved to have her with me, but I know this is something that needs to be done on my own.

Packing my bag to leave the office, I clutch my phone and consider calling V just to hear his velvet-like voice. "What the hell is wrong with you?" I mumble to myself and throw my phone in my purse, preparing for a drive I don't really want to make.

The travel to Ross' job is the longest twenty minutes of my life.

I have so many questions about my relationship and my life that I don't have the answers to, but I do know that Ross is no longer the man I agreed to marry.

I pull into the lot, park my car in the visitor's spot by the door, throw my purse on my shoulder, blow out a breath, and step out of the car. Closing the door, I feel a pair of eyes on me and whirl around to find a tall man with brown hair. I'm preparing to scream for help when I realize it's Ross' best friend.

"Shit, Brian, you scared me," I say, forcing myself to take a deep breath. His demeanor catches me off guard when his eyes travel from my feet to the top of my head. "How have you been?" I add, side-stepping away from him and my car. The corners of his lips tip upward, causing the hairs on the back of my neck to stand.

"I'm better now."

I swallow, pinching my brow together at his reply. "Well, I better get inside to see Ross. It was nice seeing you."

I quickly walk toward the glass revolving door, feeling Brian's stare blazing into my back behind me. Once I'm inside, the front desk clerk notices me, flashing a smile before nodding, giving me clearance toward the elevators. Stepping inside, I punch the button for the thirteenth floor and press my back against the wall. I can't wait to see the look on Ross' face when he realizes I called his bluff about having a client. I'm so sick of him using bullshit work excuses to get out of conflicts in our relationship.

Our dying—if not already dead—relationship.

The elevator stops, and I step off, walking toward Ross' office as I run through everything I want to tell him. I decided on the drive over that I'm not giving him a chance to speak first. I'm laying everything out on the table.

It's five thirty-one when I turn the corner to reach his office, and his secretary is still sitting at her desk adjacent his door. I grit my teeth and offer a fake smile to the woman I know is secretly trying to fuck my fiancé. She offers one back while tossing her auburn hair over her shoulder.

"Maevis, how..." Her words trail off as she studies me. "Nice to see you. Ross warned me you would be stopping by."

Warned?

Pressing my lips together, I offer another fake smile. "Yes, well, we have some things to discuss, and we agreed on this time. So, if you don't mind, I'm going inside to speak with *my fiancé.*"

I begin walking toward the door, and Mallory shoots up

from her seat, rounding the desk and blocking the door with her body. "He is in a very important meeting."

Rearing my head back at her stance in front of me, I cross my arms over my chest before taking another step toward her. "Move, or I'll move you myself."

Her eyes grow wide at the aggression pouring off me. It's not my usual nature, but if my fiancé has another woman in there, it's my right to know.

And my right to break both their fucking necks.

Shockingly, Mallory holds her stance. I reach around her, twisting the doorknob and bulldozing my way into the office. The two of us stumble through the door, my purse falling to the floor and Mallory catching herself on the doorframe before tumbling over in her high heels.

My gaze connects with Ross' before I see the back of the head of an actual client.

Ross' narrowed glare could burn through concrete as he stares into my soul with flared nostrils.

"Apologies, Mr. Stevenson. If you could excuse me for one moment," Ross says to the client before raising from his seat and walking around his desk. Mallory whispers an apology before scrambling out the door.

Ross reaches his hand out to snatch my arm and rethinks his action, putting his hand back down to his side. "I told you I had a very important client, and you decided to show up anyway?" he whispers harshly. My eyes flick to the male client in the leather chair, his dark hair falling just above his broad shoulders.

"Look at me when I'm speaking to you," Ross hisses, and my gaze connects with his again as I remain at a loss for words.

I hear the grind of leather as the client's large hands dart to the arms of the chair and squeeze tightly. "Everything okay back there?"

Those hands.

That hair.

THAT VOICE.

My breath is caught in my throat as I try convincing my brain to force my feet to move toward my stalker.

It has to be him.

"All good, Mr. Stevenson. Just tidying up some...*loose ends,*" Ross clarifies, and every muscle in my body tightens. He may as well have shoved a knife through my gut. I want to release the scream I've been holding in for so long, but I remember V's words in the doorway of my home.

"Stop depriving yourself, Maevis."

"If you don't want to discuss the deal, I can leave," the male says before standing, his hands moving to button the front of his sports coat. My lips part while I survey the back of him before Ross' glare turns so deadly, I begin to walk backwards out the office door. When I'm fully through, he brings his face to mine until we're nose to nose.

"I'll deal with you later," he hisses and slams the door in my face.

I press both palms on each side of the doorframe and rest my forehead on the wood. There are too many questions and too many variables floating through my mind.

"I told you he had a client. Should have listened. But I heard you're not good at doing that anyway."

Mallory's annoying voice pierces my ears, and my nostrils flare, invisible steam streaming out of them. I stride over until I'm directly in front of her, leaning over her desk until I'm so close, I can see it makes her uncomfortable.

I'm not sure what is slowly becoming of me, but I don't care.

"Listen here, you annoying little bitch," I snap while reaching over and grabbing the collar of her white button up undone far too low to be considered professional. "You may think I am oblivious to what you're trying to do, but I'm not. I know you're technically supposed to clock out at four o'clock. I know you stay just as late as Ross does so you can hopefully, one day, wrap those thin, pink lips around his cock, but just keep one thing in mind," I say, yanking her closer as she tries to pull back. "I'm the one with the ring. I'm the one with a fat ass. He's an ass man. These do nothing for him," I say, pointing at the perky breasts she has on display.

Releasing her, I straighten out my blouse, flash her a smile, and knock over the organizer on her desk, making every pen and pencil spill over as she scrambles to grab them.

As I turn my back to her, my eyes are rounded as I'm shocked at my own actions.

Straightening my shoulders, I stride toward the elevator, never turning back around. Once the doors close, I push the stop button to make sure no one can get on as I process what just happened. Dropping down to the corner of the elevator, I reach into my purse, pulling out my phone to call V, but I have zero reception. I clutch the phone in my hand and finally release the emotions I've been holding in for so long.

Tears fall down my face in thick, wet streams for a few minutes before I gather myself and stand. Allowing the elevator to move once again, I request for it to return me to the lobby before I make my way to the parking lot.

On the way to my car, a man in a suit catches the elevator with me right before it closes. From the moment he steps in, he begins making small talk about the weather. His eyes never leave me, and I thank God when the elevator dings to let us off at the lobby. He continues his chatter into the parking lot until we reach my car. As I wish him a good night, instead of continuing to walk to his car, he stops at mine. I can hear my own heartbeat in my ears as he continues talking. The sounds drumming in my head make me so disoriented, I place a hand on my car to stead myself.

The man takes a few more steps toward me, closing the space between us, and my breaths increase as I fumble for my keys in my purse.

"It would be a much better night if I could get your number," he says, taking a step closer until there's only an inch of space between us. From my peripheral, I can see his hand raise to touch me, and I shift my body to the side while still digging through my purse. I can barely focus as the pounding in my head increases, my surroundings blurring from the panic.

I release a nervous laugh, refusing to look up at him. "Oh, no, I'm sorry. I'm seeing someone. Engaged, actually," I inform him and finally locate my key ring. Opening my door slightly, he presses his hand to it and shuts it again causing me to take a step back.

"Engaged isn't the same as married. You don't even have a ring on your finger," he counters, and I curse *V* for taking it. "Come on, let me take you out for a drink," he insists with a thin, crooked smile.

I shake my head in protest, "No, thank you."

The man huffs a laugh before placing his bag on the ground and stepping toward me. "That's the issue with all you pretty bitches these days. You think you're worth so much more than you actually are just because of a pretty face with a nice ass."

His hand moves quickly, gripping my face. He pulls upward until I'm barely standing on my tip toes. The sun has already set, making it dark outside, and his deep brown, almost black, eyes blend with the night sky. I open my mouth to scream, and he sticks his thumb in my mouth, hooking my jaw and pressing me against my own car.

"If you scream, I'll replace my thumb with something else. Just shut the fuck up and—"

His words are cut short when I hear a loud thud and my face is no longer grasped. I snap my mouth shut as his body drops in front of me. Squeezing my eyes shut as my body shakes uncontrollably, I hear an unfamiliar voice.

"It's getting really tiring following you around the under-boss' orders. Do you ever stay out of trouble?"

I open one eye to see a tall, blond man standing in front of me. His hands are covered in tattoos, with at least four rings on each hand. Realization sets in when I see his vivid blue eyes shining bright even though it's dark out.

"It's you. You delivered the packages to my office earlier. Anika described you perfectly," I whisper on a shaky voice into the night air. The man nods and fights back a smirk. "That the name of your secretary? She talks a lot," he says, and even though I'm still shaking, I can't help but release an authentic, low laugh.

"That was *V* in there, wasn't it?" I ask the blond-haired man. He pulls his bottom lip between his teeth before his eyes flick to the building behind me and back to me without answering. "You work for him? Why is he having you follow me?"

I can see his Adam's apple bob as he swallows, and the guy who attempted to assault me groans before he's met with a foot to the gut from my new personal bodyguard.

"Are you going to answer any question I ask?"

His blue eyes soften, and one corner of his mouth twists into a half-smile as he shakes his head. I let out a groan and drop my head back to release the tension. Bringing my head back down to meet his gaze, I puff my cheeks and release another breath. "Can you at least give him a message for me?"

He nods.

"Tell *V* I'm not speaking to him anymore," I say with a raise of my chin, and the man's eyebrows shoot upward. "And tell him if he's going to play games like my fiancé, he's not actually the man I thought he was."

His brows raise even higher. "You sure you want me to relay that message to him?"

I swallow, letting my nerves get the best of me as I consider his question. He drops to the male on the ground and pulls out a syringe. "Hey! What the fuck are you doing?" I ask in panic.

He peers up at me from his crouch. "What does it look like I'm doing?"

"It looks like you're about to fucking sedate him!"

"Smart woman just like your so-called *V* said," he retorts, and I refrain from telling him to piss off. He sticks the syringe in the man's neck as he lazily tries to fight him, and the man goes limp.

Alarm floods me as I feel my pulse quicken. "Oh my God. I can't be a part of this. I was never here."

The blonde male stands as he props my assailant up against the neighboring car.

"Perfect. Do me a favor and get in your car, lock the doors, and go straight home, will ya? Make my job slightly easier tonight, if ya don't mind," he requests with a single raised brow. I don't even know his name, and like all the other men in my life, he wants to boss me around. I glare at him, flipping him off without a second thought.

He releases a low laugh and moves to open my door for me. "That's cute," he says while gesturing for me to get in.

"I'm getting in because I want to, not because you're telling me to," I mumble while sitting down and buckling myself in after starting the car. He shuts the door, and I roll down my window while putting the car in reverse. "I want you to know that I'm not a child, and I can handle myself."

He rolls his lips inward and mockingly nods his head.

"And I'm going home because I'm tired and I want to."

"Sounds like a great plan," he replies while visibly holding in a laugh.

He's getting under my skin, and he knows it. I grip the steering wheel tighter and take a deep breath before poking my head out the window to see him better. "I don't think I caught your name?" I ask as he begins walking away, leaving the man propped on top of the hood of the car next to me. My eyes roam over the man who attempted to attack me, and I question myself when I don't feel an ounce of sympathy for him—though I begin to wonder what's going to happen to him when I leave. My eyes flick back up, finding my unknown bodyguard further away now. I back my car up and pull next to him in the parking lot.

"You know you left him back there, right? There are cameras in the parking lot," I say, worry lacing my words.

"Good thing I'm an expert with computers then, huh?"

I hit the breaks the same time he stops walking and brings his head down to the height of the window.

"Go home, Maevis," he says with a serious tone. The command in his voice almost mimicking my stalker's catches me off-guard. My eyes bounce back and forth over his handsome face that Anika had perfectly described in my office.

"Your name. I didn't get your name," I say once more. He laughs and stands, turning back toward the direction we came from.

"You didn't and you won't," he calls over his shoulder before disappearing into the night.

FIFTEEN

The drive home was even worse than the drive to Ross' job.

Not only did I not get to speak my mind and figure out where we are in our relationship, the masked man I thought was a knight in shining armor is working with my asshole of a fiancé.

Behind my back.

I hate to say it, but my heart is cracking in so many places, I'm waiting for it to completely crumble.

For once, I don't care if I'm being watched as I park my car and unlock the front door. Disarming the alarm system and setting the locks back in place, I kick off my shoes and plop down on the couch with my phone in hand. As I'm about to dial Rose's number, she's already calling me.

"So, what's the verdict? Are you guys working it out, or did you come to your senses and end everything?" she rushes out, awaiting an answer I don't even have myself. I release a sigh and rip the hair-tie from my bun. But before I can tell the story of tonight's events, I hear the locks on my front door turning and clicking. My breath catches in my lungs as I await Ross bursting through the door.

How many more times will I accept his anger? How many more times will he lay his hands on me?

"Maevis, you there? Spill the beans, bitch!" Rose echoes through the phone, but I can't force myself to speak.

The front door flies open, and my breathing returns to

normal when I see dark hair and piercing green eyes behind a mask. Rose is yelling so many curse words into the phone, I can't keep up. I lick my lips as I watch the masked man I can't get out of my head slam the door shut, making me jump with a startle.

"Hang up the phone and get upstairs," he demands, pointing at the staircase. My mouth opens and closes—do I want to tell him to fuck off or agree to his command?

"Oh my God, is that him? That's not Ross' voice," Rose yells through the phone. "I swear on my life, Maevis, if you don't fuck him tonight, I'm—"

I end the call before she could finish the rest of that sentence, but it's too late. *V* is already tilting his head at her statement. I release a nervous laugh while pushing back the relentless curls from my face. "Sh-she talks crazy all the time. I have no idea what she's talking about."

V nods his head. "Upstairs. Now."

I quickly try to rush past him, but he grabs my hand and whirls me back around, flinging me to his chest and forcing me to look up at his deep-set eyes through the mask. "Does he always speak to you like that?"

I'm at a loss for words and turn to look away from him before my embarrassment swallows me whole. His other hand gently grips the back of my head, turning my focus back to him.

"Answer me."

I press both of my hands to his chest and push off him. He releases me, and I stumble backwards toward the step before his hands shoot out and catch me once more.

"Don't act like you care now. You had me fooled, just like he did. But you're working with him? I should have known a man could *never* be as virtuous as you portrayed yourself.

You're so trifling that you hide behind a mask," I scream into his face.

He may be wearing a mask, but I can see the hurt in his eyes when I compare him to Ross.

V drops his hands from steadying me at my waist, and I instantly miss the heat from his touch. He takes a step back and places a hand on the doorknob. I step forward with a hand stretched out, ready to apologize for snapping on him, but he holds a hand up.

"There's a lot you don't know, Maevis."

I study the emotions floating through his eyes. For me to have known him for such a short time, I can read his emotions through his irises far too well.

"You think I didn't want to turn around and end his fucking life? If he raised a hand to you, I wouldn't have been able to control myself," he snaps. "You have no idea what's going on."

I halt my breathing at the sight of him. The fire in his eyes as his chest rises and falls lets me know he's doing his best to clamp down the anger that is beginning to bubble over.

"Then tell me, *V*," I say in a pleading voice. "Please."

He steps forward again, raising a hand toward my face, and I flinch.

The reaction catches him off guard, and he drops his hand to his side with widened eyes. "There's not much you could ever do to piss me off, but you thinking I would *ever* lay a hand on you is one of them," he says on a soft whisper, and my lungs deflate.

He steps forward again and raises a hand, pressing it to the side of my face. This time, as hard as I try to fight it, I can't help but lean into his touch. "You don't know who or what you are, Maevis, but you at least have to know what you're worth," he says, running his thumb over my bottom lip. "And how beautiful you truly are."

His words and touch overstimulate me as my eyes fall shut and I begin to sway.

"Go to bed, Maevis."

My eyes snap open at his words. I'm nervous about Ross showing up to *'deal with me'*, and that emotion must be on my face, because *V* shakes his head, pointing at multiple corners of the house. My head swivels in each direction, my mouth dropping open further each time.

Cameras.

I turn back to him with a billion questions, but he beats me to it.

"I'm never taking my eyes off you again," he says before pulling me flat against his chest in a tight embrace and pulling me back far too quickly for my liking. His green eyes scanning over every inch of my face has me wanting to hide, a strange feeling of timidness creeping in. "You're safe," he adds, his thumb drifting over my cheekbone.

Instinct kicks in, and I raise my hand to his mask. Surprisingly, he doesn't flinch or move away from my touch. "Why are you so afraid to remove this?"

I feel the rumble in his chest as he holds back a laugh. "This mask is the only thing holding me back."

My brows pull together; I'm confused at his statement. I search his irises for an answer that isn't being offered. "Holding you back from what?" I pry. His fingers dig into my hips, and I suck in a sharp breath. My heart skips several beats when his head drops down to my ear, and his hand moves my hair away so I can hear him clearly.

"From taking you upstairs, stripping you naked, and folding you into a hundred different positions until I've seen and devoured every inch of you."

An audible pop comes from my lips parting as my body goes rigid, processing his statement.

Moving away from my ear and releasing me from his grasp, he inclines his chin toward the stairs. When I hear the locks on my door moving, my inner voice explodes in my head to ask him to stay, but my pride stomps it out. By the time I reach the top of the stairs and turn back around, he's already gone, the alarm set and locks set in place.

Dragging my feet into my bathroom, I grip the edge of the counter and stare into the mirror. My mascara has smeared over and under my eyes. My foundation is blotchy. My hair is anything but put together. Yet, despite everything being out of place, my masked admirer still told me I was beautiful.

I don't want to admit it, but it's getting harder and harder to keep my feelings at bay.

Swallowing every ounce of confusion and overwhelming emotion, I place my palm on the mirror in front of me.

Get your shit together, Maevis. You're falling for your stalker.

SIXTEEN

Waking up to over fifteen missed calls and an absurd number of texts from Ross was not how I wanted to start my day. Still, it gives me a bit of satisfaction knowing he wasn't able to reach me at his convenience. Because that's all he's ever perceived me as.

A convenience.

One quick call to my boss, and I was relieved of having to go into the office today. Nothing makes me happier than working from home in my pajamas like the hermit crab I was born to be. But three iced coffees in and two unnecessarily irate clients later, I'm back in a bitter mood.

As I stare out into the void of my bedroom window, a smile blooms as two parents hold their toddler's hands, swinging her through the air. The child's high-pitched giggles make me join in with laughter of my own.

When I was young, the good times often made the bad ones blurry as they were shoved far back into a space where I forgot them over the years. But now, the bad memories come to the forefront, in full-fledged color with sparks flying. Visuals of my father raining down fist after fist on my mother play in my head. I can hear myself screaming as I try to throw my body over her, only for my father to throw me backwards.

My parents are a force united, but every so often, my father likes to remind her of a 'woman's place'. And the older I got, the more I realized my mother was—and still is—too brainwashed to understand women were not created to serve their husbands.

As a little girl, I thrived on making my parents proud. Unfortunately, I've carried that into adulthood as well. I watch my mother and father move as one, doing their best to dictate my life because they're adamant about knowing what's best for me.

I stand, trying to fight against my memories. I press my palms into my eyes, but my brain refuses to stop searching for the deep, dark memories I've buried.

Another memory of him pressing her palm to the stovetop when dinner wasn't ready as soon as he arrived home from work has me jerking back from my desk. My head begins to pound at the absurdly painful memory of him forcing me to drop my dog off at the shelter because I received a B+ in my math class instead of an A. The memory has me breathless and doubled over my desk. The clear picture of his big, brown eyes staring up at my seven-year-old self when I set him on the desk at the shelter has me gasping for air.

These memories are the exact reason I no longer want children of my own. I spent so many years believing my mother was helpless, that she had nowhere to go. I spent so many years believing my father was loveable with a few flaws. But the entire time, she was right where she wanted to be, and my father was exactly what he was portrayed as: vile.

And as badly as I want to break free, it's engrained in me to want to make them proud, to show them their only daughter isn't a complete fuck up.

The tears I wasn't aware of soaked my keyboard as I dab at my cheeks with nearby napkins. I don't try to stop myself when the tears keep falling. Being able to release every ounce of raw emotion from the past few weeks feels like a tremendous weight being lifted from my shoulders.

The memories and heartache that climbed their way back into my mind came with a bit of clarity, and with that clarity came one realization.

I refuse to settle for a life of pain and heartache like my mother.

Finishing out my shift, I change into my favorite deep purple fitted knit dress. Doing my makeup to where I feel my best and fixing my hair into a tight bun, I finish packing every single item that belongs to Ross into a box and head out the door.

He had called me dozens more times throughout the day, and I sent every single one to voicemail without regret. But the confidence I felt during the drive here is slowly fading into the distance as I stare up at the skyscraper of his office.

I turn as I debate getting back into my car before reminding myself why I'm here.

This isn't the life I want.

My heels click along the sparkling tile of the lobby as the usual secretary smiles and nods, giving me clearance once again to the elevators. I tap the button for the thirteenth floor while juggling the box in my hand and instantly panic when I see Brian sprint-walking toward the closing doors. The predatory look on his face has me holding my breath with another spike of anxiety. In a fraction of a second, I jab the 'close' button, holding it in place until the elevator begins to move and I release a breath.

The last thing I need right now is Ross' best friend quizzing me about why I'm here, not to mention how weird he was acting the last time I saw him in the parking lot.

With my eyes clamped shut and head leaned back against the wall, I'm startled when I hear the chime of the elevator reaching the thirteenth floor. Shifting the box in my arms, I step out and prepare myself for the next obstacle: getting past Mallory. Rounding the corner, I release a refreshing breath of relief when I see she's not at her desk. The bitch finally clocking out when she's supposed to is a rarity, but I'll accept my blessing.

My ears perk up when I hear Ross aggressively speaking to someone on the phone. I raise my fist to knock on the door but quickly drop it when I remember I don't owe him any of the grace he never offered to me.

Confidently, I open the door to his office and immediately drop the box.

The room spins when I see Mallory laid across Ross' desk, her legs draped over his shoulders as he thrusts into her mercilessly. Neither of them notices I'm standing in the doorway as they continue fucking. The anger feeding through my veins is telling me to rage, to break every item in his office and set it on fire. The suspicion I've felt has me feeling a sense of relief as I continue watching my fiancé fuck his secretary without a care in the world. Every thrust he delivers reminds me of why I'm here, reminds me that he never fucked me the way he's fucking her.

The ending is what has my heart splintering into the last piece holding it together. I can feel the final crack in my chest, the sharp pieces of my heart floating through my body as I watch him finish inside her. He plants a kiss to her lips while brushing her auburn hair from her face.

After a few seconds of gathering my emotions and forcing them back into the glass bottle I keep them in, I bring my hands together in a slow clap. "Great performance, one I've never personally seen, honestly," I announce sarcastically from the doorway.

Ross' head snaps in my direction, and he quickly pulls out of Mallory while stumbling to pull his pants up from around his ankles. His whore sits up on the desk, buttoning her top with a bright, wide smile on her face that falls into a smirk with an '*I told you so*' raised brow.

"This is all the shit I wanted to give back to you before letting you know we're over," I say while pointing to the spilled items on the floor. "Enjoy fucking your whore. Send me an invite to the wedding." Ross' eyes blow wide at my statement, and I can hear him muttering something under his breath. I don't stay long enough to decipher them as I turn my back and leave his office.

I'm punching the button to the elevator on a prayer it arrives quicker than Ross can get to me, but I can already hear his footsteps.

Two hands grip my shoulders and spin me around, slamming me against the wall next to the elevator so hard, my head bounces off the surface. Stars float in my vision for a brief moment before they drift to the edges and disappear, allowing me to focus on the face of the man I was once in love with.

Ross opens his mouth to talk, but I cut him off.

"How long?" I ask, the question a whisper as my chest tightens. Ross clenches his teeth before telling me it was the first time. I hear the clicking of heels in the distance before a feminine voice joins in from around the corner.

"A year and some change," Mallory shouts, and I stop breathing.

A year?

When I snatched Mallory across the desk to threaten her yesterday, she already had him and she knew it. Whatever ounce of confidence I had left in me is now non-existent as I deflate against the wall.

Ross scrunches his face at Mallory's answer before telling her to shut the fuck up.

I try to suppress a sob, but the noise escapes me, and I push against Ross to escape his grasp. His hold on me tightens as he begins a speech I didn't want to hear.

"If you had just done what I—"

The sound of my hand connecting with the side of his face has me gasping as I watch a drop of blood trail down his cheek from a random ring I was wearing. Ross releases me, reaching up to touch the blood traveling down his face. His sneer has me recoiling against the wall, preparing for him to raise his hand in retaliation. But he grabs my hand instead, inspecting the ring on my middle finger before moving to the finger next to it.

"Where is your engagement ring, Maevis?"

Hysteria takes over me when I hear his question, and I can't suppress the maniacal laughter.

"That fucking ring better be back on your finger by the time you get home, or so help me God—"

"The wedding is off, Ross," I reiterate from earlier between laughs.

Ross produces a condescending laugh of his own. "Good luck with that, sweetheart. *You* need *me*. You're *nothing* without me."

That one little seven letter word immediately stops my laughter as I stare at him for several seconds before I remind myself of who I am. A timeline plays in my head of the woman I created within myself without his help.

"It was nice knowing you, Ross. Tell your mother she's a bitch for me," I say while turning to press the button for the elevator. The button turns red and so does my vision when Ross' hand wraps around my throat, slamming me back into the wall. The vision of my mother's abuse plays in my head as my eyes flare open and I bring my knee up between Ross' legs.

Watching him fall to the floor as I catch my breath is a moment I wish I could keep as a picture on my living room mantle. The elevator dings on arrival, and I dash to the door, stopping in front to stare at the man inside. The same blond-haired, blue-eyed man from last night is standing in the middle of the elevator, a gun in his hand. His blue eyes peer down at Ross, and a satisfied look flashes over his face, coupled with a subtle nods as Ross rolls in pain. I step inside and frantically press the button for the lobby as Ross shouts my name.

"You fucking bitch! We're not over," he yells from the floor. I press my hand to the chest of the man towering over me in the elevator when he takes a step toward Ross.

"Let's just leave," I mutter without looking up at him, but he pushes forward. "Please," I beg once more, and he takes a step back. The doors shut, and I force the fear and anxiety that was occupying my lungs out.

Hyperventilation sets in as I try to remind myself Ross was wrong. We're completely done and over. But deep in my heart, I know what's to come. I know exactly how Ross thinks and the power he has over me.

I know he won't let me go that easily.

And I know he won't forget my retaliation. The panic attack picks up when I'm reminded that Ross doesn't move on. He doesn't just forgive and forget.

He gets even.

SEVENTEEN

"How did you know?" I rush the question out as tall, blond, and handsome and I walk past the secretary staring at us with wide eyes. I panic thinking she sees his gun, but then I remember him tucking it into the waistband of his pants before we got off the elevator. She bites her lip as she scans over the man escorting me out to my car. I can't blame her; he's just as handsome as *V* without the overly dark edge.

He glances down at me and then looks back up to survey our surroundings. "You must've thought I was joking when I told you boss-man has me watching you when he can't." I swallow at his statement before he follows up. "There are cameras in the building. I tapped in and watched the entire exchange from my phone while driving here. I was hoping I could get there before he released you from the wall so I could blow his head off the moment I stepped off the elevator."

My breathing picks up as I think about Ross being dead. Would I be okay with that? Could I survive that type of trauma? I wouldn't have to deal with his bullshit anymore.

I shake away the dark thoughts floating freely through my head.

"Please tell me you didn't tell him."

"His flight just landed, but I will have to call and debrief him on—"

I step in front of him. He stops instantly and narrows his

eyes at me. While I trust him without knowing his name, he can be just as terrifying as *V* can with a single look.

"Please don't tell him. I've been defenseless enough these days. At least…" I searched for the words I wanted to string together, never taking my eyes off him. "At least don't tell him what Ross did to me. That he put his hands on me. I can't… I don't…"

I'm at a loss for words again, my heart beating rapidly in my ears as I realize what just happened.

He places a large, tattooed hand on my shoulder and drops his gaze down to mine. "I don't know how you were raised, and I don't know what you have seen or experienced, but a man raising a hand to a woman doesn't make her defenseless or weak. It makes him a pussy. Nothing less."

His words strike a chord, and I'm forcing down a sob again when my phone buzzes rapidly in my dress pocket. I drop my head back and stare at the sky when I see my mother's name across the screen. I'm convinced she and Ross speak more than we ever did.

Hell, they may even have a better relationship than we do.

"You going to answer that?" Blondie asks, glancing at the phone screen.

I click the green button on my screen and bring my phone to my ear. She speaks before I even get to say hello.

"What did you do, Maevis? Why is Ross telling me you called the wedding off? Do you realize the money and power you're walking away from? Your father and I raised you better than this."

I don't think she took a single breath between sentences. Waiting a few seconds to make sure she's done, I attempt to get her to understand my reasoning. "Mom, I…I called it off because I found him cheating with his secretary," I inform her, and I see Blondie shift from side to side.

"Maevis, men cheat. That's just what they do. You take their credit card, buy an expensive purse, and move on," she responds, and I scrunch my face. "It's better than settling for the trash you were so set on building a life with in college."

She loves bringing up my old life every chance she gets.

"He put his hands on me, Mom. More than once," I say and glance up at Blondie, who looks like he's contemplating marching back into the building. The line is silent for a few moments before my mother grunts.

"Well, what did you do or say for him to do that?"

My mouth drops open, and I know Blondie can hear her, because he snatches the phone from my grasp and ends the call. He places the phone back in my hand and reaches in his pocket, grabbing a pack of cigarettes and smacking it in his palm.

I'm stuck in a stupor. I've become accustomed to her cold demeanor when we speak, but that was a knife to the heart with a not-so-subtle twist of the blade.

How can someone who endured so much abuse at the hands of a man say that to their daughter?

Blondie places his hand on my upper back and guides me to a sleek black car in the back of the lot. "Get in," he whispers, sympathy dripping from his voice. I glance up at him with questioning eyes. "I'll drive you home, and we will get your car to you by morning," he says. I roll my lips in, fighting back more tears. His eyes grow even more sad as he runs a hand through his short hair. "I promise," he says, opening the door a bit wider. "Now, get in. Please."

EIGHTEEN

Blondie parks in front of my house, and I notice a large black figure sitting on the porch. I'm half a second away from turning and frantically telling Blondie to pull away, but the figure jolts up from the stairs, and I automatically know that stature.

The speed he's striding toward me with has my heart beating at the same speed as his footsteps.

The masked man reaches the door and snatches it open.

"Here we go," Blondie mumbles to himself while unbuckling his seatbelt and getting out of the car.

V is already reaching across me and unbuckling my seatbelt as if I'm a toddler. I try swatting his hand away, but he cuts me a glare through his mask that has me trying to blend into the seat. Once I'm unbuckled, he grabs me under both my arms and lifts me out.

"I'm fine. I just—"

"Another man had his hand around your throat. Tell me again how the fuck that equates to you being okay," he snaps. His jaw sets in a hard line while awaiting my answer. and I bite hard on the inside of my cheek.

He's right and I know it, but I don't want sympathy from anyone. His eyes are already roaming over every inch of visible skin for marks or bruises. "Tell me exactly what happened that I couldn't see on the footage you sent," he huffs at Blondie, who is leaning against the hood of his car with his arms crossed and a cigarette hanging from his lips.

"I'm sorry, what? I asked you not to tell him," I say, casting a glare at Blondie.

V's gaze turns back to me for a moment. "Was I not clear enough when I said I'm never letting you out of my sight again? And his loyalty is to *me*, not you. Of course he told me. He knows what you mean to me."

I rear my head back at his statement, pulling my brows together.

"Ryatt, I'm not going to ask you again. Tell me the details," he demands in frustration, and my head swivels to Blondie, his real name permanently registering in my head.

Our eyes connect, and he rolls his while taking another drag from his cigarette. "Thanks for telling her my name. I was enjoying not letting her know, dickhead."

I laugh and immediately try to stifle it when V cuts another glare at me.

Ryatt fills him in about what happened with Ross, and I wrap my arms around myself for comfort.

"I told you I'm good with computers. Anywhere you go with cameras, this ogre here has eyes on you, including that fucker's job," Blondie informs me, and I nod my head in understanding.

"So you're a hacker," I respond.

Ryatt shrugs his shoulders. "Call it what you will, but I always get the job done."

With every bit of information Blondie provided about the night, V fills a bit more with anger. "Thanks. I'll handle it from here. Have the rest of the night off," he says while wrapping an arm around my shoulders and turning us toward the house. I glance back at Blondie, who's stomping out his cigarette on the ground.

"That's littering, you know," I say, wrinkling my nose in disgust.

Blondie groans before bending down to pick up the smashed cigarette, and I have to hold back a smirk.

"And you're too handsome to smoke cancer sticks on the regular," I follow, and *V* tightens his grip on my shoulders while looking back to glare at his friend.

Was he jealous?

He must know his friend is a jaw-dropper—or is it just the fact that I was pointing out the obvious that he didn't like?

I'd like to say the same about *V*'s face, but I've yet to be given the privilege of seeing it.

Blondie has a wide grin on his face while walking to the driver door. "You're not too bad yourself, trouble-maker."

"That's enough," *V* barks from my side, dragging me to the house.

"Bye, Blondie! Thanks for saving my ass," I shout and note the shocked look on his face.

Once we enter the house, *V* starts moving so swiftly, I barely have time to process. He's dragging me by my hand toward the kitchen, forcing me to sit at the table while he starts rummaging through my cabinets and refrigerator.

"Ummm...what are you doing?" I ask while watching him move so fluidly through my place that I begin to wonder if it's my house or his.

"Trying to find something for you to eat in this place. Where is all the food? Please don't tell me you only eat out."

I stare at him with raised brows. "No, I just haven't really had time or made an effort to buy groceries lately."

He slams the fridge shut and pulls his phone from his pocket, dialing a number.

"Hey. I know it's late, and you're probably about to leave, but is there any way you could prepare a steak with potatoes and veggies? Send it to—" He stops talking when he sees me staring at him with wide eyes. "Breakfast food is your favorite, right?"

I nod in a stupor as he resumes his call.

"Scratch that—can you make steak and eggs with breakfast potatoes on the side? If you don't mind delivering it to my location, you can take tomorrow off as well." He thanks the person on the phone before ending the call. His eyes flick up to meet mine behind the mask, and a sense of security washes over me as he strides toward the table. "Come on," he says, offering his hand to me. "Food will be here within the hour, but let's get you washed up before then."

I put my hand in his and let him lead me up the stairs into the bathroom. Memories of our last time in here flood me, and I try my best not to get lost in them.

I'm staring in the mirror as he starts the shower then stands behind me, joining my stare in the mirror. His hands come around to the hem of my dress, and I hold my breath as he slowly lifts it over my head. Without wearing a bra underneath, I'm standing in the mirror in only my underwear. His finger slips into the band and pulls them down until they hit the floor.

My arms fly up and wrap around my chest when I finally realize I'm completely naked, as if he's never seen me before. His hands wrap around my wrists and push my arms to my sides. "There's no reason for my girl to hide herself from me," he hums in my ear, and my entire body shivers.

"I never agreed to be your girl. I don't even know what you look like behind the mask. I don't even know your name."

I can feel him stiffen behind me as he backs away. "I'll be right out here when you're done," he informs me. My hand flies out to grasp his wrist before he leaves, and I'm just as shocked when he turns to face me. His big green eyes stare at me in confusion.

"Shower with me," I say and swallow hard while waiting for his answer. I can see his eyes processing my request before he pulls his wrist from my grasp. For a moment, my heart pauses, and I prepare for him to continue out the bathroom door. But then his hands grip his shirt and lifts it over his head.

My mouth goes dry at the sight of him.

His broad shoulders are only the beginning as my gaze trails down to arms chorded with veins. My eyes wander without shame over his sculpted chest and abs. It's as if his body was made for temptation, with the perfect balance of grace and dominance. The defined lines of his abdomen have my eyes trailing lower; I wish the rest of his clothes would be gone at my command.

I lick my lips, fighting against their dryness when I can't force myself to look away. The magnetic pull I feel toward his body is about to win the fight when he nods toward the shower, instructing me to get in. I internally groan when I don't get a chance to see the lower half of him as he tucks his fingers under the waistband of his pants, but I draw in a breath when I notice he's studying me in the exact same way.

"Face the shower head," he instructs, and I do as I'm told. The hot water covers me in relaxation, and I fight not to turn around.

I hear the shower door slide open, and my lungs inflate with a deep breath when he presses his body to my back, reaching for the loofah hanging below the shower head. The size of him has me frozen—I want every inch of him to ruin me.

I watch as he squirts the bodywash onto the sponge, his arms stretched in front of me, lathering it with the palm of his hand. I relax with a drawn-out sigh when he rubs it over every inch of my body. Watching the soap rinse down the drain when he's done makes me sad—I know he's about to end the session. Reaching my hand back and up toward his face, I suppress a gasp when I feel the warmth of his skin instead of his mask.

Every fiber of my being is begging me to turn around, but I know this is him telling me he trusts me. The last thing I want is to lose the trust of the man I want so badly.

I want him to trust me as much as I trust him.

When he doesn't remove my hand, I gently roam over the structure of his face. I smile when I feel his high cheekbones, and I bite my lip when I feel how perfect and full his are with the tips of my fingers.

"*V...*" I moan into the steamed shower. "Please..."

His hands wrap around my waist and pull me into the front of him again. "Tell me what you want, Duchess."

I know he knows exactly what I want, but he's making me say it out loud. The issue is, my brain is foggy—even though I told Ross the wedding is off, does that mean we're done?

I want to be done.

I want *V*.

"You caught him fucking his secretary on his desk, Maevis," I say internally. *"You control your life, not him. You made your decision, now roll with it."*

My hands rest atop *V*'s and pull them up until they're resting over each breast. Leaning my head back with my eyes closed, I suck in a breath and release it. "I want to see you."

I can feel his chest repeatedly rise and fall as he chuckles. "Not yet, Duchess. But I can give you what else I know you crave."

My pulse quickens along with my breath as I feel the length of him harden against me. One hand releases a breast as it slides up the middle of my chest to rest on my throat. The hum of his groan has me weak in the knees. "Tell me you're my girl," he says, deliberately pressing his cock into my back. I squeeze my eyes shut, the brat in me begging me to rebel. I want to tell him I belong to no one, but right now, all I want is to forget. I want to forget about Ross. I want to forget about my family.

I want to forget everything.

His hand squeezes around my throat, and I'm scared I'm going to come without an inch of penetration. It's been months since Ross has made an advance on me, and even if he did, the intimacy between us felt nothing like this.

I press my ass into him and smirk when he releases another groan.

"Stop fucking with me, Maevis. I'm fighting every urge to be as rough as I want to be with you, but you're making it hard. *Literally and figuratively.*"

I giggle and feel another squeeze around my throat that produces a moan of my own.

"I'm your girl," I say on a breathy moan. "Yours and only yours."

He releases my throat, and his hand moves to my back, grasping the nape of my neck as the other drops back down to my hip. I can feel his full lips at my ear, and I shudder in response.

"I already knew that, Duchess. I just wanted to hear it from that pretty little mouth of yours before I'm inside you."

Before I can respond, his hand is entangling in the hair at the nape of my neck, and he thrusts me forward as my hands shoot out against the wall. I look down to see him widening his stance due to our height difference, and I gnaw on my bottom lip when I feel him hovering at my entrance.

"*V...*" I whisper on a plea.

His husky laugh fills the shower, intertwining with the

steam surrounding us before I see his knees hit the floor between mine.

I don't get a chance to question him.

I feel his tongue run up my slit, and I gasp at the feel of him between my legs, then another cry when I feel his tongue slip inside as his hand reaches around, his fingers finding my clit. My hands slip on the wall as my lower belly tightens at the overwhelming sensations.

I'm panting, on the verge of coming when he pulls away.

"What the fuck?" I nearly scream when he robs me of the orgasm threatening to rip through me.

His hand finds the back of my neck again as he widens his stance and leans over my back to reach my ear once more. "The next time I make you come, it's going to be on my cock."

A shiver runs down my spine as he trails kisses down it while pressing his tip to my entrance. "You understand that once I claim this pussy, it belongs to me, right?"

In the moment, he could've asked me to sacrifice myself, and I would have said yes. I nod repeatedly, waiting for him to give me what I need as the steam grows thicker around us.

Slowly, he presses into me, and I stiffen at his size.

"Relax for me, baby," he whispers, and I do my best to relax to accommodate him. He pushes further inside, and I cry out, trying to breathe as he stretches me. "That's my good girl," he whispers softly, and I melt into his grasp.

"A little more," he murmurs, and my eyes are about to pop out of their sockets.

MORE?

With one final thrust, he's all the way in, and I feel my knees buckle at him fully seated inside me. He catches me with an arm around my waist. Without warning, he pulls back until only the head of him is barely inside before he rams into me again. I cry out in both pain and pleasure as he finds his rhythm, immobile, held in place with one hand while his other snakes around to circle my clit.

I feel my legs weakening as the fire builds in my lower belly. "*V*, I'm going to—"

"I know, baby. It's all I've ever wanted. Don't hold back. Show me what my cock does to you," he commands, and I can't hold back any longer.

My orgasm rips through me, and he doesn't stop until I ride out my orgasm at the mercy of his pace. His thrusts become sporadic as I tighten around him, and I know he's about to find his own release.

Remembering I'm not on birth control, I snap my head up.

"Don't worry, Duchess. I already know you're not taking contraception," he grits out before smacking my ass and pulling out at the same time. I pull in a breath when I feel the hot ropes of cum on my back.

Before I straighten, I feel two fingers press into my back and run down the length of my spine. The same fingers find my lips, and I open to accept as I wrap my tongue around his fingers, tasting the release of the man whose face I've never seen. The salty taste has me humming in acceptance before I swallow, and I feel him shudder against me.

"Mmmm...I can't wait to claim that pretty little mouth," he says, pulling his fingers from my mouth with a pop.

I'm breathless and sore when he reaches back around to grab the soap again. When he's done, he instructs me to stay facing the wall as he gets out. I do as I'm told until he returns with a large towel, his mask back in place with his own towel wrapped around his waist.

My lips form a pout when I realize I still don't get to see his face, but I'm too satisfied and sore to argue as he helps me out of the shower and dries me off.

Once he wraps the towel around me, he exits the bathroom

and returns with an oversized shirt, helping me put it on. I'm embarrassed he didn't grab something sexier for me to wear and narrow my eyes when I see he's biting his lip while devouring every inch of me.

"God, you're beautiful," he says, running his thumb over the bruise still lingering underneath my eye. His eyes turn into slits of disapproval before he drops his hand from my face and crosses his arms over his chest. "Still refuse to tell me how you got that, huh?"

I glance at the floor and shake my head. "V, I'm being honest. I don't know how I got it. I just remember seeing it the next morning after a work gala with Ross. I only had a mocktail that night, so I'm not sure why I don't remember much, but I did have a long work week. Maybe I was just so tired afterwards, my brain completely shut off."

His muscles tense and relax at Ross' name, and I do everything to avoid looking at him.

"I believe you," he says, and my eyes snap up to meet his. "But that doesn't mean I won't stop until I find out for you."

I swallow and refrain from asking him what he means. Guiding me to the bed, he runs downstairs, and I hear the front door open and close. My nerves rattle when I wonder if he left without saying goodbye.

I let him fuck me, and now he's leaving. Serves me right for allowing a stalker to fuck me raw.

I'm snapped out of my internal dialogue when I hear his footsteps coming back up the stairs, and he appears in the doorway with a large brown bag.

Pulling over the small side table from the corner of the room, he unpacked the food he requested earlier on the phone. The smell is so divine, it makes me damn near drool.

"Who made this?" I ask him. I knew by the phone call that it wasn't from a restaurant.

V scratches the back of his neck as if he's embarrassed. "My personal chef," he responds and hands me a fork from the bag. He's untwisting the cap to the orange juice bottle as I stare at him.

"Are you rich or something?" I blurt out, and I wish I could take it back.

Thankfully, he laughs while setting the juice on the table, ignoring my question.

He grabs the remote from the dresser and presses buttons until he finds exactly what he knows I want after the day I've had. The theme song to The O.C. plays, and I rest back against my headboard while stuffing my mouth with breakfast food in the dead of night.

He disappears into the bathroom for a bit and returns fully dressed.

"I'll check on you in the morning. I'll set the alarm and lock the doors. Sweet dreams, Duchess," he announces with a nod, and I almost choke on my food.

"No!" I shout, food almost spraying out of my mouth. I instantly regret it, embarrassment flooding me as he tilts his head in question.

"I mean...I mean, please don't. Don't go. Just stay the night," I say on a breath. Licking my lips as I study him, waiting to see if he agrees to stay again.

"Okay. I'll be down—"

I cut him off before he tells me he's staying downstairs like last time. "Just get in the bed, *V*. We've already fucked. It's too late to act like you're some pure gentleman now."

A devious smirk spreads across my face, hoping it happens again. He shakes his head and walks to the other side of the bed, plopping down on top of the comforter.

When I finish my food, he takes the trash downstairs and

comes back up with a glass of water to set on the nightstand beside me.

Getting comfortable under the sheets, I watch as Summer Roberts reveals her Wonder Woman costume to Seth and drift off into a deep sleep as my masked stalker scrolls on his phone.

As much as I hope and pray, I doubt *V* would ever be willing to be the Seth Cohen to my Summer Roberts. Still, I feel content knowing he's next to me, if only for one night.

I can admit everything feels different since I stepped into the shower with him tonight.

Maybe it is possible to be fucked senseless.

My stomach flips at the thought of what transpired within the last few hours. Even if it is for only one night, I know I'll never be the woman I was twenty-four hours ago.

Because now, I live for me.

CHAPTER

NINETEEN

It's a funny feeling, waking up a completely different woman, one that doesn't give a fuck what anyone thinks about her anymore. It's as if overnight, I have a new outlook on life; I finally feel like I can handle whatever is thrown at me. I no longer have the weight of worrying about impressing or appeasing anyone other than myself.

Thankfully, it's the weekend, and I get to be lazy at home until my personal training session this afternoon. Rose and I have been taking boxing lessons, and our trainer doesn't let us take any weekends off. He's adamant we stick to consistency, and even though Coach Rivers is a softy at heart, his trainer voice terrifies me enough to not cancel a single session.

I roll over to an empty bed, but the scent of coffee pulls me in and lets me know *V* is still here. I exchange the oversize shirt I'm wearing for my favorite nightgown and robe before making my way downstairs for some much-needed coffee after last night's debacle.

Turning the corner, I stop cold in my tracks.

A lone chair is propped in the hallway with a person tied to it, a black bag over their head.

I begin to back up when I'm met with a hard chest to my back. I spin around to face him, searching the mask until I find the emeralds that hold zero emotion. "Coffee?" he asks while holding out one of my favorite mugs. My brain is begging me to take it as the heavenly scent floats through the air, but my

114

mouth is too dry to form words. *V* shrugs and places the mug on the table against the wall. "Take the bag off," he instructs with a nod at the chair. I open my mouth to protest, but his eyes flare, and I snap it shut.

Slowly, I pad over to the chair and remove the bag in one, swift motion, letting out a gasp as I bring my hands up to cover my mouth, stumbling backwards.

"Brian?" I whisper as I survey Ross' best friend, a gag in his mouth, bucking violently to be set free. His khaki pants are smeared with blood, his light blue tie coming undone and frayed. The highlighted hair that is usually gelled to perfection is matted with sweat.

I glance at *V* and back to Brian before shuffling back in front of him and removing the gag.

"You stupid fucking bitch. I can't wait to tell Ross the shit you've caused," he begins before *V* marches over and back-hands him, snapping his head to the side. I gasp, backing up until I feel the wall on my backside.

I watch in shock and confusion as the man I slept with last night crouches in front of Brian. "Apologize to her, or I'll send your balls to your mother in a snow globe."

Brian's eyes blow wide before mumbling an apology in my direction.

V stands, pacing back a few feet. "Brian here has something he wants to tell you."

I stare at Brian, waiting for him to speak as blood trickles down his chin from the corner of his mouth. He stares back at me with disgust before flinching when *V* takes a step toward him.

"It was me," he blurts out, spitting blood on my hardwood floor.

Confusion blooms within me at his confession. My eyes dart over to *V*, who's standing with his arms crossed over his chest and a stare that could burn a house down. I attempt to steady myself through my irregular breaths that are failing to bring me the oxygen my body is begging for. Wetting my lips, I move from the wall and take a step toward Brian. With a shaky voice accompanied by trembling hands, I ask Brian to clarify. He stares at me for a moment with a blank expression before curling his lip in a sneer.

"The bruising under your eye. It was me," he confesses and clenches his jaw.

A whimper leaves my lips as I press the back of my hand to my mouth. Last night, when *V* asked me again to tell him how I received the mark under my eye, I couldn't, because I genuinely didn't know how it happened. I went to a work party with Ross a week ago and woke up on my couch, unsure of how I got home.

"Continue," *V* hisses, bringing me back from the memory.

Brian runs his tongue across his bottom lip before turning his attention on me. "Ross slipped a roofie into your drink at the dinner last week. He lost a bet, and the prize was you. We thought he was joking, but he delivered you to my hotel room, and..."

Tears roll in thick streams down my cheeks as I listen to the story unravel.

"And what, Brian?" I ask, trying to dissolve the lump forming in my throat.

Brian rolls his eyes, as if annoyed I'm crying. I hear him mumble incoherent words under his breath that has my chest tightening. The lack of sympathy in his demeanor is gut-wrenching. With another eyeroll, he glances from *V* back to me before finally settling his gaze on the floor. "I used you exactly how I wanted. But you involuntarily hit me while you were unconscious, and I let my temper get the best of me. So, I...I hit you back."

I fall back into the wall, sliding down and gasping into the palms of my hands.

"Get up," V snaps from beside me, grabbing my upper arms and pulling me to my feet. "Do not let them see you fall," he whispers in my ear.

His words have me scrambling to gain my composure, because he's right.

How many times have I let their words and actions control me? How many times

have I let them force me back down after I've built myself up? I clench my teeth as I answer my own questions in my head.

This is what they want? To see me fall?

"While you were asleep last night, I did some digging, since you wouldn't tell me who marked you," he says while holding my gaze. "Thanks to a friend who doesn't mind getting their hands dirty, I ended up finding text messages from this sorry excuse of a man to your supposed fiancé about the encounter."

I instantly know he's talking about Blondie, and my shoulders sag from embarrassment. I've only met him a handful of times, but he must think I'm the most helpless human being at this point.

My attention is brought back to the present when Brian spits at V's feet before laughing. "And what are you going to do about it? You're so scared of us, you won't even show your face."

A grim laugh leaves V as he snatches Brian's face in a forceful hold. "The mask is for your protection, not mine, frat boy," he snaps, thrusting Brian's head back, earning a cry of pain from his victim. With an audible grunt, V brandishes the same knife he pulled on me the first time I met him, along with a gun from the backside of his jeans.

Contradictory to the smart mouth he just had, Brian now looks like he's seen a ghost as he jerks wildly in his chair.

V places the items on the table against the wall and cradles my face.

"I found the culprit, but his punishment can only be decided by you," he says before tilting his head toward the weapons on the table. "As badly as I want to rip this fucker to shreds, that is not for me to decide. You can let him walk out of here, or you can deal with him however you see fit, Duchess."

My eyes skim over the weapons on the table before glancing back at Brian, who is sweating profusely and still mumbling incoherently with his head hanging down.

V gently jerks my face to focus on him again. "You're the one building the fire, Maevis. I'm only here to provide the gasoline to keep it going."

"Maevis, don't be the dumb bitch Ross makes you out to be. Let me go, and we both can act like this never happened," Brian says from the chair, white as a ghost.

Act like this never happened?

"You assaulted me," I shout, glaring at him. He groans and rolls his head from side-to-side. "It was just pussy, Maevis. Great pussy, but pussy nonetheless. Come on, I heard you gave it up all the time in college, so what's the difference?"

V jerks toward Brian, but I catch him by the arm and pull him back toward me. The tension in his body lets me know how close he is to snapping, to taking Brian's life in the blink of an eye. My heart races at the thought of him ending a life for me, and I shake the thought away.

I look around *V* back to Brian, whose chest heaves with each worried breath.

The flame that had begun to build in my chest yesterday when I found Ross fucking his secretary was now an inferno.

The thought of all the men in my life thinking I'm nothing more than a pawn to throw around sends tremors through me.

V's green eyes flare in question when a maniacal laugh escapes from the deepest part of my soul. "You're right, Brian. It's just pussy," I say, stepping around *V* and picking up the knife. The fear on Brian's face dials my heart rate so high, I can hear the swooshing in my ears. From the corner of my eye, I can see *V* casually leaning on the back of the couch, coffee in hand, watching with intense eyes as I stand before Brian. The calmness now exuding from my stalker should be concerning, yet all I find is comfort before I return my focus to Brian.

"But what happens with *my* pussy is *my* choice," I hiss before slamming the blade of the knife into his thigh. His scream is a sweet symphony to my ears as I drop my head back, taking in a deep breath. "And I wasn't given a choice as to who shoved their dick inside *me*," I say calmly, pulling the knife from his thigh and slamming it into the other.

The blood dripping onto the floor sends my senses into overdrive as the coppery smell floats up my nostrils. I glance over at *V*, whose gaze is already set on me with a look of admiration and hunger. As if he can tell what I'm thinking, he chuckles, standing to his full height. "I know how to dispose of a body, Duchess," he says confidently.

I smile, turning back to a whimpering Brian, the smell of urine floating in the air. The poor fuck pissed himself.

"Was I the only one?" I ask while pulling the knife from his thigh, earning a guttural scream. I straighten my stance, throwing my fist into his jaw, blood splattering against the white wall. I make a mental note to thank Coach Rivers for all the boxing lessons and forced consistency.

"Yes. No... I don't know," he says between coughing fits.

"*You don't fucking know?*" I ask, throwing another satisfying punch to his jaw.

"Ross and I do it frequently, but..."

The room begins to spin. *My fiancé is taking advantage of other women—on a consistent basis.*

Ross hasn't made a move towards me in months, but he has no problem taking advantage of women? And not just women...unconscious women. How many others woke up not knowing what happened to their bodies while they were comatose?

"Who else was there that night?" I ask, staring at the blood splattered on the wall. Its crimson red is a dark contrast to the bright white paint. Brian coughs before answering, and I can tell he's stalling. "I-I'm not sure. There were a few of us in the room, but I didn't know all of them."

My head snaps back to look at him. *A few.* My fiancé let his friends defile me and then carried on with his life like I was made to serve them. I begin to tremble violently as a single tear falls down my cheek, stopping at the corner of my lips. I dart my tongue out to catch it, quickly wiping it as I vow it to be the last time any of these fuckers get any type of emotion from me.

"Maevis, I'm sorry. I really am. If you let—"

I don't want to hear the rest of his sentence, and quite frankly, I don't want to hear him breathing anymore.

The visual of the blade slicing across his throat is pure bliss.

His gurgles are the icing on the cake as I watch him struggle for air.

Untying my robe, showcasing the purple silk nightgown I threw on this morning, I straddle his lap. My gaze bores into his brown eyes as I watch the life slowly fade. I remain silent as he struggles at the hand of a woman much smaller than him while I dig my hand into his hair. Taking in the vile moment erupting in front of me, I tamp down the maniacal laughter attempting to escape. For a split moment, I wonder what's becoming of me before I brush away the thought.

I lean in closer, the blade hovering directly over his heart. "Letting you walk out of here to defile other women would be doing other women a disservice. Unfortunately for you, the old Maevis is dead," I hiss between clenched teeth, plunging the blade into his chest.

Drowsily, I climb from his lap on wobbly legs, and *V* reaches out to steady me.

I glance down at my clothes on the floor, covered in Brian's blood, before looking back up at *V*. Shock washes over me as I realize what I've done, but there are no tears, no sobbing, nor any panicked feelings consuming me. Only the ripples of electricity float through each intricate vein woven inside me.

"How do you feel?" he questions from behind his mask.

I glance around the room at the dead body strapped to the chair.

I should feel like a murderer. I should feel like a horrible person for taking the life of a man I've known for years. *A man who used me while I was unconscious.* But I don't feel an ounce of regret. The breath I take is one of ease and liberation.

A small chuckle escapes me as I register my own actions and brush my cheek with the back of my hand, smearing blood as I look into the mirror hanging on the wall.

"Alive," I answer as *V* moves to stand behind me. Wrapping his arms around my torso, he bends to rest his chin on my shoulder. His smell is so intoxicating, I want to beg him to fuck me again right here, right now. I don't even care that his cock has been in me before, I know what he looks like, or that I'm covered in the blood of the man I just murdered.

"You ready, Duchess?" he asks, tightening his grip for a second before dropping to my hips.

I know what he's insinuating. The thought of it has my body engulfed in flames of rage and revenge. But when my gaze raises to the mirror in front of me, I can't shake the fog of guilt forming in my head.

What if everything Brian told me was my fault?

I raise my fingertips to the bruise under my eye and flinch when I press too hard. Swallowing down the lump of emotions raising in my throat, I absentmindedly grab the coffee mug *V* placed on the table for me when I first arrived downstairs. It may not be as hot as when he first offered it to me, but the taste of it on my tongue sends a surge of warmth through me. My body melts into his hold as I take another sip and clear my throat.

That I believed I was in the wrong for even a fraction of a moment makes me angry at myself. None of this was my fault. None of this was my wrongdoing. And if I believe it was, that would be giving the horrid men in this world exactly what they want.

I refuse to make myself uncomfortable for anyone anymore.

I snap out of my pondering when I hear *V* reiterate his question. I place the coffee mug back on the table, my gaze connecting with his again in the mirror. I'm met with the same fire I feel burning within myself. I nod as I turn to face him, taking note of the massive amounts of blood still pouring from Brian.

I glance down at my feet, wet from the deep red that has now reached us. I follow the trail from the chair back to my feet.

A river of red from my own hand.

Not an ounce of regret passes through me as I lean my head back to look at the masked man who provided the fuel to my hidden fire. The determination that now blooms in my gut has me speaking my next words clearly and confidently.

"Let's burn it all to the fucking ground."

One of V's hands trail up my stomach, between my breasts, and settle on my throat. "That's my girl," he whispers, and I melt in his grasp. The hand wrapped around my throat is removed as he spins me back around, and I'm focused on him in the mirror as his hand rests on the edge of his mask.

I hold my breath, watching his hand work to lift the edge of the mask, his other hand tightening on my hip.

His green eyes flare, holding my gaze seconds before he completely lifts the mask from his face.

CHAPTER

TWENTY

Okay, so, maybe my knees buckled, because I'm staring up from the hardwood floor of my home.

A familiar yet unfathomably handsome face hovers over me in concern, and I blink a ridiculous number of times to focus, because there's no way this is real. There's no way he's actually here.

There's no way this is happening.

And there's absolutely no way he is this much more handsome.

"Maevis, baby, let's get you sitting upright," he says in a soothing voice, and my breath catches in my throat. How did I not recognize his voice?

Because it's way deeper than before, you idiot, I say in my head.

He lifts the upper half of my body until I'm sitting upright on the floor. His fingertips brush over my temple, pushing stray hairs away from my face, and I want to melt back into the floor. I swallow and slowly turn my head to get a better look at him. It would be an outright lie if I said his attractiveness didn't still have a hold on me.

Only this time, it's far, far worse than before.

Without the mask, his green eyes shine bright, thanks to the sunlight filtering through the curtains, as if emeralds caught in the crossfire of the beaming sun. His thick, dark lashes fan over his cheekbones each time he blinks, staring at

124

me with concern. I raise one hand to his cheek and let it drift down to his jawline that gives his face a unique, timeless appeal. My eyes drop to his lips that haven't changed since the first time I met him, his bottom one much fuller than his top.

And his scent. That delectable scent that sent waves of nostalgia and vertigo through my bones every time he came around. I should have known it was him.

"Why don't we get you cleaned up, and we can talk after," he suggests, licking his lips in the process. My eyes refuse to leave them. I haven't even had a chance to kiss them because of the mask.

I nod silently, words escaping me for the time being as I remember how we first met in the courtyard of our college campus when I dropped my books, the wind taking my papers with it. He didn't even know who I was, yet he ran in circles with me until we grabbed every piece of paper that tried to get away from me. His green eyes drank me in while chatting with me on the way to my class, exchanging phone numbers before he raced to his. From that moment on, we were inseparable until I was ripped away from him by my parents.

Two arms slip underneath my body, lifting me into the air and carrying me over to the wooden steps. I watch his tall, athletic frame saunter out of the room into the kitchen, as if there's not a dead body in the room with us. From the moment I met him, he's always had a quiet confidence in the way he carries himself. But now, with the added muscle and height, I know for a fact that he can command a room the moment he enters it.

He returns with a soaked dish towel while running a hand through his thick, slightly tousled dark hair. I thought he was unnerving with the mask, but without it, everything about him is even more intense. He exudes danger and intimidation, but I want nothing more than to be drowned in all of him.

My eyes round as he kneels in front of me, gently grabbing my face to wipe the blood from my cheek.

Brian's blood.

My gaze drifts back over to the corpse in the room, and realization sets in. Before I can stop myself, I feel the vomit rising in the back of my throat. A garbage can is thrust in front of my face, and I drop my entire head inside of it, emptying the contents of my stomach. Embarrassed, I grab the towel from his hand and wipe my mouth. "How can you be okay with a dead man several feet away from us?" I ask, staring into his hardened green eyes.

He shrugs before grabbing the towel back from me, folding it, and standing. "I see it every day in my line of business."

My jaw drops open at his reasoning. *Line of business?*

"Don't act like you can't tell I'm a different person now, Duchess," he says, using two fingers to press under my chin and close my mouth. I swallow and study the man I was forced away from in college. Vane was never purely innocent, but he was never *bad*.

Now, I'm not so sure.

He drops onto the steps next to me, and his thigh brushes mine, sending a jolt of electricity through me. Readjusting myself to face him, I have to suppress the corners of my mouth from turning upwards. But unlike me, he allows himself a small smile before erasing it from his perfect face. "Throw all your questions at me, beautiful," he says while turning his body to mimic mine.

"You let me be this close to you this entire time without telling me it was you. Why?" I asked without a second thought.

He chuckles beside me, and the butterflies that have been dormant for a bit flutter awake in my belly. "Because I knew it would throw you off. You would have been moving to impress me instead of yourself. I wanted you to ignite your own fire, Duchess."

My brow furrows at his answer. "And that. That right there. Why do you keep calling me Duchess? You never did that before."

He reaches over, taking my hand, and I hold my breath at his touch. "Because you and everything you embody should be seen as royalty, nothing less."

Tears threaten to come, and I don't need a mirror to know I'm blushing. "Vane Zorran, you never cease to amaze me, even after all these years," I reply and catch a quick, subtle smirk flit across his face.

"About that," he replies, and I have to force myself to continue breathing as my head drops into my hands. I prepare myself for another bomb of information I can't handle. "That's not my last name, by the way. It's Wrathbone."

My head pops up at the reveal. I search his emerald eyes for any trace of a lie or a joke. "Wrathbone as in the billionaires who own national casinos?"

Vane nods. "That would be the Wrathbones I'm speaking of."

Out the corner of my eye, I sneak another peak at the dead body slumped in the chair across from us and bite my bottom lip before continuing my questioning. "But you said you know how to dispose of a body. Someone who works in gaming and business wouldn't need to utilize that knowledge," I say, squinting. "You have to be lying. I've been through enough already, so please stop lying to me and tell me the truth, Vane."

I realize how easy it was for my brain to switch to his real name and suppress another smile. I observed him stiffen as he leaned in closer to me. "I may be a lot of things these days, Maevis, but a liar is not one of them."

Running my tongue across my lips, I apologized and began to fidget with my nightgown.

The palm of his hand was warm and inviting as it rested on my cheek. "Yes, my family owns casinos, but there's more that goes on underground than just gaming. And with my type of business, there most certainly can be dead bodies involved."

My eyes widen as my breaths elevate.

"If there's one thing I've learned over the years, it's that some of the kindest faces have the evilest souls underneath their skin and bones," he continues, dropping his hand from my cheek.

I stopped fidgeting to study him. His green eyes had darkened, as they never drifted away from my face. "You have a choice, Duchess. You can either stay here and continue to live this life, or you can leave with me, and I promise to bring hell to every person who has ever made you feel less than," he offers, and I bite the inside of my cheek when his palm finds my face again. "But it is your choice. It is always your choice with me."

I bring my hand up to lay atop his on my cheek, and I lean into his palm as tears roll down my face. "Why did you let me leave, Vane?" I question while trying to suppress a sob. "I told you my parents were making me leave, and you never tried to get me to stay. Why?"

His long, dark lashes fluttered closed for a few seconds.

"I would have gone anywhere with you, and you know that," I add without looking away.

His jaw flexes, and he drops his hand from my face again. "Because I knew I would need to leave for training soon. I was never going to get the chance to finish college. My family only let me live out my college dreams for a moment as a courtesy before I had to take over the family business. I knew I wasn't in the position to save you from the hellhole you've been dealing with."

My eyes roam over his face for any trace of lies or deception, but I can tell he's being truthful.

"You know how when bad people do bad things and the authorities take days, months, or years to find them? Sometimes, the cases even going cold?" he questions, and I nod.

"Well, the casinos bring those people to us rather than us having to track them down most of the time. Much sooner than the police would." My eyes bulge. "Underneath our casinos is illegal betting and gambling. It's where the high-rollers come in, and with the high rollers come the *really* bad people. I'm not talking stealing or fraud. I'm talking kidnapping, assault, torture, trafficking. All the things that make it a terrifying world for everyone, but especially women and children."

My breathing turns rapid as I listen.

"I'm the last person in the chain they see when they won't confess what they've done," he says, placing a hand on my thigh. "And that's further down underground, below the illegal betting and gambling. If they don't accidentally turn themselves in via gambling, my men hunt them down."

"So you make them talk. You're like...the final boss in videogames," I confirm, and he releases a subtle laugh.

"Yea, I guess you could say that. I'm the final boss who gets them to talk," he confirms, and his eyes flick back up to mine. "And I haven't failed yet."

The confidence in his statement sends my heart rate soaring. Taking a few deep breaths, I force myself to ask a question I tried to forget. "When you were begging me for money back in college, you didn't really need it, did you?" I ask and bite my lower lip, waiting for him to answer. Slowly, he shakes his head with saddened eyes, and I drop my shoulders.

"I couldn't watch you ruin yourself with any drug you could get your hands on. I knew that without any money, you couldn't buy them. You were too innocent to offer anything else in exchange for them," he clarifies, and I stare at the ceiling to fight back the tears.

I had let myself spiral in college, getting my hands on any drug money could buy that didn't involve needles. The stress of being the perfect daughter was eating me alive, and I needed a temporary high too many times to count. I never went home to visit my parents, so they never got a chance to pick up on my addictions.

But Vane knew. He saw every withdrawal firsthand.

If it weren't for him basically depleting my funds when he would beg me for money for food and clothes in exchange for tutoring me in math, who knows how far on the deep end I would be today?

Who knows if I would even be alive?

I blink through the tears when I see him reach into his pocket for a phone. He types for a moment before he turns the phone around and places it in both of my hands. I glance over at a bank account with thousands of dollars and back up at him with a confused expression.

"It's yours," he says, and I almost drop the phone. After a moment, realization smacks me in the face when I see my name across the top of the screen. A whimper slips from my lips.

"This is all the money I loaned to you in college," I say on a forced whisper, waiting for him to confirm. When he nods with a crooked smile, my tears turn to waterfalls. His hands slip around my waist as he pulls me into his lap and tucks my head into his chest. I feel his lips press into my hair before he speaks.

"I had nothing to give you at the time, and I knew...I knew I had to find a way to get you away from your family. Maevis, there's so much I have to tell you, but not here. Not like this. Let's dispose of the piece of shit strapped to that chair and get you out of here," he offers, and I raise my head to look at him.

Another crooked smile stretches across his face. "If you want to, that is."

I run my thumb across his full bottom lip and feel my shoulders relax at the feel of his face beneath my fingertips. "I don't want this life anymore. I want to be in control of myself."

He nods his head, taking his phone back and dialing a number. "Code blue. We need a quick cleanup," he says into the speaker, and shock runs through me.

He really is who he says he is.

"You go upstairs, take a quick shower, and get into something comfortable. Pack a bag while you're up there. You'll be staying at my place for a bit," he says, and the command in his voice has a warm, unfamiliar sensation slithering over my body. I stand, making my way up the stairs, but midway up, I glance back to look at him. His vivid green eyes are locked on me, his lips curling into a full-blown smile.

I produce a smile of my own as the butterflies in my stomach fully extend their wings this time. It's in this very moment I know…

I know I'll never be able to live without him again.

I know I'll never want to know what a life without him is like again.

And I know I'm in for the ride of my life.

TWENTY-ONE

I can hear rustling and movements of additional feet downstairs as I change into leggings and an oversized hoodie. My mind races as I try to figure out what I got myself into. Outside of committing murder, one other thing is for sure.

I feel absolutely liberated.

My entire life has consisted of me being a robot. But now... now, I feel like I'm in charge of all the controls.

The swirling thoughts of how I'm going to avoid prison time for murdering a rapist subside as they change to thoughts about Vane. He looks so different yet exactly the same. I always found him attractive, but now, he looks like a god among mortals.

The smell of bleach floats upstairs, and my eyes begin to water. I quickly finish packing my bag of essentials for a few days and head downstairs. I stop at the top of the stairs when I notice two men putting Brian's limbs in a black garbage bag.

Arms and legs that are no longer attached to his body.

I feel the bile rising in my throat, but I stop myself.

Both men crane their necks to look at me when they notice me frozen on the stairs.

"This the Duchess, boss?" one of the men asks in a thick Boston accent. My eyes drift over to Vane sitting next to Blondie, the two of them studying a tablet intensely. His gaze connects with mine as he runs his tongue across his bottom lip.

"That's her. She has clearance for everything. She can be trusted."

My heart flutters irregularly at those four words.

Blondie offers me a nod in greeting when I make it to the bottom of the stairs. Seeing them next to each other has wicked thoughts running through my head. I can only imagine what being satisfied by both at the same time would be like. Vane clears his throat, bringing me out of my stupor, and I realize how hard I'm staring.

"Care to voice whatever you're fantasizing about in that pretty little head of yours, Duchess?" Vane asks in a gravelly tone that makes me flinch in embarrassment.

The man with a Boston accent chuckles but stops when Blondie and Vane cut him a glare. My phone buzzes repeatedly in my pocket, and I open it to see eight texts from Rose.

Everything ok?

Girl, where ru?

Please don't make me drive over there...

Unless ur in bed with your masked murderer?

I want to watch!

I roll my eyes and crack a smile at her ridiculousness. I take a moment to make sure I don't say anything that could get me caught before I reply.

All good! I'm sorry, but I'm going to miss our session this morning. I don't feel good at all.

Coach Rivers is going to make me do triple the number of push-ups if I go by myself. I think I'm going to be sick too. *wink emoji*

I laugh and put my phone back in the front pocket of my

hoodie. The sense of ease I had from talking to Rose is quickly gone when I look up to notice Vane's glare. Tilting his head, he raises a brow, and I quickly understand he thinks I'm texting Ross. I drop my bag and raise both my palms.

"There's no way in hell you think I'm texting him," I say. Vane only tilts his head further to the side, and now, Blondie is staring at me just as intently. "I was texting my best friend, Rose. I swear, you can even look if you want to." I reach in my pocket to hand him my phone, but he holds his hand up, stopping me.

"I have no desire to go through your phone like a child. I'm just making sure you're not moving backwards," Vane explains calmly.

Blondie rubs his hands on his thighs. "Rose... That the friend I always see you with?" he asks with a look of lust in his eyes, and I glare back at him. He laughs while sticking a cigarette in his mouth and bringing the lighter to the tip.

I march up to him and snatch the cigarette out of his mouth. "Not in here! Have you lost your fucking mind?"

He stands, towering over me with a smile. "Never had it to begin with princess."

"He's not wrong," Vane adds, standing from the couch as well. I notice he's about an inch taller than Blondie, and I swallow hard while looking between the two of them. They both stare at me for a moment with a confused expression before Blondie turns to Vane.

"That asshole who offered you the three foreign women in exchange for six million comes in tonight. I'm going to go prepare the interrogation room for that."

I can see Vane visibly grit his teeth. My stomach twists in knots when I replay Blondie's words in my head. How can people be so cruel? I cringe and wrap an arm around my stomach.

"Did you ensure he's bringing the women so we can get them help and back to their families?" he asks, and Blondie nods.

"Sure did," he confirms while swaying from side to side.

"Why do you look so happy about bringing this fucker in?" Vane asks skeptically.

"Because I lost in Warzone ten times in a row before I came here. I need to let out some aggression."

My mouth drops open, and for the first time since college, I hear Vane let out a loud, legitimate laugh. Blondie joins in, and they smack each other on the back. When they settle their laughing bout, Vane turns toward my shocked face. "Come on, let's head back to my place. The guys will handle the rest of the cleanup. You can trust them in your home. Ryatt will stay behind until they're done here as well," he says and nods to the men, who nod back at me with a tip of their baseball caps.

I take one last look in the doorway and race toward the mirror hanging on the wall where the two men are working. Bending, I pick up the mask that hid Vane from me over the past few days. I straighten to see him staring at me with a furrowed brow.

"I would feel weird leaving it behind," I say, feeling embarrassed and holding up the mask.

Blondie laughs while Vane shakes his head with a smirk. "Let's go, Duchess," he says while holding his hand out for me. I stride back over to him, placing my hand in his without hesitating and heading out the door of a home I have a feeling I won't be seeing for a long time.

CHAPTER

TWENTY-TWO

Leaving my home, Vane guided me down the steps to a sleek, black Audi R8—aka, money.

And lots of it.

"Where's my car?" I ask, looking up and down the street.

"In my driveway," Vane responds without missing a beat. I crane my head in his direction with squinted eyes.

"Blondie said he would make sure my car was brought here last night," I say, crossing my arms over my chest.

Vane saunters over, towering over me. "Wrong. He said we would get it to you by morning. He never said *where,*" he concluded and turns toward his car. I glare at his back while running through my conversation with Blondie last night and realizing he's right.

Picking up the pace, I pass him, getting to the car first. Reaching for the door I felt a smack on the top of my hand. Snapping my eyes up, I'm met with Vane's green ones glowering at me as he reaches for the door handle and pulls it open. I bite my bottom lip and place my hand in his.

"I meant what I said about knowing your worth," Vane hisses while leaning into the car and reaching over to fasten my seatbelt.

"Thank you," I whisper, trying to calm my racing heart. Racking my brain, I try to remember if Ross had ever opened my door for me, let alone buckle me in.

I startle when I hear him open the driver side door. When

he's seated next to me, I catch myself gawking and snap out of it when he turns his head in my direction. I can see a deep grin on his face as he waits for me to look at him.

"Are you going to keep acting like you're not attracted to me?" he asks, pressing the circular button to start the car with a childish grin. I clear my throat to gather my thoughts.

"What makes you think I'm attracted to you?" I question and quickly glance out the window to avoid eye contact.

He scoffs and shifts the car into drive. "I don't need you to tell me you're attracted to me. Your body told me all I needed to know last night, Duchess."

My eyes nearly bulge from my head and fall between the seats.

"And I don't need to tell you how badly I'm attracted to you. If you can't see that, I'll show it to you over and over," he says in a low, rough tone. A single large hand reaches out to rest atop my thigh, and I catch my breath. "Until your body physically can't take it any longer and it's ingrained in your thoughts."

My thighs clench at his statement, and I close my eyes to steady my breathing.

The rest of the car ride is silent, with Vane's hand resting on my thigh. I know the touch should feel possessive—and it does—but I've evaluated every emotion in my body, and not a single one resents the feeling. I've spent years with Ross and never felt protected or safe. I've only been reconnected with Vane for a few days, without even knowing it was him, and I feel like he is the safest space I've ever known.

The car halts at a black metal gate, and a device scans Vane's face for access. Slowly, it swings open, and we move uphill. My gaze sweeps over the mansion that comes into view, and I press myself into the leather seat with a feeling like I don't belong.

As we follow along the never-ending driveway, I can't help but take in the architecture. The deep, dark aesthetic fits perfectly with Vane's entire personality, and it almost makes me chuckle in the seat next to him.

Vane pulls up to the double front doors and puts the car in park before getting out and rushing around to my side. I know better now than to open the door on my own after getting my hand playfully smacked back at my house.

He opens the door and holds his hand out for me to grab. A playful smirk flits across his face when he notices I didn't try to open the door on my own. He pulls me into him with a subtle tug, his lips find my ear, and a shudder radiates down my spine.

"Good girl," he whispers with a kiss to my temple.

I gaze up at him, my jaw slackened, before he pulls me by the hand toward the front steps of his home. One of the doors swings open, a short woman with a long black braid falling over her shoulder loudly scolding Vane. When she notices me, her eyes widen and then soften as she smooths out her apron.

"You must be the Duchess," she says, her eyes gleaming.

Vane groans next to me. "Beverly, don't start with your nonsense," he says and kisses her atop her head. "But yes, this is her. She will need a few things while she's here, if you don't mind."

She slaps at Vane's arm to let me go and links her own arm through mine. I catch a glimpse of Vane rubbing his arm where she hit him with a grin on his face.

"Of course, of course," she says. "How long will you be staying with us, gorgeous? Are there any specific foods you don't like? Any that are your favorite? What brand of shampoo and conditioner do you use?"

Her questions are rapid fire, and I don't get a chance to

answer any of them before we halt in the foyer. "My...you are even more beautiful than Vane described you."

"Okay, Bev. You're acting like I talked about her every day. Relax," Vane hisses from the door as he shuts it behind him.

The woman rolls her eyes. "Because he did." My gaze drifts over to him, my brows shooting up and relaxing when I look back at the woman. "But anyway, how about you make me a list, and I will get everything you need? Write down your clothing sizes as well, down to the underwear," she says. "If you wear them. Heavens knows I don't anymore."

Vane groans again while offering me a sheepish grin. His embarrassment has a laugh bubbling within me that I can barely contain.

"What? A woman has to let it breathe every so often," she says, and I nearly yelp with laughter.

"Okay, I think Maevis has heard enough for the moment. I'll get her list over to you today. Thank you," he says, grabbing my hand and pulling me up the grand staircase.

"I'll have lunch prepared within the hour!" she calls out as we ascend the stairs.

I offer a smile and wave that she returns with an even wider smile. My eyes roam my surroundings quickly as my legs jump from step to step while trying to take everything in as quickly as I can. The chandelier hanging in the middle of the foyer between the staircases. The white and gray marble flooring shined to perfection. The expensive-looking paintings hanging on the walls. I blink, trying not to think about the price of everything.

"Who is she?" I stammer when we stop at the top of the stairs.

Vane never releases my hand as he leads us toward a room at the end of the hall. "She's family. Not literally, but she's taken care of my siblings and me since we were children."

He has siblings?

I was preparing to ask him to elaborate on his siblings when I realize I didn't grab my bag from the house. "Shit, I forgot—"

"Your bag," he finishes my sentence for me. "I know. Ryatt said he would drop it off later."

I thank him as he opens the door, and I freeze. His bedroom is a view straight out of a romance comedy with a twist of darkness. The four-post bed is against the far wall with red and black sheets. A matching bench sits at the foot. My gaze drifts over to the large black dresser that has multiple pieces of jewelry strewn across it along with an old-school alarm clock.

Vane walks over to the long curtains and snatches them open, revealing a balcony with two chairs and a table. I follow behind him and sit in the metal chair he pulls out for me. "I have to take care of a few things at the casino. I'll send Bev up in a bit to check on you."

I stare up at him, almost wanting to beg for him not to leave me even though I know I'm safe here. "I don't need anything," I reply and watch as his face turns to stone, making me swallow and avert my gaze.

"You need to eat, Maevis. Don't make me miss a very important meeting to make sure you take care of yourself," he says in a lethal tone.

I clear my throat and look back up at him. "Would that meeting have anything to do with the guy Blondie mentioned and possible torturing?" I ask with a tilt of my head. Vane runs a hand across his forehead and down his face before opening one of the drawers to his dresser. He lifts his hoodie and shirt over his head, and I do my best not to drool.

When we had sex in the shower, I never got to see his face or his body. His back is full of ridges and bulges where his muscles protrude. After grabbing the last piece of clothing, he turns around, and I drop my gaze to the floor.

I hear him release a subtle laugh as he makes his way back to me. "You can look as much as you want, Duchess. I'm all yours."

Heat washes over me in waves. He's saying he's mine without asking for anything in return.

I feel two fingers under my chin as he raises my head to look at him. "What's on your mind, baby?" he quizzes while sliding his sweatpants down and stepping out of them.

I'm begging the fog in my mind to dissipate, but the sight of him almost naked in front of me won't allow for it. I clear my throat once more after I'm done eye-fucking him and run my hand across the smooth concrete table. "I just... I have a lot of questions. Are you sure I can stay here while you're gone?" I ask.

He pulls on his dress pants and fastens them without breaking eye contact. Placing two hands on the table, he dips his head to level with mine. "I promise you that after this meeting, I will come back to this very spot, and you can ask me whatever questions you have," he says in a soothing tone, and I wet my lips.

"And so there's no confusion, don't ever ask me again if you're allowed to do something. I don't own you, and you're not beneath me unless we're fucking. What's mine is yours. You have full reign of this house and all my cars," he says before a small smile blooms on his perfect face. "And full reign of me as well."

My breaths and words are in a jumble in the middle of my throat when I try to respond.

He straightens, putting on his shirt and fastening the buttons followed by buckling his belt. He glances down at the watch on his wrist for the time, and I grimace in awe.

Is that a fucking Patek Philippe?

I am nowhere near broke, but I am also nowhere near rich as fuck. That watch alone oozes *rich as fuck.*

"Six o'clock," he says and throws on his suit jacket. "I'll meet you back here for dinner then. We can watch the sunset together."

I nod my head with a smile as he kisses the top of my head. "Be safe," I say.

"I will," he responds, tucking his phone in his pocket and turning away from me.

Without a second thought, I blurt out my next statement. "Come back to me."

Vane freezes in the doorway of the balcony, and I'm terrified it was a step beyond his boundaries. We're not in a relationship. Hell, I don't even know what we are, and I just gave him a command as if he's my husband.

He turns his head over his shoulder, a lone, large hand gripping the doorframe. "Always."

My heart flutters so fast and hard, I'm afraid Beverly will find me dead when he leaves and have to call an ambulance.

And without another word, he's gone, and I'm alone on the balcony of the man I thought I would never see again.

CHAPTER
TWENTY-THREE

(VANE)

My knuckles are snow white thanks to how tightly I have to grip the steering wheel to convince myself not to turn around and head straight back to her. The way her body molded with mine when I finally claimed her in the shower is a feeling I've never felt. And her eyes. *Those big, brown eyes.* Every single time they stare up at me, I feel like I'm about to lose control.

I should have kissed her on the balcony.

Thanks to that stupid mask, I wasn't awarded the luxury of her full lips pressed to mine. Even in college, we never took that step. We may have cuddled to watch a movie or two, but nothing beyond that. God knows I wanted to, but she was just so innocent, so...pure.

Have I had my share of women? Absolutely.

Did I have feelings for any of them? Fuck no.

I forget I'm behind the wheel and daydream about what she looks like while coming. Now that I don't have to wear that fucking mask around her, I can stare into that gorgeous face while I make her scream out for any god of her choosing.

Was the mask dramatic? Probably.

But I wanted her to find her true self without doing it because she knew it was me. I wanted her to fall for me, not my face or my body or my money. I'm not stupid—I know I'm attractive. I know money can get the pants off quite a few people in less than five seconds—but I wanted Maevis to find her own fire with just a slight push from me.

A car horn blares from behind me, and I'm snapped back to reality when I realize my car is barely moving. Speeding up, I wave my hand in apology, even though they can't see me through the tint of my windows.

I've never let anyone have any type of hold over me, but one look from Maevis with those brown eyes, and I'm like Olaf when he stepped into the fucking sun.

Reminder to myself to stop with the Frozen references.

The first time I ever laid eyes on her again after college, I think my heart stopped.

I know it was wrong to let her leave, but I knew there was nothing I could give her with where I was in life. I knew she deserved so much more, was owed so much more, but I had refused to let her go without stopping the drug use. She was far too intelligent for that stupid shit.

I refuse to let the love of my life live in fear and harm.

The first time I saw how her fiancé treated her, I wanted to break his fucking neck right there. But the woman I know Maevis to be would want to do it herself once she found out the type of scum he is.

The flashback of her ending Brian's life gets my cock hard when I picture her covered in his blood. *I should have fucked her right then and there.* I'm jarred back to the present when I slightly swerve and the car next to me lays on the horn.

She has a hold over me even when she's not here.

I'm so fucked.

CHAPTER
TWENTY-FOUR

Pulling up to High Roller's Haven never brings me joy. None of the casinos we own do, but this one is the darkest. I watch as patrons walk through the doors, ready to throw their money away, but I could care less. I know there's an asshole who needs to be dealt with below ground.

I drive around to the back of the parking garage and turn my face toward the scanner to be let into the underground tunnel. It beeps, and the garage door raises, presenting two armed guards who nod when they see my car and plates, moving to the sides to let me in.

When I arrive at the first door, I park the car, and the usual valet jumps over the rail to assist me. "Hey there, Mr. Wrath-bone. Hope you're having a good day," he says in his always-cheerful tone. Typically, it would annoy me, but I know he's Ryatt's nephew and offer him a smile instead. His poor, innocent soul doesn't know what happens down here. We don't let him beyond the hallway past his break room.

"You're cheerful as always," I say and take my wallet out to slip him a hundred-dollar bill. I know we pay him a handsome hourly wage, but he's a good kid, working to save for his first car. "Take care of her for me, like always," I add and toss him the keys.

I'd be lying if I said I didn't enjoy the way his eyes light up every time he knows he gets to drive it.

I wait until he starts the car before heading down the long, dark hallway to the familiar red door. Punching in the code I created, I swing the door open and am immediately met with an outcry of pain.

Thank God for soundproofing.

Rounding the first corner, I look through the double-sided mirror to see Ryatt deliver another punch to the man sitting in a chair in the middle of the room. Pressing the button next to the window, I speak, "Has he given you what we need yet?"

Ryatt turns toward the window, and I see he still has all his rings on. I can't stop the chuckle I release into my hand.

Fucker shows zero mercy.

And that's why he's my best friend.

"He refuses to speak at all. I'm actually kind of impressed," he says and turns back toward the man. I cringe when I see the man spit on Ryatt's favorite pair of shoes. My best friend looks down, and I press the button again before he has the chance to knock him unconscious and this takes even longer.

I'm not trying to be late getting back to Maevis.

"Let it go for now. It's my turn."

Ryatt smiles menacingly. "Good luck, fucker."

I press my palm against the scanner next to the metal door and walk in. The man's right eye is already swollen shut, but I see one dark brown eye follow my every movement.

"I'm not afraid of you," he spits.

I shrug out of my suit jacket and hang it on a hook near the door. "Is that why you think I'm here? To scare you?" The man licks his lips and looks from me to Ryatt. "You had your chance with him. You should've talked, and this could've been much easier for both of us."

He jerks in his chair, trying to break the zip ties keeping

him in place. I hit the keypad on the wall, and a drawer pops out. I grab my favorite piece of interrogation equipment and stick it in my back pocket.

"You want out of those zip ties?" I ask the man, who eyes me suspiciously.

"Obviously. Why the fuck would I want to be tied to a chair bolted to the ground?" he replies, and my face turns to stone as I raise a brow.

"I tell you what. You answer one little question for me, and I'll release you from that chair. Sound like a deal?"

I can see the man's chest rise and fall while mulling over my offer. He knows just as well as I do that nothing in this field is as easy as it seems—but he also knows he doesn't have many options here.

"Deal," he says reluctantly.

"Good boy," I reply, and I can see him grit his teeth at my response.

I pace toward him, stopping five feet away and leaning back on the metal table. "Why did you follow Maevis Moore to her car that night and attempt to sexually assault her?"

My own question makes me feel warm. The thought of another man putting their hands on *my girl* makes me want to go on a rampage.

He stares at me for a moment before laughing. "Does this girl have kryptonite pussy or something? Everything revolves around her," he says, and I can't stop myself when my fist connects with his jaw.

"Sorry about that. I don't like when people don't answer the simple fucking questions I ask. Let's try again, shall we?"

He has a coughing fit while blood dribbles down his chin. His lone open eye locates my hand that slowly balls into a fist again when he doesn't start talking. "Alright, alight," he says while licking his lips again. "Her parents hired me."

I have to refrain from letting the confusion I feel inside play across my face. Why would her own parents hire someone to harm her? For once in my life, I'm truly baffled.

"Hired you for what? My patience is wearing thin here," I reply and run my fingers across my brow in annoyance. I hate when people don't give me what I want quickly and efficiently.

"They said her current guy was dropping the ball, so they wanted me to handle it a different route," he rushes out. I tilt my head, insinuating for him to continue. "Since he wasn't doing his job of bringing the families together through marriage, they decided to go the other route and have me sell her to the highest bidder. With her name and bloodline, they knew they could make millions in a single night."

My brows come together in confusion. "Her name? Her family name is nothing. What weight does that last name hold around here?"

The man stares at me blankly before bursting into laughter. "You don't know?" he asks, looking at me with a menacing stare. "Oh, now this is getting good." He breaks out into a hysterical laugh that sends me over the edge.

Reaching into my pocket, I pull out the brass knuckles I pocketed when I entered the room. His eyes blow wide when I slide them onto my fingers.

Blood spills everywhere from the way his face splits open, and a few teeth fall to the floor. He's attempting to pass out when Ryatt pulls his head up by his hair, smacking him on the opposite cheek. "Wake the fuck up, bitch boy," he says, smacking him again, and his eye flutters open.

"Unless you want that a second time to the other side, I suggest you just fucking talk," I growl.

After a moment of collecting himself, he starts talking again.

"Those aren't her real parents," he speaks, barely audible

through what could be a broken jaw, and my blood runs cold. "I don't know if the details of the murders are accurate, but those very people had her real parents murdered in cold blood. I'm not sure why, but after they murdered them, they found her in the bassinet, and they couldn't bring themselves to leave or kill her, so they took her as collateral. Figured they could profit off her once she was older. This current boy toy of hers was supposed to help unite two wealthy families. They can't access any of her parents' money without her, as her name is on everything at every bank, domestically and internationally."

Not many things leave me in a stupor, but this is one of them. How could I have missed this? They covered their tracks so well, I never even thought something like this was happening. Maevis even looks like the two people posing as her parents. I looked them up online years ago.

"What is her real family name?"

"Fuck if I know. All I know is that there's some serious cash to the bitch's name," he says, followed by a choking laugh. Without hesitation, my foot finds the middle of his chest. The air is knocked out of him, but I continue.

"Does she know?"

The man gasps for air, fighting for a single breath to answer. "Does she know what?"

"Does she fucking know they're not her real parents? Does she know her biological parents were murdered?" I shout back at him.

He spits blood onto the floor and focuses back on me. "No. She doesn't know."

I don't show it, but every ounce of air escapes my lungs until the room spins for a moment, and I grip the edge of the table behind me. I hear Ryatt mutter a hundred expletives behind me.

"Hey man, you said you'd let me go after one question, and that was way more than one. You're a man of your word, aren't ya?" he rushes out, his one eye roaming over both of us.

Finding my composure, I stand upright and remove the brass knuckles, placing them on the table. "You're right. I am a man of my word. But there are a few things here I can't let go."

He jerks in the chair again and stares at me with peeled back lips. Ryatt hands me a folder, and I'm sick to my stomach when I open it. Holding up a single picture, I ask my question.

"Does she look familiar?"

His eye widens, and he looks away.

"How about them?" I ask and hold up a picture of ten-year-old twin boys.

I've done a lot of dark things in my lifetime, but I have never harmed a child or woman, and I'll be damned if I release someone who has back out into the world.

"Grab the gag for me," I instruct Ryatt and watch his eyes light up. He brings it back from one of the nearby stations and hands it to me. Without instructions, he stands behind the man and holds his head steady. He jerks violently as I pry his mouth open and place the metal gag inside, winding it until his mouth is open as wide as the gag allows.

Walking back over to the station where the metal device came from, I grab a pair of plyers.

When I'm back in front of him, I grip his jaw and read a name from the folder. "Gavin Derosen," I say and find a single tooth with the metal plyers. Clamping them down, I twist and pull until I hear cracking and pluck the tooth from his gums. Blood pools in his mouth while he cries out in pain. Dropping the tooth to the floor, I continue the same routine. "Elisabeth Collins," I announce and rip out another tooth. Tears stream down his face, and I notice him attempting to beg through a broken jaw and the gag.

I drop the plyers to the floor.

"Are you fucking begging? Did they beg for their lives when you sold them off and did God knows what else to them before you handed them over?" I hold up a collage of their pictures from the folder. "You know what? Cut the zip ties," I instruct Ryatt and unbutton my shirt, throwing it on the table.

Ryatt hesitates but pulls out his knife when I cut him a hard glare. He cuts both zip ties, and the idiot bolts toward the door that remains locked without one of us opening it. Realizing he's cornered, he eyes the tools and makes a dash for it.

But I'm faster.

Sliding the brass knuckles back on my fingers, I hit him directly in the back of the head and watch him fall to the floor. Ryatt kicks him over onto his back, and I climb on top of him. "Not only did you participate in trafficking, but you touched *my girl,*" I hiss and punch the brass knuckles into his rib cage. I throw my head back when I hear a satisfying crack and see blood spurt from his mouth. "And no one who touches what is mine lives to tell the tale."

The room turns to a blur, the edges of my vision blackening when I land blow after blow to his head and body with the metal attached to my fist. Ugly thoughts of Maevis being auctioned off as if she's not a person fill me, thoughts of her being defiled when she's not even conscious enough to fight back.

The vivid pictures of her being harmed in a way I can't erase from her memory pierce my soul, and I can't back out of the dark place as I rain down hit after hit. If he had successfully taken Maevis that night in the parking lot, only God knows what would have happened to *my girl.*

I'm lost in a deep, dark realm until Ryatt is pulling me from an unrecognizable body sprawled and limp beneath me. His face is so smashed in, it looks like ground beef when I come to.

"He's dead, Vane. He's dead. Come on bro, get up. Find yourself," Ryatt says while hoisting me off the dead male. I realize he's right and find my footing, stepping away from the body that is nothing but ground meat and blood now.

Ryatt lights a cigarette, takes a puff, and passes it to me. Taking a drag and handing it back to him, I step over to the table and grab a towel to wipe myself off.

I don't smoke, but I need something to take the edge off and stop me from bashing the fucker's head in again. Well, what's left of it anyway.

I'm focused on my best friend while he stands over the dead body, pulling a black and white bandana from his back pocket. "Wipe yourself off. You're bleeding," he says and throws it on top of the man with a laugh.

Amusement seeps its way into my bones, and I crack a smile.

Son of a bitch is crazy, but I love him.

The dread settles back in when I realize what I have to do. My heart has a small, thin fracture when I accept I'm going to have to be the one to completely shatter Maevis' world.

CHAPTER
TWENTY-FIVE

(MAEVIS)

Is it weird wandering around someone else's home like you live there? *Yes.*

Is said home the size of a mall? *Yes.*

Is it normal to have already gotten lost four times? *I'm not sure.*

Poor Beverly has found me wandering with a lost look on my face four times now. On this final adventure, she guided me back to the main foyer to save me any more embarrassment.

"How about some cookies?" she asks in a sweet, soothing voice—unlike the voice she used on Vane when we first arrived. I can already tell she's like a mother figure to him.

"That sounds delicious," I reply as she links her arm through mine and guides me to the kitchen. I prop myself on top of a stool at the island.

"Coffee? Tea? Water?"

I decide on water. Thanking her, she gets to work on the cookies. We make small talk for a while, feeling each other out. She slices some lemon and slides the small, white saucer over to me across the island.

There are exactly three slices.

The same number I always ask for at every restaurant I go to. I slowly glance from the saucer back up to her.

"I don't think you know how often he has spoken about

you, dear. He's missed you all these years," she says with a deep, warm smile. I'm about to move our conversation toward Vane, but a voice from the backyard calls for her. I turn and see a gardener waving a rake in the air. She mutters something under her breath and smiles softly at me. She pulls the cookies from the oven and sets them atop the counter. "Let them cool for a few minutes. After that, they're all yours."

I thank her and watch as she makes her way out to the large backyard of the mansion, the only place I haven't explored so far.

Consistently glancing at my watch like a restless child, I snatch a cookie from the tray when I think they're cool enough and devour it. It almost melts in my mouth, and I grab another one, eating it in seconds.

"You know, you could have just told her you were hungry, and she would have made an actual meal for you instead of a treat," a deep, tired voice booms from the doorway. I drop the remainder of my sweet treat on the counter and snap my head around to glare at Vane, but my mouth drops open when I see his hands and the deep-set bags under his eyes.

His knuckles are bloody, his green eyes far past tired and his dark hair tousled. I notice a blotch of red near his temple, and my heartbeat loses its rhythm. "Is that bl—" I start to question.

"It's not mine, Duchess. I'm okay."

I narrow my eyes, and he mimics the look. "I thought I told you I'd meet you where I left you."

His statement makes my glare disappear for a moment before it settles on my face again. "I'm aware, but I'm right here. Beverly offered a snack, and I can't tell her sweet self no. Not to mention, they're fucking delicious, so there's that. I'm in the house regardless. Calm down, *Boss Man*."

His eyes flare and drop back down into a glare. His eyes

could burn a hole through concrete like Clark Kent, but I stand my ground, reaching for another cookie. I jump when I see him quickly glide from the doorway to the island. I don't have time to process his movements as he plucks me from the stool and places me on top of the counter.

"In here, I'll make an exception. But out in the real world, if I tell you to stay or meet me somewhere, you better fucking do it. Do we have an understanding, Duchess?" he says in a steely voice, and I smell the hint of menthol on his breath and scrunch my nose.

He wraps an arm around my waist and pulls me into him until my legs are nearly wrapped around his hips. I wet my lips and nod like an adolescent child being reprimanded by a parent.

He runs his thumb across my bottom lip. "That's my good girl."

My body melts at the sound of his praise, and I'm met with the softness of his lips pressing into mine. I get lost in the moment, my hands weaving into his thick, dark hair.

So long.

For so long, I've waited to feel his lips pressed to mine, to know if I would feel the same electricity float through me from just his touch. But this...this is an explosive feeling I've never felt, an emotion that is unexplainable through words.

His hands slither their way under my shirt, and it's in this moment I realize we're in his kitchen, where Beverly and the gardener can see us. I grab both of his forearms and push them down. "Beverly said she would be back in a bit," I tell him, pulling my lips further away.

"She's seen worse," he replies, attempting to pull me back into him. I resist and furrow my brow in his direction. "Are you telling me you bring women here often? Am I just another little toy for you to use up and throw away when you're done?"

For the first time, I watch his green eyes turn dark as night, and I hold my breath.

"Is that what you truly think? Because I know you have to feel what I just felt," he questions, and I shake my head slowly. "Whatever piece of pussy was in this house was a momentary replacement for you. For one moment. Every moment I was fucking them, your face was the only one I pictured. So, tell me, Duchess: did you remain squeaky clean while we were apart?"

I freeze at his question.

"That's all the answer I need," he replies. "Would you like to know why I never attempted to claim this back in college?" His hand moves between my legs, and I release a whimper I wish I could take back as I try to hold my ground. He moves his lips to my ear, and I shiver at his cool breath on my skin. "Because I knew if I had a taste, I'd never be able to let you go."

My eyes connect with his once more, and whatever remaining breath I'm holding onto is forced from my lungs. "Vane…" I whisper.

His tongue runs across my bottom lip, and I moan, not caring who can hear me anymore. Without warning, he plants a kiss on my lips and pulls away, the warmth of his body going with him. "Bev will have dinner ready soon. Let's make our way back to the balcony. I promised you a sunset."

Sad that the moment is gone but happy at the light back in his eyes, I place my hand in his and let him lift me from the island. Letting him guide me back to his room and out onto the balcony has me wishing we stopped at his bed, but I don't voice my desire.

Vane pulls my chair out, and I thank him while sitting. Dropping down into the seat across from me, he lets out a long sigh. I can tell he's tired, but I don't know from what.

"Vane?" I question with worried eyes. "Are you okay?"

His line of vision darts from the open field over to me.

"You've waited for me all day, and that's your first question?" he asks with a subtle laugh. "I'm okay, Duchess. Just a lot on my mind." We're quiet for a while before he turns toward me and chews on his bottom lip. "What's your first question?"

I bite my cheek and figure it's better to start with a bang. "What did you do at the casino that justifies blood being smattered on your face? Exactly *how* do you get them to talk?" I ask with a quick glance at his temple, where the blood has dried and crusted over.

Vane's face hardens, and he leans back in his chair. "I can't answer that," he replies with a stony face, and I'm taken aback.

"Why can't you?" I reply in a hushed tone.

He studies me for a moment, his emerald eyes roaming across every inch of my face, settling on my lips before he finds my gaze again. "Because it's not something you can handle. It's not something I want you to handle. I have enough people who think I'm a monster. Hell, *I* think I'm a monster." He studies me for a moment longer in an eerie silence. "I *know* I'm a monster."

My brows draw together, and I lean over the table. "You get to stalk me and everything else that comes with it, but I don't get to know what you do at your *job* in detail?" I'm so sick of everyone in my life acting like they need to coddle me. His expression never changes, but I notice the rapid tick in his defined jawline, and I huff a laugh. "You think you're some kind of savior or something?"

"Maevis, you know I don't think that. You—"

"I didn't need saving, Vane. I was doing just fine getting myself out of that relationship, and I'll continue being just fine on my own."

I push my chair back and stare him in the eyes. "Last chance. Are you going to treat me like a child or be honest with me?"

He peels his upper lip back, flashing his straight, white teeth.

Narrowing my eyes, I shake my head at his lack of response and stand. "Fuck you, Vane."

I get a foot through the doorway before I jump at the harsh demand in his voice. "Sit down, Maevis."

I don't turn around, terrified of what he will look like. Shaking my head, I reply, "You don't get to tell me what to do. You're not my parent."

"You're a grown fucking woman, Maevis. Parents or not, they shouldn't have been dictating what you do either. But the difference between me and them is that when I tell you to do something, it's in your best interest."

His words are the perfect strike. I know deep in my heart— deep in my bones—that he's telling the truth.

"Sit down and drop the attitude before I fuck it out of you."

I swallow down the arousal and panic rising from his threat. "And if I don't?"

"Have you ever been chased, Duchess? Because if I chase you and I catch you, there's going to be a lot less talking and a lot more fucking. How about we do the talking first?" he replies with a thin, sinister smile. I muster a deep breath until my lungs fully expand and turn around, making my way back to my seat.

"You're insufferable when you don't get your way," I tell him and scoot back up to the table. He cocks a brow, still wearing the same smirk. "I'll make up for it later."

My heart flutters, and I force myself to look away, over the rails of the balcony. As much as I want to be mad at him, it's so hard to commit when everything about him brings me comfort. "We need to talk..." he says hesitantly. "About you."

My head snaps up. "What about me?"

His tongue darts out between his lips before he releases a

breath and reaches into his pocket. My nose scrunches when he pulls out a pack of cigarettes and a lighter. He notes my reaction and rolls his eyes, placing both items on top of the table and running both of his hands through his hair.

"What do you know about your parents?"

My heartbeat increases with every blink, and I struggle to focus. With one solid study of his demeanor, I know by the look in Vane's eyes that my life is never going to be the same.

CHAPTER
TWENTY-SIX

When the fog floats from my head and I come back to reality, I sit back in my chair and cross a leg over my knee. "They're my parents...I know as much as I can. What do you know about yours?"

I note another tick of his jaw. "Before they died or after?"

His reply has me feeling like the biggest asshole. My shoulders sag when I see the quick flash of hurt across his face. "I'm sorry, Vane. I-I didn't know."

He folds his hands on top of the table and leans in. "It's okay, baby. I know you didn't mean it like that. But I need you to answer my question."

I look down, studying my fingers before peering back up at him. "I know just about as much as any kid would. Nothing out of the ordinary, I guess."

When he doesn't reply, my nerves begin gnawing at my insides. "Vane, what's this about? Has something happened to them? Did Ross do—"

"No. They're fine. But I need to know something."

I nod my head and brace myself for whatever question he's about to throw my way.

"Have you ever...have you ever found yourself unrelatable to them? As if you don't have any of their characteristics?"

I stare blankly for a moment, followed by an outburst of laughter.

Vane produces a blank stare of his own, allowing me to wipe my tears before cocking his head to the side. "Unrelatable?" I reply with both eyebrows raised. "I'm nothing like my parents. They don't like sports, I love sports. I love all types of music, they only like Mozart and Al Di Meola. I love watching action movies, and they tell me they rot my brain. I want to be the breadwinner in my family one day, and they tell me a woman should stay in her place. There's nothing...the same... about..."

I trail off as the dots start to connect in my head.

"Vane?" I question softly, feeling slightly dizzy from how fast my heart is pumping. "W-what are you trying to get at? Do you know something I don't?"

His expression turns sorrowful, and I curl into myself in the chair. I slowly shake my head.

"You're wrong. Whatever you're about to say, you're wrong. I look exactly like my parents. I grew up with them."

He reaches a hand across the table to touch my arm, but I snatch it away. "I don't know what kind of game you're playing to fuck with my head, but I'm not falling for it," I snap, averting my gaze to the landscape over the balcony. My mind is jumbled with a hundred different thoughts and scenarios, but I've been here before. The number of times Ross would twist stories and events to make me think I was in the wrong or crazy sends me into a deeper frenzy. Through disoriented eyes, I focus on Vane again. "You men are all the same. Ross used to play these exact—"

"I'm going to stop you right there. Do not now, or ever, compare me to him, or it's the last time you'll ever see me," Vane bites out, and my glare softens. "Do you really think I want to hurt you, Maevis? After doing everything I could to open your fucking eyes to the piece of shit you were about to be tied down to?" He jolts up from his seat, pacing the balcony. "I was going to try to break this to you softly, but clearly, that's not the route you're going to let me take. So, here goes."

I sit in silence as he lays everything out for me, an elaborate story about how my biological parents were murdered, a plan by my adoptive parents to marry me off for money, and how I have millions under my name in banks around the world.

When he's done speaking, I stare at him as he does the same. Moments later, I break out into hysterical laughter, waiting for him to conclude the joke. Instead, his expression hardens, and he points further over the balcony. "You see Beverly over there with the gardener?"

"Yeeeessss," I draw out.

"She's the only motherly figure I have left, one of three people I would lay my life down for," he says, and I immediately wonder who the other two people are. *Does it include me? What about his siblings?*

"Every ounce of information I just gave you, I put on her life. May lightning strike if a single lie was told."

I choke on air at his statement and immediately realize how serious he is. Involuntarily, my body accepts the anxiety breaking its way in, and I stumble from the chair and fall to my knees, where Vane meets me. I'm hyperventilating as he pulls me to his chest and cradles me on the floor. "Maevis, I'm here. You're safe, I promise. I'm here."

I hear his words, but they're not registering. Everything I've ever known is a lie, and I can't stop the questions.

"Why would they murder my biological parents?"

"Why did they lie to me all these years?"

"Does Ross know? He had to have known."

"Who am I?"

I cry in Vane's arms for what feels like hours when I notice the sun has set.

Between the sobs, I realize Beverly came in with trays. I shut my eyes and continue crying to avoid looking at her out of embarrassment.

"Maevis, baby, I'm going to move us to the bed," I hear him say through the now-muffled sobs. The strong woman I found this morning is already hiding in her shadows.

Vane transfers me to his bed and brings the trays in from the balcony. "You need to eat an actual meal," he says and uncovers one of them. The food smells amazing, but I try to push it away. "Nope, you're eating. Your stomach has made twenty different noises within the last hour. Eat, and then, we can try talking again."

I give him the best evil stare I can muster but pick up the fork and dig in to the roasted chicken and potatoes. I would be lying if I said it doesn't bring me comfort to feel a warm, homecooked meal in my belly. When I finish, I'm embarrassed to notice there isn't a single crumb left on my plate. I glance over at Vane to see he finished his meal at the same time and is studying my plate to make sure I ate.

"Good girl."

My heart flutters, but those two words earn a tiny rumble of a laugh while he gathers the trays and sets them on a table beside the door. I spot my bag I had forgotten at my house next to the table. Vane notices my gaze and turns back to me. "Ryatt gave it to me at the casino."

So Blondie was there too.

The thought makes the anger return. Vane quickly reads my expression and holds his hands up. "Duchess, I promise to share everything about my life with you in due time, but right now, we need to take care of *you.*"

As much as I want to yell at him in protest, I can't. I can hear the sincerity in his voice.

Scooting off the bed, I head over to my bag and pull my phone out to see an ungodly number of phone calls and texts from Ross that I ignore. But my heart sinks when I see how many attempts I've missed from Rose. I shoot her a quick text to let her know I'm okay before looking up at Vane, who wandered over next to me.

"Can I be honest for a moment?" I ask, now staring down at my feet.

"Always," he replies, using two fingers to tilt my chin up toward him. I get lost in his eyes, in everything about him.

"I want to forget about everything. Forget about what you just told me, my life before yesterday, everything. For just an hour, I want to be stress free."

Vane studies my face before releasing me and bending down to pull a familiar box from my bag. The ribbon sends my heart rate into orbit. He lifts the top and pulls the lingerie from the box with a deep, mischievous grin.

"Why'd you pack this?" he questions, keeping his eyes on me.

I don't need a mirror to know my cheeks are now the color of roses. "I-I don't know. I'm not sure. Honestly, it was a mistake. I thought it was something else," I ramble. I cringe at my own lie that he can easily detect.

Dropping the lingerie he purchased for me back into the box, he puts the lid back on it and thrusts it in my direction. "You sure about that, Duchess?"

His question sends a surge of heat between my thighs that quickly spreads through the rest of my body. Dipping down, he pulls out the black heels I packed last minute, and I know my lie has exploded in my face.

"Put it on," he demands while licking his lips.

I swallow, glancing from the box with the shoes stacked on top and back to him. He cocks a brow, and I hesitantly grab the box between my hands, careful to balance the shoes on top. He raises a hand, pointing to the bathroom.

I flick the light on in the bathroom and close the door without turning around.

Should I be doing this when I just received a shitload of dreadful information? No.

Can I stop thinking about what it would be like to fuck Vane without the mask? No.

There's nothing in my current scenario I can change or fix in this very moment, so I swiftly remove my clothes and open the box. I slip on the lingerie he sent to my office and allow myself a quick glance in the large mirror. I gasp at the image.

The black lace molds to my body in all the right place, and I instantly regret not grabbing my bag with my makeup case.

Folding my clothes and placing them on the counter, I slip on the heels, automatically adding multiple inches to my height. The image sends a shudder through me. Forcing myself, I make my way to the door and grasp the handle, refusing to turn it.

"I can hear you at the door, Duchess," Vane's voice carries from the other side, and I coerce myself to continue breathing.

"I don't...I don't have any makeup on, Vane," I admit and bite my bottom lip. I'm aware I haven't had any makeup on this entire time, and I love feeling free around him, but how can I be sexy to a man of his caliber without it?

"And is that supposed to be an issue?" he replies, sending a million butterflies flapping their wings in my lower belly. I shut my eyes, mulling over all the times Ross demanded I put on makeup and style my hair *properly.*

"Get out here, Maevis," he growls, and I snap my eyes open,

twisting the doorhandle on a lone, deep breath and stepping out.

The look on his face is engulfed by desire and lust. He's drinking me in like an iced sweet tea on a sweltering summer day.

And I'm ready for him to savor all of me.

(MAEVIS)

"Beautiful," he whispers, and I cast my eyes down toward the floor.

"Eyes on me, Duchess," he breathes, just inches away from me, and I snap them up, tilting my head back to see his face. His hand reaches underneath my jaw, cupping it. "Your natural beauty would bring any real man to his knees," he says while grabbing my hand and taking a step back from me. He motions for me to turn, and I smile bashfully as I spin before he slams me into his chest, tightening his grip.

"Do you know how long I've waited to feel you back in my arms?" he whispers while hovering over my lips. His fingers run from the base of my neck, down my spine, and end with a smack to my ass has me yelping.

"Vane," I moan, and he presses a finger to my lips.

"I'm not ignorant to the stress I just threw at you on the balcony. But it's late, and I can't have you going to bed like that," he says. I swallow, trying to figure out what he means. "So, I'm going to help you relieve some of that stress."

My mouth runs dry, my tongue darting out to wet my lips.

I'm hoisted into the air as Vane wraps my legs around his waist and plants another smack to the underside of my ass. The sensation sends another wave of heat to my core. Walking us over to the bed, he gently lays me on my back while holding my stare. Dropping a kiss to my forehead, he stands and unbuttons his shirt. He glances over me again with lust-filled eyes, and I snap my legs shut.

"You know I respect you, right, Duchess?"

His question confuses me as I stare at his upper body, free from his shirt. He cocks his head, waiting for an answer.

"Y-yes. I know," I answer in a breathy tone.

Vane unbuckles his belt and pulls it from the loops in one, swift motion. Bending, he tucks one hand behind my ass and hovers over me. "Good. Because I've waited too long to feel myself inside you again. So, for the next little while, it's going to seem like I don't."

My eyes widen, and I feel his hand grip me, flipping me onto my stomach. Before I can get a word out, I feel the leather of his belt wrap around my throat, and I surge forward to escape—

unsuccessfully. His arm wraps around my waist, holding me in place as I feel his breath on my ear. "What's your safe word, Maevis?"

I blink profusely, trying to understand why I'm so turned on by this moment.

Because it's what turns you on but your fiancé refused to partici-pate, you idiot, the voice in my head bites out.

Vane's grip around my waist tightens when I don't answer, forcing additional air from my lungs. "Raspberries," I blurt out and drop my head down.

I fucking hate raspberries, so it only seemed right.

A light, husky chuckle sounds from him. "Alright, Duchess. Raspberries it is." He places the belt through the metal of the buckle without fastening it and lets the slack fall.

"If you move, I spank you," he growls, and I let my eyes fall close on a shaky breath. "And I promise to leave my mark each and *every* time."

I don't need to check to know how wet I am. I can feel it dripping down the inside of my thighs. I fail to suppress a shudder when he pulls me to all fours and spreads my knees. The warmth of his hands sends sparks up my thighs, directly to my core.

Is he? He can't be doing what I think he's doing.

"You're so ready for me," Vane groans while running his fingers through the juices on my thighs. He brings the same fingers around to my face. "Suck."

My mouth drops open at his command, but I do as I'm told and wrap my lips around his fingers, sucking and licking until every last drop is gone. I can feel him shudder when my lips release his fingers. "That's my good girl," he proclaims and proceeds to run the same fingers down my spine and over my ass, ending at my entrance. It's in this moment I realize there's a slit perfectly stitched into the lingerie, giving him easy access to the most intimate part of me.

"Vane," I murmur, followed by a whimper, and I drop my head between my shoulders.

"No need to beg, Duchess. I'm going to give you exactly what you want," he says in a steely voice. "Right after I show my appreciation for this perfect pussy."

I press my face into the sheets to suppress the moan I can feel rising in my throat at his words. But the restraint ends when I feel his fingers circle around my clit, and my body bucks forward.

Smack.

My eyes bulge at the sting and flutter closed when I feel his tongue glide across the area he just smacked. His fingers continue their assault on my clit through the lace of my lingerie, and I force myself not to jerk forward at the sensation. A groan slips between my lips when I feel his fingers make their way back to my entrance, pushing the fabric to the side and dipping a single digit inside me. Slowly, he works a second one in, and I throw my head back on another involuntary moan.

"The prettiest song I've ever heard," he whispers and thrusts a third in, forcing a cry from my lips as I fist the sheets. "Too much, baby? If you can't take it, I understand," he antagonizes me while slowly threatening to remove his fingers.

"No!" I shout. "I mean, yes. Yes, I can take it. Please don't... please don't stop."

The begging makes me groan in embarrassment. He has me at his mercy and he knows it.

Vane curls his fingers, finding the spot made for sending me to another dimension, and he doesn't let up. My legs begin to quiver when he picks up the pace, and I prepare to freefall, but I snap my eyes open when he quickly pulls his fingers away.

Peeking over my shoulder with the most vicious glare I can conjure I snap. "What the fuck, Vane?"

He's removing the remainder of his clothes, and I gasp when the length of him is released from his boxers.

How did I take that in the shower?

"You ready for me, baby?" he asks while stroking himself, and I know for a fact I've never been more ready in my life. I nod twice. I feel both of his hands grip the lace fabric and pull until it rips away. I gasp, slightly hurt—I had fallen in love with the ensemble.

"Don't worry, I'll replace it," he assures me while gripping the slack of the belt. Hooking one arm around my hips, he drags me to the edge of the bed, and I brace when I feel the head of his cock align with my entrance. I take a deep breath and cry out at the pain and pleasure of him forcing his way into me.

"Shhhhh. Save that for when all of me is settled inside this warm, wet pussy," he says, and I freeze.

That wasn't all of him?

I don't have time to catch my breath before he pulls out and drives back into me until he's fully seated. I feel the belt tighten around my throat. The lack of air combined with the pleasure of being stretched wide has me tightening around the thickness of him.

"Fuck, Maevis. I can barely fuck you if you keep gripping my cock that tight," he says on a ragged breath, and I mutter an apology. I feel him adjust his stance and tighten his grip on the belt strap. "Don't be sorry for your body molding to mine, sweetheart."

He begins pounding into me, and my eyes roll to the back of my head from the perfect fit. I reach my hand between my legs to find my clit, but it's smacked away, along with another slap on my ass cheek.

"Vane," I cry out, and he tightens the belt.

"Your job is to provide me this pussy and receive pleasure, not to pleasure yourself," he hisses and picks up the pace while reaching his other hand around to pinch my nipple before finding my clit. I throw my head back and beg him to grant me the release that's building.

"How close are you, baby?" he asks, continuing his assault on my clit yet steadily hitting my sweet spot. My pussy tightens around him with each drive. He pulls the belt taut once more, and oxygen becomes foreign to me. The pleasure overrides the panic, sending me into a euphoric state. I can feel the orgasm that's about to rip through me when Vane stops his stride and pulls out of me.

I drop down to my stomach when he releases the slack of

the belt. When he grabs my thighs and flipping me over to face him, his gaze is locked on me before he pulls my knees apart and studies the most intimate part of me.

"I promised myself the next time I made you orgasm, I was going to drink in what you look like while I did it," he huffs, removing the belt from my throat. "Open for me, Duchess."

I watch him stroke himself for a moment before I spread my legs wider.

He moans while pumping his cock. "Perfect," he croaks, never taking his eyes from my entrance. He climbs on top of me, his hands finding my ankles to place them over his shoulders.

"Take a deep breath for me," Vane murmurs.

My lips pop open, and I stare into his green eyes as he presses into my entrance. The width of him feels foreign, even though he was just inside me moments ago. I sigh with pleasure as I stretch to accommodate him as he slides deeper.

"Vane, I'm not going to last," I rush out on a breath.

"I don't need you to last. I need you to milk the cum from my cock, because I'm not pulling out," he grits out, dropping my legs from his shoulders as the room begins to spin.

"Come for me, Maevis. If this perfect pussy is mine, *come. For. Me.*"

His words are my ethereal ending as I tighten around him, releasing every ounce of stress through the unreal orgasm that rips through me. I attempt to shut my eyes when his hand grips my face. Slowly, they flutter open to see Vane above me, his gaze heavy and unyielding with the dark intensity surrounding his jaded eyes. His lips barely hover above mine when his hand drops from my face and wraps around my throat. "You look at me when I'm fucking you."

"*Oh God,*" I scream, and he releases a throaty laugh.

"He can't help you right now."

My orgasm reaches its peak as my back arches and my legs lock around Vane's torso. Just as he had promised, his eyes never veer from my face as I lose all control.

"That's my girl," a strained voice declares while kissing every inch of my neck and collarbone. He brings his face back to mine and licks my bottom lip, continuing each stroke as I ride out the rest of my orgasm.

"My turn," he whispers into my ear, followed by a kiss right below it.

Before I can say anything, Vane is pumping into me again at an even faster speed, and I experience something I've never felt. I can feel the tension building in my lower belly *again*. "Vane, I'm going to—"

There's no way I'm about to orgasm twice in a row.

"That was always the plan, baby. Come again for daddy," he says with a smack to the side of my ass. The edges of my vision begin to blur when the release catches me. Vane's movements become rigid, losing his specific rhythm as he continues slamming into me. His moans grow louder, and I can feel his body relax as he releases inside me.

Another first.

When he finishes, his lips crash to mine, and his mouth drops to each of my nipples. When I'm down from my high he pulls out, wrapping the covers around me and kissing my temple.

We stare at each other for a moment as he lays on his side, his hand brushing over my hair and down the side of my face. The silence should bother me. With anyone else, it *would* bother me. But not with him.

Not with Vane.

The only things I feel in this moment are comfort, satisfaction, and the throbbing between my thighs.

He flashes a smile and jumps off the bed. "I'll run us a bath."

Lying limp, I can only stare at him as he disappears into the bathroom. Within seconds, my eyes bulge when I replay what just happened.

I let him wrap a fucking belt around my throat.

TWENTY-EIGHT

(MAEVIS)

Seated in Vane's oversized bathtub between his legs was not where I saw myself a year ago. *But it's the only place I want to be right now.* We've been sitting in comfortable silence for at least fifteen minutes, the back of my head resting on his firm chest, his corded arms around my middle.

The steady rhythm of his breathing calms every bit of stress I walked into his home with earlier.

"I'm sorry," Vane says on a hum behind me, and I sit up, spilling some of the water over the edge of the tub in an effort to see his face. He pulls me back against his chest instead.

"Sorry for what?" I question, pressing myself into him as much as I can. He sucks in a deep breath, rubbing a calloused hand over my arm and resting it on my stomach. "I didn't give you a true chance to ask all your questions. I kind of just jumped right into the new information about you," he says and stretches his legs out further in front of us. "Ask away, Duchess. Just...just not about how I get them to talk."

While I truly want to know what goes on behind closed doors at the casino, I let it go and relax into him. Lacing my fingers with his beneath the water, I nod a few times and decide on my first question.

"Why do you do it?"

I feel him stiffen behind me and reach down to rest my hand on his thigh. Instantly, I feel him relax under my touch.

"Because I witnessed things growing up I never want anyone else to endure."

Now, it's my turn to go rigid.

He places his hand atop mine and runs it up the length of my arm again. "My father wasn't a good man, and he definitely didn't have any respect for anyone." He paused to take a deep breath. "The one time I snuck off to make a call to the police, they turned around and contacted my dad. Apparently, they were working together. I ended up with one of the worst beatings I've ever taken."

I notice I haven't been breathing and suck in a breath.

"If this is too dark for you, we can talk about something else, Maevis. You asked, and I just wanted to be transparent with you," he explains softly, shifting behind me. I shake my head and urge him to go on. He's silent for a moment, and I can tell he's contemplating if he should say something. "I helped two get away when I was ten years old. Helped her and her brother escape trafficking before my father returned," he rushes out on a breath, cutting me off. "The beating I took was worth it. I always wonder if they would remember me if I saw them today."

I'm speechless. "I remember his belt hitting me straight across the face, and I stayed standing," he said with a dark laugh. The barely visible mark under his eye plays in my mind, and I sit up slightly.

"Vane...I'm so sorry."

He squeezes me with the arm still wrapped around my waist. "I'm sorry I got dark so quickly. What else do you want to know?"

I turn just enough to see his face and run my fingers over the faint silver scar underneath his eye. The touch has him holding his breath as he knits his brows and relaxes imme-diately.

"I've never been afraid of the dark," I reassure him with a soft smile.

He places a light, sensual kiss on my lips, pulling away and turning me back around. "Good, because there wasn't much light in my life until you came back into it," he says and urges me to continue my questions.

It's hard to remember my next one when my heart is threatening to break through my ribcage.

"What about money? Does that play a part in what you do at all?"

"I didn't need any money when I decided on this venture. When my father was murdered, my mother gave me more than enough to never have to work another day in my life," he clarifies.

"But you...you have even more now from the casino, right? Does it come with getting the bad people to talk?" I ask and immediately regret it, wondering if I'm prying too much.

Vane never skips a beat. "I get no money for making them talk, just a small sliver of happiness and sense of pride knowing I took one more asshole off the streets." A moment of silence passes before he speaks again. "But the money that comes in from the gambling is nice."

Raising a hand from the warm water and waving it around the room, I laugh. "Gee, I would have never guessed."

His chest vibrates with laughter, and it makes me smile. "Money is nothing without someone to share it with."

That statement sends the butterflies in my stomach into a frenzy. I begin fidgeting with my hands under the water as I think about how he came back into my life. He grabs both of my hands, settling my nerves once again. "Any other questions for me, Duchess?"

I lick my lips and dive into the question gnawing at me. "Do you...do you kill often?"

There's a stretch of silence, and I shut my eyes, hoping I didn't go too far again. His arms tighten around me, and I wonder if he's scared his answer will have me running for the hills. "Yes. Never women. Never any children," he replies on a sigh. "I know there's a place in hell for me, and I'll gladly burn if that means I can make this world a safer place, ending one predator at a time."

"Guess we will burn together after what I did to Brian," I say without thinking.

I can feel Vane shrug behind me. "He got off easy, if you ask me. And you'd look hot surrounded by flames, so I wouldn't worry about it too much."

We both laugh, and I shove an elbow into his ribs for his remark. When the laughter subsides, anxiety creeps its way in. I'm in the arms of a man my parents forced me away from and had zero contact with for years. Yet, I've never felt this safe or confident.

"Vane?" I whisper into the room.

"Yes, Maevis?"

I run my tongue across my bottom lip, worried I might not want the answer to my next question. "What do you know about my real parents?"

Again, Vane stiffens behind me but tries to mask it by running his hands over my thighs. His touch has me melting into him once again.

"Nothing more than the name that comes with them," he replies, and my eyes bulge. I never considered he would know their names. "Devereaux is their family name. Very well known for trade and charity, lots of money and power," he says, fidgeting under the water. "But I can search for more info if you'd like."

I think for a moment. Am I ready to know more about the parents I lost before I got to know them? Did they love me? Did they die thinking about me?

Devereaux.

Tears spring to my eyes, and I hold them back. "I would appreciate that."

An hour later, we're drying off and putting clothes on in his bathroom. Running my fingers through my curls, I connect with his eyes in the mirror before muttering the words.

"I guess I should get home before it gets any later." I avert my gaze when I see his narrow.

"You'll stay here tonight," he replies while hanging his towel on the hook. I open my mouth to protest, feeling like a burden, but he cuts me off. "That's an order, Maevis. I'm not going to argue with you when I know you're not going to win."

I'm caught off guard, and now, it's my turn to narrow my gaze at him. Pulling my tank top over my head, I point a finger in his direction, which causes him to tilt his head and arch his brows.

"You don't order me to do a damn thing."

His tongue darts out to wet his lips, and I drop my hand. "There's the fire that keeps fighting to burn."

I roll my eyes, placing one hand on my hip and resting the other on the countertop. "I have a home, Vane."

"And if you wish to go back tomorrow, you can," he replies and grabs my towel from the counter, hanging it next to his. When he turns around, he walks over to me, resting his hands on my hips. "Additional security cameras are being installed as we speak, so I don't have to worry about your well-being when I'm not with you."

I blink frantically, trying to wrap my mind around him taking the authority to install *more* cameras in my house without my permission. As badly as I want to tell him he has no right, the heat between my thighs says differently. I should be annoyed with how overprotective he is, but it's a new feature I've never experienced, to feel like I'm so important to him, he has to take such an initiative. It makes me smile on the inside.

Guiding me to the bed, he lifts the covers and waits for me to crawl underneath. I watch him go to the closet and bite my lip at the way his sweatpants hang off his hips.

"Weighted blanket and white noise, right?" he questions from the closet, and my mouth pops open.

He remembers.

I nod, and he produces a smile that could light up a room.

When he climbs into bed, I turn toward the window and push my ass into him when he wraps his arm around me. I hear him growl and fail to suppress a giggle when I realize he can't deal with the friction. "You're playing with fire, Duchess," he says and grips my hip to stop me from grinding against him. "You need your rest. I promise I'll never get tired of fucking you, but you need to sleep," he says, and I huff in response.

"I have a question," Vane announces, and I turn to face him. His green eyes are locked on mine, and I can't help but melt into the sheets. "What do you want, Maevis? Do you want to go back to your old life? Or is this where you want to be?"

My breathing flat lines, and I raise my hand to rest on his cheek. "I would rather die than be anywhere but here."

Vane shuts his eyes at my answer and opens them to kiss me, embracing me so tightly, I'm scared he might break my spine. When he releases me, he searches my eyes again. "What do you want to do about everyone in your life who doesn't value you? I can't make decisions for you, Duchess. Talk to me."

I squint, thinking before I answer such a serious question.

Finding his gaze again, I know exactly what I want. "I want to see them pay. For all of them to pay," I say and watch his expression intensify. "To never... I want them to suffer and never walk this Earth again. And I'll do it myself if I have to."

Vane lifts his hand to push a stray curl away from my face and tucks it behind my ear. "Your wish is my command."

My lips curl into a smile, and I scoot closer to him until our chests are pressed together.

"Why did you look for me?"

Vane is caught off guard but never pulls away from me. He presses his lips to mine and turns the light off on the bedside table.

"Who said I ever lost sight of you?"

My heart skips several beats as a single tear falls down my cheek, and I nuzzle my head under his chin. I have so many questions, but I embrace the warmth of his body and accept my safe haven as I drift into a deep sleep.

CHAPTER
TWENTY-NINE

Sunlight begins to flood the room when I notice I'm still wrapped in the warmth of Vane. I must have shifted in my sleep, because my back is pressed to his front, his chin on top of my head. For the first time in a long time, I feel well rested and...*happy*.

I'm not sure if feeling happy is justified after yesterday, but I don't dwell on it for too long.

Vane shifts behind me, and my senses are awakened when I feel his hardness pressing into my back. He groans, and I feel his hand run down the length of my stomach, resting at the apex of my thighs. I let my eyes flutter shut and release a hum I can't contain. His touch and the smell of him send me somewhere I never want to return from.

He takes in a long breath, his face buried in my hair, before planting a kiss on my shoulder, sending a shudder through me. "How did you sleep, baby?" he asks, placing another kiss on the top of my spine.

I roll over. "Amazing. I may need this exact bed at my place." His thumb runs down the length of my spine. "Or you can just make this one yours and this place your home," he says without breaking eye contact.

I swallow, wondering if my heart is going to kickstart itself or if I'm about to flatline in this bed I've already become attached to.

"I know I'm moving fast, but I'm not sorry about it," he adds when I stare at him with wide eyes. "Just something to think about."

The only issue is, I can't think.

I knew the moment I laid eyes on Vane in college that he was special to me.

He looks so different now. How can he be even more attractive than before? And he's so much...darker. But I'll happily embrace his darkness if it means he'll never leave me again.

He pulls his arm from around my waist, and I whimper at the loss of warmth that comes with his touch, but I'm suppressing a smirk when his large frame crawls on top of me, holding himself up on his elbows.

"Since you got your rest, I think it's only right I make sure you're fully awake for the day ahead," he says with a playful smirk. My toes curl at the mere sight of him hovering above me. My lip is crushed between my teeth as I suppress a smile before Vane dips his head, forcing his tongue between my lips to set it free. I moan when his lips leave mine to find my throat, traveling between my breasts and making their way down.

The sensation increases when he snatches my legs apart and his face disappears between my thighs. I can't stop myself from moaning his name the moment the tip of his tongue meets my mound. His hands splay across my belly, my legs on his shoulders, my hands instinctively moving to his hair. I feel the fire burning in my lower belly, and I'm thrown off when my phone buzzes on the nearby nightstand. Whoever it is has now called multiple times, and Vane's head darts up, his lips glistening with my arousal.

"Answer it," he says, and I look at him like he's crazy until one eyebrow shoots up. "I'm sure it's him. Answer it."

The command in his voice has me stretching my arm as far as I can to pick up the phone. Ross' name flashes across the screen, and my heart can't decide if it wants to halt from panic or speed up from the excitement of Vane between my legs as I'm about to answer my ex-fiancé.

"*Now*," Vane barks from between my thighs, and I jolt.

When I click the green circle, Ross begins shouting in my ear before I can say hello. "Where are you, Maevis?" he shouts into the phone.

My eyes connect with Vane's smirking face before his head dips back down and he continues his assault. My back nearly bows off the bed, but he places his hands back on my stomach to keep me in place.

Gathering myself, I respond to Ross, "N-none of your business."

There's a moment of silence, and I hear mumbling in the background. "Your parents beg to differ," he replies, and I can hear the smugness in his tone. Vane dips his tongue inside me, and I clap my hand over my mouth.

"You don't know what my parents think. We're over," I say as quick as I can and bite my hand. There's fumbling with the phone, and a female voice comes through the speaker, making me freeze.

"Get your ass down here now, you spoiled little brat," my mother hisses through the phone. My mouth pops open, and Vane brings his head up when he hears her voice. "Your father and I are at Ross' office; he's filled us in on everything going on. Thankfully, he's already told me you resigned from your job, since that position has made you forget your role as a woman."

I shoot straight up, and Vane follows, dropping my legs from his shoulders with narrowed eyes. Ross jumps back on the phone, repeating my name. "You didn't," I whisper, tears welling in my eyes.

"You were worried about the wrong things, Maevis. I logged into your email and sent them your letter of resignation. It's better this way. I can take care of you, and you'll have a clearer mind," he tries to reason. My chest feels tight as I wonder how I can fix everything with the job I worked so hard for while I listen to him repeat my name.

"I fucking hate you," I say in a hushed tone.

Vane reaches up, grabbing the phone, and ends the call before handing it back to me. He runs the back of his hand across his mouth and sits as I frantically check my outgoing emails.

Sure enough, the email is right there, as if I sent it. My boss already replied, upset and partially irate at my random departure after he advocated for me so many times. I drop my phone and stare at the wall before I scream in aggravation. Vane wraps his arms around me, pulling me as close as possible.

"Maevis, we will fix this. I promise."

My mind is racing a million miles a minute while I try to process another piece of my world crumbling. I bite my lower lip, trying to figure out how I got here. My life was anything but great, but at least I had my career going for me.

I freeze when a lone thought pops into my head.

Vane.

My life was a shit show, but it has only become worse since Vane came back into my life—

or at least the way he went about it.

I wiggle my way out of his arms and hop off the bed. "None of this would have happened if you hadn't stalked me."

The words even hurt me, and I instantly wish I could take them back. Vane stiffens but says nothing in reply. I can see his Adam's apple bob as he swallows the pain, waiting for me to follow up. "I know my life wasn't great, but I didn't have to deal with...with..." I feel the sting of tears rimming my eyes. "With so much fucking confusion and..."

Vane slides off the bed, standing with his arms at his sides while studying me for a moment. "Then go to him."

Vane's words are like a bullet to my heart, ripping through each artery as I stare at him through thick tears that eventually fall down my cheeks. Silently, I grab my duffle bag and change clothes in the bathroom. Dropping the bag by the door, I turn toward Vane without knowing what to say, but he speaks for me.

"If you want to go back to him and live the handmaid's tale, go do that. But don't act like this is my fault. Don't act like he wouldn't be doing this had I never showed up. Don't act like this is unfolding because of me," he bites out, and I can barely breathe. "Your car is parked in the driveway, but don't call for me when he batters you into the good little wife he demands you be."

"Vane, I didn't mean I want him. I—"

"You said what you wanted to say. I understand, Duchess," he cuts me off, staring straight through my soul. "You're not a hostage. Your car is in the driveway, and your keys are by the door. Do as you wish."

His words are cool, calm, and collected. I open my mouth to speak, but then I shut it and hang my head, making my way to the door.

"Maevis," Vane calls, and my name on his lips stops me cold in my tracks. "Don't let them put out the fire you've built."

I feel my heart flutter, and I take a deep breath before opening the door and walking out into the hall.

CHAPTER
THIRTY

I step in and out of Vane's front door so many times, Beverly asks if I was okay. My heart splinters in every direction when she nearly begs for me to stay. Hugging her, I run to my car without the overnight bag I had packed but refused to grab, not wanting to have to face Vane again.

If I went this many years without him, I could do it again.

I know it's a lie, but it's one I have to accept for the time being while Ross dangles my career in my face. Ross has always had a good relationship with the owner of Stark Financial, and I'm wondering if he's already talked to him, which would make it even harder to get my job back.

Pulling into the parking lot of Ross' job gives me goosebumps, but I jump out, knowing I'm going to have to face my demons alone. *I would give anything to have Vane by my side right now.* To march in with him by my side and tell them to go fuck themselves.

But that isn't an option, because I *need* my job. I don't want to depend on a man for the rest of my life, even though I know Vane could provide for me and is willing to do so. I know I could find another job; I just don't *want* to. I worked hard to get where I am, and I'll be damned if this asshole takes it away from me.

When I'm finally on the elevator watching the numbers

light up toward the thirteenth floor, my anxiety kicks in, and I have to force myself not to hyperventilate. I tuck my phone into the back pocket of my jeans to ensure I don't call Vane. Stepping off the elevator and rounding the corner, I see Mallory sitting behind the desk with the smuggest look on her face. She opens her mouth to speak, but I hold up a hand.

"Shove a dick in it, bitch."

There *is* a small spark of joy in seeing her expression fall flat. I'm not even shocked Ross didn't bother to fire her after what I witnessed.

My entire life is a joke at this point.

As soon as I open the door, words are shouted at me from every angle. My father is sitting next to my mother, continuously questioning where my head is at. My mother is shouting over him, asking where my morals are and if I need to see a therapist. Ross' father stands at a distance, throwing a look of disgust in my direction, adding additional insults between questions.

The ringing in my ears finally stops when Ross demands quiet as he stalks over to me. He reaches toward my arms, and I step back, accidentally closing the door behind me.

"Where have you been?" he asks, and I swallow, preparing whatever lie I can muster on such short notice. There's no way in hell I'm about to give up information on Vane. I can only imagine my parents piecing together the puzzle.

My mother steps up, making zero effort to defend me, and pushes Ross out of the way. "I don't know what has gotten into you, but you better get your shit together. Ross has been nothing but patient with you, and this is how you repay him?" she questions.

Astonished, I step away from the door, inches away from her. "I told you he *laid his hands on me*, and this is what you have to say about me deciding to walk away?"

"I'm sure you deserved it with that smart mouth of yours," Ross' mother counters, and I peel my lips back. When my father studies me in turn and shrugs, I feel my heart finally shatter.

No one in this room cares about me.

No one in this room is willing to fight for me.

And I just walked away from the one person who never lost sight of me.

I pull in a shaky breath before focusing back on Ross. "We're over. This relationship is over. Don't call me, don't text me, don't even look in my direction if we cross paths. You had no right to do what you did. And you," I say, pointing at Ross' mother. "Your son isn't as innocent as you think—working late nights, fucking his secretary behind my back."

She lifts her shoulders. "My son has a right to seek a little release from a deserving girl if he desires. He is the bread-winner of the relationship, after all, especially under current circumstances."

My mouth drops open, and I feel the fire Vane told me not to let go of slowly fizzling out.

I'm nothing but a joke to them.

"Why don't we start over, Maevis? I know you lost your ring, so I had a replica made," Ross announces and grips my hand, shoving a ring on my finger as I try to pull away.

My mother marches up to me, gripping my face. "You will figure this relationship out. You will marry him on the chosen date. And you will bear his children before you fuck up this family name, Maevis Moore."

Hearing her say my last name makes me cringe. I desperately want to correct her.

Devereaux. My fucking last name is Devereaux.

"Don't forget the prenup," Ross' mother chimes in.

I grit my teeth and snatch my face from my mother's grip.

"I'm not your fucking pawn to move around however you see fit to win whatever game you're playing."

Before I can blink, my mother's hand clashes with the side of my face, forcing my head to the side. Without looking back up, I swing open the door and rush down the hall, ignoring Mallory's remarks.

Frantically, I push the button for the elevator, but it's not quick enough. I feel my mother's grip on my arm. Ripping it away, I glare at her. "You don't get to make decisions for me anymore. You chose every path for me in life, down to who I could and couldn't date in college. You forced me to come home just to get me away from a guy who wasn't even bad for me. Meanwhile, you introduce me to a man who does nothing but belittle and abuse me." She falls silent while I continue to glare at her. "I know things you think I don't know, *Mother.*"

I study her as her face hardens, running through every possible outcome of this conversation.

"And exactly what is it that you know, *daughter?*" she replies, and the anger in my chest blooms so large, I can barely contain it. As badly as I want to lay everything out on the table right here, right now, I'm still too afraid to do so.

"*When does it stop?*" I shout in her face.

"You were going to throw your life away for the wrong guy. Your father and I know what is best for you."

A sarcastic laugh erupts from me when I notice how she defaults back to the same old argument. I continue punching the button for the elevator that just won't fucking show up. "Okay, and so what? I would have been loved unconditionally. You don't even love Dad. And I'm not entirely sure he loves you either."

Another hand connects with my face, and my maniacal laughter continues. "I don't take back what I said. You would rather see me with someone for money than to truly be loved by a man who would have burned the world down for me. And now, here I am. Is this what you wanted?"

Flames burn in my mother's eyes as she turns her nose up, her upper lip twitching at my response. Ross rounds the corner, and I drop my head back, praying the elevator door opens. "Have you talked some sense into her yet?" he questions, his hands in the pockets of his dress pants. My father and Ross' mother are right behind him, my anxiety at an all-time high.

Somehow, I feel a flicker of the small fire left inside me and glance around. *Why am I so afraid of them? Why do I keep running away from what I know now?*

Fuck it.

"You're so concerned with me taking on his last name," I say while nodding in Ross' direction. "Tell me, what would my name be changing from—Moore or Devereux?" I question and watch everyone's faces fall in astonishment. Squaring my shoulders, I place a hand on the wall and ask again. "I'm nothing like any of you. *Be honest with me for once in your lives. Are you my biological parents?*"

I catch myself shouting, emotions running high. I'm unsure which emotions have bundled together, and I'm me preparing to lose my shit as I clear my throat and take a step back.

A deep, incongruous laugh erupts then. I shout my question once more and get a small bit of satisfaction when Ross' mother and Mallory both jump.

"Ross, handle your soon-to-be wife," my father spits and ushers everyone back into the office except for Ross and my mother. My eyes flare in his direction, but he only shakes his head in disapproval and follows the others back down the hall. I hit the elevator button a thousand times more and step back when Ross gets in my face.

"Listen here, you spoiled little bitch," he spits and grips my shirt by the collar. Panicked eyes fall on my mother, who stands by idly, her arms crossed over her chest. "We have more pressing matters than your little temper tantrum. Brian is missing; no one has heard from him."

Laughter creeps its way up my throat and out my mouth, and Ross yanks me further into him. "You stupid whore. You think that's funny? I'll show you wh—"

His words are cut short by the ding of the elevator stopping at our floor. Ross releases me, and I stumble backwards toward the wall. The door opens, and cigarette smoke snakes its way into the hall.

It can't be.

A black combat boot steps out from the elevator, and all the air rushes from my lungs. A tall, muscular build steps out of the elevator in all black, a hooded sweatshirt pulled over his face. The only visible part is the cigarette hanging between his lips.

"Get in the elevator, Maevis," he commands, and my heart kickstarts back to life. I would know that voice anywhere.

I slide across the wall until I reach Vane, who pulls me behind him.

"Who the fuck is this?" Ross snaps, and I see Vane's shoulders vibrate from laughter as he slowly pulls down his hood.

I would pay thousands of dollars to see Ross' confusion and baffled reaction again as Vane reveals his identity.

"I'm the rebound she picked up when she left you for a real man who can please her," Vane says, never taking his eyes off Ross. My gaze flicks over to my mother, who is now unable to close her mouth.

"You son of a bitch. I made deals with you, possibly the biggest business deal ever, and this is how you repay me? We're business partners, and you—"

"We were *never* partners. It's called being used. And from

what I've heard, that's something you like to do a lot. It doesn't feel so great when you're on the other end, does it?" Vane replies in his calm voice that sends shivers down my spine.

I notice Ross' hands ball into fists and take a step toward Vane. I may not be sure of a lot of things in my life, but I am positive this isn't a fight Ross would win. Yet, I can't help myself from moving closer to Vane, as if I can protect him from harm.

Vane cuts me a glare over his shoulder to get in the elevator my foot is propping open. "I'm not leaving you," I whisper and see him subtly shake his head.

"I don't know who you think you are, but striding in here with a cigarette between your lips and a hood doesn't make you look as badass as you think. Ross, call security," my mother demands with a sneer. "This one here is almost as bad as the one who left you in college."

Vane releases a lower, menacing, grim laugh that scares even me.

Taking a long drag of his cigarette, he drops it to the ground and stomps it out in the carpet; I chew on my bottom lip to suppress a laugh from the look of horror on Ross' face. Vane places his hands in his pockets while focusing on my mother.

"First off, I never left. You forced *her* to leave *me*. Second off, fuck you."

I hold my breath while analyzing the shocked look on her face when she realizes what Vane just revealed. It feels good hearing someone speak to her the way she speaks to me.

"I'm her mother. You can't speak to me like that," she stutters with eyes full of horror.

"If you were her real mother who treated her with the kindness and respect she deserves, I wouldn't. But you know as well as I do that you're not and you don't. So, go back into that office before you see something you don't want to see," Vane says without missing a beat. When she doesn't move, Vane shouts his command again; my mother jumps and quickly walks back towards the office.

To my surprise, Ross stands his ground, looking around Vane to settle his gaze on me. "That's my bitch. We're engaged," he says, pointing at me, and I narrow my eyes.

"Fuck you, Ross," I hiss, still holding the elevator open.

Vane looks back at me and down to my hand with the ring Ross shoved on it moments earlier. "This tiny ass diamond right here?" Vane asks and grabs my hand, ripping the ring off. "Ya know, the strangest thing is, I have one that looks exactly like it."

My eyes round when Vane produces my original engagement ring from his pocket.

"With a face and pussy like hers, she deserves three times the carats," he says and turns, dropping both rings down the slot of the elevator shaft in the floor. My mouth drops open when I hear the tiny clinking of them falling into the abyss.

Ross lunges toward the elevator, but Vane is quicker, catching him by the collar of his button-down shirt and bringing him inches away from his face, pulling a gun from his back pocket.

I yelp at the sight of it and throw my hand over my mouth. "Vane, don't! Come on, let's go," I beg from the door of the elevator.

Do I care about Ross' life? No.

Am I terrified security would come up on the opposite elevator and see a gun being held to his head by Vane? Yes.

Ross is nearly five inches shorter than Vane and has to crane his neck to look up at him. "If you come near her again, I'll blow your fucking head off," he says to a now nearly shaking Ross.

"Not so tough with a gun to your head now, are you?" Vane questions, followed by a wicked laugh. "Don't worry, the devil never lets you know when he's coming. I won't kill you here."

I fight to keep the panic from rising in my throat as Vane shoves his gun into Ross' head again, making me flinch.

"Maevis, baby, take the pack of cigarettes from my back pocket and hand me one, will ya?"

With shaky hands, I fumble to grab the pack of cigarettes and pull one from the box before putting it back. As much as I detest cigarettes, now is not the time to beg him to quit. I place the single cigarette between his lips and wait silently.

"Got a light?" he asks Ross, who looks just as confused as I am before shaking his head. "Jesus, you really are useless, aren't you?" Vane questions before turning towards me again. "Mind grabbing the lighter from my front pocket?"

Trying to calm my shaky hands, I retrieve the lighter and light the cigarette. Everyone from Ross' office comes rushing around the corner, and his mother screams in terror.

"Bloody hell, shut the fuck up, will ya? Causing attention and shit," Vane mutters around the lit cigarette in his mouth. I have to force myself not to laugh as I watch the cigarette bounce.

Still holding on to Ross' collar, Vane tucks away the gun and takes a drag of the cigarette. Mallory gasps loudly as she rounds the corner and claps both hands over her mouth. I roll my eyes at the sight of her, and for a moment, I wish I could have her in the same position Vane has Ross.

The second elevator door dings, and my heart stops.

Security. We're so fucked.

But confusion envelopes me when Rose steps out into the hallway, surveying the entire situation before her eyes land on Vane and her brows shoot straight up. "Yeah...I see why you gave into fucking your stalker," she says with an approving nod.

I smack my palm to my forehead. "Get in the elevator, Rose."

"You should have answered your phone. Thank God I remembered you shared your location with me," she says, walking over to me like this is a normal day. I squint when she doesn't even acknowledge the additional people in the hallway. Stepping around Ross, she looks him in the eye. "Pussy," she hisses.

I snatch her into the elevator with me. "I'll explain later," I tell her on a rushed breath.

"Is tall, dark, and broody coming with us?"

Vane casts a quizzical look at Rose, who offers a smirk, and I roll my eyes.

He takes one last drag of his cigarette and focuses on Ross. "You or any of these assholes behind you bother her again, I'll kill you all. But just in case you forget..."

Vane presses the ember of the cigarette into the side of Ross' neck, and I throw my hands over my ears at the scream. Dropping Ross to the floor as he writhes in pain, Vane steps into the elevator with us and plants a heavy kiss on my lips.

"Maevis, you get your ass back out here right now," I hear my father yell as the doors begin to close. "You'll both pay for this. This isn't over, do you hear me?"

I know it's not over, and it never will be.

THIRTY-ONE

(VANE)

Maevis' entire family plus that frat boy's is going to come for us.

And I don't give a single fuck.

I've waited far too long to have Maevis back in my life, and I refuse to let her be taken advantage of by two families who don't deserve her. All they care about is her inheritance. Her parents were good people who fucked around in things they couldn't defend themselves from.

The elevator passes the fourth floor, and I realize her little friend has been staring at me the whole way down. "Can I help you?" I ask, looking down at the petite redhead with large hazel eyes. She cocks a brow, her arms folded across her chest.

"How do I know you're not going to kill both of us after stalking her?"

Her question forces a wide grin to my face. "I guess that's something you're just going to have to trust me on, isn't it?"

She glares back at me. "Just because you look intimidating, wore a mask, and stalked my best friend doesn't make me afraid of you. You can still be a little bitch until proven otherwise."

My mouth opens to reply, but my head can't comprehend the amount of sass that's coming from such a tiny woman. The elevator stops on the main level with an accompanying ding, bringing me out of my stupor. The door slides open, and another short girl with dark curls and flawless brown skin stands there with her phone in her hand.

"Son of a bitch, Rose. I thought he kidnapped you too. Do you not know how to answer a—"

She stops laying into Rose when she notices me in the corner of the elevator, Maevis tucked under my arm. I look from her to Rose and down to Maevis. "How many of you are there?" I ask on a grumble.

"Well, there's three here currently, so that would make…" the newest girl remarks from outside the elevator as we shuffle into the lobby.

"Fantastic. Another smart-mouthed short one to add to the pile," I say, flashing her a glare.

She huffs while smacking her lips together and moving toward Maevis, grabbing both of her arms. "Are you okay?" she asks frantically.

"With the way the dark one here just held a gun to her fiancé's head, I don't think I'd be okay if I were her," Rose remarks from behind us, and I cast another glare in her direction.

Maevis' two friends mimic my glare, sending it right back, and I narrow my eyes. Typically, if I give that look to someone, they curl in on themselves, but these women don't give a single fuck. I'm being ganged up on by a group of women who are infinitely smaller than me.

"Ex-fiancé. Please don't forget the *ex* part," Maevis scolds, and warmth slowly spreads through me. The newest girl— Anika?—opens her mouth to speak again, and I cut her off.

"Parking lot. Now."

The three of them snap their mouths shut and stare at me.

"Oh, he's one of those, I see. Listen here, John Wick," Anika says while Rose puts her hand over her mouth to stop her. I cock my head to the side.

Rose produces a nervous laugh. "S-she talks a lot. Like, a lot."

"I can tell," I reply. "Car. Now."

"Vane, I don't really want to leave my friends," Maevis starts, and I bring my fingers to my temples.

"Maevis, there is still a lot you don't know, and I am not letting you out of my sight right now," I say in an agitated tone. Maevis opens her mouth to protest again, and I step toward her, opening the car door. "Get in the fucking car. I won't repeat myself again."

She looks from me to her friends and back again. Her shoulders drop, defeated, and my gut twists. I would never come between a woman and her friends, but her safety is my number one priority right now. Leaning down to buckle her in, I whisper an apology, and she grumbles her disapproval. Her two friends glare daggers at me when I close her door and walk around to the passenger side, but I don't care.

I wrap my hand around the door handle and freeze. Cold seeps into my skin, down to my bones. Something feels off, but I can't exactly pinpoint it.

I look back toward Anika and Rose, watching quietly until I notice the car they're headed towards. The *very* isolated car in the lot. I swivel my body, looking for anything to confirm my suspicion. When my gaze lands on a security camera, I look for another, then another. I scope out five cameras and curse under my breath—every single one of them is conveniently pointed away from the corner of the lot where they're parked.

My gaze travels back to her friends, and panic travels through me as time slows. Releasing the door handle, I point at Maevis through the car window. "Do not to get out of the car."

I study her startled expression that falls into a worried one for a moment before I step away from the car.

How long were we upstairs?

How long was their car left with no one in it?

That car isn't equipped with the same security sensors as mine.

"Stop!" I shout from twenty feet away. Both girls look back at me with sneers on their faces.

I could be wrong. My intuition could be completely wrong, but it's never failed me before.

"Don't go any closer to the fucking car!" I shout again as Maevis opens the passenger door of my car.

Why won't she just listen for once?

Both women continue walking away from me. I know it's only a short amount of time before they reach their car. Knowing they won't listen to me, I draw my gun from my back and point it at them.

The safety is on, but they don't need to know that.

"Vane! What the hell are you doing?" Maevis shouts.

"Your friends don't like to listen," I say through gritted teeth.

Both women drop everything they have and put their hands in the air.

"Maevis, I told you he was fucking crazy! He's a stalker, for crying out loud," Rose shouts with fear in her eyes. Sadness pierces my bones for a moment at the sight of them looking at me like I'll hurt them. They don't know me well enough to know I would never harm a woman, and in this moment, it's working in my favor.

"Walk this way," I say while holding the gun steady. The two women glance at each other and slowly begin moving towards me. "Faster," I demand, waving the gun, and they flinch. Another pang of guilt pierces my heart, but only for a split second, because when they're ten feet away from me, the car bursts into flames.

Once the commotion stops, I put my gun away and extending my hands out to help them from where they fell to the ground. With rounded eyes and mouths wide open, they take my hands and stand.

"Will you *please* get in the damn car now?" I ask with a raised brow. Without speaking, they nod and rush over to my car, where Maevis stands with her arms out to embrace them.

"*Women,*" I mumble to myself.

And silently thank God for them.

The car ride to my house was silent.

Well, aside from Anika chattering about how she was almost done paying off her car that was now blown to pieces. When I couldn't handle her rambling anymore, I told her I'd buy her a new one. The tears in her eyes pulled at my ice-covered heart, and I threw a very small half smile in the rear-view mirror—but I erased it quickly when a call from Ryatt flashed across the car screen.

I press accept. "What ya got for me?"

"The info you asked me to dig into. All of it, plus more," he replies, and I can hear the smugness in his voice. It's always a game for my best friend to see how quick he can access information I have a hard time getting. The line is silent for a moment before he clears his throat. "I think...I think that maybe you might want to be briefed on this information asap. Maybe who it involves should be present as well."

My hands tightly grip the steering wheel, and I end the call.

"What was that about?" Maevis asks, voice wavering, and I

glance over at her. The absolute perfection that she is makes me swallow hard. I take a quick peek at her friends in the backseat through the mirror and then turn back to Maevis.

"Can you trust them?" I ask, not caring if they get offended. They look at each other before settling their gaze on Maevis, who nods.

"I'm not talking about *can you trust them with a secret*, Maevis. I am asking you, do you trust them with your life? Would you trust them to take a bullet for you?"

I can see her swallow while mulling over my question. She turns to look back at them. "I...I know I would take a bullet for both of them."

They both reach into the front seat to grab her. "And I would for you too," Rose replies. "You don't deserve anything they've put you through."

"I mean, I would take a bullet for you, but like...it can be somewhere I choose, right?" Anika asks, and everyone in the car groans.

I turn the car around, making a U-turn at the stoplight.

"We're going to the casino."

CHAPTER

THIRTY-TWO

(MAEVIS)

My heart thumps hard in my chest, and it feels like it's going to travel up my throat at any moment. He's taking us to the casino after a call from Blondie—deep in my soul, I know it has to do with my biological parents. But this is what I asked for, isn't it? I asked Vane to find out whatever he could about them, and he's about to deliver.

But what could be so serious that we need to know *now?*

Vane pulls us into the back of the casino to an underground garage locked by facial recognition.

"I just want you to know that I'm living my Jason Bourne fantasy right now," Anika announces from the backseat, and I snort.

Once Vane pulls the car underground, the large metal door falls behind us, and my breathing picks up. Vane's hand finds its way to my thigh, and he squeezes lightly. "You're okay, Duchess. I promise. Anyone down here is here to protect you, just like I would."

His words send a wave of calmness through me, and it settles in my belly.

The car rounds a corner in the tunnel and stops where a young man stands; his eyes brighten when he sees Vane's car. I can only assume that with the tinted windows, he doesn't know the three of us are in here as well.

203

Vane hops out of the car and helps Rose and Anika from the backseat before making his way around to me. I smile. Ross never even gave my friends the time of day, yet Vane is extending the same kindness toward them as he does me.

"Hey, boss! Ryatt let me know you'd be bringing three guests. Can I help any of you gorgeous ladies?" the young man asks, and Vane ruffles top of his head, messing up the kid's hair.

"You're too young for them. Don't even start your shit today," Vane says with a laugh, and the kid produces a sheepish smile as Vane hands him the keys and a hundred-dollar bill.

Opening the metal door, Vane ushers the three of us through, and Anika can't help but to comment. "You know this could get our black card revoked, right? Following a white man who stalked you into an underground room no one knows about."

"Shut the fuck up," I whisper laugh to Anika, but I can see Vane's shoulders shudder while trying to contain his laughter as well. He leads us through another door, and I catch up to him. "Thank you for saving my friends. I don't know what I would do without them."

I look up at him with a closed-lip smile. His green eyes search my face as we walk, and he licks his lips. "You're welcome, Duchess. Losing a friend isn't something I'd wish on anyone. It's a terrible feeling."

The pain in his reply penetrates me, and I almost stumble while walking. He opens the last door, and when we shuffle in, I see Blondie standing over a table, blood smeared on his purple shirt. When our eyes connect, he nods.

"Blondie," I say in greeting, and he rolls his eyes.

"Jesus, are they all hot like this?" Anika asks under her breath next to me at the same time as Rose stumbles through the door. Her deep red waves fall into her face, and she glances up while trying to push them out of view.

"I knew these heels would be the death of ...." She trails off when her gaze falls on Blondie. I look from her to him to find he's staring at her while running his tongue across his bottom lip.

"Going to introduce me to your friends, Maevis?" Blondie asks while cleaning off the tool in front of him. I introduce Anika, and when I get to Rose, he comes around the table and stops a few feet away from us.

"Hi," he says in a low tone, and Rose rears her head back.

"Nope. I've seen how crazy he is," she says while pointing at Vane. "And if you're his friend, that means you probably match his crazy."

Ryatt sucks in his bottom lip and picks up a rag from a nearby table, wiping his hands. "Have it your way, short stack."

The nickname has all of us choking on a laugh as Rose stares at him, dumbfounded.

Vane is the only one who doesn't have a reaction. Walking over to the long table on the other side of the room, he sits down and gestures for everyone to do the same. "What's the info you had for us?" he asks Blondie, who eyes my two friends.

Vane notices where his stare lands. "Maevis says she trusts them, and I trust Maevis. So, they have full clearance for the conversation."

"Umm, okay," Blondie responds, and Rose purses her lips to sass him.

Grabbing a seat across the table from Vane, he studies me for a moment before running his hand through his blonde hair. After relaxing in his chair, he folds his hands on top of the table and begins twisting his fingers. "Your parents...your *biological* parents were good people, Maevis. Very, very good people, and I just want to make sure you know that before I continue."

I press my tongue into the inside of my cheek and prepare myself for everything he's about to tell me. I requested Vane get whatever information he could on my parents, and that includes the good with the bad.

"They were known for saving women and children from the hands of wicked people. Additionally, with all the money they had, they tracked down those vile people and..." He trailed off while biting the corner of his bottom lip.

I groaned, waiting for him to continue.

"And they would kill them to rid this world of any evil. Kind of like what this guy here does," he says with a nod in Vane's direction. My eyes flick toward him, and I notice he has barely moved. He's so lost in thought, so still, I can barely see him breathing.

"So, what happened to them?" I follow up when I finally pull my gaze from Vane.

Blondie scratches the back of his neck, refusing to make eye contact with me. I fight back the tears threatening to fall. "It's okay. However bad it is, you can tell me. Just tell me...please."

Blondie's eyes snap up to meet mine. "From what I read, you were their world. You were everything they hoped for. Everything they prayed for."

I choke a bit, continuing to fight back the tears. "I need to know exactly what happened that lead to their death."

Blondie tries to hide his flinch and runs a hand across his brow. "Your biological parents were going to expose your adoptive parents for human trafficking, fraud, and racketeering," he says, and I see him swallow as my stomach twists and turns, waiting for him to provide more information. "They found out they were about to be exposed, found out who was going to do it, and put a plan in action to..."

I feel the tear roll down my cheek but refuse to swipe it

away. Rose's hand rubs circles on my upper back as Anika places her hand on my leg under the table.

"They waited until the middle of the night, called in a professional assassin to take them out. They were usually very good about being alert, but they were preoccupied with you," he says, flashing me a pitiful smile. "You were just a newborn, and they were most likely off due to a lack of sleep and didn't even have their alarm system set."

Tears fall in heavy streams down my face now, my body vibrating from trying to hold in the sobs. I blink a few times to get a clear view and notice Vane clenching his jaw so tightly, a visible tick pops through.

"That's enough information," he growls from the end of the table, and I shake my head.

"No. Tell me everything. Tell me every single thing they did," I hiss.

Blondie glances over at Vane and tries reasoning with me. "Maevis, I don't think that's something you want to hear. I don't want—"

"I don't care what you think, Ryatt. They were my parents, and I want to know," I bite back at him, realizing I used his real name. His deep blue eyes widen.

"Tell me exactly how they were killed and how I ended up with those two low-lives as my parents," I snap again, standing from my seat and backing away. Vane scoots his seat back, and I cut him a glare that glues him to his chair.

Blondie clears his throat and presses his back into his seat. "They, along with the assassin they hired, pulled your father out of bed and executed him in front of your mother while begging for her life and yours," he mumbles.

"Go on," I say through clenched teeth.

"They pulled your mother..." Blondie looks away before

continuing, and my heart splits directly in half. My chest feels so heavy, I can barely breathe.

"They pulled your mother out of bed and assaulted her... repeatedly. They beat her so badly, she could barely open her eyes," he finishes while rocking back and forth in his chair. "They went to nursery, took you from your crib, and brought you back into the room, where they asked her to choose between her life and yours."

Involuntarily, my back hit something hard as I teeter backwards. At some point, Vane must have ignored my glare and moved to stand behind me, because his arms are now wrapped around my shoulders as I lose my balance. Blondie finally looks up at me with a cold, hard stare that lets me know he's just as sick to his stomach as I am.

"She chose you, Maevis, and they executed her with a knife to the throat. They took you knowing how much of an asset you would be in the future."

My knees buckle, and Vane holds me up, turning me around to face him.

"Do not. Do not fall to your knees and give them the satisfaction of your pain," he says in my ear while tightening his grip. "Look at me."

His words are a distant ringing in the void. My mother was executed in the same room as me, and there was nothing I could do. Did I hear her screams as a baby? Did I cry knowing she was leaving this world?

"*For fuck's sake, Maevis. Look. At. Me.*"

I snap back to reality and focus on the two emeralds staring down through my blurred vision. From the corner of my eyes, I can see Rose and Anika swiping away tears of their own.

"You know the story. You know what happened to the people who loved you the most. But that is only the beginning. Now, pull yourself together and *write the fucking ending*," Vane hisses, eyes glaring into me. The feel of his hands on my face sends warmth through me. I search his face for a moment, looking for the strength I need to pull myself together.

And it's there. Everything I need to push forward is staring back at me through darkened emeralds. I hold his stare for a bit longer, feeding off his strength to help me focus on the present.

Like a knob turning off a faucet, my sobs stop altogether. Squaring my shoulders, I nod my head as he wipes away the remaining tears. As much as I want to cry the pain away, he's right. Tears won't bring my parents back.

Nothing will.

But I know the rage that slightly blossomed within me when I ended Brian's life healed a small part of me, and I am certain the rage I felt then can't hold a flame to the rage I feel in this moment. When I finally pull myself together, Vane releases me, and Blondie calls my name.

Turning around to face him again, I see him rounding the table.

"I gathered most of this information from your aunt. Your mother's sister is a very hard woman to track down, but she was the only living relative I could find. I didn't tell her I knew where you were or that you're alive, because that's not my place. But if you ever want to get in contact with her…" Blondie trails off, handing me a folded piece of paper. "She also provided this. If you don't want it, I'll shred it, but I figured you might want to keep it."

Flipping it over, my lungs squeeze tight. My shoulders begin to shake but I hold myself together as I scan over the picture. Rose and Anika rush to my side, wrapping their arms around my shoulders while Vane backs away to give us a moment.

"That's a beautiful family," Rose whispers next to me, and I force down a sob.

"Your mother is your twin," Anika adds with a loving giggle.

I lean into both of them for support as Vane makes his way back to the table and flips open a folder.

My eyes refuse to leave the photo. My mother is cradling me, staring down at her newborn baby, my father standing two feet away, staring at the two of us as if we're his world. I swallow down every bit of emotion threatening to consume me and look up at Blondie.

"Thank you. For everything."

He looks down at me with sadness etched on his handsome face. After a few seconds, he nods and walks over to Vane's side. I narrow my eyes when I notice how intently Vane is reading whatever document is laid out in front of him.

"There's one small detail he left out," Vane says, closing the folder on the table.

Our gazes connect, and I wait for him to continue. He runs a large hand over the folder and pushes it toward the center of the table.

"Your biological parents killed my father."

The blood drains from my face, and I feel both of my friends' grips tighten on my shoulders as Vane stares me down in the middle of a cold, silent room.

THIRTY-THREE

(VANE)

I can see the fear in Maevis' large brown eyes.

Fear of me.

And it breaks my heart to know she can even feel that emotion toward me. I told her how horrible my father was, but I can tell she's wondering if I still cared about him being murdered.

She doesn't know he would beat the shit out of my mother and me whenever he felt like it. She doesn't know the other horrible things he did. She doesn't know that nearly every night, I would pray he wouldn't come home.

The look on her face makes me want to hold her until she knows there will *never* be a reason to fear me.

Other people? Yes. They should fear me. But not Maevis.

Anika and Rose step in front of their friend to shield her, and I roll my lips in to keep from smirking.

"If you want to get to her, you have to go through us first," Rose says with her arms crossed over her chest.

"Wow. I don't know if we will ever manage," Ryatt replies sarcastically from beside me, and I have to look down to keep from laughing.

"Oh, shut up already. We're not scared of a Machine Gun Kelly wannabe," Anika snaps to defend Rose, and I shut my mouth quickly. The look of shock on his face is one I'll never forget.

Holding up both hands, I explain myself and my piece-of-shit father to Maevis' bodyguards. "Ladies, let's calm down here. First off, I never in my life would lay hands on a woman. Secondly, my father was a piece of shit."

The flashes of shock on Anika and Rose's faces are expected, but the only face I can focus on is Maevis'. I want to explain everything about my family to her, but only her, not here with her friends.

"Why don't we go back to my place and talk about it?" I ask Maevis, who takes a step toward me, but Anika pushes her back.

"Uh-uh. Who's to say he won't take you back to his place and murder you?" she asks, and fire shoots through my veins. My eyes turn to slits as I glare at her.

"That broody, bad-boy glare has no effect on us. Anika has a point," Rose follows up. "We came here with you, but we don't know you well enough to let her leave with you."

I look from Maevis to her friends and back, flashing a look that's begging for her to back me up.

"Guys, if he wanted to kill us, he could do it right here. We're literally underground in a concealed room," Maevis reasons, and I raise a brow while nodding a few times. I never thought about how dangerous this entire meeting could have been for them if I was someone else.

Rose and Anika consider their friend's statement and agree after a few whispers between the three of them.

"She is required to share her location with us at all times," Rose states, and I roll my eyes.

"And she is required to keep this in her purse," Anika says while running over to her bag on the table. She pulls an air tag from the bottom of it and runs back over to Maevis, placing it in her hand. "Just in case like…you get kidnapped or something. I don't know, these two seem like they get into a lot of shit."

Ryatt and I look at each other with a quick grin before focusing back on the three women.

"I'll take the two of you home, and Vane can take Maevis back to his place," Ryatt offers.

"My house. We're going to my house," Maevis says, and I groan. She has to be the most defiant woman I have ever met. I finally mutter an agreement to go back to her house at the same time Rose begins protesting Ryatt's offer.

"I am not getting in a car with him. What if he doesn't even take us home?"

Ryatt barks a laugh next to me. "I will do anything you want me to do if it means you'll shut the fuck up."

Rose rears her head back with a look of surprise, and Anika hollows out both of her cheeks as she holds in her laugh.

After a few more moments of bickering, the five of us leave the room to collect our cars. Rose and Ryatt were still bickering when his car pulls out with the three of them in it.

Once Maevis and I are out of the tunnel and on the road to her house, I know her questions are going to start like rapid fire. I hear her clear her throat and grip the steering wheel a little tighter as I prepare myself.

"So…" she starts, and I stare at the road ahead of me. "About your father. What did you mean back there?"

"Exactly what I said," I reply, a bit too harshly. My stomach twists when I see her shift in her seat. I'm not used to having to change my tone, but I will for her. "I'm sorry," I say and rest a hand on her thigh.

I breathe easy again when I feel her relax under my touch. After taking a few moments to collect my thoughts, I spill details about the abuse, punishments, and nefarious actions of the man I still despise, flowing from my mouth like a river. My jaw tightens from how many times I grit my teeth. When I'm done speaking, Maevis sits in silence, and my chest tightens.

Did I say too much?

Were the details I gave her too much for her to handle?

I instantly want to retract everything that came out of my mouth for the past ten minutes. I refuse to look over at her, afraid of the assumed disgusted look on her face.

What if she thinks I'll be exactly like him over time?

But I stiffen in my seat when I feel a small hand on the back of my head, weaving through my hair and massaging my scalp. I swallow before I sneak a glance at the beautiful woman in my passenger seat.

Her bright brown eyes are gazing at me like a baby deer in an open forest.

It's taking every ounce of strength and willpower to not pull this car over right here and drag her into the backseat. "I don't need any sympathy," I say in a low voice.

Her hand drops to my thigh, and I suppress a shudder when my body realizes how close she is to my cock already straining against my pants.

"I know," she replies in a low, honey-covered voice that has me growing harder for her. "But that doesn't mean you don't deserve it. That doesn't mean I can't feel the hurt you experienced. And that doesn't mean I can't support you while you share some of your darkest times with me."

I swallow and firmly press my palms into the wheel, twisting my head from side to side and cracking my neck.

This fucking woman will be the end of me.

She removes her hand from my thigh. "So…what happened to your mother?"

Her question feels like a giant cement slab has been dropped on top of my chest. I don't speak of my mother because the thought of her no longer being on this Earth is still too much to bear, but I owe it to Maevis to be open and honest with her about every aspect of my life.

"She couldn't accept the life she had to deal with when they killed my father. All his wrongdoings fell to her. She couldn't understand how such a loving man could turn so cold over time. The stress killed her. Slowly...but it ended her through cancer," I rush out as quickly as I can. He hid almost everything from her, but not me, and she found out just how evil my father was toward the end.

"I'm sorry," Maevis whispers in a hoarse voice next to me.

The rest of the car ride is a comfortable silence neither she nor I break. I'm convinced she's as deep in thought about her life as I am about mine. Every part of me knew I shouldn't bring her into this soulless, dark life, but I can't help but be selfish. I can't imagine living another five years, another month, or another second without her in my life.

I bite the inside of my cheeks until I feel the taste of copper; I know that not only will her family come for us, but that piece of shit ex-fiancé's family will as well. I'm not worried about either of them compared to my circle. What I *am* terrified of is something happening to Maevis. She's going to start looking for another job soon—which annoys me—and I won't be able to keep an eye on her.

My spine straightens as an idea pops into my head. A slow, deep grin crawling across my face as I pull in front of her house.

"What are you smiling about over there?" Maevis asks with a small, fragile smile on her petite face. A lone, free-falling curl rests on the side of her face, and my heart races as I think about wrapping more of them around my hand and pulling tight while driving into her wet—

"Vane?" she follows up, snatching me from my lewd thoughts.

Reaching to tuck that lone curl behind her ear, I press my back into the seat and put the car in park. "Just thinking about what you look like naked, Duchess."

My smirk deepens when I see the slight redness on her cheeks bloom.

Stepping out of the car and opening her door, I help her out and hold her hand the entire way to her porch. I let her search in her purse for the house keys instead of taking mine out and watch as she grips the key in her hand before staring up at me. "They're going to come for us, aren't they?" she asks, and I nod in response. Maevis darts her tongue out, licking her lips as her brow creases. "I don't think I'd like to die yet. I think I'd rather spend time seeing where we end up together."

Her statement sends scorching heat through me, and my arms shoot out to grip her around the waist. Dipping my head low to press my forehead to hers, I stare into her glowing brown eyes that are as wide as they'll go. "In order for you to die, I would have to already be dead, Duchess. I refuse to live another second of this life without you at my side. If that means I have to kill anyone who comes in the way of that, I'll gladly commit the sin."

THIRTY-FOUR

(MAEVIS)

My heart is in my throat as Vane's words play in my head over and over.

I'll gladly commit the sin.

Disarming my alarm, I kick off my shoes and drop my purse into the nearby loveseat. When I look up, my eye quickly catches on a new addition to the room. Taking a few steps forward, I notice a small red dot blinking back at me. I whip around to meet Vane, and my nose collides with his chest.

"Is that a new fucking camera?" I shout, pointing to the corner of the room behind me.

Vane swivels his head to look around like he's never seen the device before and pokes out his bottom lip like he's impressed. "Looks like that's exactly what it is," he replies with a devious grin.

I cut my eyes to a glare while holding his stare. "You can't just keep installing more and more cameras in my house without asking, Vane," I snap. "And what about privacy?"

He takes a step in my direction, and I take one back. Raising a brow, he takes another step toward me and snatches my bicep when I try to mimic his action. Pulling me into him, he searches my eyes. "So now I need permission to make sure my girl is safe?"

I try to reply, but incoherent words are the only things that come out.

"Not to mention, I warned you. Did you think I was bluffing?" he adds, and my eyes roam the room. I completely forgot.

He releases his grip and turns me around, pulling my back to his front. "Here, here, and here," he says, pointing in different directions. "I have eyes in every single direction in every room of this house. If you're going to be mine, I'm going to know exactly what you're doing every moment I am not with you. I am going to be reassured you're *safe*."

My chest rises and falls rapidly as I make sure to choose my next words carefully. "You keep saying that word," I whisper.

"What word?" Vane asks, confusion etched in his voice.

I wet my lips again and swallow, preparing for whatever punishment comes with my next statement. "*Mine,*" I say even quieter than the previous whisper.

Vane's grip tightens on my shoulders. "Are you telling me you're not mine, Duchess?"

I clear my throat and wiggle out of his grasp to turn and face him. "I'm saying you have never officially asked me to be *yours*. What makes you think you have some sort of claim over me just because I let you fuck me? That's not how that works, Vane. It could have just been a hookup or a friends-with-benefits type of moment."

The word vomit is out before I can stop myself, and I struggle to fill my lungs with air while staring into the deep, dark green eyes staring back at me with zero emotion.

"So, what is it, Maevis? You want me to ask you to be my *girlfriend* like we're in fucking high school? You want me to bring you a bouquet of flowers and ask to go steady? Is that what you want?"

I stand in front of him, blinking rapidly while trying to figure out how to answer him. I jump when his large hand grasps my chin, craning my neck back to look up at him. A deep growl vibrates in his throat, and I jerk my head back but barely move as his grip tightens.

"How about I show you that you're mine?"

My eyes blow wide. "Vane, I—"

I don't get to finish my sentence as I'm lifted into the air and thrown over his shoulder. "Vane, put me down," I screech and feel a small sting on my left ass cheek. "Did you just smack me?"

Another smack to the same ass cheek sends pain radiating through me, and I yelp in response. He begins ascending the stairs, and I press my palms into his back to lift my head up. "Vane, put me down right now. I'm not joking anymore."

Smack. Smack. Smack.

Three hits in a row to the same ass cheek have me screaming in legitimate pain, yet I can feel myself getting wet. I hate myself for it.

"I'll show you exactly who you belong to. *The adult way,*" he growls before kicking open my bedroom door. He throws me on the bed and begins walking away.

"Where are you going?" I ask frantically. My eyes following him as he turns around, standing in front of the lone chair in the room.

"Right here, Duchess," he replies with fire in his eyes, dropping down to occupy the chair. "Now, strip."

Blood drains from my face at his command. I study him as he begins clicking away on his phone until music plays and he sets it on the side table.

"Don't make me ask twice," he warns, unbuckling his belt and pulling it from the loops in one swipe.

Memories of that same belt wrapped around my throat has me scrambling to the edge of the bed, sliding off until my feet hit the ground. Staring at the floor, I can hear my heartbeat in my ears and slowly raise my gaze to meet his. He quirks his brow and cocks his head to the side, his belt hanging from one hand off to the side of the chair.

I swallow, hoping to wet my throat that now feels like a thousand dust particles have stationed in it. Reaching up, I quickly pull down one strap of the sundress I have on, and Vane launches forward in his seat. "Slowly...Duchess."

I bite my bottom lip and nod in understanding.

Every fiber of my body is telling me to ignore his commands and run for the door, but the pulsing between my legs is begging me to do whatever he tells me so I can get the reward I know my body craves. But if he wants to play this game, I'm going to give it right back to him.

He's playing checkers, and I'm going to play chess like a pro in central park.

Slowly, I move the other strap down and let my dress fall just below my breasts as they bounce free. Noting the tick in Vane's jaw at the preview, I smirk and raise a brow that has a flash of surprise bolting across his face before it vanishes just as quickly as it arrived.

That's right, fucker. You wanted a show, you got one.

I rub both hands over my breasts and twirl around to face the bed. Placing my palms on the edge, I bend over slightly and begin shimmying out of the sundress until I feel it fall to the middle of my thighs.

"Maevis..." I hear Vane groan from the corner, and I glance at him over my shoulder while reaching up to remove the hair tie holding my hair on top of my head. Removing it, I shake my head until every single curl falls free over my shoulders and down my back.

"This is what you wanted, right?" I question with a hint of seduction while holding his gaze over my shoulder. Shimmying a little more, I feel the dress hit the floor. Vane is so entranced with the show, he lets the belt slip from his grasp but refuses to look down and pick it up, afraid to miss a millisecond of the show. I slightly spread my legs and bend all the way over in nothing but my lace thong as I remove the dress from around my ankles. My heart skips a few beats when I see both his hands grip the arms of the chair, the upholstery groaning under his grasp.

"You're poking the bear, Maevis. A *very* hungry bear."

I let an alluring laugh release from my lips as I turn around to face him and stare directly into his eyes. Without breaking eye contact, I press two fingers into my mouth, straight to the back of my throat, and take them back out. I note him jerking forward in his chair as I begin making a trail down my chin, to my throat, down the middle of my breasts before sitting on the bed and crawling backwards.

"And what kind of woman would I be if I didn't let the bear feast?" I whisper and bend my legs, spreading them as wide as they'll go while keeping my eyes level with his. When I truly focus on him, heat surges through me. I survey his peeled back lips while he fidgets in the chair. His eyes roam over every inch of me as he removes his shirt and begins unbuttoning his pants.

He begins making strides toward the bed as his pants hang from his hips, showcasing the deep V to my favorite part. When he reaches me, without hesitation, he hooks his hand under the lace thong and rips it away in one swift motion as I gasp. His hands reach back down, hooking under my thighs and yanking me to the edge of the bed. A hand shoots back out and wraps around my throat as he maneuvers his way between my thighs and leans over until his lips are hovering over mine.

"Remember that safe word?" he asks, and I can't answer because I'm so entranced in his smell, his confidence, his masculinity. "Focus, Maevis," he growls, and I nod in answer before whispering the safe word.

"Good. Because I'm not going to show you an ounce of mercy."

"Vane, I—"

His hand squeezes my throat and releases. Even though it was for only a second, I suck in air like my life depends on it.

"You're done talking, Maevis," he hisses before hooking my thighs again and dropping to his knees. The sight of him at my core sends an inferno of flames through every inch of my body. "First, I'm going to have the meal I've been yearning for since the first time I tasted you on my tongue," he says before he flicks his tongue at my clit. I bow off the bed, causing him to press a hand to the middle of my chest and forcing me back down.

Slightly lifting my head from the bed until I find his gaze, I force myself to breathe at the visual of him basically salivating between my thighs. He releases a low, devilish chuckle before the darkness consumes him, his eyes darkening even more. His next words let me know I am truly and utterly fucked.

"And then, I'm going to fuck you until you understil you understand exactly who you belong to, Duchess."

(MAEVIS)

Is it normal for a woman to have back-to-back orgasms from just oral sex?

My head is spinning as I rapidly blink while trying to bring myself back within Earth's orbit.

"Vane, I need a break. I need—"

I feel a sharp sting on the inside of my thigh that causes my eyes to fly open and prop myself up on my elbows. He's staring back at me with pure dominance in his gaze.

"I'll tell you when I'm done. You'll never get a break from me, Duchess," he says and dips his head back between my thighs to continue his assault. A deep, muffled moan escapes when I feel two thick fingers slide into me, finding the spot that makes me completely melt. I'm on the verge of climaxing again when he quickly removes his fingers and stands at the foot of the bed.

"The next time you come, it'll be on my cock."

My heart rate spikes as he removes the rest of his clothing, allowing the length of him to spring free from the restraint of his jeans. Flashbacks play in my head from the first time we were together in this very bed.

But now, it just feels... different.

I'm damn near panting at the sight of him spitting on his

cock and stroking it while climbing on top of the bed until he hovers over me. When he brings his face down just above mine, I hold my breath. "You're so convinced you're not mine until I ask you, right, Duchess?" he asks with a look in his eyes I can't read.

I dart my tongue out to lick my lips, and his eyes flick down to it, pulling a sound from him I've never heard before.

"By the time this is over, you'll know exactly who you belong to."

Before I can say anything, he flips me over onto my stomach. My face is buried in the comforter when I feel him fist a handful of my hair and yank my head backwards. "I'm going to bury my cock so deep inside you, until you believe deep in your soul that you and I were created for each other," he breathes in my ear, and the coolness sends shivers down my spine. "Now, relax for me, Duchess."

In an instant, he shoves inside me.

This was anything but slow and steady. His cock slams in and out of me so quickly, I can barely catch my breath between each thrust.

"Who do you belong to?" he questions on each drive, and I try to drop my head back down onto the bed. His hand winds tighter in my hair, pulling me back toward him. I let out a yelp of pain mixed with insurmountable pleasure.

"*Answer me*," he snaps, but I keep my lips sealed. I refuse to give in that easily. He catches on to my defiance and lets out a husky laugh. "Your torture, not mine, baby."

Smack.

I cry out as the sting of pain spreads throughout my left ass cheek. Quietly, I'm grateful it's not the same side he assaulted on our way up here. He asks the same question four times, and each time I don't answer, he smacks my ass harder.

"I love a brat from time to time," he says, delivering another smack to my ass, and I buck forward.

The stings are starting to make me numb, but I feel the sweat forming while trying to acclimate to his domination. His thrusts slow, and he releases my hair from his grasp until I finally drop my head down onto the mattress.

"You're sweating, sweetheart," I hear him say on a triumphant laugh, and I clench my teeth in an attempt to gather my thoughts.

"Vane..." I hiss while peeking at him over my shoulder. His hands slide from my shoulders, to my rib cage, down to my waist before I feel two fingers start at the top of my spine and glide down to the base.

Is he gathering my fucking sweat?

"Is this for me?" he asks before plunging both fingers into his mouth and sucking as hard as he can. He pops them out, holding my stare from over my shoulder and slowly brandishing a smirk. "We're just getting started, Maevis."

I feel him pull out, forcing a gasp from my lips as he flips me over onto my back and places my legs on his shoulders. "Here's your chance to tap out, Duchess. What's it going to be?"

My heart is threatening to hammer out of my chest while I stare at him above me. Do I think I can take whatever he's about to give me? Absolutely not.

Am I going to tap out and give him the satisfaction of winning? Absolutely not.

I'm a brat until the very end.

"Do your best, asshole," I whisper with a devilish smirk.

His brows shoot upward, and he reaches out a hand to move the hair from my face. "I want to make sure you can see me while I break every single part of you."

My mouth drops open at the same time he drives into me so hard and deep, I'm convinced I'm going to split in half. My eyes flick back up to him, and I notice he's still staring directly into my eyes.

"I'm not even going to ask the question anymore. You'll break soon enough," he says while continuing to pump in and out of me. I close my eyes, attempting to keep my screams bottled inside, when I feel his hand wrap around my throat. "No, the fuck you don't, Duchess. Look at me when I'm fucking you."

And that was the push to send me tumbling over the edge.

Every muscle in my body tenses so tightly, I feared I would crack all 206 bones. My legs begin to shake, my breathing ragged.

"There it is," Vane croaks, gripping my throat even tighter. "Let's see how quickly you come without air."

My eyes feel like they're going to pop out of my head. I knew Vane had a dark side, I just didn't know *how* dark. Unfortunately for me, every single move since throwing me over his shoulder downstairs has awoken every kink I didn't know was buried deep down inside.

The edges of my vision begin fading to black, and just when I think I'm about to pass out, Vane releases my throat. I gasp for air, and his hands grip my waist, fucking me into oblivion as the fire in my lower belly explodes and I feel myself tighten around his cock.

"Vane," I cry out, completely giving in to him as an orgasm rips through me like I've never felt before.

Bringing his face down, less than an inch from mine, he holds my stare. "Eyes on me, Duchess. I'm right here."

His thrusts become more sporadic as he's about to reach his own climax, and I ride out my own. "Tell me where you want it," he hisses between jerky thrusts, trying to hold himself together. Shock sweeps through me at his question.

I don't want him to pull out.

Quickly, I wrap my legs around him, and as if a hex has been cast over me, I can't stop myself. "Every single drop is mine, and I'm yours."

A growl vibrates through his chest, and he pulls my head to his shoulder, delivering thrust after thrust. I can't stop myself from biting his shoulder from the sensitivity of him rubbing against my clit as he finishes inside me.

Pulling out, he drops down next to me, panting. I snap my eyes shut when I realize he won. *I willingly told him in a moment of ecstasy that I was his.* I smack my hand to my forehead, and he rolls to his side, pulling my hand from my face.

"Don't tell me you regret me coming inside you. It's a little late now," he jokes with a half-smile. I snap my eyes open and roll on my side to face him. "I regret nothing with you, Vane. I just realized I caved. I didn't even make you beg in the slightest," I admit while poking out my bottom lip. I laugh when he uses his fingers to gently tuck my lip back in.

"I'm sorry, Duchess. If it makes you feel any better, I plan on asking a more serious question when you're ready," he says as he wraps an arm around my waist. "But I wasn't going to give you an option to not be mine. I knew the moment I laid eyes on you in college that your fate was sealed."

He presses his lips to mine, and his heat transfers to me, restarting my body as I try to press so far into him, I hope we meld into one. Everything is moving so fast while the world as I know it crumbles around me, but I wouldn't want to live through this dumpster fire with anyone else.

Vane drops to his back, reaching for the remote on the nightstand. He presses buttons until he brings up The O.C. and pauses before starting it. "What do you want to do about your job, Duchess? I know how much you loved it," he says with a kiss to my forehead. My heart skips a beat when thinking about how I lost everything I worked so hard for at Stark Financial. I know he can sense my hurt as he tucks his fingers under my chin and lifts it so I look directly at him.

"You know I can take care of you, Maevis. You don't have to work another day in your life," he hums while stroking the side of my face.

I smile and place my hand on top of his. "I appreciate you so much for that, but I can't see myself not working," I say, glancing away for a quick moment. "I think I'd be okay with not working if I had kids in the future, but not right now."

I realize what I said after the fact and stiffen.

What if he doesn't want kids? Oh God... What a stupid thing to say after having the best sex of my life. Hell...I don't even want kids. Didn't want kids? What is happening?

Did I just go against everything I believe? I pride myself in loving my job and working my way up the ladder through hard work and consistency, and now I just blurted about being okay with putting all of that to the side to pop out babies I've never wanted?

Can lifelong desires change when you connect with someone so strongly?

Vane pulls me closer to him and kisses me again, harder this time. "Maevis, baby. The day you let me get you pregnant is the day I do a backflip off my car. You sacrificing yourself... your body to give me a child is the greatest gift you could offer to a man. I would gladly make you a stay-at-home wife to care for our little one if you wish."

Butterflies flutter in my belly and make their way up my throat as tears rim my eyes. Vane gives me one last peck on the lips before pulling me into his side and starting my comfort show. "I've never seen a single episode of this, so here goes nothing," he notes.

As the intro music plays, I bite my lower lip. "Honestly, I wouldn't mind running my own business one day. Wishful thinking, I know," I mutter quietly and feel Vane chuckle next to me.

"Anything is possible when you're as beautiful and brilliant as you, Duchess."

(VANE)

The very idea that had me unexpectedly smiling and antsy in the car is sparked back to life again while talking to Maevis about the job her asshole of an ex ripped away from her. If my girl wants to own a business, she'll own a fucking business.

Maevis is tucked into my side, my body begging me not to leave her, but I have to sneak away for a moment to execute my plan.

Slowly, I peel away from her and pull the covers over her naked body. Throwing on my boxers, I sneak downstairs to grab my laptop out of my bag. Taking a seat on the couch, I open it and get to work. It took about an hour to send the necessary emails and make about ten calls in the middle of the night, but with the business I'm in, it's rare the people I know are sleeping anyway.

After speaking with the last piece of the puzzle, I call Ryatt to make a wire transfer for me. As usual, he picks up after one ring.

"What's wrong? Maevis wouldn't let you fuck? I charge $100 an hour for phone sex, buddy," he says on the other end, and I hear a woman giggle in the background.

I sit up straighter and tilt my head to the side. "Was that a woman?"

Ryatt clears his voice, and I hear a door close behind him.

In all my years of being friends with him, I have never known him to take a woman back to his actual home. "Mind your business, asshat. What do you need?" he asks, and I roll my eyes.

"I need you to wire transfer twenty-three million dollars within the hour," I say with a command in my voice that lets him know the timeframe is not up for negotiation. He's silent for a moment before clearing his throat again.

"I can do that for ya. Everything okay?" he asks, and I can hear the concern in his voice. Ryatt may not be blood, but I know I can count on him as if he were.

"Everything is fantastic," I reply, thinking about how I plan on fucking Maevis on the kitchen counter in the morning. "I'll send you the information for the transfer once we hang up."

He agrees, and we disconnect the call at the same time. Closing my laptop after sending the information, I go to head back upstairs to Maevis when I notice a black SUV slowly pass by the front of her home.

I groan and rub my hand over my forehead. I'm being careless by agreeing to stay at her place instead of mine with twenty-four-seven security and a better system. I grab my gun from my bag and head back upstairs, slowly slipping back into bed and placing the gun in the nearby nightstand.

Rolling over, I stare at Maevis, sound asleep. Her mouth is slightly open, her full lips puffed out, and I fight myself not to shove my cock between them while she sleeps.

What the fuck is wrong with me?

Snapping out of my lust-filled state, I bring myself back to the gloom of the present. I know it's only a matter of time before both families send their people after us. I hope Maevis knows that if it comes down to me having to sacrifice myself for her, I'll give my life a thousand times over.

I place my arm around her waist and pull her into me,

tamping down the anger threatening to keep me awake. I'm aware Ross likes to play games, but he's playing checkers while I'm playing chess.

CHAPTER
THIRTY-SEVEN

(MAEVIS)

Every time I fall asleep in Vane's arms, it's the deepest, most comfortable sleep of my life. But this time, my body is begging me to wake up. Even though I feel the surge of electricity floating up from between my thighs, I'm in such a euphoric state, I can't will myself to open my eyes. I can feel my breaths climbing as I squirm. Alarms blare in my head when I feel large hands press into my thighs to halt my movement.

My eyes snap open, and I hear nothing but birds chirping and the sound of Vane's faint, soft moans from between my thighs.

Oh my God.

He started eating me out while I was sleeping.

I blink a hundred times, trying to figure out why anger isn't part of what I'm feeling; rather, it's satisfaction.

I try to squirm again, but Vane's hands hold my legs in place over his shoulders. One hand slithers its way up my stomach, between my breasts, and wraps around my throat, squeezing tightly before wandering back down to wrap around my thigh.

"Vane, I was sleeping..." I say on a moan.

This man's tongue will be my undoing.

"I know," he quickly mumbles and gets back to moving his

tongue in perfect circles around my clit. My back bows off the bed, and he presses me back down.

My phone buzzes next to me, and I ignore it, letting it go to voicemail.

"You can't just... I didn't even know you...." I can't form words. Pulling my legs from his shoulders, he presses them back toward my body and holds them as wide as they'll go. He nips at my clit with his teeth, and I'm consumed with the pain mixed with pleasure as he licks it all away. Popping his head up while licking his lips, he stares at me. The sun shines into the room, and his green eyes are brighter than ever in the morning light.

"Are you telling me I can't taste my girl whenever I want?"

I stare at him dumbfoundedly. There was no way I was ever going to decline him using me this way. Hell...I could have woken up with his dick inside me and been completely fine. I don't think there will ever be a day I will say no to Vane. My lower belly tightens at the thought of him having his way with me while I'm asleep. It tightens even more when he dips back between my legs and plunges his tongue inside my pussy.

"Vane, I'm going to—"

"It would be your second one, Duchess. You already came while you were asleep," he cuts me off, and I hear him groan in appreciation as he sucks.

Just when I'm about to orgasm, my phone buzzes rapidly on the nightstand again.

"Answer it," Vane demands. When I don't move to grab the phone, he halts the movement of his tongue, and I whine in protest. He slaps the inside of my thigh, and I yelp as he commands me once again to answer the call.

I grab the phone from the stand, and my eyes grow wide at the name flashing across. I don't want to have this same encounter again. "I-It's Ross. I don't want—"

"Answer. The Fucking. Call."

Vane's frustration grows, and his fingers dig harder into my thighs. I know I'll have bruises of his fingertips, and part of me questions my sanity when the thought turns me on.

Answering the call, Ross begins screaming before I even press the phone to my ear. "You sneaky fucking bitch," he shouts, and I pull the phone away from my ear for a moment.

"W-what?" I stutter back into the phone as Vane lines his fingers up with my entrance, causing a welcoming panic in my voice.

"My business, you cunt!" he shouts again into the phone, and I squint at his statement. "It's been bought out, and it's under your fucking name, Maevis. You better have a good explanation for this shit, because once my father gets ahold of you, you're dead, you and that fucker you're letting use you."

My heart is beating a million miles an hour from Vane's assault between my legs and the information I just learned. "Ross, I...I don't know what you're talking about."

He begins screaming expletives into the phone again, and I flinch at the names he calls me.

"I could have any girl in the world, and I am *still* choosing you, Maevis," he follows up in a softer tone. I grind my teeth, remembering how much of a narcissist he is and how often he would pull this tactic in our relationship. I open my mouth to tell him to fuck off at the same time that Vane's fingers hit the perfect spot, and a moan escapes me instead. I clap my hand over my mouth, but it's too late. Ross heard the sound Vane forced out of me, and before I can think of an excuse, the phone is being snatched out of my hand.

I sit up to see Vane wiping my juices from his mouth and pressing the phone to his ear.

"Ross? Hey there, buddy," Vane says, and my mouth drops open. "Maevis is a little busy right now with my tongue between her thighs. Mind if we talk about this later? If you want to work for her, job openings will be posted soon."

Vane ends the call, looks directly into my eyes, and snaps my phone in half.

I gasp, lunging toward him in the process.

He drops both halves to the floor without looking away from me.

"A new one is already on the way here for you anyway," he says with a shrug. "You've needed a new phone number for a while now. That way, only the people you want to speak to will have access to you."

I want to be mad at him for destroying my property, but he has a very valid point. The only reason Ross was even able to call me just now was because he had my phone number and I hadn't even thought to block him. Now, I don't have to be bothered blocking anyone because I will have an entirely different number. My focus is solely on Vane, who is still on his knees and shirtless in bed. I move to draw my knees up to my chest, but he grabs the bottom of my legs.

"Where do you think you're going? I'm still owed one more orgasm," he says with a smile, dragging me back toward him. I jokingly squirm and swat at him.

"Vane! Wait! I need to know what the hell he was talking about," I plead, and he releases me with an annoyed eyeroll.

"Well, what did he say?" he asks on an exasperated breath.

I explain what Ross said happened to his business. Skepticism creeps in when Vane doesn't look the least bit confused or question what I said.

"Sounds like he's found himself in a bit of a situation," Vane says while walking over to his pile of stuff on the chair and grabbing his pocketknife before sitting back down.

"Vane...what aren't you telling me?" I ask, pulling the covers over me and glaring at him.

"Don't give me that look," he reprimands, and I swallow when he stands with the knife, closing it and throwing it back on the chair behind him. He grabs a shirt and pulls it over his head, and I immediately miss seeing the top half of him naked. He stares, and I can see his eyes softening while his gaze washes over me.

"I did it," he says and walks over to sit on the edge of the bed.

I'm too stunned to speak. I was convinced Ross was making up some bullshit to get me to speak to him. "You…did what…exactly?" I ask while trying to piece it all together.

"I bought out his business and placed it under your name," he clarifies with a shrug. "You said you wanted to own your own business last night. I made it happen this morning. Is that an issue?"

I open and close my mouth, my pulse increasing by the second. When no words come out, Vane walks around to my side of the bed. He bends down, cupping my face while forcing me to look at him. His tongue runs between his lips, and I melt a little further into his hands.

"I plan on giving you the world, but we'll start small," he explains, and my eyebrows shoot up to my hairline.

"Did you just call purchasing a business *small*?" I question, and a genuine laugh erupts from him.

Vane frees my face from his grasp and runs a hand over the top of my head, smoothing my hair back. "With a face and heart like yours, you have no idea what you could get a man to give you," he says with a broad smile. "Not to mention that pussy."

I'm speechless as he plants a subtle kiss on my lips. When he pulls away, I jokingly smack his chest, and he wraps me in a bear hug, lifting me from the bed while kissing my neck and making me squirm.

"Your friends won't stop badgering Ryatt about you. Seems he gave them his number in case anything happened. Meet me downstairs in twenty minutes. Apparently, Rose says you have a training session you can't miss," he says as he sets me down.

I'll be damned if I'm late and have to hear Coach Rivers bark commands for an overdose of push-ups.

CHAPTER

THIRTY-EIGHT

(MAEVIS)

I should have known Rose and Anika wouldn't stop bugging both men until they knew I was alive and breathing. And I definitely should have known Rose wasn't willing to show up to our personal training session alone.

Throwing on some workout clothes, I scramble down the steps to meet Vane.

He's standing in his typical ensemble, black jeans and a dark grey tee. He grabs his black zip-up hoodie from the back of the chair before handing me my purse. At the very top is a brand-new phone flashing the time. My eyes bounce from the phone to Vane, who's looking back at me without any type of expression.

"One of my men dropped it off this morning. Should have all your important numbers and information already stored, along with any pictures you had on your phone."

"How much do I owe you?" I ask, holding the sleek, new phone in my hand. I'm bursting with happiness on the inside because I noticed the deep purple of the back panel.

Vane squints while slightly scrunching his nose at my question.

"Are you asking *me* how much *you* owe for a phone *I* broke?" he asks, placing a hand on the wall and leaning into it while rubbing his chin with the other. "And let's be clear, even

239

if I didn't break it, there is no way in hell I would ever have you pay for something."

I swallow, watching him scold me for my question while marveling in his masculinity. His scent of musk and pine casts a spell over me I can't break. The only response I can offer to his statement is a quick peck on the lips and a smile.

Opening the door, he ushers me to his car while lecturing me about only giving my number out to people I want to have it. Once Vane starts driving, I unlock the phone to set up a passcode and shot over a text in a group chat with Anika and Rose, whose numbers were already saved.

Vane pulls directly up to the gym and parks the car in the nearest spot. I don't even bother asking how he knew where I work out, because at this point, there's probably nothing he doesn't know about me.

I fiddle with both my hands while staring down in my lap.

"Speak, Duchess," Vane says from next to me, placing his hand on my thigh. "You're doing that thing you do with your hands when you're nervous. What's on your mind?"

I press my lips together and stare out the window for a moment before twisting to look at him. "I want to go in by myself. I don't want you to have to constantly watch over me like a fawn who can barely walk."

Vane's eyes narrow, and I can tell he's about to protest my request when I see Coach Rivers walking toward the entrance. His gaze bounces from me to Vane and back. Vane isn't small by any means, but I know he's impressed with Coach River's stature when his lips fall into a thin line and he nods multiple times.

"I'm assuming that's your trainer?" he asks, and I confirm.

"Has he ever made a pass at you?" he questions, and I punch him in the arm before realizing what I've done. Vane slowly looks over at me and smirks. "Guess the training is working. That punch had a little kick to it."

A blush creeps onto my face when he rubs his arm and looks back over to Coach Rivers, who nods at Vane.

"I'll be back in one hour, Maevis. Don't make me come in there and get you."

A wide, genuine smile spreads across my face before I lean over and kiss his cheek. "Good luck getting past my friends first," I say and quickly dash out of the car while hearing Vane curse under his breath.

"New boy toy?" Coach Rivers asks when I reach him, and I snort.

"Something like that," I reply as Vane winks at me and speeds off.

Coach Rivers holds the door open for me, and I walk in with my bag and new phone in tow. My mouth drops open at the person standing with Rose.

"How the hell did you get her to come with?" I ask in literal shock.

Anika is standing next to Rose with an annoyed look on her face, looking down at her phone and eating a blueberry muffin with a matcha close by. "I lost a bet last night at the bar. And she won't let me back out, so now I have to take part in this stupid—"

Her statement is cut short when her eyes flick up to see Coach Rivers.

The two of them are staring at each other like they're long-lost soul mates. The electricity between them is so strong, the hairs stand up on my own arms. For the first time ever, I see Coach Rivers produce a small half smile that pulls up one side of his mouth.

He strides over to Anika, sticking out his hand and offering a greeting. She stands up straight, and, in true Anika fashion, she shoves the rest of the blueberry muffin in her mouth to shake his hand.

The three of us begin stretching before starting our session, and I quickly inform Rose and Anika of everything that happened since we separated at the casino.

Minus the hot sex details—even though I'm sure they would enjoy it.

We're in the middle of jump squats, Anika cursing everyone out for making her come, when the front door slams open.

"No fucking way," Rose hisses, and Anika grabs me, pulling me behind the boxing ring. Coach Rivers looks back at me being put into hiding and narrows his eyes. "Crazy and abusive ex-fiancé who can't understand she's done with him," Rose quickly explains, and Coach Rivers' brows shoot up.

"Abusive?" he asks with his head cocked to the side, and Rose nods adamantly.

Rose joins us as Coach Rivers stalks to the front of the gym, where the front desk clerks are trying to tell Ross that he can't enter the gym without a membership. He takes cash out of his wallet and throws it at the two women, who flinch at his aggression.

Ross never sees Coach Rivers coming from behind when he's grabbed by the back of his button down, yanked backwards, and slammed into the nearest table.

"I don't think I've ever been this turned on before. Would it be abuse if I wanted him to slam me like that?" Anika whispers to us, and Rose smacks her on the back of the head to shut up.

Ross scuffles under the hold he's been placed in. Annoyed, Coach Rivers picks him up again and slams him on top of the table, a loud cracking resounding through the gym. I wonder if it was the table or Ross' back as he cries out in pain.

"I don't know what country club you think you're at, but

we don't treat women like that around here," Coach Rivers shouts over Ross. "Now, I'm going to let you get up, and you're going to calm the fuck down. Understood?"

Ross stops struggling and nods in agreement. He jumps off the table once he's released, smoothing out his clothing and sneering at everyone staring at him.

"I know that bitch is in here," he snaps while searching the gym with roaming eyes.

Coach Rivers steps toward him, and Ross takes a step back. "Uh-uh. Not in here. Not in my place. You speak about women with respect. But from what I hear, you don't know much about that."

Watching Coach Rivers stand up for me sends a million emotions through my system. I'm grateful to have him in my corner, but I'm also tired of having to have everyone else protect me.

"I'm so sick of hiding," I say, my eyes connecting with Anika's, who poked her bottom lip out and tilts her head from side-to-side.

"Then don't," she replies.

The three of us stand at the same time, and Ross' eyes dart directly to me. He steps forward, preparing to come for me as Coach Rivers presses his hand into his chest and pushes him backwards. I make my way over to them with my friends directly behind me.

"I told you days ago that it's over, Ross. You can't keep doing this," I say, frustration lacing my tone.

He releases a maniacal laugh. "You don't know the first thing about running a business."

I hold my stance, even though he's right. I have absolutely no idea how to run a business on my own, but that doesn't mean I can't learn.

"No, but my boyfriend does," I say before analyzing my words. It's the first official time I've called him that out loud.

Ross rears his head back at my statement. "My mother always said you were a whore. I've never known her to be wrong."

"Have you seen your mother? She couldn't be a whore even if she wanted to with that stiff ass wig she wears," Anika remarks from behind me, and I have to bite my cheek to keep my serious stance. Meanwhile, Rose begins cackling with Anika behind me.

Ross analyzes Anika, and my stomach sinks to my ass—I know he's going to try to hurt her emotionally rather than physically. "It's always the biggest one in the group who wants—"

Crack.

Coach Rivers' fist connects with Ross' face before he can finish his statement. I rush over to Coach's side and look down at Ross, who dropped to his knees at the pain.

"You never know when to shut the fuck up," I comment and send my fist into his jaw, knocking him sideways.

"Great form, Maevis," Coach comments, arms crossed over his chest.

Anika and Rose flank my sides now, and I know they're not going to pass up a chance to put Ross in his place.

"Big or small, my face card is never going to decline, pussy," Anika says before sending her foot directly between Ross' legs.

Rose hovers over Ross, spitting directly on him. "That's for abusing my friend, asshole," she says with a satisfied smirk.

Grabbing Ross by the collar, Coach Rivers drags him back through the front door while he groans in pain.

Satisfying? *Absolutely.*

Liberating? *Absolutely.*

Is it going to land me in even more trouble than before? *Fuck yeah.*

CHAPTER
THIRTY-NINE

(MAEVIS)

I'm convinced Vane had Blondie tap into the cameras at the gym or did it himself, because less than thirty seconds after the whole ordeal with Ross, my phone is buzzing like crazy. Vane doesn't greet me when I answer, just telling me he would be here in less than two minutes to pick me up. I cringe when he hangs up without saying anything else.

"He's coming to get you, isn't he?" Rose asks, biting her lip with worry. I nod and turn back to Coach Rivers, who's glancing over me with concern.

"Restraining order, Maevis. It's necessary. I don't care how much pull that nepo baby has," he snaps, nothing but worry sketched across his face.

I don't know what came over me, but something I have never done happens within the blink of an eye. I run towards him and wrap my arms around his large frame as tight as I can. I feel him stiffen under my hold and then relax as he returns the embrace.

"Okay...I think that's enough," Anika says, jealousy dripping from her voice.

Rose and I both rolls our eyes at the same time Vane's sleek black car pulls in front.

"I think we've had enough excitement for one day," Coach Rivers announces. "Let's end today's session. No charge."

We grab our belongings and thank him as we headed out the door. I catch him gently grabbing Anika's wrist just before she could step out of the gym, whispering something in her ear. Pulling his phone from his pocket, he hands it to her while trying to hide a smile as she taps away on his screen, most likely giving him her phone number.

"You sure you're okay, babe?" Rose asks me with concern in her tone as we leave.

Vane rolls his window down, shooting a glare in my direction. "She's perfectly fine. Get in the car, Maevis."

"I wasn't asking you, tall, dark, and broody," Rose spits in his direction, waiting for me to answer her question.

"I'm okay. I promise. You have my new number, and I have yours. I'm good," I affirm as I walk around to the passenger door. When Rose and Anika walk away, Anika sticking her tongue out at Vane, my brain flashes a warning sign that Vane is legitimately pissed at me. He never lets me open my own door.

Once I'm in the car, he waits until I buckle myself in before he peels out of the parking lot. I'm hoping if I speak first, it'll release some of the tension. I look over at him and whisper his name. He doesn't even look in my direction, and my heart plummets. I try again, and he pulls the car over into a restaurant parking lot, slamming his fist into the steering wheel. Memories of Ross getting physical with me flash over my vision, and I press myself against the car door.

"God damnit, Maevis. He could have walked in there with a gun and blew your fucking head off. All of you—he could have killed all of you! You are so fucking lucky he's a pussy, because—"

He stops ranting, and I unclench my eyes to peek through them. When he realizes how terrified I am, sympathy washes over him. "Baby, I am not going to hurt you. I could never," he whispers and instantly looks like he regrets his outburst.

"I-I know. I just..." I attempt to reply, but the tears build so quickly as fog fills my brain.

Vane unbuckles his seatbelt and then mine, pulling me into his lap. Silently, he begins rubbing my back as heavy tears fall.

"You get nervous you're going to have to live through what he did to you all over again," Vane finishes my sentence for me, and I nod twice. "Maevis, I'm just upset with myself for letting you go in there without me. I would literally put a gun to my head and pull the trigger before ever laying a hand on you," he says, planting a kiss to the top of my head. "The bedroom doesn't count, though. Sorry, not sorry."

I can't help but laugh, and he squeezes me so tight, I cough.

"Sorry, sorry," he mumbles, pulling away and studying my face.

Without warning, our mouths collide. My breath is pulled from the intensity of our kiss as his hands wander, and I welcome them. The windows begin to fog right when he pulls his mouth from mine, his chest heaving.

"I cannot lose you again, Maevis. I can't and I won't. You're done going anywhere by yourself until he's six feet under. All of them will be six feet under," he says, placing me back in the passenger seat and buckling me in. My breaths are just as rapid as his, and my body yearns for his touch, but I remain silent as he starts driving again.

"We're going back to your house to get whatever else you need. After that, we're going to my place and staying there. Don't even try arguing with me. You won't win," he says without a glance in my direction.

As badly as I want to argue for my independence, I know he's right.

I'm the safest at his place, in his arms.

CHAPTER

FORTY

(MAEVIS)

Walking into my house is a bittersweet moment because I know it's the last visit for a long time.

If ever again.

Vane is already checking the cameras to make sure everything is still working properly, even though we won't be here. "Do you ever just relax and let your guard down?" I ask him, and he glares at me.

"When it comes to you? I did it once this morning, and look what happened," he replies, and my shoulders sag. Once again, he's right. "When it comes to my girl, I'm not fucking up again."

"Your girl, huh?" I tease and watch his jaw set as he clenches his teeth.

"You remember what happened last time you defied me when we had this convo?" he asks, and my pussy instantly throbs at the memory. I stick my tongue out at him and march upstairs to begin packing.

Throwing my favorite articles of clothing into a large suitcase has me smiling as I think about how badly Ross is spiraling without his beloved business.

Serves him right.

I finish packing the last of my important toiletries when

249

Vane comes strolling into the bedroom, his eyes locked on me. "What are you thinking about?" he asks.

"Wondering how the fuck I'm going to run a business I know nothing about," I reply honestly. I don't know a single thing about the business Ross and his father ran.

"Well, you know finance pretty well, and that head on your shoulders runs better than either of theirs did. I'm sure with the right employees and a little help on the side, you will be just fine," he says, walking over to zip up my bag for me and carry it to the door.

He returns to me, wrapping his arms around my waist and forcing me to my back on the bed. "Since we won't be back here, one last time on this bed won't hurt, right?" he asks while running his tongue across my bottom lip, making me shudder.

My hands are already tangled in his hair, his hands running up my stomach to my breasts, when he stops and sits up on his knees.

"What? What's wrong? Did I do something?" I ask him in a panic.

He raises his index finger to the middle of his lips. "Quiet, Duchess. You hear that?" he asks in a hushed voice. His eyes roam around the room before he's getting off the bed to the dresser where he set his gun. Vane's phone goes off with a buzz, and he answers it quietly. I can hear Blondie shouting through the speaker.

"Get the fuck out of there. They're surrounding the house."

"Ryatt, get Rose and Anika and take them to safety. You and I both know they will start with those closest to her," Vane snaps.

A loud bang echoes through the room as the door flies open.

Too late.

A large man with a gun stands in the doorway, and I watch

him collapse as Vane pulls his trigger. A single bullet to the man's head has him gone in an instant. As badly as I want to scream at the brain matter splattered on my wall, I keep my mouth clamped shut and my eyes on Vane.

Multiple footsteps pound downstairs and make their way up the steps.

Vane quickly glances out my bedroom window and rushes over to snatch me off the bed, moving us through the bathroom door just as smoke begins to fill the bedroom. I hear him press the lock into place, and my breaths come short.

"Maevis, look at me. *Look at me*," he snaps as I shake in fear.

I force myself to look at him with tears in my eyes. I thought I was tough enough to live by his side in this lifestyle, but I'm not the girl he needs. I can't handle this.

"They're going to take us. There are too many of them, and my men won't get here in time," he rushes out. "If we're lucky, they will keep us together. If not, I will find you. I found you once, and I will do it again. I won't let anything happen to you."

I let out a wail, and he claps his hand over my mouth at the same time that the bathroom door breaks open. Vane raises his gun to an empty doorway as a small metal ball rolls in.

"Gas," he says as he focuses his eyes on mine and brings me to his chest.

CHAPTER
FORTY-ONE

(MAEVIS)

I want to open my eyes more than anything, but my brain isn't following my commands.

Maevis.

My back is against something cool and hard, and my wrists ache. Why is it so fucking cold?

Maevis.

Even though I'm uncomfortable, my body is begging me to continue sleeping as my brain shouts for me to open my eyes.

Maevis.

Where is Vane? Wherever he is, he will find me. I can go back to resting for just a bit longer.

Maevis!

My eyes snap open, and panic instantly rises. Every single alarm goes off in my head, and they get louder when my eyes land on Vane. He's tied to a metal chair bolted to the cement ground beneath us. His right eye is swollen shut, and blood is crusted on his face.

A cry escapes my throat before I can stop it, and Vane is begging me to be quiet while reassuring me he's okay. "Baby, baby, listen to me. Please, if you want us to live, you have to listen to me with a clear head. I promise, I look worse than I am," he begs me, and I suppress the cries that want to escape me, even though the tears fall in silence.

"We're going to get out of this," he says at the same time we see three men in black ski masks walk past the glass window. "Fuck...it's too late. Okay, Maevis, baby, listen. You have to remember, it's just pain."

"*What?*" I shout accidentally.

My eyes roam over the room, and I notice a table like Vane has at the casino filled with sharp tools and syringes. My heart races when I realize what he's implying. "Vane, I am not built for this. I am not strong enough to be by your side. I can't—"

"You don't have a choice at the moment, and I'm sorry, but shut the fuck up. If you can handle the bullshit you've lived through your entire life, you can make it through this," he rushes out, and I look away as more tears fall.

"Don't you dare, Maevis. Eyes on me," Vane snaps, and I turn my head back toward him. "You've come this far without letting them break you. Do not break now."

The large metal door opens, and the three men in ski masks come in, followed by Ross in a dark grey suit. He never looks at Vane but makes a beeline straight to me. I force myself to stand up straight against the pillar I'm tied to. My wrists scream in agony as I slide them up the stone where they're tied behind me, but I refuse to have him tower over me while I sit on the floor.

He stops less than a foot away, and I can hear Vane shouting for him to move. One of the men deliver a punch to the side of Vane's face, and it takes everything for me not to drop back down to the ground with the way his head snaps to the side. Still, I don't make a sound. I don't even let a tear drop.

"*Do not break now.*"

Ross raises the back of his fingers to my cheek, and I stand frozen as he caresses it.

"You know, your coach and friends really did a number on me earlier today. Nothing a little makeup can't fix," he says while tilting his head to the side. "I really thought you'd make a great bride, Maevis. I hope you know that."

My reflexes kick in, and spit flies straight into Ross' eye from my mouth.

"Go to hell," I say with a shit-eating grin.

Ross never removes his hand from my cheek as he bites his lip, spit trailing down his face. Holding my stare for a moment, he nods. His next movement is so quick, I don't even have time to flinch in preparation.

My face stings as I see stars.

Not the first time he's slapped me, probably not the last.

Smack.

Nope...definitely not the last.

"You son of a bitch," Vane shouts, and I cast a look at him to shut up before he gets punched again.

Ross grips my face so hard with one hand, I'm convinced my teeth will poke through my cheeks. "I cannot wait for you to be my bitch for the rest of your pathetic life. And the best part? The people who claimed to be your parents your whole life don't give a single fuck as long as they get a check."

My heartbeat stutters and my breaths turn rapid, but I refuse to give this asshole fresh tears. I hold his gaze until he drops his hand, and I note the taste of iron on my tongue from his blows to my face.

"Now, I know it won't be easy to get you to leave your little boy toy here. And as much as I would love to start off by slitting his throat, which I will eventually, I think the only way to get what I need is to torture him," Ross says while walking over to the tools on the table.

"He won't cave to your bullshit," I snap at Ross between deep breaths.

Slowly, he turns his gaze over to Vane, then to me. A crazed smile blooms across his face while he picks up a pair of pliers.

"No, he won't. He was brought up around this type of setting, from what I've researched."

He walks over to where Vane is tied to the chair, one man holding Vane's head back while placing a metal device in his mouth to keep it open. Ross examines the pliers once more while standing in front of Vane and casts a look in my direction. Swiftly, Ross pulls a knife from the table next to him and slams it into Vane's leg. My screams intwine with Vane's as the room spins.

Ross observes me with a broad, sinister smile as I continue to cry, watching Vane writhe in pain. With a nod in my direction, his three words pierce me to my core.

"But you will."

FORTY-TWO

(MAEVIS)

I make it two teeth in before I throw up at the sound of Vane's agony.

When he begins choking on his own blood, my breaths turn shallow, and I blink rapidly to keep from passing out. Ross has pulled out two of Vane's back teeth and doesn't show any signs of stopping until I speak.

You have to remember, it's just pain.

The men refuse to let him lift his head up to keep from asphyxiating on his own blood, and Ross glances at me, waiting to see if I'll speak. When I don't, he shrugs with a smile and waves the pliers in the air before forcing them into the front of Vane's mouth this time. I can't handle anymore.

"Stop!" I shout, causing everyone to freeze. "Please, just stop. Let him breathe...please."

Ross glares at me before instructing man to release Vane's head.

I watch on strangled breaths as Vane quickly brings his head forward, letting the blood drip from his mouth onto his lap and the floor below.

It's okay, he's okay. He's alive I tell myself over and over in my head.

But for how much longer if I don't give in?

"Too much blood for you, my love?" Ross asks, and I hear a

snarl from Vane, which results in his head being snatched back again by the man behind him. "Imagine how much blood there will be if I pull this knife from his femoral artery," he says while wrapping his hand around the handle. Vane jerks in the chair.

"Just tell me what you want, Ross," I beg from where I stand, keeping my eyes on the blade in Vane's thigh. "Leave him alone and just tell me what you want."

Ross throws his head back, an impressed expression on his face. "After all this time, I would think you'd know what I want, Maevis baby," he says while striding over to me, pliers still in hand. "Say you'll come home to Daddy."

My stare turns ablaze, and I know Ross can see it in my eyes. Shrugging, he raises the pliers and turns back toward Vane.

"Stop. Stop, alright. Just...take that thing out of his mouth," I say. When they do, Vane instantly starts shouting at me to stop, but I know what I need to do, what I have to say.

And I know full well it's going to break my heart along with his.

"We both know this was never going to work out, Vane. We were living a dream filled with lust. There's no point in you acting like you care for me any longer than you have to. I know you're in it for the same reason Ross is. I might as well choose the lesser of two evils," I rush out on a breath before I can't force myself to deliver the lie.

The instant hurt on Vane's face is enough to have me pulling my own teeth out with the tool in Ross' hand.

"Don't do this," Vane says, leaning forward in the chair. I can hear the pain from his teeth slurring his words. Forcing myself to look away from him before I confess to lying in front of everyone, I focus on Ross, who is smiling from ear to ear.

"I knew you would come to your senses, baby," he says,

walking over to me and placing a hand on the side of my neck. I have to steel myself to stop from headbutting him.

"I'll sign everything over to you, including myself, as long as you release him," I say and watch Ross' face fall. "We may not love each other, but he's still an old friend, Ross. Let him go, and you can have whatever you need."

Ross grinds his teeth and steps away from me, going over to a different table and grabbing a manilla folder. "Release her and bring her over," Ross snaps at the men.

Moments later, my wrists are freed, and I'm manhandled over to the table. Forced into a cold metal chair, I clench my eyes shut at Vane's shouts. "Maevis, don't agree or sign a single fucking thing he gives you," he shouts once more, and my heart skips a few beats at the anger in his voice.

"Sign here, here, and here," Ross instructs while laying papers in front of me.

"W-what are they for?" I question while picking up the pen.

"Do not sign shit, Maevis," Vane roars, and I hear another fist connect with his face. I flinch, but I refuse to turn around to look. If I see the pain he's in, I'll cave, and we will never make it out of here alive.

"This one is for all assets to be signed over to me, this one is for all accounts your parents left to be in my name, and this one is our marriage license, dated for today," he says while flashing a giant smile. My head snaps up to meet his eyes, and he wiggles his brows. "Don't worry, I already ordered a replacement for the ring you loved so much."

Vane is full on shouting at Ross, who turns to pick up a nearby knife.

"Stop! We had a deal," I say, standing from the chair before one of the men force me back down.

Ross stops in his tracks, and I see his shoulders rise and fall on a breath. "Then hurry up and sign. My patience is wearing thin with this one."

My hand shakes as I sign on each dotted line.

The third document is the hardest to sign, my vision of walking down the aisle toward Vane nothing but a daydream now. When I finish, Ross drops the knife and holds out both arms. "See? All this torturing and violence for nothing. Now get over here to your husband, sweetheart."

The swooshing of my heart is so loud in my head, I sway when I stand, and the man behind me roughly grips my arm to lead me over to Ross. Wrapping his arms around me, he presses his nose to my hair and breaths in deeply.

"You know I can't let him go," he whispers before spinning me around, clapping a hand over my mouth, and forcing me to look at Vane with wide eyes.

"String him up, boys," he instructs the masked man next to Vane as I scream into Ross' hand.

"Have some fun first," he adds as I look on in horror. Fists fly into Vane as he remains strapped to his chair. With each hit, my lungs lose more air from the screams muffled by Ross' hand.

With each blow, Vane's eyes find mine while Ross drags me backwards toward the door. Even as I'm kicking and screaming, my gaze never leaves Vane as I panic that I'll never see him again, that he won't leave this room alive. The men begin tying a thick, brown rope around his legs, and my heart stops.

They're going to hang him upside down...

The last fist I see lands in his ribs, and I hear an audible crack.

Angst jolts through me as Vane's eyes fill with fire, and then Ross pulls me through the doorway and out of sight.

CHAPTER
FORTY-THREE

(VANE)

Does it hurt? *I've had worse.*

Does seeing him drag Maevis from the room hurt even more? *Yes.*

I spit out the blood pooling in my mouth and allow myself a deep breath before opening my eyes to a spinning room. My legs already feel like they're about to dislocate as I hang upside down from the steel beam in the middle of the room. One of the men laughs while flipping a knife in the air, trying to intimidate me.

But they've never met my father.

I'd rather be stabbed in the femoral artery four times than spend another minute in the same room as that man. This is light work compared to being the offspring of that son-of-a-bitch.

"Should we place bets on how long he has once we make the cut?" the same man questions while still flipping the knife.

I've seen a lot of injuries in my line of work. I've seen a lot of unethical things done in my lifetime to get a man to talk. But in this very moment, I have no idea where they're going with my torture.

The man with the knife walks over to me, dropping down to a squat and removing his ski mask. He pats the side of my face with his hand, "I have to be honest with you. I've heard a lot about you over the years, and I never thought a piece of pussy would be your downfall. I'm a little disappointed."

Making sure to burn the memory of his face into my mind, I spit directly between his eyes before smiling. The look on his face is the icing on the cake until he stands and sends his fist into my stomach. Coughing and fighting to not throw up, I force myself to laugh as he squats back down.

"When you die, I'll make sure to have a crack at that bitch when Ross sluts her out," he says with an even wider smile.

Whatever pain I felt prior to his statement dissolves in that moment. There's not much that can get under my skin, but I know it's the truth. Ross doesn't love Maevis, and he will do whatever he can to make her suffer for the rest of her life because she embarrassed him.

In a flash, the masked man flicks his wrist and makes a small incision on the side of my neck.

Bleeding out.

They're going to have me bleed out slowly instead of pulling the knife from my thigh and speeding it up.

I can't help but smile, a simple raise of a brow and nod to say touché in their choice of death. Standing, the man presses his boot to my forehead and kicks me backwards, sending me spinning in the center of the room.

"I'll give it twenty minutes before we're hauling his body out of here," one of the men says, and I hear him slap money down onto a table.

I can feel myself getting more lightheaded by the second from the blows I've taken and blood rushing to my head. I can only pray my saving grace walks through that door.

Am I a man of God? No. Do I believe in God? More or less. I do believe in a higher power, and I'm praying my ass off for him or her to answer me in this moment.

At least ten minutes pass, and Maevis' face and bright

smile play in my mind while I listen to the masked men place bets on my life. I force myself to keep wiggling as much as I can to stay conscious while the blood drips down my face and onto the floor from the cut on my neck.

But I'm losing the battle as my eyelids threaten to fall heavy.

With my wrists still tied behind me, I move my arms around to make sure my watch is still in place and take a deep breath when I can feel it wrapped snuggly around my wrist.

Amateurs.

The men go silent, and I can only assume that with my eyes closed, they think I've passed out.

"Ah shit, boys... I don't think any of us are going to win," one of the men says when a loud bang rings out through the room.

My eyes fly open to see Ryatt standing in the doorway, eyes wide with fear at the amount of blood on the floor. Giving a subtle nod as a greeting, he releases a breath. The masked men were so enthralled with their bets, they left their weapons on the opposite table. As they scramble to grab their guns, four more of my men enter, releasing rapid fire into the room and hitting their targets with every single bullet.

I'm barely conscious enough to see my captors laid out in their own blood, my eyes roaming to find Ryatt in the chaos. "You're late," I mutter with a cough, doing my best to keep my eyes open.

"Right on time, motherfucker," he replies while rushing over to me. "Had to scare ya just a bit."

In my head, I laugh, but I know I can't form another word or sound.

"Cut him down!" Ryatt shouts while surveying the cut on my neck. "Lance, please tell me you can fix this," he mutters to the guy next to him. Lance is my medic who knows everything there is to know about situations like this. He's never failed us, and I'm counting on him right now.

"I... Listen, Ryatt, that's a lot of blood loss. We need to get him out of here and somewhere safe, and I'm not sure—"

Ryatt grabs our medic by the collar, staring into his soul with fire-filled eyes. "I don't care if you have to play God himself. You save my fucking brother, or I'll end your life right here."

My men cut me down, releasing my hands from behind my back, and slowly lower me to the floor. Lance begins barking commands, and my men move quickly. I scan the room for the man who threatened to assault Maevis, and satisfaction blooms in my chest when I locate him near the door, wheezing and trying to crawl out.

Pushing my men away from me, I get on my hands and knees, crawling toward him as my medic and Ryatt shout at me to stop moving. But they're voices in the wind as I focus on my goal. A trail of blood follows me as I grab the same knife that was used on me. I grip the back of his shirt, flipping him over and crawling on top of him. I can feel the sweat forming at my hairline when our eyes connect.

"What's your name?" I ask the man, whose eyes are as large as saucers.

"M-M-Mark," he responds.

"Got a last name, Mark?"

"L-Lasso. Mark Lasso," he says, wetting his lips in the process. "L-Listen, man, I was only doing what I was told. I had no intentions of hurting your girl."

"I know, Mark," I say, offering a sincere smile. "Because you were never going to get the chance to do it."

He starts bucking beneath me as I instruct Ryatt to bring me the same metal device they used to hold my mouth open.

Ryatt forces it into the man's mouth as he's held down by another one of my men.

"I'm going to make sure that even in whatever afterlife you experience, no woman has to deal with hearing your annoying fucking voice," I say with a sadistic smile before I grab his tongue. His screams are so loud, everyone in the room winces from the high pitch. Once his tongue is completely severed, I hold it in front of his eyes and shove it to the back of his throat.

"Just want to make sure her name never falls from your tongue again," I say and attempt to stand, stumbling as sweat falls down my face and back. I know I'm going to pass out, but I don't care, just as long as this fucker suffers. "Oh...one more thing," I add, grabbing the knife from the floor and plunging it into his thigh before removing it quickly.

Watching him squirm on the concrete is like watching the sunrise on the beach in Maevis' arms. I wince at the pain from my ribs as the room begins to spin, my vision blurry. A searing, sharp pain shoots through my leg, and I glance down at the knife still sticking from my thigh.

"I think I'd like that help now," I mumble to Ryatt as he catches me in his arms and my vision goes black.

CHAPTER
FORTY-FOUR

(VANE)

"Hey, sweetie," Maevis whispers while running her hand through my hair.

I want to respond to her, but I can't. All I can do is stare at her beautiful face as she looks at me like I'm the only thing she's ever loved.

"I need you…"

I mouth a response, but words don't come out.

"I need you…"

She repeats herself, eyes wide with fear when I can't respond. I feel my heart skip a few beats when I see the panic in her eyes.

"I need you to wake up, Vane. Wake up!" she shouts before a hand wraps around her mouth and she's lifted away from me while kicking her feet. I try reaching for her through my weakness. Her muffled screams have my heart about to explode in my chest when I finally produce her name from my throat—but she's already dragged away into the void.

I shoot upwards and feel a tug in the middle of my arm before I realize I'm in bed with tubes and cords surrounding me.

"Hey, hey, chill. You're at the casino," Ryatt says from the corner of the room, setting his laptop down and making his way over to me.

"How long have I been asleep?" I ask, running my hands down my face.

"Twelvish hours," he replies, already pressing me back down onto the bed. "We're looking for her, Vane. You need to relax."

Pushing him away, I rip the needle from my vein and sit up. "Fuck you. If it were someone you loved, would you lay in a bed?" I ask him at the same time as Rose rushes around the corner.

"He loves someone? Who?" she asks, eyes darting from Ryatt to me. I narrow my eyes at the two of them.

"You brought her here?" I ask in confusion.

"She was already with me."

I tilt my head, trying to figure out why she would already be with him when it finally clicks, and my eyebrows raise expeditiously.

"Anyway," Ryatt says with a narrowed look that could cut glass. "I think I located her thirty seconds before you woke up, and you're not going to like it," he says while walking to his laptop and handing it over to me. "I'm assuming she doesn't know you placed a tracker on her?"

I cut him a glare, ignoring Rose's shocked face, and study the computer screen.

"You're welcome for forcing you to always wear your watch, by the way. Otherwise, I'm not sure you would have received that blood transfusion in time. I'll take that bonus in the form of a Ferrari. All black, cream interior. No rush, though," Ryatt says, and I fake lunge at him, causing him to flinch jokingly.

I glance over to the side table where I see clean clothes and begin throwing them on over my boxers. I stiffen in shock from the pain surrounding my ribs but continue moving. "He took her out of the fucking state?" I ask through gritted teeth.

Feeling a pulsing in my leg, I looking down to see the bandage on my thigh where the knife once was.

Ryatt nods. "I just now found her when you woke up. The tracker was having issues locating her in the air, I guess."

"How quickly can we get to her?"

"Roughly two hours by plane," he answers, and I groan. Anger consumes me, and I trash every piece of equipment and breakable thing in the room. Ryatt stands in front of Rose, pushing her behind him to avoid flying debris. When I finish my assault on the room, he instructs Rose to stay in the corner as he makes his way over to me.

Falling to my hands and knees, I force myself to breathe.

I can feel his hand on my shoulder as he drops to his knees to meet me.

"I've never seen you like this, Vane. You really love this girl, don't you?"

I turn my head to face him. "I will take my gun to my own head if anything happens to her."

Ryatt's eyes widen and narrow before softening slightly. "We'll get her back."

"You better pray, for their sake and mine, that we do," I hiss.

Ryatt nods his head in understanding, rising to his feet and making a call to prepare the private jet. In the meantime, I have a fantastic idea.

"We need to make a stop along the way," I say, a devilish smile spreading across my face. Rose cringes, and Ryatt gives me a look—he knows nothing good ever comes when I produce a smile like this one.

Ross may be an asshole, but he's a smart man.

And if I'm going to get my future wife back, I'm going to need leverage.

FORTY-FIVE

(MAEVIS)

I fought with everything I had as Ross dragged me away from Vane, and he ended up having to drug me. Whatever his men injected into me has my head pounding as I force my eyes open. Licking my overly dry lips, panic floods me when I realize I'm on a plane. I attempt to stand and am immediately snatched back down. I blink a few times before looking down, noticing a thick black rope binding me to the seat.

"Hey there, baby," Ross greets me, rounding the seat and sitting in front of me with a drink in hand. My only response is to stare at the audacity of him acting like this is a regular stroll in the park.

"Sorry about the restraints. With the way you were acting back there, I didn't want to take a chance in the air." He gives a nonchalant smile I want to slap right off his face.

"Have you lost your fucking mind?" I ask through clenched teeth.

"No, but I think you've lost yours. Attempting to throw your life away *again* for the same low-life you did back in college? Well, you would have had it not been for your parents," he says with a smug look. "I understand how good looking he is, but dear God, Maevis, have some common sense. I can take better care of you. I can give you what you need. Just pop out a few babies and be a good bitch for once, and you can live a life of luxury."

His statement has me seeing red, and the way he speaks about Vane makes me want to break his neck. Maybe he wasn't wrong about needing to restrain me. I knew I lost myself back when I killed Brian, but while I lost myself, I found my soul.

Vane made it out of there. He had to. He wouldn't leave me to live this life without him.

What would he want me to do in this situation?

Ross studies me, waiting for me to lash out at him for insinuating I be his breeding toy for the rest of my life and be content with it.

So, play along with that narrative, I hear Vane's smooth velvet voice whisper in my head.

Taking a deep breath, I relax my shoulders and press back into the seat. Ross' eyes narrow for a split second at my response. He always believed I was stupid, that I was incapable of making the right decisions for myself. So, I'll give him the Maevis he believes me to be.

"You were right..." I say while staring down into my lap. "I should have known you were the only one who truly wanted me. Vane wanted to get married as soon as possible, I'm assuming for the same reason as you—so he could have access to my inheritance."

Ross laughs, taking a sip of his alcohol. "I could have told you that. Maevis, baby...be honest with yourself. With that hair and the weight you've kept on, do you really think men would just be throwing themselves at you?"

My blood boils, but I bite my tongue so hard, I taste the tang of blood. Instead of answering, I just nod my head to avoid blowing my cover.

"Lucky for you, I'm taking you to your favorite place in the world."

Nashville. He has to be taking me to Nashville. Did I ever tell Vane how much I love it there?

"It's just a short stop for a day or two before the paperwork is completed for our marriage and we can leave the country for a bit. Don't worry, I'm working on your passport as well. What do you say about conceiving in a different country?" he asks while standing to run his knuckles over my cheek. I force myself to give him a look of lust.

His eyes trail down to my lips. "God, those lips may be the only perfect thing about you."

Fight or flight creeps in when he begins unzipping his pants while licking his lips.

The pilot's door opens, causing us both to jump. "Sir, we will be landing in ten minutes."

Ross thanks the pilot and sits back down in the seat across from me. "Guess there's more than enough time to take advantage of that mouth once we're there," he comments, typing away on his phone.

Once we land, I realize instead of Nashville, he took me to Gatlinburg.

The fucker couldn't even remember my favorite place.

Making me promise to be a *good girl*, he had his men release me from the restraints and guide me off the plane into a black SUV with deeply tinted windows.

Arriving at a large, luxurious cabin in the woods, I realize how hard it will be for Vane to find me here.

"Isn't this great? No phone, no laptop, no technology for you. Just nature and your future husband once the marriage license is processed," Ross says, wrapping his arms around me from behind. I have to make sure not to step out of his embrace. He plants kisses down the side of my neck to my shoulder.

"Do you mind if I run to the bathroom? Long flight," I say, turning around to face him while making sure to force a fake smile.

He scowls and relaxes before releasing me and stepping back. "I'm warning you now, Maevis. The place is surrounded with security, so don't try anything stupid."

I shake my head. "I told you, I'm yours. I signed the papers... I already made my choice. I just really need to pee."

His shoulders relax, and he points me in the direction of the bathroom, informing me that fresh clothes should already be laid out on the bed in the adjacent bedroom as well. "When you come out, I'll be ready to utilize that mouth of yours," he adds on, and I force the bile back down my throat at the thought.

While he is an asshole, I'm thankful for new clothes. Grabbing them off the bed, I race to the bathroom and close the door, locking it in place. Dropping down to the floor in the corner of the room, I pull at my hair while wondering how I'm going to get myself out of this mess.

I rest my head against the cool wall and shut my eyes to envision Vane's handsome face. I smile and relax at the thought of lounging in his arms, lying in bed, waiting for the sun to rise.

There's no other option but to get out of here alive. I refuse to die without feeling his touch, his warmth, one last time. I don't care if that means I have to kill every motherfucker behind that door to get back to him. I open my eyes with a sense of control, knowing I'm not afraid to fight my way out of here.

"You lying fucking bitch," I hear Ross shout as he begins pounding on the other side of the wooden door, making me

jolt upright. "I'm going to make sure you never see daylight when I'm done with you," he yells, and I shuffle to stand, leaning against the counter.

I jump when the door flies open from multiple kicks, and one of his men are standing there. Ross pushes him aside and comes running at me. I move to run around him as he catches me with a fist full of my hair and tosses me backwards. My head knocks against the corner of the sink, and blood instantly trickles from the open wound.

Putting my hands up in defense, I beg him. "Ross, what the hell is going on? I just came in to change and—"

"I am so sick of your lies," he snaps and sends a kick into my stomach that has me falling to my side on the floor. As I gasp for air from the blow, he grabs me by my hair again and drags me over to the toilet.

"I'll fucking kill you," he roars before shoving my head into the water.

Flailing my arms around, I attempt to grab his hand holding me down. After what feels like an eternity he pulls my head from the water. Instantly, I begin to gasp for air like my life depends on it—because it does.

"You signed the fucking papers under a different name?" he questions loudly and shoves my head back in the toilet. I begin flailing again when he holds me under for an ungodly amount of time and my lungs begin to burn.

Snatching my head up, he shakes me back and forth. "And not just any name. You gave yourself *his* last name?" he questions with anger before quickly pushing me back into the bowl of water.

This time, I know I won't survive without taking a breath. My lungs burn as if a blowtorch is being held against them.

Use your fucking head, Maevis. I just need a little more time, I hear Vane say in my head, and a lightbulb switches on.

Instead of flailing my arms, I reach around the base of the toilet until I feel the metal piece I'm searching for, pressing until I hear it flush. My lungs draw in air just before Ross pulls me up and throws me to the corner of the room. I slide in water, the back of my head smacking against the wall so I see stars.

Ross is still berating me as I force myself to stand. His words go in one ear and out the other as I make a dash out the door, avoiding his man standing next to him. I make it halfway to the front door when another man tackles me from behind.

"Get off her," Ross demands and replaces the man's weight with his. I try wrestling him before he pins my arms to my chest, bringing his face just above mine. "You're done, you little conniving bitch. I tried, Maevis. I tried to offer you the life women would dream of, but you insist on betraying me every chance you get," he says with a forceful slap to my cheek, making my head twist to the side.

"Now, my men are going to clean you up, and they have my full permission to use you however they see fit. It seems you need a little lesson in obedience," Ross informs me, and I buck my hips to get him off me. While still straddling me, he slaps me again so hard, my vision blurs and I go limp. "Don't worry, they'll pull out. My baby is the only one you'll be carrying *very* soon," he whispers in my ear at the same time his phone begins ringing in his back pocket.

He stands from crushing me with his weight, and I gasp for air.

Two men grab me off the floor, dragging me toward the room. Ross answers the phone while adjusting his clothes, and my heart surges to my throat when I hear the deep, loud voice come through the speaker. Pressing my feet into the floor, I go dead weight and scream Vane's name to ensure he hears me. The larger man hits me, knocking me to the ground, but I can hear Vane shouting before a woman's voice comes from the other end.

Her frantic voice, filled with fear, echoes as Ross scowls, his eyes a fiery gaze that won't leave me. And when the screams come through the phone again, my heart pumps rapid-fire.

Vane has Ross' mother.

(VANE)

Am I proud I broke into an older couple's home and held them at gunpoint? *No.*

Would I do it again if it meant I had a surefire way to keep Maevis alive? *Absolutely.*

Ross' parents were so high and mighty, they don't even have a proper security system. It took Ryatt less than a minute to disable it along with their cameras without sending a notification to alert them.

I've never tortured a woman, and I still don't have it in me to do it.

Rose refused to stay behind, and when we got here, I had whispered in our huddle that I can't hurt his mother because it goes against what I do. Rose rolled her eyes, walked right up to where she was tied up, and backhanded her.

"I think I just got instantly hard," Ryatt whispers, and I tell him to shut up.

"He won't torture you, but I damn sure will for everything you put my best friend through," Rose hisses in the woman's face as her husband jolts in his seat, duct tape over his mouth. Walking over to replace Rose, I squat in front of the woman and attempt to reason with her to avoid any more harm.

"Listen, Margaret. All I want is for Maevis to get back to

me. Unfortunately, your son thinks he has some sort of claim over her. Now if—"

The woman kicks her foot out to hit me in the face, and I dodge it narrowly. Anger rises in me at her attempt, and I bare my teeth. "Fuck this. Rose, how open are you to torture?"

Rose tilts her head from left to right and shrugs. "Anything to get my bestie back," she responds while flipping off Ross' mother with both hands.

My eyebrows shoot up, and I shrug. "Fantastic. Ryatt, grab her the knife from my bag," I instruct him, and he hands Rose the knife with sparkles in his eyes that makes me twist my face in annoyance.

How the fuck did these two end up together?

I walk around behind his mother, holding her head back. "Cut her tongue out, since she's no use to us."

Her husband begins violently jerking in the chair next to hers. Rose rips the tape off his mouth. "Wanna tell your wife to stop being a dumb bitch and call her son?"

Ross' father begins cursing, telling his wife to cooperate. When she continues to refuse, Rose straddles her lap and grabs her jaw, attempting to get her tongue as the father shouts in protest. Sweat begins to bead at Margaret's hairline, and she finally caves when Rose says she will settle for an eye and holds the blade less than an inch away from the woman's right socket.

"Figured you'd see it our way," Rose says, hopping off the woman's lap and slapping the tape back on the man's mouth. I force myself to close my mouth as I stare at the pint-sized girl who's acting like she's the head of this operation.

His mother instructs us on where to find her phone, and I press Ross' number with a smug facial expression. When he answers, anger is the only emotion I feel at his voice.

"Where the fuck is my girl?" I shout into the phone before I can stop myself. Before Ross can answer, I hear Maevis scream my name in the background, and my heart shatters into a million pieces.

Without another word, I hold the phone up to his mother's mouth, and she begins begging for his help.

Snatching the phone back, I release a laugh into the speaker. "I propose a little meeting. What do you say, Ross?" I ask with a smugness in my tone. Within seconds, he's agreeing to meet, giving his exact location, as if I didn't already have it. The fucker doesn't know we're already on the plane toward him.

"Ross, he has us on a plane! You know how terrified I am of these things," his mother screams, and Rose backhands her as a warning to shut up. Once Ross agrees to meet in three hours, he tries to end the call, but I halt him.

"Put Maevis on the phone," I snap, and Ross refuses. "Then say goodbye to your father," I reply, and his mother begins shouting that I have both of them, causing Ross to fold and grant me my request.

"Maevis, baby, I'm coming for you. I'm coming," I rush out, trying to control my emotions when I hear her voice on the other end.

"I know, Vane. I never doubted it," she says on a whisper, and I can hear the terror in her voice.

I swallow before asking the next question, wondering if I want the answer. "Did he put his hands on you?"

Silence falls on the other end, and I can only imagine Ross giving her a look.

"Maevis, did he or any of his men put their fucking hands on you?"

A muffled cry is heard on the other end, and I clamp my teeth together so harshly, my jaw aches when I hear them take the phone from her. Ross' voice echoes through the speaker, informing me the conversation is done.

Turning around to face his parents, I raise the gun.

"I don't need to ask any more questions. Her silence speaks volumes. Every time you lay a hand on her, I kill someone close to you," I tell him as he begins speaking nonsense into the phone.

Nonsense I don't give a single fuck about right now.

"One parent is better than none," I say before three shots ring out, and I end the call.

CHAPTER

FORTY-SEVEN

(VANE)

Ross' father lays limp in the seat of my private jet as his wife screams next to him.

Part of me hates the way I can't find an ounce of empathy. The other part of me wants to laugh, because she wants empathy as a person who took part in murdering two very good-hearted people. Did she pull the trigger? No, but she knew the plan and helped orchestrate it. Maevis' parents didn't deserve what happened to them, but these two deserve everything they get.

"Get this motherfucker out of here," I say with a wave of my gun.

My gaze flicks up to Ryatt, who is looking at me like I'm crazy. Maybe I am. Hell, I know I am. But right now is not the time for a speech.

"Vane, we're on a fucking plane," he exclaims with a worried look on his face. "What do you want us to do? Open the door and throw him out?"

Ross' mother screams even louder, and it takes everything in me not to finish her off as well. Sometimes, I hate my own rule and small number of morals I have left. I release a breath and pinch the bridge of my nose. "Throw him in the bathroom or back room for all I care. He's getting blood all over the place."

279

His mother's screams are getting on my fucking nerves. I glance over at Rose, who is studying me even harder than Ryatt. I tilt my head and raise a brow, waiting for her to lecture me.

"You could've just suffocated him or something way less dramatic to avoid the mess," she says before plopping down in her seat and opening a bag of chips. "Not to mention if a single shot would have missed and punctured the plane, we would all be falling to our deaths right now. A little *overkill*, don't you think?"

My mouth refuses to close as I stare, wondering who the fuck this woman is that she could care less about witnessing a murder, let alone willing to eat right next to a dead body and a woman screaming her head off.

"For the love of God," Rose snaps, slamming her chips down on the table in front of her and grabbing a silk scarf from her purse. Strutting over to Ross' mother, she shoves the scarf in her mouth, snatches the duct tape from the mouth of his father's dead body, and slaps it over Margaret's lips.

I watch Rose with confusion as she drops back down in her seat and goes back to eating her chips, scrolling on her phone. "How far are we from my best friend?" she asks nonchalantly, and I inform her we're thirty minutes out.

Ross' mother is staring at me with wide eyes, tears streaming down her face as my men begin moving the body like I requested. I force myself to move in front of her, dropping into a squat and staring into her deep brown eyes. "I want you to know that every single time your son lays a hand on my girl, I'm going to kill someone he loves. So far, you're up next on that list. Let's hope he got the message loud and clear."

She starts kicking, aiming for my face and body, but my reaction time is too quick as I stand, giving her a few pats on the cheek before making my way over to Ryatt, who witnessed the interaction. "Vane, not that it wasn't justified, but maybe..." he begins one of his rare lectures, and I don't feel like hearing it, so I cut him off before he goes any further.

"I don't regret it," I say, walking past him to grab a water and gripping the back of a seat due to turbulence.

"Vane, where the fuck is your head at? We're going to get her back," Ryatt continues, but his voice is a faint whisper compared to the clutter of nonsense I have going on in my head. What if Ross heard those shots and decided to retaliate by killing Maevis? My heart beats faster at the thought of losing her while my best friend is still lecturing me in the background. When I hear him start about how Maevis and I aren't even official and I'm going crazy, my focus returns, and I step to him.

"I fucking love her," I snap with my lips peeled back. "Do you know what that means? Do you?"

He blinks at me, remaining silent as my chest heaves. When he crosses his arms over his chest and widens his stance, I know he's giving me the floor to continue.

"He has her at his mercy, doing God knows what to her, because she traded herself for me. *For me.* A nobody. Do you know how many people have sacrificed themselves for me? Do you?" I snap, having to turn my head away from him as emotions start flying high, emotions I haven't felt since adolescence. I refuse to let them reach the surface.

"The answer is none," I force an answer to my own question with a hoarseness to my voice.

Grounding myself, I turn back to look at my best friend, who is staring at me with his large blue eyes holding an amount of sympathy I've never seen from him before. Without a word, he raises his hand and places it firmly on my shoulder. We stand silent for a moment, staring at each other while I force myself to stop grinding my teeth at the pain of worrying about Maevis.

"I'll kill him if anything happens to her. All of them. I'll kill all of them," I declare without a second thought. I can see Rose watching us out of the corner of my eye, but she doesn't say anything. I don't even think she is considering judging me when it comes to her best friend.

Ryatt nods a few times before squeezing my shoulder. "Then we go get her and use this bitch as leverage," he says while nodding toward Ross' mother. Relief blooms in my chest, knowing my best friend still has my back.

"We have to get her back. I let my guard down back at her place, and they took the opportunity. This is my fault... We have to bring her back, Ryatt," I plead and instantly bite my cheek to avoid those foreign emotions from breaking free.

He pats my shoulder a few times before dropping his arms to his side and shrugging.

"Let's go get your future wife."

FORTY-EIGHT

(MAEVIS)

My heartbeat is nonexistent since hearing the gunshots ring through the speaker of Ross' phone. He hasn't said a word since the line went dead, and for the first time in a long time, I'm genuinely terrified of what his next move will be.

His hand tightens around the thin phone in his hand as his gaze moves to me with an unreadable emotion. Raising both my hands up in protest, I take a step backwards, but he moves so quickly, I stumble back, and one of his men grips me by my hair, holding me in place.

In the blink of an eye, Ross pulls a gun from his back pocket and raises it to my forehead. Despite fighting my emotions, I can't stop myself from trembling at the feeling of the cool metal resting against my skin with my eyes clamped shut.

"Ross, please... I don't—"

"Shut. The fuck. Up. Shut up!" he spits back at me, causing me to flinch.

The front door flies open, and three friends of Ross' I've seen before walk in.

"Sorry we're late. Our cocaine dealer was running behind and—" one of them states before stopping in their tracks. "Holy shit, bro, what's going on? I thought we were here for a gang bang, not a murder."

The men produce a nervous laughter, and I lick my lips, concentrating on pleading my case.

"Ross, don't do this. You heard him—he said he'll kill someone close to you every time you lay a hand on me," I try to reason, but he presses the gun harder into my forehead. My knees go weak from panic, but I force myself to remain standing.

"Yea? And what will he do if I blow your fucking head off right here? Huh? What will he do if his little fuck toy is dead?" he asks with anger in his eyes.

"Probably go on a killing spree if he's anything like you," one of his friends chimes in behind him with a chuckle.

Without a second thought, Ross turns, removing the gun from my head and pointing it at his friend, pulling the trigger.

Everyone in the room jumps as the body falls to the floor with a bullet wound to the middle of his forehead. The other two press themselves against the wall next to the door, shouting at Ross to put the gun down and asking what's gotten into him.

"He talks too much," Ross explains and turns back to me with the gun at his side, instructing his guy to release my hair.

"He said I can't lay a hand on you. He didn't say anything about anyone else having their way with you," he clarifies, and my pulse races. "Chase and Jake, take her to the room and do what I called you here for, just like back at the hotel."

Just like back at the hotel.

Brian had let me know he took advantage of me before I killed him, but he said he couldn't recall if there were any others there. My eyes flick back and forth between the two men who could care less about the dead body on the floor.

Excitement dances in their eyes as they walk toward me.

"Don't touch me," I say and attempt to run, but one of them grabs me around the waist and lifts me into the air. I manage to kick the other one in the chest, watching as he falls to the floor, attempting to catch his breath.

"You bitch," he mutters through gasps. Standing, he grasps my face and presses his lips to mine. "It's going to be fun with you being awake this time," he says, and tears spring to my eyes as I begin kicking and screaming while being carried to the room.

My eyes find Ross, who stands with his arms hanging at his side and a devilish grin on his face. My anger surges when he raises a hand to wave goodbye.

Do not let them know you're scared, I hear Vane's voice in my head and clamp my mouth shut.

Fine.

They want to play? I'll play.

(MAEVIS)

Vane will come for me. I know he will. I just need to stay alive long enough for him to get to me, and then I'll be free.

The repulsive man carrying me throws me onto the bed, and I crawl backwards toward the headboard.

"That Ross is giving us free range on his bitch is hilarious," he comments and the other laughs.

Ross opens the door just enough to stick his head through. "When you're done with her, make sure you lock the door behind you. And don't come in her. I need to be the one to get her pregnant, unfortunately."

My breaths pick up as I watch him toss one of the men a key before he closes the door again.

The two men focus back on me as the other pats his pockets and groans in annoyance. "I forgot the handcuffs and drugs in the car. Be right back," he says with a wink. The other focuses on me with a wide smile as he removes his clothing, and I look away in disgust.

"You can either take your clothes off, or I can rip them off you," he says, and I flip my middle finger at him. He raises both brows, crawling on top of the bed. "Heard you have the perfect lips for sucking dick. I didn't get to find out last time because you weren't conscious."

I jump off the bed and run toward the door, but he grabs

my wrist and yanks me backwards. Holding a knife to my throat, he presses his chest to my backside. "You are way less combative when you're asleep. Hopefully, Jack has something to help you relax a bit."

Coach Rivers only taught me and Rose a few self-defense classes, but during that time, he taught us what to do if someone was holding us from behind.

I'm not sure how much time I have left before the other guy returns, but I toss up a prayer before grabbing his wrist and bending it back as I duck underneath his arm. Never letting go of his hand gripping the knife, I twist it until the tip is facing his chest and run towards him with all my might until he hits the back wall. The knife presses into his chest, sending blood down his naked body.

My eyes find his as the look of shock settles on his face, and I pull the knife from his chest, allowing him to bleed out as he slides down the wall. Whatever artery I hit was a good one, as his eyes instantly gloss over, and he slumps to the side.

My brain is telling me to throw up at the sight of a dead man, but I've been here before, and I don't regret it. I'm snapped back to reality when I remember a second man is coming back for me. Taking my chances, I wipe the knife on the bed sheets and keep it gripped in my hand as I crack the door open and look around. The hall looks clear, though I hear Ross speaking on the phone somewhere.

"He's probably killed both of my parents by now, and I'm just sitting here, letting her get fucked by two men at once. I should walk right in there and end her," I hear him say. "I might as well let her suffer a little longer before I decide."

Ross and my family have taken everything from me, but I refuse to let this asshole take my life without a fight. I steady myself, sucking in a deep breath, and dart toward the back door. I can only assume his additional men took a break, since I'm supposed to be with his two friends.

Reaching the back door, I snatch it open and run like hell down the steps of the back porch and around the corner, smacking right into a man's chest, the one who was planning to assault me back in the room. He quickly notes the knife in my hand, grabbing my wrist and bending it on an angle that's so painful, I drop to my knees and release it. The knife clatters on the ground, and he grabs it. Forcing me to my feet, he wraps an arm around me, hoisting me into the air and out toward the woods. My instincts are to scream, but I stop when I realize that will only bring additional attention I don't want.

No one here will save me.

A few yards into the wooded area, I'm thrown to the ground as he wrestles me down and climbs on top of me. Sticks, rocks, and dirt dig into my back as I claw at his face until he presses the tip of the knife to my throat. I still under his threat, and a smile spreads on his narrow face.

"Fucking you in the woods was not on my to-do list today, but when God grants me a gift, who am I to not accept?" he says and brings the knife to the hem of my shirt, pulling up until it exposes my bare chest. He lifts a brow, licking his lips. "My momma always said a true whore never wears a bra, just to make sure she's always ready. I can appreciate that."

I shut my eyes, looking away from him to prepare for the assault I'm about to endure at the hands of yet another man. He's too much to buck off, and screaming will only cause me more harm. I'll let him finish his assault and work on a plan from there.

I melt into the ground, and I feel a single tear slide down the side of my cheek.

"No need to cry, baby. I'll make sure it feels good," he says, and I grind my teeth.

I can feel his hands sliding up my waist toward my chest when I hear boots crunching on the ground. My eyes snap open to see my assailant hovering over my breast, another man standing behind him, holding a gun to the back of his head. I blink back the tears, focusing on the face behind the man, and my heart surges into overdrive.

Vane.

"Get up," he growls at the man on top of me. "And drop the knife."

The male stands, dropping the knife next to me and turning around to face Vane, whose eyes are so dark with rage, even I'm terrified. I scramble to my feet, and Vane gestures for me to stand behind him. My arms fly up to cover my bare chest as I rush behind him.

"How far did he go with you?" Vane asks, not moving the gun or his gaze.

"H-he didn't. He didn't get to... I mean, he didn't do what they were trying to do." I take a deep breath. "Ross instructed two of them to have their way with me, but I killed one of them, and then this one found me and brought me out here to finish the job, I guess."

I can see Vane's shoulders tense, and the guy begins pleading his case. But he only gets a few words in before Vane pulls the trigger, and the man falls to the ground. Vane pulls the trigger three more times, pointing at the man's crotch, and I wince.

"Silencers are a beautiful thing," Vane comments before turning around to face me.

Tears begin to fall before I can stop them, and I run at Vane, wrapping my arms around him. I give in to my emotions when he wraps his arms around me so tight, I can barely breathe. When he finally releases me and we stare into each other's eyes, I beg him to get us out of here. He's silent as he removes his hoodie, pulling it over my head.

"We have to go. They're going to start looking for me. There are a lot of them," I beg and pull on Vane's hand, who doesn't move an inch.

Shaking his head, he checks the chamber of his gun for remaining bullets, closes it, and reaches down to grab the shirt of the man he just killed. "We have unfinished business," he says, dragging the dead body back toward the cabin.

FIFTY

(MAEVIS)

We walk up the steps of the back porch, and the thuds of the dead body Vane is dragging up the stairs sound. I catch a peak at the side of the house, where bodies are sprawled across the lawn like Halloween decorations. Vane's unit must have either killed or briefly silenced Ross' men. I spot Blondie a few feet away, and he smiles with a wink before kicking a man in the head and going right back to business.

My ears perk up when I hear Ross yelling inside the cabin.

He must be on the phone, because I can hear him explaining how he lost track of me. The door is still slightly ajar, and I look over my shoulder at Vane for an action plan. Without pause, he throws the body through the door and points the gun directly at my ex-fiancé.

Ross stops in his tracks, and I freeze as well when I hear the female voice shouting on the other end of the phone.

"I don't know what is going on, but the papers are signed, right? That's all we needed, but you better find that unthankful bitch, or the deal is over and you're as good as dead," I hear my mother scream into Ross' ear.

He didn't have the balls to tell them my signatures were null and void.

"Hang up the phone," Vane instructs, and Ross opens his mouth to say something, but Vane shakes his head and points the gun lower. "If you utter a single word, I'll blow out both your knee caps."

Ross removes the phone from his ear and ends the call with my mother still shouting at him.

"Where's my mother? My father? We had a fucking deal!" Ross shouts toward me. A shiver runs down my spine when I look over at Vane, and his expression never falters. I can't read what his next move is going to be, and anxiety begins creeping its way in. A split-second passes, and I see Vane's trigger finger pull backwards, shooting Ross directly in the knee.

"You didn't utter a word like I requested, so I'll spare the other knee," Vane says before putting the gun away.

Blondie comes rushing through the front door and surveys Ross on the ground. "Shit, I missed it? That's not fair."

I hear a tiny voice with a southern accent come from behind the door, and my eyes blow wide. *There's absolutely no way she came here for me.* The lump in my throat grows by the second until I hear her clearly.

"Can I bring this bitch in now?" Rose shouts from outside and pushes the door in with her foot. She's standing there with Ross' mother, whose hands are tied in front of her, mouth taped, while two of Vane's men flank them. When my gaze connects with Rose's, she hands the woman off to one of the men and sprints over to me. A thousand questions run through my mind, the main one being *why is she here?* followed by *how is she here?* We lock in an embrace that I don't want to release until she squeezes too tight, and I flinch. The reaction catches her attention, and she pulls back to look over me, her face twisting in disapproval.

When Vane found me, the sun had already begun to set, leaving little light for him to see any bruises or cuts. Vane notices Rose's face and gently pushes her out of the way to study me. Anger quickly takes over, and I reach out to stop him, but I'm not quick enough.

He's already on top of Ross, choking him. I watch Vane's rage play out in silence as my nerves consume me. Ross' face turns a mix of purple and blue, and it should make me concerned, but a flood of satisfaction and joy washes over me. Then, I snap back to reality and realize if he kills him, we won't get any of the answers we need.

I'm behind Vane, begging for him to let Ross go and trying to reason with him.

"Come on, man. Get up," Blondie is on the other side of Vane, trying to reason with him. "Let Maevis decide his fate."

I'm wrestling with a million thoughts before I wrap my arms around Vane's torso. "Vane, please. We need answers, and we won't get them if he's dead. I'm here. I'm right here."

Vane snaps out of his rage-fueled rampage and looks back at me with fury still in his eyes. I grab his hands and gently pull them from Ross' throat. "It's okay, baby. I'm okay, I promise. You're here now, and I'm okay. Let's finish this the right way," I say in a soothing voice.

Slowly, he stands from straddling Ross, who is now choking and gasping for air. His mother must have a gag in her mouth, because she's trying to scream, but all I hear are muffled noises.

Blondie pulls up two wooden chairs from the dining table and faces them toward each other. Rose forces Ross' mother into one chair, and a man ties her to it while Blondie pulls Ross up into the opposite chair. He zip ties his hands behind it, doing the same for his legs.

"Let's begin, shall we?" Vane asks.

CHAPTER

FIFTY-ONE

(MAEVIS)

Vane instructed Blondie to remove the gag from Margaret's mouth, and the moment he did, instant regret washed over everyone's faces.

"All of this over a simple-minded whore who can't keep her legs closed?" she shouts without sucking in a breath. Without a second thought, I step toward her, ready to smack every taste she's ever had out of her mouth. But before I can take one more stride, Rose marches up to her and slaps her right across the face.

I blink and study my best friend, who returns to my side, crossing her arms over her chest and popping her hip out to match my stance. "What's gotten into you?" I ask her with an astonished half-smile.

"I don't appreciate arrogant, snobby ass bitches making my best friend's life hell," she replies nonchalantly, and my heart grows ten times in the moment.

Ross' mother still sits shell-shocked, strapped to the chair, while Ross throws every curse word in Rose's direction.

"Now that we've got the bullshit out of the way, let's start with an easy question," Vane proposes, standing in the middle of the two people I hate most. "Where are Maevis' parents?"

"Dead," Ross replies with a laugh.

My heart stills when I realize he's referencing my biological

294

parents. But his nefarious behavior is short-lived when the butt of Vane's gun connects with the side of his head. A trail of blood drips down the side of his face as Vane towers over Ross, outrage swirling in his irises with his lips peeled back.

"I know you're used to being able to talk to people however you want. I know you think you have some sort of power over Maevis. But we're going to get something very, *very* clear right here, right now," he snaps, dropping down so his face is directly in front of Ross'. "I'm not afraid to look you in the eye while I end your life, and I'm not afraid to end hers while you watch," he declares, pointing the gun directly at his mother.

I don't give a damn about either of their lives anymore, but my heart hammers in my chest all the same.

"Now, I'll ask one more time. I suggest you forego the bullshit and just answer the question. I'm sure everyone in this room would thank me for silencing this arrogant bitch. Where the fuck are the people who kidnapped an innocent baby and turned her life into a living hell?" Vane snaps.

"They're out of the country," he answers reluctantly.

"And that would be where exactly?" Vane follows up, only receiving a grunt from Ross without an answer.

Vane sends a cue to Blondie, who damn near jumps with joy as he grabs a hammer from a nearby bag and makes his way over. Putting the hammer on the floor, Blondie begins removing Ross' shoes. Sweat falls from my ex-fiancé's forehead, and my own palms become wet as I try to figure out what is going on.

"I don't ask twice when I need information. Last time was a courtesy I won't offer again," Vane announces with a nod at Blondie, who is already squatting with the hammer back in his hand. He offers Ross a malicious smile before raising the hammer and bringing it down on his big toe.

The sound of bones cracking make me stand up straight,

and an audible gasp comes from Rose as her eyes pop. Ross' mother screams but clamps her mouth shut when Rose shoots her a warning glare.

"I'm tempted to reach down that bitch's throat and cut her vocal cords," my best friend mumbles, and I don't know if I should be more in awe of her or Vane at the moment.

Vane doesn't repeat his question; he just stares at Ross, who's screaming and squirming in pain before finally focusing on Vane. "Prague. They're in fucking Prague, you psychotic asshole.".

"Now that wasn't so bad, was it?" Vane asks with a hand on Ross' shoulder. "Next question. I know you know their plans. What are they?"

Ross glares at Vane without an answer, and I have to give it to him: for the amount of pain I know he's in, he's doing his best to hold his ground. But Vane could care less as he nods in understanding—Ross is refusing to give information. Blondie and Vane communicate without words. Unsure of their telepathic message, I glance between the two before Blondie moves over to Ross' mother and begins removing her heels. Automatically, she starts screaming, tears rolling down her cheeks.

I know I should feel remorseful, but right now, all I feel is excitement.

"Stop! Stop! I'll talk, I'll talk. Just please, please leave her alone. She doesn't deserve this," Ross begs while pulling at his restraints. His statement makes all of us roll our eyes, but Blondie halts his assault and allows for him to speak. "Maevis' parents are planning to kill her off since she already signed everything over to me. Well...at least that was the plan before I discovered the conniving little bitch signed the documents with *your* last name."

Vane's gaze instantly finds mine, his green eyes surging with admiration and a hint of warmth.

Is it possible to want to fuck someone in such a serious situation?

I notice a quick smile flash across his face with a look of hunger in his eyes before his mask falls back into place.

"The deal is to split the estate and assets of her biological parents between my family and them with a sixty-five/thirty-five split, them getting the larger half," Ross finishes explaining and pulling on his restraints again. "Maevis, baby... Sweetheart. Please. You have to understand, I did all of this for us. I never meant for—"

Blood flies across the hardwood floor.

Vane pistol-whipped Ross right in the mouth. Two teeth clatter onto the floor, sliding over to his mother's bare feet.

"You don't speak her fucking name without her permission, you piece-of-shit," Vane barks, spitting in his face and striding over to me with fire in his eyes. "It's your decision from here, Duchess. Ryatt was right—the outcome of their lives is not my call to make," he says, grabbing my hand and wrapping it around the handle of the gun while making sure it's still pointed down.

My heart is hammering so hard, I'm terrified it will leap up my throat and out of my mouth.

Wetting my lips, I force my legs to move until I'm standing directly in front of Ross. He opens his mouth, and I see two teeth missing on the side as blood drips from the corner.

"You, your family, and my parents took everything from me," I whisper as he clamps his eyes shut and looks away. "All I did was love you, and instead, you helped the people who took my real parents' lives. The life I was supposed to have crumbled at the hands of the people you helped. The people you were more loyal to than me."

Ross' eyes fly open, large and brown just like I remember them. "We can still have our happy ending, Maevis. Don't let this asshole tell you any differently. I did all of this against my will. I never meant to hurt you. Baby, I am so sorry. I'll get the help I need, and I can promise you, it will never happen again. I promise to make it up to you, to love you and treat you like you deserve."

Annoyance is curling its way around me when I hear his mother, still berating me like their lives aren't on the line. She's throwing out every insult I can think of as Rose threatens her, moving closer after each sentence.

"Maevis, baby, let me go, and we can kill them together, walk right out of here and live our lives like we were created to do. Have my children like you were created to do."

His words send a burst of fire and outrage through my heart, my vision turning red.

After all this, he still thinks I'm nothing more than a breeding machine, still thinks I'm worth nothing more than being his wife. Taking a deep breath, I tame the fire in my veins for a brief moment and focus on the man before me, the one I was so sure I'd spend my life with just a short time ago.

Slowly, a genuine, wide smile spreads across my face, and I detect the panic in Vane's face when I take a step toward Ross. I rest my palm on Ross' cheek, and Vane stiffens the moment I offer him my touch.

Margaret's voice still rings behind me, throwing insult after insult my way.

Ross' eyes find mine, and in an instant, superiority washes over him. "I knew you were still mine. Turn that gun on the fucker who got into your head and release me and your mother-in-law so we can get the fuck out of here, baby."

Slowly, I lean down, kissing him on his temple, my eyes connecting with Vane for a split second. He looks like he's going to burn everything and everyone in the room. Sliding my lips down to Ross' ear, I whisper the secret I've held in for long enough.

"I killed Brian."

Ross goes rigid under my touch, pulling his head away and bucking in his chair.

"You did *what*?"

"I killed your best friend. Right after he let me know you drugged me and let him fuck me while I was unconscious. Right after he let me know he wasn't the only one you let use me against my will."

Confusion disappears from Ross' face, replaced by dread. A vein pops in his neck as he offers reason after reason, lie after lie. "Maevis, I would never. You killed an innocent man. Are you fucking crazy?"

A wicked laugh escapes me, and I double over as the room falls silent. Straightening my spine and wiping away the tears from laughter, I study the man I believed would one day be my husband. "Even now, you're still programmed to lie. You sent your men to fuck me when we first got here. One of them even admitted it would be *different with me awake.*"

Ross' Adam's apple bobs as he forces a swallow, realizing his lies aren't holding up. Casting his gaze down, he whispers an apology before looking back up at me. "Maevis, I was stupid. I was...I was under the influence, and I don't know what got into me."

Stepping away from him, I nod my head rapidly. Visions of him fucking his secretary on his desk play like a movie in my head. Turning around and raising the gun toward Ross, I hear his mother plead for his life behind me while continuing to berate me. My gaze connects with Vane, who looks at me with a swirl of different emotions.

"*Always your choice,*" he mouths, and a smile flits across my face.

"As badly as I want to kill you," I say, studying Ross' sweat-covered face as he trembles in his chair, "I'd rather you feel the pain I still carry every fucking day thanks to you."

In the blink of an eye, I turn around, the barrel of the silencer pointed directly at his irritating fucking mother. The look of shock and horror on her face is one I will never forget as Ross screams. His terrified voice sounds like a sweet symphony I could listen to every day of my life.

And even though it's a song I never want to stop, I'll never forget the tranquility that sweeps over me when I pull the trigger.

CHAPTER

FIFTY-TWO

(MAEVIS)

At the long, dark wooden table, the four of us sit and discuss our plan to the background music of Ross' endless wailing.

For years I had to deal with him and his mother berating me. I took each and every little jab in stride because I thought I loved Ross.

Truly, I did love Ross.

But it's not the kind of love I would wish on anyone.

I look back over to Vane, who is staring at me with steady, dark eyes. I can tell he's wondering if I regret my decision, so I offer a faint smile that leads to a smirk. His shoulders noticeably relax, and that's when it hits me.

Vane is wondering if him coming back into my life is changing me into someone I don't want to be.

I take my phone out of my pocket and type out a quick text.

Vane pulls his phone from his pocket, flicks the screen with his thumb, and reads the text. I can see the smile crack on his perfect face before he slides the phone back into his pocket, looking up at me and sending a quick, *sexy as fuck* wink my way. I pop the little bubble Vane and I are living in to focus back on the plan.

"The bodies can be taken care of in under an hour," Blondie states.

Rose sits across from him, watching his every move with a

301

neutral expression. There's something going on between them, but I can't quite pinpoint it.

"Which brings us to our next task," Blondie says and turns to look at me. "Your parents. Do we have to call them your parents? Because honestly, I don't think they deserve that title."

I stare at him while processing his words. He is one-hundred percent right. Why am I still calling them my parents when they murdered *my real parents* in cold blood? I swallow down the pain and hurt and begin nodding my head.

"The Moores. Call them The Moores."

Everyone at the table furrows their brows for a moment but shrug in agreement.

They're probably wondering why I continue to give them the same last name as me, but I no longer claim that name. I don't care what any legal document says. The moment I get back home, I'm changing it to Devereux.

"So, next task. The Moores," Blondie says, cracking a smile as Ross' shouts fill the room again.

"I have that handled," Vane chimes in.

My eyes snap up to him, slightly narrowing and relaxing when he sends another wink across the table at me.

"Then please tell me we can move on with this crybaby bitch over here so I know what silence is again," Rose petitions, throwing her thumb over her shoulder toward Ross. I bite my cheek to keep from laughing, and I'm instantly disgusted when Blondie looks at her like he's going to fuck her on the table in front of all of us.

"Okay, what is this?" I ask, pointing between the two of them, and Rose stiffens with wide eyes.

"Nothing," she replies far too quickly. Her face drops back to neutral.

Blondie grunts next to me, and his tongue darts out to his

bottom lip, licking it while studying Rose. "Nothing, indeed," he agrees, and Rose sends a piercing look across the table at him before pulling out her phone and typing away.

Vane stands from his seat, sliding the gun over to me. "Safety is on, but once again, it's your decision," he says with a nod in Ross' direction.

Flashbacks play in my head from the day I murdered his best friend, Brian. His blood pooling on the floor around me. His lifeless body slouching in the chair where Vane had tied him up and presented him to me like the most important gift on Christmas morning. When it was all said and done, I remember Vane's arms wrapping around me, pulling my back to his front as we both stare into the mirror on the wall.

"How do you feel?" Vane had asked me without breaking eye contact in the mirror.

That moment was the first moment of full clarity I had in my entire life.

Alive, I had replied while staring back into those deep emeralds that held the key to my heart from the very beginning. That revelation still hasn't changed.

Grabbing the gun from the table with my head held high, I walk over to Ross, who is now covered in sweat, blood, snot, and tears. I study him for a moment before his brown eyes land on me, casting the nastiest glare I've ever seen someone produce.

And I can't quite blame him.

Narrowing his eyes even further, he spits at me, and I dodge to the right on impulse, avoiding his disgusting assault. My brows raise as I analyze him with a tilt of my head.

"I just want to know one thing before we proceed," I announce, and Ross' eyes flare.

"You don't have the balls to pull that trigger, you dumb bitch. My mother was right. She was always right about you.

You came from nothing, and you will always be nothing," he spat back at me.

Vane strides toward us quicker than lightening, and I press my hand into his hard chest to stop him. Vane relaxes under my touch but never takes his heated glare off Ross.

Dramatically, I turn my body in his mother's direction and wave the gun toward her. "She said that about me?" I ask, a shocked look on my face. "I am truly and honestly appalled. She was such a nice lady."

Ross' lips peel back, showing his bright, white teeth.

"Emphasis on *was*, because she's not doing much talking right now. Want to add anything into this convo, Margaret?" I ask the dead body behind me.

"Speak now, or forever hold your peace."

Ross begins writhing and shouting, doing anything and everything he can in hopes of being able to break his restraints. Vane runs his hand down the side of his face and over his mouth in an attempt to wipe his smile off his face. Rose's laughter explodes throughout the room, and I crack a smile in Ross' direction I can't hold back.

"I think she's asleep. Anyway, back to you," I say, taking a step toward Ross. I press the silencer to the middle of his forehead, and he freezes, never taking his eyes from mine. "It's different when the roles are reversed, huh?" I question when I survey his shocked expression. "I'm going to ask you a question. You answer honestly, I'll let you live, and Vane will figure out a way for you to leave without ever coming back."

"What the actual fuck? Maevis—" Vane begins to protest, taking a step towards me, but I hold a hand up to cut him off. His green eyes flare with fire from the corner of my eye, but I ignore it. A quick glance at Blondie and Rose show the distraught looks on their faces before focusing back on Ross.

"You have a deal," he says, licking his lips in anticipation.

I release a low, disgruntled laugh. "Figured you would say that," I say, dropping the barrel from his forehead and taking a step closer. "How many men did you let assault me while I was unconscious when you drugged me?"

Ross' eyes bulge so far out of his head, he looks like a tree frog.

He begins mumbling incoherent words, and I press the silencer back to his head. "Does that mean you're unwilling to answer the question? Works for me," I say and release the safety with a clicking sound. He pulls his head away and frantically begs me to move the barrel.

"I need a fucking answer, momma's boy," I snap, pressing the barrel harder into his head.

"Twenty-two!" he shouts. "Ish... Twenty-two-ish," he confirms, and I drop the gun to my side, staring at him in disbelief.

I shake my head, trying to remove the fog filling it. "No, that's not....that's not even possible," I say, my eyes shifting over to Vane, who looks like he's going to rip Ross' head from his body.

"You asked how many I let *assault* you, not *fuck* you. Now release me," Ross snaps, and on impulse, I send the butt of the gun into his nose. Blood sprays me, but I don't even blink as the crimson drips down my face.

The room falls silent even though I know everyone is talking. My vision refuses to process any color but red.

I aim the gun in his direction, pulling the trigger twice through the red haze taking over my vision. Ross' screams calm me in the moment, and I shake my head, turning to Vane, who is clenching his jaw so tightly, I'm afraid he's going to break his own bones.

"I'm okay," I whisper, trying to convince him and myself. "I got this."

Vane nods his head, his fists clenched at his sides. "I know."

Turning back to face Ross, with two bullet holes in the wall behind him where I aimed, I roll my lips inward and inhale a deep, calming breath through my nose.

"You lying bitch! You said you would let me go!" he screeches from the chair, and on a breath, I shrug.

"Looks like we're both liars now, huh?"

His eyes widen with anger as he releases a scream so loud, I wait for glass to break. When he stops, I nod my head in amazement.

"Now that you've gotten that out of your system," I follow up, "as much as I know it would feel amazing to end your life by my hand..."

His focus snaps to my face, his breathing picking up in panic.

"I'm going to let you die at the hands of the man I love, the man I never stopped loving from the moment he handed me his pencil in accounting my freshman year of college," I say with a lump in my throat as I hold the gun out for Vane to take.

When I don't feel him take the gun from my hand, I turn to look at him. A flood of emotions plays across his face that I can't quite read, and for a split second, I swear I can see tears rimming both of his eyes before he coughs into his fist and moves toward me. A small smile blooms on my face before fading when I see his eyes darken.

Taking the gun, he holds it at his side while grasping my chin with his free hand. "You sure about this, Duchess?"

I nod in confirmation without a single doubt in my mind.

"I love you, Maevis, from the moment I laid eyes on you. I will die before I ever let you out of my life again."

My heart pounds in my chest, threatening to end my life

right here if it goes any harder. I want to say the words back, but my brain is short-circuiting, trying to process it all.

Vane turns toward Blondie, releasing my chin. "Cut his restraints."

Shock and confusion wash over me as Vane walks over to the table, setting the gun down.

"You're going to let him go?" I question in panic.

His eyes connect with mine. "Did I not just tell you I love you? You said he could die by my hand. I'm not giving him the satisfaction of the easy way out with a bullet."

I stand in silence, at a loss for words as he strides back in front of Ross, who is now free from his restraints and attempting to stand. Ross eyes the front door, and Vane releases a low laugh.

"You'll never make it," he taunts Ross, who throws an off-balance fist toward him.

Vane catches the blow in his palm, delivering a punch of his own to Ross' gut, which has him doubling over and dropping to the ground. Vane grabs him by the hair, pulling his head back.

"You loved putting your hands on my girl, right?" he questions, releasing his head and throwing his knee into Ross' chin. Blood falls onto the floor, and so does Ross.

"This is getting good," Rose chimes in from the side with a soft, giddy clap of her hands.

Vane towers over Ross, gripping his hair once more and using it to twist his head in my direction. "You see how little she is compared to you? And you still put your hands on a fucking woman," he shouts, kicking Ross repeatedly until the blood falling from his mouth becomes a puddle.

"Be a man and get the fuck up," Vane demands, pulling on Ross' shirt until he stands on his one good leg. Holding him by the collar, Vane lands punch after punch to his face until his nose is so smashed in, he's barely recognizable.

He drops Ross back down into the chair and instructs Blondie to replace the restraints. Ross is so disoriented, he makes zero effort to fight back.

Vane glances at Ross' mother with a look of disgust. "Get this bitch out of here," he snaps at his men once Ross is restrained again. Blood and spit fall from Ross' mouth as he cries out when his mother is dragged from the room.

Could they have carried her? Absolutely.

But Vane's men knew the visual Vane wanted ingrained in Ross' head.

And they delivered.

Vane walks back over to the gun on the table. Grasping it in his hand, he makes his way back to me without breaking eye contact.

"Turn around and face him," Vane instructs me, and my lungs constrict, pushing every last bit of air from my body. I swallow, doing as he instructs because I trust him more than myself.

I feel him tower behind me as his chest presses into my back, his long arms wrapping around my front. "Wrap your hands around the grip, Duchess," he whispers in my ear, sending shivers down my spine. I do as I'm told and wrap my hands around the grip, melting into his chest when his large hands fall on top of mine so we're both firmly holding the gun.

He plants a kiss to the top of my head. "Good girl."

I know I shouldn't be turned on, but my legs feel like Jello.

"We're in this together," he says as Ross spits up blood, wet cough after wet cough.

"Until the very end," I say on a shaky breath.

Studying us with the eye that isn't swollen from Vane's

assault, Ross' chest heaves as he stares down the barrel of the silencer.

"You'll both rot in hell for this," he sputters from his chair with another cough.

Our grips tighten.

"As long as we're together," I say before our trigger fingers pull back, and a bullet lands directly between Ross' big, brown eyes that once held my future.

CHAPTER
FIFTY-THREE

(MAEVIS)

Watching Ross' eyes glaze over as death consumed him was a bittersweet moment. I wanted him to die a much more agonizing death, but knowing he was forced to watch as Vane and I pulled the trigger was better than any death I could have hoped for him.

As we boarded Vane's private jet—one I didn't even know he had—I sat down across from him, his gaze never leaving me. Rose occupied the seat next to me near the window, as if she didn't just witness everything back at the cabin. Blondie sat across from her, eyeing her like she was the last meal he was ever going to have.

The plane ascends as we sit in a comfortable silence, waiting for it to level out.

"Since we didn't get to discuss it back there, what's the official plan?" Rose asks while picking at her nails. Blondie continues eye-fucking her for a bit before laying out the plan for us.

I'm busy observing the luxurious private jet when my gaze lands on Vane. I bite my lip when I notice the devious smirk on his perfect face. Blondie's voice fades into the background when I glance down at Vane's lap. His hand pats his thigh twice, instructing me to sit, and I happily oblige.

"We're going to stop for fuel along the way, but after that, we're going straight to Prague," he details, and I shift on his lap to look at him. "This ends now. They're going to get what they deserve." His gaze drifts over to our two friends.

"I...kinda sorta have a warrant in Prague," Blondie comments, scratching his chin with a twisted face and glancing over at Rose, whose eyebrows reach her hairline. "Okay, maybe a bit more than a warrant. More along the lines of a very powerful family who can't wait to get their lick back waiting for me to step foot on their territory again. Don't ask," he adds with an embarrassed chuckle.

"I should probably get back to work before I'm fired," Rose says with a worried look.

"You could come work for me. Apparently, I own Ross' business now?" I say skeptically, and Rose's mouth drops open before she squints her eyes. "Ya know, usually, I would have a billion questions to throw at you, but I'd much rather send in a letter of resignation and report for duty at Maevis Industries or whatever the fuck you plan on calling it."

I laugh with my palm to my forehead.

"Can I request a two-week vacation first, though? These past forty-eight hours have been...a lot," she says.

"Vacation request granted," I announce and roll my eyes. I look over at Blondie, who's eye fucking her in silence. "That. That right there," I say, pointing at him. "Stop eye fucking my best friend."

His head snaps over to me, and a devilish grin creeps onto his face. "You two have a lot of catching up to do."

A deep blush blooms on Rose's face, her eyes flaring at Blondie's statement. "You're fucking irritating, you know that?"

"You're delicious, you know that?" he replies, and Rose's eyes round and dart over at me. A nervous laugh sounds before she kicks Blondie in the leg and urges him to shut up. But that only heightens his theatrics as his tongue darts out toward her. Rose steps over me to stomp toward the bathroom, Blondie following after her. I stand to rescue her, but Vane snatches me back down onto his lap.

"First question," he asks in a low, gravelly tone that sends my core into overdrive. "Are you sure about this?"

I nod. "They deserve to pay for what they did to the only parents who ever loved me."

Vane nods in agreement. "Second question," he follows up in a deep, lust-filled voice that sends my core into overdrive. "Have you ever been a part of the mile high club?"

I swallow at his question and inform him I have not. I fidget, my pussy pulsing at the sound of his voice playing over and over in my head.

His hand creeps under my hoodie and finds my breast, pinching my nipple with the perfect pressure, pulling a moan from my lips as my eyes dart toward the bathroom where Rose and Blondie have disappeared.

A muffled moan filters through the door, and I drag in a breath.

"Sounds like they're doing just fine. Your best friend might have even beat you to it," Vane says before standing and lifting me over his shoulder.

"Vane, wait! You can't just—"

A smack lands to the back of my thigh, and I snap my mouth shut.

"You already agreed to be mine. I can pleasure this perfect body however the fuck I want."

I can feel myself getting wetter by the second. The moment he steps into the bedroom of his private jet, I know he's going to stick to his word.

When he throws me onto the bed, I squeal.

I have this man for the rest of my life.

CHAPTER
FIFTY-FOUR

(MAEVIS)

At our layover, a separate jet was already waiting for Blondie and Rose to take them back to Chicago. I hugged my best friend tight, thanking her for everything and demanding an explanation when I got home. When it came time to say bye to Blondie, I begged him to watch over her for me. He vowed to protect her before hugging me so tight, my back cracked.

I woke up at our destination to Vane planting kisses along my neck. The mile high club induction was one I will never forget. I'm still recovering from every position Vane threw me in like I was nothing more than a ragdoll. This second nap left me feeling groggy.

And I craved more.

"Rise and shine, Duchess."

My eyes flutter open, and I sit up in the overly comfortable bed.

"Fresh clothes are ready for you on the side over there. Let's hurry up and get this over with so I can have you all to myself," he says before planting one last, soft kiss to my lips and heading back into the cabin.

Before we left Nashville, Vane's men dissected Ross' phone. I cringed when they held the phone up to his dead body for facial recognition to unlock it.

They were able to track down the last phone call,

pinpointing exactly where the Moores are staying. His men transferred everything from his phone so we knew exactly when they returned to their hotel room.

Little did they know, we would already be waiting for them when they did.

CHAPTER

FIFTY-FIVE

(VANE)

I see Maevis' concern sketched across her beautiful, tanned face as we wait in the bathroom of their hotel suite. Even though my men are downstairs—disguised as civilians so they could alert me that the targets are on the way up—my own heart flutters when a room key unlocks the door from the other side. Their laughter fills the room as if they hadn't just put their so-called daughter through hell and back.

Hell, her entire life, if we're being honest.

But all that stops here. It stops today.

Her angelic face turns to meet mine, and the only thing I can do is focus on those full, soft lips of hers. Blinking and looking away barely helps; I have to force myself to focus on the task at hand instead of lifting her, setting her on this counter, spreading her legs as far as they'll go, and devouring her until she sings my name.

"Vane, are you okay?" she asks in a whisper I can barely hear.

A smile blooms across my face. I've done shit like this damn near my entire life, and she wants to know if I'm okay?

I place a kiss on her forehead and assure her I'm okay.

"You ready?" I whisper, partially afraid of her answer. What if she backs out? This is a walk in the park for me, but for her... She's new to all of this. She could back out, and I couldn't

315

even be mad at her for it. Her eyes never leave mine as I crouch down, pulling my gun from my back pocket and handing her my extra from the duffle bag on the floor.

"Until the very end," she whispers with a broad, bright smile, and the heart once frozen melts in a split second. I reach for the handle of the door, and just before I turn it, her hand grips my bicep, stopping me. I turn to face her, panic threading through my lungs. Then, I notice the smile still plastered on her face.

"Whatever happens out there," she says on a swallow, "thank you."

My brow pinches.

"Thank you for helping me. Thank you for guiding me but never forcing me. Thank you for helping me see what I deserved in this lifetime. Thank you for...for coming back for me."

Releasing the door handle, I turn to her, pulling her into my chest and staring into her bright eyes. The feel of her against me is something I never want to lose. In this moment, I know I'm going to be raw and honest with her as I lift her onto the granite countertop, cupping her beautiful face. I run through the memories of her having coffee by herself at her favorite shop and wanting to sit at the table with her. The memories of her walking into work with worry etched across her face, how I wanted to tell her how amazing she is at what she does. My chest tightens.

"I never left you, Duchess. I watched you every moment of every day. I tracked you every single place you went. I watched you at work. I even watched when you went to that fucker's house and never left."

She tenses for a moment, her eyes widening at my statement, and I don't regret telling her the truth about how deep my stalking went.

"I may have waited far too long to pry my way back into your life, but there was never a moment I wasn't going to make you mine."

Her small hand rises, pressing into my cheek before gently moving to the side of my neck and to my chest. A single tear falls from her eye, and I swipe it with my thumb.

"I love you, Vane. I should have said it back at the cabin because I knew. I've always known, but I was just... I love you," she rushes out, a huge smile playing on her face. I don't try to hide the smile blooming in my heart at those three words finally leaving her lips.

"I know, Duchess. I love you too," I reply, giving her lips the attention they deserve with my own. We finally separate in a lust-filled haze around, grins plastered on our faces before I move back into action.

"Now, let's go murder the fuckers who took everything from you so we can start our life together."

The smile drops from her face, a serious, stone mask falling into place. Our foreheads press together one last time before I swivel back to the door, turning the handle slowly to avoid any sound. Cracking it, I see the two of them pouring a glass of wine at the island of the suite, and I turn back to Maevis with a nod.

Opening the door all the way, we silently move out of the bathroom, guns drawn.

"Good afternoon, Mom and Dad," Maevis singsongs from my side, and they both jump, wine spilling everywhere.

Maevis' father raises a gun of his own that must have been hidden under the counter. And not just any gun—a suppressor is attached, just like mine.

I swept the entire suit for weapons. What the actual fuck?

"Shoot her," Maevis' mom shouts, red wine splattered

across her white sundress. "We already have the signatures we need. *Kill her.*"

Maevis' father steadies his gun, and I line mine up directly with the center of his forehead.

"Maevis, we had everything set up for you to live a beautiful life. Why couldn't you just fall in line?" her father questions with anguish. "Where is Ross?"

"Dead," Maevis deadpans. That would normally bring a smile on my face, but a gun is pointed at the love of my life, and I'm not about to break character.

Her parents' faces drop at her answer, and her mother bangs her fists on the counter. "You stupid little brat. Do you know what you've done? Do you know what his parents will do to you when they find out? What they'll do to *us*?"

"They won't do anything, because they're dead too," she informs them, and their mouths drop so far open, they almost bounce off the counter.

I was prepared for a verbal response instead of the one we get.

My heart races at the sound of her father pulling the trigger, the gun pointed straight for her chest. I don't second guess my action. I don't even wonder if she'll hate me for exchanging my life for hers. All I know in the millisecond of making my decision is that I promised I would die before I live this life without her.

Her scream is the last thing I hear as a bullet pierces my flesh.

FIFTY-SIX

(VANE)

"No, no, no, no... Vane, please. Why would you do that? Oh my God, no, please...." I hear Maevis cry above me. The room spins for a moment, and she's dragged from on top of me by her hair.

The idiots don't even take the time to see if the gunshot wound was fatal.

It wasn't.

My left shoulder throbs, but I've been through worse.

Without a second thought, I pull the knife from my ankle and slice straight through her father's Achille's tendon. An ear-piercing scream echoes through the suite as he releases Maevis. I wrestle the gun from his hand, shooting him in both knees with zero regret. I had signaled my men from the device in my pocket the moment her father raised the gun. Three of them burst through the door, swiftly silencing her father with a gag.

"I wouldn't scream anymore, if I were you," Maevis snarls, her gun aimed directly at her mother, whose hands are raised in front of her in surrender. "Couch. *Now!*"

I watch the gun shake as her hands tremble in concern. Her focus bounce back and forth from me to her mother with a worried brow. "Keep your fucking hands exactly where I can see them, or I swear on my life, I will kill you right here."

I feel dizzy as I stand and grip the edge of the counter for balance. My men are on me instantly, dropping the med kit they seemingly knew to bring. Within minutes, I'm bandaged up—a clean shot.

In and out the back.

Not the first time. Probably not the last.

Maevis' father is dragged over to the couch next to his wife. Maevis stands across from them on the other side of the coffee table, gun drawn, her eyes flicking from them to me repeatedly, her breathing heavy from worry. "You took everything from me," she hisses at them.

Instructing my men to wait in the hall, I walk behind Maevis, my hands on her shoulders. "Maevis, baby...I'm okay," I whisper, but she's already snapped.

"No! They were going to take you from me," she shouts again. This time, fresh tears roll down her cheeks. "They took my parents from me, and now, they almost took. I thought...I thought—"

Her words trail off, and I grab the gun from her hand. Lowering the weapon, I turn her to face me, leaning in so only she can hear me. "Wipe those fucking tears from your face. I told you, do not let them see you crumble. I'm fine, you're fine. Now turn the fuck back around and be the woman I know you are. For me, for yourself, and for your parents, who deserved so much better. Give them the justice they deserve."

Her gaze snaps up to meet mine.

And as if the other half of her sprang back to life, her hands dart up to her adorable face, swiping at the tears as her brown eyes harden into something fierce. She nods once, taking the gun back.

"I got this," she hums before turning back around to face them, gun at her side.

She studies them in silence for a moment as her father

groans. My gaze focuses on his blood leaking all over the white couch and onto his wife.

"You took everything from me, beginning with my biological parents because you knew you could never be who they were. As strong as they were. As caring as they were. As...as amazing as I've heard they were," she says with a steady, calculated tone.

"Your parents were useless trash who wanted to make the world *a better place* like fucking idiots," the woman barks from the couch.

And for the first time in my life, I flinch from sudden movement.

Maevis raises her arm so quickly, I didn't realize it happened until blood is leaking from her father's side.

"You scream, and I put one between his eyes. You speak ill of my parents again, and I will put one between your eyes. Are we clear?" Maevis snaps, sobs coming from the couch while the woman nods her head and applies pressure to her husband's wound.

This isn't the time or place for it, but my cock is hard as fuck in my pants.

"Since you don't seem to show any remorse, I'm going to do you exactly how you did them," Maevis declares with her chin held high. "I'm going to make you suffer."

That's my girl.

CHAPTER
FIFTY-SEVEN

(VANE)

"You're doing all of this for nothing, Maevis," her so-called father rasps. "The papers were already sent to our attorneys. Every asset, every dollar, every title your parents left you is ours."

The woman flashes us a devilish grin despite being covered in her husband's blood.

"Did you even bother reading the signature? Did your beloved Ross even bother telling you what he discovered?" Maevis questioned cooly without moving.

"The signatures were signed Maevis *Wrathbone*. Last time I checked, that isn't my legal last name."

"Yet," I interject, and their eyes flare with hatred. I sneak a quick peek at Maevis, who flashes a smile at my input as warmth spreads throughout my chest.

"Those contracts are as good as dead, just like him once he bleeds out," Maevis says, returning to her cold demeanor while pointing the gun in his direction. "Unless we let you go, that is. Let me hear you beg, dearest Mother."

I blink rapidly at Maevis' demand. My girl has become a cold-hearted killer in the past few days, and I don't know if I should be proud or scared.

"You can't be serious," the woman whispers from the

couch, and Maevis takes a step forward, raising the silenced gun.

"Both of you, beg for your fucking lives, just as my parents did."

Between their begging and hushed sobs, Maevis asks me to grab the folded paper she had shoved into the duffle bag. Keeping my eyes on the couch, I use my foot to drag the duffle bag out and find the folded paper. When I bring it over to Maevis, she takes a deep breath and unfolds it. The picture Ryatt had given her back at the casino sits in Maevis' shaky hand.

"You see them?" she asks, holding up the picture toward the couch. White hot anger blooms when I see the hurt on Maevis' face. "You'll never be like either of them."

"Take back what's yours, Duchess," I say, loud enough for them to hear me. I watch as Maevis' spine straightens, her shoulders setting and her chin raising high. The begging begins from the couch again before it's silenced by the gun in her hand.

Gradually, their bodies slump, their heads connecting.

They weren't perfect gunshots to the forehead, but my girl still got the job done on shaky hands.

She shifts the safety back into place, setting the gun down on the coffee table, and I catch her as she stumbles backwards. The picture of her perfect little family falls from her grasp to the floor. I can see the sweat beading at her hairline, and I know something was wrong. When she falls back into my arms, I grab her around the waist and feel something warm and wet.

Blood drains from my face as I lay her on the floor, pulling up her hoodie to reveal a gunshot wound to the lower side of her abdomen.

I'm not a crier, never have been. I can barely show emotion when needed.

But in this moment, when the love of my life is pale and her eyes have a distant look to them, I cry like a baby.

I shout for my men with whatever ounce of breath I have left.

"Maevis, baby, please. Don't do this to me. Don't you dare do this. You made me a fucking promise. *We're in this together, until the very end.*"

CHAPTER
FIFTY-EIGHT

(MAEVIS)

Life is a funny thing.

One moment, you're about to marry a lying, conniving, manipulating, asshat of a man.

The next moment, you're being stalked and end up falling in love with said stalker. And somehow, after that, you become a cold-blooded killer in a foreign country.

And after that...you feel a rush of both fear and calm as blood seeps out of you, and you're convinced you're about to die after killing your fraudulent parents when you didn't even know you were adopted until a few days ago.

I hear beeping and murmurs, though my eyes are too weak to open.

The murmurs fade, and I feel a dip in what must be a bed I'm lying in. A large, familiar hand wraps around mine, and the warmth of it surges through my hand and lands right in the middle of my chest. The familiar touch blooms some sort of fireball that refuses to die down. And as if everything snaps into place, my eyes fly open to find Vane staring at the TV in the corner.

I work my throat for a moment, preparing to speak through the dryness I feel when I swallow. My gaze floats over to the television, where The O.C. is playing my favorite episode, where Summer dresses up as Wonder Woman to win over Seth.

"They get married in the end, ya know," I finally rasp, and Vane snaps his head toward me so quickly, I get whiplash.

He grips my face, and, without saying a word, he kisses me a hundred times.

"Maevis, oh my God, baby. I can't... I don't... They said you would pull through, but having you lay here silent for days.... I don't ever want to experience this again," he says before kissing me again.

"How bad was it?" I question and instantly get a glare from the man I love.

"You lost a lot of blood. The doctor said one more minute without added pressure, and you wouldn't have..."

His words trail off, and I reach up to rest my palm on his cheek.

"I don't want to think about it," he finishes, and I let him know we don't have to talk about it.

"Why didn't you say something?" he questions, sadness in his deep, green eyes. It's in this moment I note the lines of exhaustion on his face. The unfamiliar bags under his eyes let me know he hasn't slept.

"Because I know you would have rushed me out of there, and we were there to finish a job. I wasn't leaving until I finished what I went there...what *we* went there to do," I said on a serious tone with a matching look, letting him know I don't regret my decision.

The hardness in his gaze melted away, his shoulders losing the tenseness from seconds before. "You know you're going to get punished for that when you're fully healed, right?"

Butterflies flap their wings in my belly at his tone.

"Looking forward to it," I reply, but I freeze when I glance at the hand resting on his cheek. When I pull it away, my eyes widen at the way the diamond on my ring finger shines under the hospital lighting. "Vane, is this..."

"An engagement ring? Yes."

His answer forces the air from my lungs. Did he propose and I don't remember? Sadness washes over me at the thought.

"If you're wondering if you don't remember the proposal, don't worry. There wasn't one," he says with a smirk. "I sent my men out to find a ring similar to the ones you saved on your Pinterest board."

My eyes squint in confusion. "How did you see my—"

"Maevis... how many times do I have to tell you: there's nothing you can hide from me," he says, cutting me off. "Anyway, I was never giving you an option to be my wife. Of course, you can have whatever type of wedding you want, big or small, but there will be a wedding."

My heart rate escalates on the monitor.

I didn't need a proposal. He's right: I would marry him with or without a ring. We could go to the courthouse as soon as we're back and I would be completely fine with that. My gaze flicks back up at him from the ring I could only dream about.

"What about babies?" I question with a raised brow. I didn't want any with Ross, but now, I can't imagine not carrying Vane's children.

A look takes over his eyes, darkness mixed with lust, and I swallow.

"If you think I don't plan on seeing that belly pregnant with my child, you've lost your mind," he says in a husky tone.

Am I cleared to fuck yet? Probably not.

"But travel first. Enjoying each other first. Giving you everything you've ever deserved in this lifetime first and more," he says, grasping my hand and planting a kiss on each knuckle. "And once you let me know you're ready after all that,

I'll give you as many babies as you want. And if you change your mind, I won't care as long as I have you."

I wanted to give a smart-ass remark, but all I could do was release the tears I was holding onto, tears of joy and happiness at the weight being lifted from my shoulders. I asked if he would lay next to me, and with a wide smile, he slid in as I scooted over.

Reaching into his pocket, he handed me a folded piece of paper, and immediately, I knew what it was. Unfolding it, I studied my parent's faces.

My real parents.

The love they shared in this photo is the only thing I ever wanted for myself. And as if Vane could read my mind, he presses his lips to my temple.

In this moment, from a hospital bed with multiple beeping machines, I'm sure more than I have ever been in my life that I'm right where I'm destined to be.

EPILOGUE

(MAEVIS)

Without question, I sell my place and move in with Vane—he offered on the plane ride back home from Prague to Chicago last year. Even though it's a big change, there isn't a single moment I've regretted my decision.

While Vane begged me for a big, elaborate wedding, I opted for a much smaller, intimate one right in our backyard with those closest to us.

But right now, my heart pounds in my chest with the anxiety gnawing its way through my skin as I stare at myself in the mirror. I jump when Bev knocks frantically on the bathroom door. "For heaven's sake, Maevis, let me in if you're not going to say anything!" she begs.

A wide, genuine smile spreads across my face. I may have lost my parents when I was a baby, but Beverly has been the mother I never got to experience. I unlock the door and snatch her inside with a laugh. "Hush, will you?" I request while waving the pregnancy test box at her.

"Well, what's it say?" she questions, peaking over my shoulder.

I bite my lip and look over at her. "I don't know. I'm too scared to look. Will you?"

I've been nauseous the past week, ever since we got back from a spontaneous trip to Ireland. I thought it was food poisoning, and Beverly finally forced me to take the test.

Her tiny, frail hand lifts the stick, comparing it to the directions on the box. Then, she squeals, and I clap my hand over her mouth.

"Everything okay in there, baby?" Vane shouts from downstairs, and our eyes bulge, connecting in the mirror.

"Yes!" I shout back. "Lady things!"

He must accept my answer, because I could hear him go back to talking with Blondie.

The door flies open then, and Rose waltzes in without invitation. "What are we fawning over?" she asks before her eyes land on the pregnancy test. My hand leaves Beverly's mouth and claps over Rose's just in time before she squeals.

"Shut up, shut up, shut up!" I hiss at Rose while trying not to laugh. "Vane has no idea."

The three of us jump up and down as a small bit of panic raises inside me. I know my world is about to flip upside down again, but this time, it will be in a good way.

After making the two women swear to secrecy until I tell Vane, we make our way back downstairs. Unfortunately, we must not have masked our discovery well, because both men stare at the three of us with contorted faces.

"Why do the three of you look like you just witnessed the most life-changing thing in that bathroom?" Vane questions, looking me over from head to toe.

Beverly huffs, breaking away from the group and turning toward the kitchen. "You ask too many questions."

Rose and I break out into laughter as Vane stares at her in shock.

The doorbell rings, and Vane opens it to find Anika talking Coach River's ear off about some sort of new matcha she wants to try down the street. When she notices the door, she barges in and wraps me and Rose in a hug. "It's been way too long," she sings with a smile.

"It's been two days," Rose forces out through the squeeze of the embrace.

"Yeah, well...same thing"

She and Coach Rivers, who now insists we call him Maverick, settles in with us at the table.

After dinner, Maverick and Anika make their way out onto the patio in the backyard. I scan the room for Blondie and Rose, who have once again snuck away. It's been a year, and they still haven't admitted to being in a relationship, but I'm not stupid. I'm determined to drag answers from them soon.

I'm sipping my after-dinner coffee when Vane sneaks up, wrapping his arms around me. "Are you happy, Duchess?" he questions, placing three sensual kisses down the side of my throat as my head leans back to rest on his shoulder.

"What kind of question is that? My husband gives me the best orgasms and takes me on trips," I tease as he turns me around.

His face lights with laughter before he presses his forehead to mine in a gentle gesture. "I mean it, Duchess. Are you happy?" he asks again with a look of intensity that is begging me to reassure him. A lock of hair falls across his brow, and I reach up, pushing it back from his ungodly handsome face before assuring him that I never want to lose what we have.

"I do have a question, though," I add, and his expression turns serious. "Why do you still call me Duchess?" It's been over a year, and I've never questioned the nickname again until now.

His eyes light up like the night sky on the Fourth of July. "The title signifies a woman of high rank," he says with a kiss to the hollow of my neck. "It signifies a woman strong enough to be a leader."

Another kiss to the side of my neck.

"It signifies a woman who can command anyone or anything."

Another kiss right below my ear that has my breathing turning rapid.

"It signifies royalty, and that's exactly what you are to me. Royalty who deserves the finest things in life," he says, lifting me in the air as I wrap my legs around his torso and set my coffee down. He walks us up the long staircase of the house, kissing me the entire time.

"Vane! Our friends are here, and they're waiting for—"

"Our very grown friends. With their very own grown relationships. They can wait an hour," he says once we reach the door of our bedroom.

"An hour?" I protest at the same time we hear a moan come from the guest bedroom down the hall. I know instantly that it's Rose, and the two of us laugh when we hear a grunt from Ryatt.

Vane presses another kiss to my lips, trailing down to my collarbone. "Vane, wait. There's something I need to tell you," I say on a breathy moan.

He groans, our eyes connecting. "Can it wait until after my cock is settled inside my wife?"

A rush of heat overcomes me and I force back down the secret I was going to reveal to him. I wasn't going anywhere, neither was he, and neither was our future baby. "It can wait," I say on a strangled whisper as a hand creeps under my dress, a growl releasing from his throat when he notices I opted out of underwear for today. Finding my slit and two fingers enter me, causing me to slouch against him at the sensation of his touch.

"Maevis, baby...you know I respect you, right?" he asks, and I pop my head back up to level with his gaze. He's only asked me this question once before, and the actions afterward were something I want to relive instantly.

I nod, a teasing grin sliding across my face.

"Perfect. Because for the next hour, it's going to seem like I don't," he responds, matching my smile before biting me on my shoulder. Both pain and pleasure explode through me as he kicks our door open, shutting it with his foot and turning the lock.

As I land on the bed, I look up to see his emerald eyes shining in the dim light of the room. Dragging me up toward the headboard, he strides over to the dresser. When I see him pull out two bundles of black rope, I stand to run for the door. Hooking me around the waist, he wrestles me back down, straddling me to keep me in place. Making quick work of his job, he ties my wrists to the two top posts of the bed.

I tug at them, knowing damn well I don't want to go anywhere. We've done a lot of things in this room, but he has yet to tie me up.

I shut my eyes, begging for the pulsing in my pussy to stop —it doesn't.

"Look at you... God, you're perfect. I hope you know that," he says in a low, rough voice that has arousal leaking between my thighs. He pulls two more bundles of rope from the dresser and ties each leg to the last two bed posts, forcing me to be spread wide for him.

Pushing up my sundress, he smiles—no underwear. "Just how I like it. Always ready for me." He plunges two fingers inside me, bringing them back out to hold them up to the light. "You see this, baby? I haven't even done anything yet, and you're already soaked for me."

He pushes both fingers into his mouth, cleaning them with his tongue. Throwing his head back when he's done, he hums his approval. "Sweet as ever. I could have this for breakfast, lunch, and dinner."

A moan escapes me. "Vane, please... I need this."

A husky laugh releases from him. "Careful what you ask for, baby. You know I aim to please," he says and forces three fingers inside me without warning. I writhe on the bed, and his stare connects with mine as he bends down, his mouth wrapping around my clit and sucking hard between tender circular motions with his tongue.

"Oh fuck... I'm already going to—"

He pulls his hand and mouth away from me with a raised brow.

"You son of a bitch," I hiss as he denies me the orgasm that is right there, ready to overtake me.

"Whose good girl are you?"

A devious smile crosses over my face, and a smack hits my pussy, pulling a cry from the sting. But pleasure surges through me at the speed of light, suppressing the pain.

Slap.

I cry out again from the denial of my release.

"Yours! I'm your good girl," I shout, begging lacing my words.

His tongue connects with my clit again, and the vibration of his laughter pushes me over the edge. I'm tumbling into the darkness of ecstasy. My orgasm rips through me as his other hand reaches up, shoving four of his fingers into my mouth and down my throat, making my eyes roll back as I ride out my release.

"Good girl," he hums while licking up every last drop.

"You know...it may be a first...but I think it's time to see if we can get four in this tight little pussy," Vane growls while studying my drenched slit. My head snaps up from the pillow in protest, and a large hand comes down in the middle of my breasts. "You're lucky I don't go straight to fisting you, Duchess. Now, shut the fuck up and let me stretch my wife wide."

My breathing threatens to cease when I think about the size of his hands.

"What's your favorite number?" he questions.

He knows the answer, but I say it anyway. "N-nine," I stutter, darting my tongue out to wet my lips. I can feel the sweat on my body as I squirm, still pulling the ropes.

"Stay still, or I swear, my entire fist will make its way into this warm, wet cunt, Maevis."

His command has me freezing. The only thing moving is my chest from the deep, frantic breaths I can't stop.

"Nine. That's the perfect number of times to come, don't you think? We will put you at one out of nine so far. Your friends won't mind waiting a little longer, right?" he questions, running his tongue across his lower lip, where the aftermath of my arousal glistens.

Shock at the thought of coming nine times has me unable to reply, but he doesn't wait any longer. I hear the cap of the lube flip open before he pours it over my most sensitive area. I can't stop the sharp intake of breath that comes when his fingers spread it over every inch of my pussy.

"Take a deep breath for me, sweetheart," he says on a long exhale, and I follow his request.

His fingers push into me....

One.

Two.

Three.

And then the fourth as he turns his hand so his fingers rub perfectly against my g-spot. I bolt my upper back off the bed, and his hand presses me back down with a growl. Slowly, that hand creeps down to my stomach, over my navel, and right above where his hand is inside me.

"I want to feel myself working you from the inside. Is that okay, baby?"

Our eyes connect as his mouth assaults my clit with his fingers still inside of me. I nod my head slowly; I know my body isn't ready for what I'm about to experience as he presses his hand down where his fingers are perfectly curled inside me. I can't help but squirm as my second orgasm already creeps its way into my lower belly.

I hear Vane tsk twice at my movement.

"That's such a shame you moved. I believe I promised you something if you didn't obey. Such a little brat for me." He sighs with a devilish grin, and my core tightens when he slightly pulls out and I feel the fifth finger force its way inside me.

Panic floods me as my eyes roll to the back of my head and I realize what I'm about to experience for the first time.

But I also know I'm about to be handled...

Exactly. The way. I like.

Acknowledgments

The acknowledgements for this book are going to be slightly different than my last ones because not only do I need to acknowledge everyone who helped make this book possible, I need to thank those who helped me through a very dark time in my life.

As my author note stated, writing a book from the deepest, darkest parts of your soul can drain you. This was a time when I desperately needed my inner circle. They show up for me even when they don't know it, and I'm forever grateful for the people listed below.

Mom and Dad: I think it goes without saying that you know exactly what time I'm referring to. You are the best parents a girl could ever ask for. Thank you for helping to watch baby boy while I worked to get this done. Thank you for being the rocks I needed to get me out of the darkness during that awful life lesson. I love both of you more than you'll ever know. I am hoping and praying you didn't read this book and just skipped straight to this part. But if you didn't...I am so sorry, and let's pretend like this never happened LOL.

Rhea: GIRL. I don't know what I would have done without you during THAT time. You literally had to drag me out of my house and right to meeting my future husband. I love you so, so much! Thank you for being the perfect best friend in the darkest of times.

Britt: Thank you so much for all the coffee and shopping

trips when I needed a break from the writing cave. You are the best sister a girl could ask for (aside from forcing me into debt for concert tickets LOL). I love you!

Liz & Jo: Best I can do is...say I love you both more than you'll ever know. Liz, thank you for beta reading and letting me know this isn't dark to your standards (multiple times!). Jo, thank you for guiding me into this new genre and being the sweet one in the group. And even though I'm Jo's favorite... Actually, I'll just leave it there. LOL

Meg: Thank you for holding my hand over text messages and phone calls when my panic and anxiety took over. I have told you this a thousand times, but: you're stuck with me forever!!! Love ya!

Janna: You already know how much you mean to me, but I will say it here: thank you, thank you, thank you for your expertise!!! I promise to work on getting my tenses under control... I'm lying, but I love you and I'm sorry. **kisses**

Alexa: You're definitely the one reading and editing this...so hopefully, the tense is right LOL. I'm so glad we connected, because you're stuck to me like glue now, babes. I appreciate you and love ya!

My ARC Readers: Thank you so, so much for taking a chance on me in a new genre before anyone else. I hope you understand how much I appreciate you. I don't have words to express my gratitude for giving me your time and attention. Thank you!

My Readers: I HAVE READERS? What is this life? Every single one of you makes me happier than you will ever know. Never in this lifetime did I think I would have people to read novels I wrote. Time and time again, you show up for and support me throughout this journey, and I am still in disbelief. Thank you for giving me your time and trusting me to provide you with a story that will keep your attention. Please know I will forever cherish every single one of you!

Andrew/Sir Hubbington: Always the very best for last. Words cannot explain how much I love and appreciate you. You were the light above that deep, dark hole I couldn't pull myself out of. There is no one in this world who understands me the way you do. Thank you for supporting me. Thank you for believing in me. Thank you for telling me to shut up when I said I wanted to give up. You and baby boy are my world. There is nothing in this universe I wouldn't do for you. In this lifetime and the next, you are my person. I love you!

About the Author

O'Junea Brown is an emerging author of Romantasy and Dark Romance. A Fate of Onyx and Ivory is her first published novel with many more to come. She was born and raised in the suburbs of Chicago, Illinois.

She loves her books, comics, video games, sports (go Cubs!), and anything fitness related. O'Junea has a bit too much dark humor and somewhat of a sailor's mouth, but her husband loves her the way that she is and that's all that matters.

Her baby boy and dog Khloe are her only babies.

Follow her on Instagram and TikTok at @ojunea.brown